About t

Maisey Yates is a *New Y...*
of over one hundred ron...
writing strong, hard-w...
princes or multigeneratio...
getting lost in fictional worlds. An avid knitter with a
dangerous yarn addiction and an aversion to housework,
Maisey lives with her husband and three kids in rural
Oregon. Check out her website, maiseyyates.com or
find her on Facebook.

Maya Blake's writing dream started at thirteen. She
eventually realised her dream when she received 'The
Call' in 2012. Maya lives in England with her husband,
kids and an endless supply of books. Contact Maya:
mayabauthor.blogspot.com
twitter.com/mayablake
facebook.com/maya.blake.94

When Canadian **Dani Collins** found romance novels
in high school she wondered how one trained for such
an awesome job. She wrote for over two decades
without publishing, but remained inspired by the
romance message that if you hang in there you'll find a
happy ending. In May 2012, Mills & Boon bought her
manuscript in a two-book deal. She's since published
more than forty books with Mills & Boon and is
definitely living happily ever after.

Royal Scandals

Royal Scandals: The Playboy Prince

MAISEY YATES

MAYA BLAKE

DANI COLLINS

MILLS & BOON

First Published in Great Britain 2022
By Mills & Boon, an imprint of HarperCollins*Publishers,* Ltd
1 London Bridge Street, London, SE1 9GF

www.harpercollins.co.uk

HarperCollins*Publishers*
1st Floor, Watermarque Building,
Ringsend Road, Dublin 4, Ireland

ROYAL SCANDALS: THE PLAYBOY PRINCE © 2022 Harlequin Books S.A.

Crowning His Convenient Princess © 2019 Maisey Yates
Sheikh's Pregnant Cinderella © 2018 Harlequin Books S.A.
Sheikh's Princess of Convenience © 2018 Harlequin Books S.A.

Special thanks and acknowledgement are given to Maya Blake for her contribution to the *Bound to the Desert King* series
Special thanks and acknowledgement are given to Dani Collins for her contribution to the *Bound to the Desert King* series

ISBN: 978-0-263-30408-4

MIX
Paper from
responsible sources
FSC™ C007454

CROWNING HIS CONVENIENT PRINCESS

MAISEY YATES

For Mr H, my 4th and 5th Grade teacher. I remember you teaching us about pseudonyms, and you said if we didn't use one you might be able to find us and read our books someday if we ever became authors. Unless we wrote romance, which you didn't read. Now you're mentioned in a romance—bet you didn't see that coming.

CHAPTER ONE

LATIKA BAKSHMI TOOK a deep breath before steeling herself to open the door. She knew exactly what she would find behind it.

Or rather, *who*.

Prince Gunnar von Bjornland, her boss's brother, dissolute rake, and general disgrace to his country. A man she despised with every fiber of her being. And, a man who was her current project.

Queen Astrid, who was not just her boss, but also her friend and confidant, had asked her to take on the task of reforming Gunnar, and she was going to do it.

In a minute.

"Stop lurking outside my door."

She jolted. "How did you know I was outside the door?"

The door swung open, revealing a man who was more Viking God than mere mortal. His blond hair was pushed back from his face, a slightly darker beard covering his jaw. His light blue eyes were the color of ice, but somehow contained heat nonetheless.

And his *body*.

It was an assault to all her good sense and she hated and loved it in equal measure. She both prayed he would find some sense of decorum in himself and learn to put on a shirt whenever they might encounter one another.

And prayed he would not.

Ever.

His chest was broad, and currently bare, a light dusting of hair over the toned, taut skin there. He took a breath, his well-defined abs shifting as he stepped to the side, as if allowing her entry into his bedchamber.

"How did you know I was out here?" She asked again, not making the move toward entering.

"I could feel the tension radiating through the door. And only you give off tension quite like that, Latika."

"Ah, yes," she said, giving a slight nod of her head. "You're very funny."

"I can *hear* you. You do not wear sensible shoes, like my sister. You wear those hard, spiky heels, and they make a very particular sound on the marble. I suppose, were I given to any great sense of shame, I would be concerned that sound can travel so freely through my bedroom door. One assumes then the sound can travel out just as well."

"A *grave* concern for you," she said, clipped. "I can only imagine."

He shrugged a broad shoulder, making all the muscles in his body shift and bunch. "It isn't really."

"It should be." She looked around the room. There were no signs of recent debauchery, at least. By that she meant, there wasn't a redhead or a blonde lying sprawled out in his bed, or anything quite like that.

However, the bed was unmade, and he had clearly just arisen from it, and likely just pulled the jeans he was wearing on.

It made her wonder if there was anything underneath.

She gritted her teeth, angry with herself without thought. "Astrid has asked me…"

"I would like you to find me a wife," he said, cutting her off and silencing her effectively.

"You… What?"

"I would like you to find me a wife. I understand that my reputation has become of some concern to Astrid. She's married, had a child, and our nation is on the brink of a great and modern future the likes of which would probably make my father rotate in his grave were he not so busy burning in hell."

"Astrid has asked me to help you reform," she finished.

"I know," he said. "And I think there's only one way to do that."

She had expected resistance. She had expected him to balk. To banter. To use excessive double entendre. She had not expected him to see her coming, to anticipate her words, and raise her.

"Why? Why are you suddenly interested in marriage?"

"I didn't say I was suddenly interested in marriage. But I do know that a fairytale is the quickest way to capture the hearts of the people. Is it not?"

"Well, judging by your sister's experience, I would say you are correct enough."

"I am not the heir. That is something that has always sat comfortably with me, but the burden that Astrid carries does not. And for my part, if I can alleviate some of what she carries, then I will do it. I can see that the simplest way will be for me to find a wife."

"A bizarre leap in logic."

"I know you don't respect me, Latika, and I have

never asked you to. Moreover, I've never behaved in a way that might invite you to. Oddly, though it may seem to you, I'm not overly concerned with your approval. But, I do wish to make Astrid happy, and I do wish to bolster the standing of my country in the world. So, you must help me find a wife."

"Is there a particular brand name you are drawn to?" she asked, her tone caustic.

"Yes," he said, not missing a beat. "I would prefer a philanthropist. I do not require that she be in mint condition, so to speak."

It took her a moment to catch his meaning. "You do not expect a virgin? How progressive of you."

"Well," he said. "As I myself am not a virgin, it seems a bit of a double standard to demand my wife come to me untouched."

She tried to keep the flush out of her face, and tried to keep her tone sharp. "You are not untouched?"

The corner of his wicked mouth turned up. "I've been touched one or two times."

"Shocking," she returned.

"I expect that you possess ample channels through which you might find a woman interested in marrying me."

The very idea of arranging marriages didn't sit very well with Latika. Not given her experience surrounding such things. Of course, Gunnar didn't know anything about her real life. Or her real identity. Fishing around in the sorts of circles that might require him to find a wife in might present a problem for her as well.

Considering she was technically in hiding.

But then, she could find ways to be discreet. Find

ways to make sure that she avoided any places that might be problematic.

Just one grim corner of Europe, and the East Coast of the United States. She imagined that Gunnar wouldn't mind her fishing around for an English debutante, rather than looking on the Upper Eastside of New York City.

"Blonde? Redheaded? Brunette? Do you have a preference?"

"None," he said.

"You don't have a type?" she pressed.

"*Female* covers it."

She fought against rolling her eyes. Instead, she made a very officious note on her clipboard. Then treated him to a smile. "A female philanthropist. Hymen not required."

"In fact, I would prefer that there were no hymen present at all," he said. "I'm not a patient man. I'd rather not have to instruct a woman on how to please me."

"Indeed," she said flatly. And she managed to hold back: *that rules me out handily then.*

As if she would ever, in a million years, with flying pigs in the sky, consider being Gunnar's bride.

He turned away from her, his broad back filling her vision. His muscles moved in very interesting ways and she attempted to study the ceiling, rather than his skin.

But it was hard, because his skin was so much more compelling.

And he began to move around the room. He opened up a dresser, pulled out a T-shirt, and shrugged it over his body.

Something about the flex of those muscles caused an answering flex between her thighs, and she did her best to ignore it.

Her emotions were so very charged in his presence, always. And it was her preference to play off the heat as anger. And to pretend that there was no other layer to it.

That there was no part of her—not even a tiny part—that wished to bite down on that insolent mouth of his.

And then bite his chest.

And then lick it.

No. No part of her at all.

She forced a smile. "Anything else?"

"No. I believe that covers it."

"Then I shall begin putting out inquiries, Your Highness. And very soon, I will have found a wife for you."

"It may also bear mentioning," he said, "That I am the owner of my own multibillion-dollar company."

Latika froze. "You… You're what?"

"Yes. I suppose it's about time that came out."

"How… How did you keep that a secret?"

"No one is looking for that bit of dirt. Honestly, it isn't dirt. Why would anyone care? My company has a name, obviously, and *my* name is buried beneath it. But the only thing anyone is ever interested in is who I'm sleeping with. Not the fact that I am the CEO of a multibillion-dollar corporation that deals in green building."

"I…"

"It's part of revamping my reputation, Latika. These things must be made public. I assume you're the person to speak to about the press release regarding that as well."

"I will take care of it," she said, blinking.

"See that you do."

Those blue eyes caught hers and held for a moment, and Latika did her best not to pay attention to the slight shift she felt in her stomach. Did her best to ignore the fact that suddenly the air felt a little bit thicker.

And she really tried not to examine what any of this new information—that he was not going into any of this kicking and screaming, that he had an endeavor that went somewhere beyond gambling and whoring—made her feel.

She was much more comfortable when she disdained Gunnar.

Anything else was unacceptable.

Prince Gunnar von Bjornland had settled into debauchery for far too long. He was at an end with it.

It had been one thing to engage in it when his father was living, and indeed it was something that he had enjoyed.

To throw in the face of his father, even as the old man attempted to sabotage Astrid. Their father was a relic of the highest order. A man who had not been able to fathom that a woman could possibly do a good job of running the country, regardless of the fact that there were many examples that proved they could, and just fine thank you.

No, his father had never gotten over the fact that his heir was a woman. And the fact that his only son had refused to take his side and engage in a coup, overthrowing his twin had been something that the old man could not accept even in the end.

Gunnar had never risen to his father's bait, and to the contrary, had taken a perverse kind of delight in behaving in every way that Astrid did not.

As his sister had lived a serious and contemplative life, dedicating herself to service, Gunnar had waged an all-out war against propriety.

He had taken every sacred tradition and broken it at least once, had taken delight in running roughshod over deeply revered customs, and in general putting Bjornland on the world stage in the context of his behavior.

He had imagined that if nothing else he would be a rather colorful footnote in history.

But of course, it had never been enough for his mind. Hence the secret business endeavor.

But now that Astrid was Queen, and now that various and sundry accusations were being thrown at him as the narrative around his country shifted, he could see that it was time for a change.

This latest debacle had only served to highlight it.

A woman had come forward alleging that he was the father of her child. And no matter that Gunnar had never seen the woman before, there had also been a seed of doubt in him. He always used protection. But condoms weren't entirely reliable, and he'd had to concede that there was a possibility the child could be his, no matter that he was always as responsible as a man could be while being indiscriminate.

The headlines had been scathing, the very fact that a paternity test had been conducted had been cause for scorn among the people.

And now the conversation had become that Astrid could not control her wayward brother. That her own brother despised every value held dear by the country. And when that had been aimed at his father, Gunnar had been happy enough.

But his entire reason for his behavior, his entire reason for being, had been to protect Astrid. Astrid was a strong woman, and always had been, but there had been a war waging beneath the surface of the polished exterior of the palace that she'd had no idea existed.

A war that Gunnar had been on the frontlines of.

He had always protected her. And if protecting his sister now demanded he behave differently, so he would.

And if it meant employing the use of his sister's delectable, and irritating, assistant, then he would do so.

Latika might be delectable, but she was also as stiff as a plank of wood and no less bland.

She was beautiful. There was no argument to be had about that.

In fact, she was uncommonly lovely, and he had always found it a strange thing that a woman of such brilliant beauty be relegated to such a *beige* sort of job.

Though, he imagined a great many people would not find being personal assistant to a queen a *beige sort of job*. But in his world it certainly was.

A woman like her should be wrapped in silk, should be in jewels.

She should spend hours soaking in perfumed baths, readying herself for a lover.

She should *not* spend hours contemplating the merit of clipboards. Though, he had a feeling that was how she spent much of her time.

Her beauty was, in the end, a terrible farce anyway. She looked like a woman built for such things, with her generous mouth and beautiful curves, but she was through and through a woman of practicality and severity.

And he did his very best not to think about how much he would like to test that severity.

He did his very best not to think about just how satisfying it would be to tease that mouth out of that firm unnatural line she kept it in, and torment her until it became a soft "O" of pleasure.

Yes, he did his best not to ponder that.

His world was changing. He would need to find a wife, and he would need to be faithful to that wife.

The very idea of such a chore set his teeth on edge. He could think of no woman at all that would amuse him for the rest of his life, and if he quit engaging in risky behaviors such as racing cars around the autobahn and jumping out of helicopters, his life would likely have a longer expectancy.

Really, this was a terrible plan, but it was the only way he could see to help Astrid.

Though she did not know it, his life had been devoted to that protection.

He would not falter now.

Marriage was, in the grand scheme of things a small price to pay. And for her he would do it. Perhaps not happily, but it would be done.

Because Gunnar von Bjornland might never be King, but he was the master of his own life. And once he set his mind to something, he would damn well see it done.

This was no exception.

CHAPTER TWO

"HERE YOU HAVE IT," Latika said, setting a stack of folders onto Gunnar's desk. "Veritable binders of women."

He looked at the stack, then back up at Latika, one elbow resting on the desk, one brow raised in an impudent manner. "I'm rather insulted you have brought me so much choice," he said.

Latika blinked. "How is that insulting?"

"I should think that the criteria for becoming my bride would be so exacting that you would have little more than a slim volume to present me with."

"I should have thought you would want choice," she said, bristling against his rather pronounced lack of gratitude.

She had gone to a lot of trouble to dig up so many eligible women, lacking in scandal and in possession of beauty.

"I haven't time to do so much reading," he said.

"Do you find it so laborious? To read profiles on women you might marry."

"I find it *boring*."

"I have here in these folders options, for a woman that you might be tasked with sleeping with for the rest of your life. How is it you find that dull?" she pressed.

"When one turns sex into homework even that can be boring."

He was *impossible*. He was impossible, and he was ridiculous, and she had half a mind to kill him where he sat. She could do it with a letter opener, a paperweight or half a dozen other items on his desk.

As solid as her friendship with Astrid was, she had a feeling that Astrid would take a dim view to Latika assassinating her brother. Just maybe. If Astrid only knew the surrounding story she might forgive her.

"Who do you think the top five are?" he asked. "Use your knowledge of me to guess who I might find the most likely five."

"Gunnar," she said, keeping her tone frosty. "If I had that kind of insight into who you are as a person… Well, I would probably throw myself off the nearest cliff."

"A test then." He folded his large hands in front of him and it didn't escape her notice they were scarred. Odd for a man of his position, she would think. "Who do *you* think my top five would be?"

Latika gritted her teeth. She would lie back and think of Bjornland. She would do her very best to remind herself she worked for the palace.

And this was service to Astrid.

And for Astrid, she could do anything. The other woman had essentially saved Latika's life. And it was something that she was not going to forget anytime soon. Or ever. She was eternally grateful for all that Astrid had done. Working with Gunnar on this marriage project was a small thing to ask.

"All right," she said, doing her best to cover up just how aggrieved she felt. "If I had to choose, I would choose not so much to please *you*, but to give maximum improvement to your reputation, and to the reputation of the country. Therefore, we can set aside your personal preferences as secondary."

He rubbed his chin, the light in his blue eyes wicked. "*Can* we?"

"Yes," she said decisively. "This marriage is for the country, after all."

"And yet, I feel that if I am to be shackled to one woman for the rest of my life, it will have to be a marriage bed that I enjoy the idea of being shackled to." His lips curved upward. "Rather, a woman not averse to being shackled to the marriage bed for my pleasure. I've never been one who enjoyed being shackled. But I have nothing against doing a bit of shackling."

Yet again, she ignored the searing heat in her body, and affected an incredibly bored expression. "Yes, yes. I and the rest of the world are aware of the fact that you are shocking, and love to engage in *edgy* sexual activity. I promise you that if a double entendre presents itself you do not have to be so obvious as to speak it."

"Oh, but I enjoy being obvious."

"Do you?" she asked. "Because I would say that the fact you own your own company was not obvious at all."

She hadn't intended to bring that up.

In fact, she had every intention of ignoring it completely in the conversation today, if only to spite him slightly. And herself. Because the fact that he was a secret mogul fascinated her. And the one thing she was eternally trying to ignore when it came to Gunnar was her fascination with him. And anything that seemed to foster further fascination she resented.

There was something about him that enticed her to act in ways she knew she should not. She didn't like it.

It made her feel like she was not above the rest of the female population of the world in any way at all. And she liked to think that she wasn't that basic.

"That's the trick," he said. "Be obvious enough over here that you can have your secrets where you choose."

"I see." She took a breath. "Well. That aside." She shuffled through the folder and plucked out one. "I would choose…these."

"Explanations," he demanded, taking the stack of folders in his hand. "Or do I have to do everything myself."

"You have done absolutely nothing for yourself since I walked in," she said.

"That isn't true. I've been breathing the entire time. I'm keeping myself alive. For which you and the rest of the world should be supremely grateful."

"I'm about to expire from gratitude," she said. "The first candidate is Hannah Whitman, an English rose. She will compliment you well. Though, your progeny will likely burst into flames in the sun."

He laughed, explosive and deep, hitting her in unexpected places.

"Well," he said. "Melanin deficit aside, she is pretty. And what attributes do you suppose she would bring to our alliance?"

"She's extremely wealthy in her own right, her family is very successful in manufacturing. She has started several charities, with a focus on educating children with special needs. She is more than willing to do the work, not simply write a check."

"I imagine that means there are many photographs of her with grateful children."

"You are correct. She is a light to all the world."

"Well, I have always thought that one's wife should be able to double as a flashlight."

"Best of all," Latika continued, "she's scandal free."

"Excellent. Because I have enough scandals for ten people. It's one thing I do not need a wife to bring to our marriage."

"Next is Lily Addington."

"Another Brit?"

"Yes. Her family owns horses."

He frowned. "That sounds like an awful lot of time spent at racetracks."

"Would you not find that enjoyable?"

"No. I prefer my gambling to take place in a casino. It's much more civilized."

"All right. Bim Attah. She is a Nigerian heiress and UN ambassador for women's rights. She has a PhD from Oxford, and has been instrumental in supplying feminine hygiene products to impoverished girls throughout the world."

He leaned back in his chair, placing his hands behind his head. "She sounds a bit overqualified, don't you think? PhD. I'm not sure I'm equal to that task."

"You have a title. I suspect that in many ways that outstrips a PhD."

"One you are born with," he pointed out. "One you must work for."

She arched a brow. "Shall I take her off the list?"

"Oh, no," he said. "I feel nothing if not entitled to things that might be too good for me. Leave her on the list."

She cycled through the rest of them quickly with Gunnar vetoing all but numbers one and three.

"Okay," she said, sighing heavily. "I will attempt to

arrange a meeting for you. Whatever you do, try not to be yourself when you meet them."

"I never am," Gunnar said. "Why, when there are so many other interesting people to choose to be?"

Latika gritted her teeth. "Why indeed."

She turned away from him, and her phone buzzed in her hand. She looked down and saw that it was an unknown number.

"Oh, don't decline the call on account of me," Gunter said. "There's no need to worry about manners in my presence."

"I wouldn't," she said, answering the phone decisively. It had nothing to do with her anyway. She worked for Astrid, and she couldn't afford to miss any kind of communication just in case.

"Hello?"

"Latika Bakshmi."

The voice was strange, low and husky, and something about the accent sent a familiar sliver of dread beneath Latika's skin.

"Yes?"

"Check your email."

The line went dead. Latika lowered the phone and stared at it, feeling like she lost herself for a full thirty seconds. She had no sense of where she was, or what she was doing.

Until she felt the intensity of Gunnar's gaze on the side of her face. She looked toward him. "What?"

"Are you all right?"

"I'm fine."

"You've gone very pale."

"No. A strange phone call. Likely a prank of some kind." She tried to force a smile. In spite of herself, she swallowed hard and guided her thumb over the email icon on her phone.

She prayed that Gunnar didn't notice the slight tremble in her hands.

She did indeed have a new email.

From an address she didn't recognize. She opened the email, it had one line of text. And a photograph.

So there you are.

And beneath those words was a picture. Zoomed in tightly and cropped close. Latika could just see the edge of Astrid's dress, and that gave her an indication of the event.

The wedding.

Astrid and Mauro's wedding. Latika had been standing just behind the Queen, and she had been sure that she was not in any sort of limelight position. She had been with Astrid for nearly four years and never had been.

But they had found her. Finally.

She swallowed hard, fear like lead in her stomach.

The worst part was, it hadn't been her parents who had found her. She was sure of that. Because while her parents would have happily hauled her away from her newfound life, they wouldn't engage in this level of theatrics. That she knew.

They would still cling to the idea that this was all for her own good, for their own good as well, but also for hers. They would lie to her, lie to themselves, all the while using soft, soothing voices and telling her to think of the future.

No, this kind of threatening language was definitely

the work of the man who was supposed to be her husband by now.

The man she had run away from.

The man she would rather die than find herself joined to.

Latika took a breath and put her hands down, holding her phone closely to her thigh.

"What is it?" Gunnar asked.

"Nothing," she said. "I will make the necessary inquiries, and make arrangements for you to meet these women. In fact, I think we will organize a ball."

"A ball?"

"Yes. For all the eligible ladies in the file."

"I said that I'm only interested in these two."

"But why limit your options, Your Highness. You're correct. The chemistry that you may feel with one of them is important to explore. Allow me to take care of it. I will handle everything."

Her mind was spinning as she walked out of Gunnar's office. On the one hand, creating such a spectacle around the country at this time was possibly unwise. But on the other hand… Well, on the other hand an event like this would necessitate an increase in security. And with so many eyes on the country, she imagined that Ragnar would be loath to attempt to take her now.

No, he preferred to do things secretly. In the dark of night, essentially.

His position as Norwegian nobility mattered far too much for him to go and create bad blood between himself and the Royals in Bjornland.

And in truth, Latika had counted on that. Always. When she had first come to Astrid for the job, it had been on her mind. The fact that Bjornland was politically involved with Norway, and that it would put Ragnar in a bad position should he cross the Queen, had mattered to her.

Because she needed protection.

The palace guards would provide it. The increased attention would provide it. She had to believe that.

The alternative was far too awful to consider.

CHAPTER THREE

THE ENSUING WEEK was a whirlwind. At least, it looked as though it were one for Latika.

Gunnar did nothing but sit back and enjoy the show.

Over breakfast one morning, Astrid commented on it. "I don't think I've ever seen her work so hard at anything. And that's saying quite a bit."

"Yes, she has taken control of the task admirably," he said, not rising to his sister's bait. Because he knew there was bait. Even if he wasn't sure what the hook buried in said bait was meant to drag him toward.

"Are you assisting her at all?" Astrid asked.

"Do *you* assist her in the planning of parties?"

Astrid gave him an icy look. "She is *my* assistant."

At that moment, Astrid's husband came into the room holding Gunnar's nephew. It had taken Gunnar a time to accept his brother-in-law. He had not trusted the man at first, but then, given the way that his sister had met him, Gunnar felt he could hardly be blamed.

Astrid had engaged in subterfuge, essentially tricking Mauro into getting her pregnant. And when he had discovered the ruse, Mauro had been decisive in his action. He had demanded that Astrid marry him, and that, was what Gunnar had taken exception to.

The man was common born, and it wasn't as if Gunnar was any sort of snob, but he had grave concerns about anyone seeking to use his sister. As it had turned out, his feelings for Astrid had been genuine and their marriage had become a very happy one.

But, Gunnar was still getting used to the situation.

"That's different," Astrid said, rising from her seat and crossing the room, giving Mauro a kiss on the cheek before taking her son into her arms. "You should be helping her. Since she is helping you clean up your mess."

For Astrid.

He wasn't going to say that. He didn't care what anyone thought of him. And were it not for his sister, he would happily go on not caring.

"I'm sorry, what exactly did you want me to do?" he asked. "Ensure that the punch is spiked?"

"I don't know, something that wouldn't send my assistant to an early grave. Since I am quite attached to her."

"Yes," he said. "Something that I'm not sure I understand. You seem more fond of her than you are of me at times. And yet, for all I can tell, Latika seems to lack a sense of fun, or humor."

"That's a phenomenon that only presents itself in your presence, Gunnar. I find her amusing and delightful." His sister's gaze was glued to him. "Perhaps it's just you."

"Everybody likes me."

"Everyone thinks you can do something for them. That's different. I don't think Latika cares one way or the other whether or not you can do something for her."

That wasn't true. Everyone was an opportunist. And

everyone would use a person if the need was great enough. He'd learned that early, and he'd learned it well.

Nothing could insulate you when someone decided to use you as a tool. Not even family. Not even blood.

"She works for you. If she needs a favor… You're the one she'll go to," he pointed out.

"Are you implying she doesn't actually *like* me?"

"Did you not just imply that none of my friends actually like me?"

"Are either of you going to threaten to have the guards shoot the other this time?" Mauro asked, his brother-in-law's expression one of amusement.

"Probably not," Astrid said.

"The two of you make me so sad that I was an only child," Mauro said.

"I can see where you would be jealous," Astrid responded serenely.

They settled in to eat breakfast then, and Gunnar was bemused by the domesticity before him. It was difficult to imagine himself settling into such a life.

And yet, he didn't think it would make him entirely miserable. Of course, he would never feel for his wife the way that Mauro and Astrid seemed to feel for each other.

And there would be no children in his marriage.

The line was guaranteed to continue without his help, and he was not the heir. Therefore the task wasn't his.

After the childhood he'd endured, he had no interest in exploring the relationship between a parent and child again. Even from the opposite side.

The door opened, and Latika entered, her black hair swept back into a twist, her makeup sedate. And yet, she glowed. He ignored the tightness that he felt in his stomach. In his groin.

"I do hope I'm not interrupting," she said. "Queen Astrid, we have an appointment with your stylist. We must ensure that you are appropriately outfitted for the ball."

"What about me?" Gunnar asked.

"You will wear a black suit," Latika said, each word crisp.

She was like a tart apple. Then he desperately wanted to take a bite of her.

It was a shame. For with this new endeavor now before him, he never would.

For years now, his dearest fantasy had been getting down on his knees before his sister's prim assistant, pushing one of her tight pencil skirts up around her hips and draping her legs over his shoulder, her back against the wall, as he licked his way into her center.

As if she sensed his thoughts, her gaze landed on his, locked there. She looked startled, like a deer caught in the headlights.

"It seems to me that you are avoiding having to dress me," he said.

"I'm not avoiding anything," she said. "Believe me, Gunnar, if you required dressing, I would accommodate. I'm sorry if that wounds your fragile masculinity in any way."

"Good to know," he said.

On a tightlipped smile, Latika turned and walked out of the room.

Astrid fixed her cold gaze on him. "Can you not deliberately poke at her with a stick?"

"I'm not poking her."

"You're a pain in the ass. She's been through enough without you harping on her constantly. Be a decent human being."

"That is, dear sister, the point of all of this."

If he could not fashion himself into a decent human in the realest sense, he would make himself look like one.

In his world, facade was better than reality anyway.

Two hours after the encounter with Gunnar in the dining room had left Latika trembling and feeling hollowed out, she found herself standing in Astrid's chamber while her friend tried on a myriad of dresses.

"It seems strange," Astrid said, currently admiring a white gown with delicate silver beading that clung to her curves. "To draw attention to myself on what should be a ball in my brother's honor."

"Yes," Latika said. "I can see that. But you know, it is about improving the way people look at all of Bjornland. We have essentially put out a call to all the eligible ladies of the world that Prince Gunnar is looking to settle down. The media attention alone demands that you shine above all else. Especially all those eligible ladies. It won't do to have anyone in attendance be more beautiful than the Queen."

Astrid laughed. "I imagine there will be a great many women there who are more beautiful. My brother attracts rare beauties like honey attracts bees."

"Yes," Latika said. "Pity he is not actually sweet."

"I don't think anyone would find him half so compelling if he were."

Compelling.

That was an appropriate word for the man.

Of course, there were other words too. None of them fit for polite company.

"I think this color washes me out," Astrid said. She looked over at the rack that was entirely filled with gowns. "And that orange would be hideous on me. It would look lovely on you."

She gestured to a gown with a long bodice and a full, sheer skirt that gathered at the side, with a close fitted lining beneath. It was orange, with shimmering gold geometric detail over the top of it.

And, Latika *knew* she would look good in it.

But, she needed stay in the background. Desperately.

"I think I will opt for something black," she said decisively.

"Well," Astrid said. "I will not. I would look like a ghost."

Astrid sighed and then looked over at Latika thoughtfully. "Are you all right?"

"I'm fine," Latika said.

"You don't look fine. In fact, you seem very tense. And not simply because you're planning a party. Usually, you enjoy that."

"Well, it's just Gunnar. You know he and I don't exactly see eye to eye. But it's normal. Nothing out of the ordinary." Except the threats to her safety. But she was choosing to handle that herself.

Astrid blinked. "Yes. I do know that the two of you get on like angry ants trapped in a jar. I also don't think that's the real problem."

"Why?" Latika asked.

"Because I know you. Because we're friends. Latika, don't you trust me?"

Latika shifted uncomfortably. "Of course I do."

"Are you upset about Gunnar getting married?"

Latika sputtered. "What?"

"I'm not a fool," Astrid said. "I know that he irritates you, but I also know that there is something underneath that. I can never tell if the two of you are going to start yelling at each other, or start tearing each other's clothes off."

Latika stiffened, her face getting hot. The fact that Astrid had noticed that she carried some sort of shameful...fascination with Gunnar was truly alarming. It was somewhat refreshing to be able to be alarmed about something other than the email she'd received a few days ago, though, she would not have chosen this. "I can honestly say that I am not upset about Gunnar choosing to get married."

"Then what is it? Please don't tell me it's to do with your parents."

Latika sighed. "Not as such."

"It's related to that, though."

"I... I have reason to believe that my former fiancé knows where I am."

"Latika, that's terrible. You should have told me immediately. I will do whatever I have to, to protect you."

"And I will do whatever I need to, to protect *you*. You don't need to worry about me, or the issues that I'm having. The scandals in my life were never meant to touch you."

"That's not how friendship works," Astrid said. "Yes, you have been an employee, but more than that. And you know it. You are the single best friend I've ever had. It's because of you that I found my husband."

"In fairness," Latika said, "it was highly unlikely any of that would work, and I feel it was only a stroke of incredible luck that saw it all come together. Or fate, perhaps. But either way, I cannot take credit. And had everything gone awry, I would have been responsible for your most disastrous decision ever. We could have damaged the whole of the country over a one-night stand."

"But it was meant to be," Astrid said. "And you trusted me. You trusted me when I said I needed your help, and believe me, the people in my life who have trusted me, who have taken me at my word, have been in short supply. For the most part, people have doubted I know my own mind because I am a woman. Really, only you and Gunnar, and my mother, ever treated me as though I had the head on my shoulders required to run a country. Or, to make any decisions on my own."

"Yes," Latika said. "Well."

It was one of the difficult things about Gunnar. He had always been incredibly supportive of his sister. And though he had been angry over the incident with Mauro, and Latika colluding with Astrid to sneak her into his club so that she might engage his services in the making of an heir, in many ways, Latika couldn't blame him. And indeed, would possibly respect him less if he'd had no issue with it whatsoever.

Latika had helped Astrid accomplish that for her own reasons, but it certainly wasn't in the interest of her finding love with Mauro. No. It was only that she understood what it was like to feel that you had no power in your own life.

An ancient law written into the code of the land of Bjornland had stated that the Queen could declare herself the sole parent of her issue. With that goal in mind, Astrid had set out to get pregnant by the most disreputable man on the planet, thinking he would want nothing to do with the child. Of course, he had. And Astrid had not ended up with a child, and no man, but with a husband. One that she loved very dearly. Nothing had gone quite as they planned, but in many ways, it had gone better.

Latika had never seen Astrid so happy.

And that—she had concluded—was what happened when people were allowed to live. To make their own choices.

To make their own *mistakes*.

Sometimes even a mistake—in the end—was perfectly all right because it led you to where you had always been meant to be.

But choice, that was what Latika wanted. Eventually. A life of her choosing, with a man of her choosing.

She wanted children.

Watching Astrid with Mauro all those desires had only become more pronounced.

She was tired of surviving.

And with Ragnar coming after her those dreams seemed farther away than ever. Dreams other people took for granted.

"What can I do to protect you?" Astrid said. "Your problems are mine. Because we are friends."

"Honestly, this ball is going to offer me a modicum of protection I would not have access to if it weren't for my position here. We will, of course have to increase security. Seeing as we are inviting every eligible woman in the world to come and have a chance with Gunnar. And those who haven't met him will surely jump at the opportunity."

Astrid erupted into a peal of laughter. "You do protest too much, Latika."

"Perhaps my protestations are honest," she said.

"You find my brother attractive. Whether you want to admit it or not."

"A spider can be beautiful in its web," Latika said. "But that doesn't mean I want it on my skin."

Astrid shook her head. "But see, that's where you have him wrong. He's not a spider. Any more than you're a fly. A predator, possibly. But maybe more like the wolves we have here in the mountains. Deadly if necessary, surely. But more than willing to put everything on the line to protect his pack. Gunnar is a true alpha. Leader and protector."

"Perhaps that's the problem," Latika said. "It is difficult for two alphas to get involved."

"That would be the story of my marriage," Astrid said. "But what Mauro and I have learned is that sometimes it can be quite pleasurable to let the other take the lead."

"Yes, well." Latika firmed her lips into a straight line. "I will take the lead by finding some other woman for Gunnar to harass."

"Are you sure you don't want to wear this?" Astrid asked, gesturing to the orange gown again.

"No," Latika returned. "I am not one of the women vying for your brother's attention, and I will not dress like one. It would have to be a moment of true crisis in order for me to turn to him."

"Well, let us hope we had don't have any crises ahead of us."

CHAPTER FOUR

THE EVENING OF the ball, everything was going according to plan. Latika could find no fault with anything.

And she ignored the orange and gold gown that Astrid had sent up for her, in favor of a long, formfitting black dress and simple gold accessories. She would look appropriate, and she would *blend*.

And that was the idea.

She bustled around, making sure that everything was in place, pacing the length of the ornate ballroom, examining it from the gilt-edged ceilings, all the way down to the marble floors.

The massive, golden chandelier was lit, and it was like a sun burning brightly at the center of the room. Perfect. Gleaming and lovely. And in the next twenty minutes the ball would be full of fluttering flowers, all vying for Gunnar's attention.

She heard footsteps on the marble floor, and turned.

And there he was.

He was devastating in that custom cut black suit, the one she had dismissed with a wave of her hand, saying that men needn't be so concerned with such things.

There was nothing *plain* about Gunnar in a black

suit. He was a weapon against all good sense, his broad shoulders waging war on every prudent thought.

His hair was still overlong, brushed away from his face, his beard just a bit unkempt.

And it put her in the mind of a Norse marauder, and she found that however she tried, she could not dislike the image.

And for the first time, a strange pain hollowed out her stomach.

Another woman would dance in his arms tonight. Another woman would dance with him from tonight, possibly into forever.

And she would never know what it was like to be held by those strong arms.

She clenched her teeth. That was an empty fantasy, driven by hormones. And she was not a slave to her hormones. She was a woman who never had such a luxury. She had been driven by the need to survive. By the need to press forward, always, and make for herself a life that she could not only stand, but that she enjoyed.

She had found a way to live.

It might not be her ideal life, yet. But it was wonderful.

And she was only ever proud of herself for that fact.

Gunnar served no purpose. Attraction to Gunnar served no purpose.

She did not even like the man.

"You have done a spectacular job," he said, and she ignored the slight thrill of pleasure that went through her midsection.

"Thank you," she said.

"Soon, I will be like a steak put out before the dogs."

The wicked glint in his eye bade her stomach turn over. She ignored the sensation.

"You will find there are no dogs here. Only a wolf," she said, harking back to Astrid's earlier words.

He grinned, and Latika thought it was decidedly wolfish. "Perhaps."

"Sheep," Latika said. "Sheep going before a wolf."

"Very evocative. Does that make you Little Red Riding Hood in this fairytale of a metaphor? Because I must tell you, I feel my mouth is all the better to eat you with."

And that was when she realized, he was not simply engaging in empty banter. No, there was a gleam in his blue eyes that spoke of intent. But there was no point to him making sexual promises toward her. Not when tonight, of all nights, moved any possibility of something happening between them out of reach.

She ignored the jolt of irritation that she felt over that. The intense regret.

Every time he had ever traded barbs with her she had assumed it was simply who he was, what he did.

She had never once thought that he might… That he might actually want her.

"I am not anyone's version of a fairytale. And you would find, that I bite back."

He moved closer to her, and a thrill shot down her spine. "Pity for you, that what you intended as a threat only sounds like a promise to me. I like a woman who gives as good as she gets."

"Then I suggest you find one here in the room full of them."

"I doubt there will be one sharp as you."

"The trade-offs you make for respectability," she said.

She turned away from him and began to busy herself with details that did not need her attention.

"Are you not respectable?"

"That depends, I suppose," she said, "on your definition of respectability."

Those blue eyes regarded her with open interest. "Someday, I should like to find out."

She locked her teeth together. So tight her jaw ached. "Oh, but there is no someday. For you are getting married. And we all know your life will end as we know it."

"A tragedy," he said.

"Well," she said, brushing her hands down the front of her dress. "It's time to bring in the staff. And then it will be time to open up the doors. I suggest you get in position."

He arched a brow, a wicked smile curving his lips. "Missionary? Did you have something else in mind," he said.

Latika ignored the sharp shock of pleasure that shot straight down through her core. It was wrong for them to talk like this—worse to be talking like this tonight. Though in some ways, it pushed it further out of the realm of possibility than ever. Which made it...almost less wrong maybe? Or less dangerous.

"You will look a bit silly in missionary position on your own," she shot back, unwilling to let him see that he had affected her.

"I suppose that depends on who you ask."

The doors opened then, and the staff began to filter inside. Latika managed to busy herself and soon her interaction with Gunnar was forgotten. She had work to do. It distracted her, both from the strange sensation she felt whenever she was around the man, and from the underlying sense of fear she'd been feeling ever since she received that email.

The many, many palace guards in attendance made her feel safe.

No one would do anything to her while she was here.

She repeated all those things to herself as she made sure the food was in place, as she made sure all was well. And then, went back to the antechamber to ensure that everything was ready for Astrid to make her appearance.

Several guests arrived before the Queen was to be seated. And Latika had the task of making sure that Astrid's entrance went smoothly, and according to plan.

Astrid and Mauro looked beautiful, the pair of them absolute perfection. Astrid had ended up choosing a deep emerald gown, and her husband was in a black suit. Mauro was a handsome man. There was no denying it. Tall, dark and Mediterranean, with wicked eyes and a mouth that looked like it was made for sin.

And yet, it was no particular sin that called to Latika. No, there was something about the cold, wild beauty that Gunnar possessed that seemed to ignite thoughts of sin.

Sin that sorely tempted her.

She put her head down, resolutely making her way through the ballroom, now filled with women that were bedecked as tropical birds, fluttering about in bright colors.

She knew that Gunnar had expressed a preference for two women in particular, but the guests did not. And every one woman—single or not—had dressed to impress him.

Latika cued everyone to Astrid and Mauro's entrance, and the royal couple alit, walking through the crowd and taking their positions in their honored seats.

It was all going so smoothly Latika wanted to celebrate. That was the thing. She might not have a husband or children yet. She might not be fully living the life of her choice, but she was living well.

She'd been seen by her parents as a bargaining chip. Her only value had been how she could marry. And here she was, operating in a very stressful and important career.

And she did it well.

She allowed that to buoy her mood. To take away the sour feelings that had begun to roil in her stomach earlier.

With them settled, Latika felt the need to check on the kitchen. She turned and slipped out a side entrance, heading down the hall. And what she saw there made her stomach twist. It was him.

Ragnar.

He didn't have the decency to be hideous. No, instead he was a severe looking older man with salt-and-pepper hair and a neat beard. He was handsome. And a great many women—regardless of their age—would have been thrilled with his attentions. But Latika knew how cruel he could be. And she knew that a life with him would be equal to misery.

The fact that he had come after her after all this time, likely less out of an attraction for her specifically, and more because he wished her harm, sent fear rattling through her.

"My dear, Latika," he said. "It has been quite some time."

"Not accidentally," she said, stopping in her tracks

and beginning to edge back toward the ballroom. There was security there. And she would be able to call for help.

"Do not think I'm so foolish as to try and take you from the palace. I simply wanted you to know how close I am. If you try to leave the country, my agents will intercept you. And I know you are here. Ultimately, as long as I can reach you, you are not safe. I will have you brought back to Norway, and married to me before you could ever protest."

"And why would I marry you?" She asked, fighting to keep her composure.

He liked fear. He liked to cause pain.

She would allow him to see neither in her.

"Because you will find the alternatives so unpleasant. You have made for yourself a little problem here. You thought that by making yourself invisible you would become invisible to me, but you are not just invisible to me, but the whole world. And that is where you have failed yourself, my darling girl. Because when I take you, I will be able to hide you. Your Queen may miss you, but how will she mobilize forces beyond the borders of her country? The public outcry will never be sufficient enough."

The words settled down to her bones, the truth of them making her feel fear. Real and heavy.

He continued. "I have you between a rock wall and me. And you know that it is true. For now... I will be here all night."

"I can have you removed," she said, craning her neck.

"I have done nothing," he said. "And my removal would create an international incident. As you well know. I know you do not wish for an incident. You are too smart of a girl for something like that." She swallowed hard, and turned and fled, running back into the ballroom, shutting the door behind her, pressing her hand to her chest.

And she saw Gunnar. At the center of the room dancing with a woman. The brilliant Nigerian activist.

And suddenly, she had an idea.

Times were desperate. And so was she.

She made her way across the ballroom, heading toward the opposite door she had just come in. A door that would take her away from Ragnar.

With purpose, Latika left the ballroom, and headed toward her room.

Though she didn't know it at the time, Astrid had given her an escape. And Latika knew well enough to take it.

Gunnar was dancing with his third potential bride of the night when a hush fell over the ballroom. He turned, following the gazes of everyone in the room. And there he saw her. Standing at the entrance to the ballroom, dressed in orange and gold, her black hair a glossy wave over one side of her shoulder.

Latika.

She did not look like an assistant. She looked like a princess.

And when she began to descend the stairs, the crowd parted for her as if she was. And then she looked at him. Deliberately. Intentionally.

And a fire ignited in his gut.

He had no idea what game she was playing. He had made it plain earlier that he was attracted to her, because he had never been the sort of man to be coy about such things.

She looked completely different than she had earlier. Though, she had still been delectable in the slinky black dress she'd been wearing, it was the sort of dress designed to make her blend in. And had she been a different woman, it might have been successful. For him, Latika would never blend in.

His greatest concern in life at this moment was that she would go on always as an unanswered need.

And he was not a man who understood denial. Not in his adult life. When he'd escaped his father's power, when it had become clear to the man that Gunnar could not be manipulated, and when it would have taken the involvement of palace guards to continue his grand experiments on Gunnar, Gunnar had taken the chance to escape into a world of sensual pleasures.

Food. Drink. Women.

Luxurious surroundings.

Most of his time spent in warm climates rather than the harsh chill of Bjornland.

He had forgotten denial. He had forgotten need.

Until her.

And while he had no moral qualms about taking Latika to his bed between now and his wedding, he did feel that perhaps the ball where he was supposed to meet his future wife was perhaps not the ideal venue for such an encounter to begin. But Latika didn't seem to agree.

She crossed the room, heading straight toward him, the expression on her face one of seductive intensity.

He wanted her. And he had, ever since she had come into his sister's employ. Every time they had sparred, it had only increased his desire for her.

And now, she paraded herself before him. As if she thought he would not be able to take action here. As if she thought he would be leashed.

"If you would excuse me," he said to his partner, a woman whose name he could no longer recall.

He stepped away from her, making his way toward Latika. And much to his shock, she increased her pace and nearly flung herself into his arms. "I would be delighted to dance with you," she said.

"What are you doing?" he murmured.

"I am sorry," she said. "You have no idea how much. But I need you. Desperately. And I think that I will not harm your objective. I think that I will further your cause."

"Do you?" he asked, keeping his voice low.

"I need you to marry me," she said. "And I need you to announce it now."

"Latika…"

And then, she did something truly shocking. She launched herself forward, and captured his mouth with her own.

Gunnar was a difficult man to surprise, indeed, until this moment he would have said it was impossible.

People were boring in their predictability.

And up until this point, Latika had been scarcely different.

She had bantered with him. She had brought their exchanges of wit to the edge of propriety, but she had never crossed it. And while he found her enjoyable, she had never truly shocked him.

But in this moment, she turned the whole ballroom—maybe the world—on its head.

There was something desperate in her kiss, and he

responded to it. He wrapped his arm around her waist, pressing her tightly against his body, forgetting they had an audience. Because what else mattered when he was finally tasting this woman that had vexed him for years.

He took control of the kiss, tightening his hold on her and angling his head, taking advantage of her surprise, of her slightly parted lips, and slipping his tongue between them.

She gasped, and he took it deeper.

And only then did he fully realize that while he might have ensnared her at this very moment, she had caught him in her trap.

"Everyone has seen," she said. "If you were to reverse course now, no one would believe you. You have clearly staked your claim on me."

"Minx," he said. "Was this your game all along?"

"I promise you it was not."

"Does my sister know that you are little more than a fortune hunter?"

"Your sister knows the truth."

He looked over at Astrid, who was seated in her throne still, watching what was taking place before her with a surprising amount of equanimity. If Astrid suspected that Latika was trying to snare him as a fortune hunter in some way, he knew that she would be on her feet.

That she would have crossed the room, making her way to him, and to Latika, demanding that the farce be ended.

But she was not. Instead, she was sitting and watching. Waiting. Clearly.

"You must say that you'll marry me," she said. "Because if you do not, there is another man here. And he is going to take me away. Not from here, but if I ever set foot outside the palace, he has promised that he will take me. If I ever leave the safety of your land. And he said… He said that my anonymity is what has cursed me, and he is not wrong. If I were to go missing, no one would know. No one would care. But if I was your wife… Gunnar, if I was your wife not only would I improve your standing in the world, but you would save me from this man. If I was your wife, I could hardly go missing without notice. Then he could not force me to marry him. I need you to protect me."

On this, Gunnar did not need a moment to think. They could work out the details later, and they would, but if what Latika said was true, she needed protection. And it was no matter to him which woman in this room he married. It might as well be the one who needed help. It might as well be the one who lit his body on fire.

"Very well," he said. "You have yourself a fiancé." He took her hand and led her over to where Astrid sat. Latika, for her part, was ashen at his side, and did not look the part of blushing bride at all. She was going to have to work on that.

"I have an announcement for you to make," he said to his sister. "It seems that I did not have to look far and wide to find my bride, as she was here the entire time."

Astrid's gaze shot to Latika. "Are you in danger?"

"I will be. If measures are not taken."

"Hello," Gunnar said. "I am the measures being taken. I assume you know about this?"

"Yes," Astrid said.

"We will speak later," he said to his sister. "For now, just make the announcement."

"I think, it's time for you to make your own."

Gunnar turned toward the crowd of people. He was not a stranger to being the center of attention, and in fact, in many venues had courted it. But never here in Astrid's domain. He had been very careful about that fact. That he never assume too much authority in his sister's presence.

Mostly, because it had angered their father.

But he was certain. Certain in this decision, whatever the eventual outcome would be.

There was no other logical choice.

"Thank you all for coming tonight. It is with great pleasure that I am able to announce that I have decided to marry. Especially in a room full of such suitable people. I will marry Latika Bakshmi in two weeks' time. You have my permission to spread the news far and wide, and to publish photographs everywhere. After all, you do know I like the show."

And with that, he grabbed Latika, and pulled her close, kissing her fiercely on the mouth. He might be aiming for a kind of propriety, but he would never be tame.

And that was something Latika would learn. He would help her, but he would never belong to her.

For he belonged to no one.

Not to Bjornland.

Not to his father.

What he did, he did because he *chose* to do it.

He had not gotten where he was by being weak.

He was unable to be brainwashed. Either by verbal suggestion or physical torture.

He'd proved that.

And he'd hidden it.

Because the only other alternative was for Astrid to

know just how desperate their father had been to have her ousted.

And he would never do that to her either.

The only line his father had was that of assassinating his own daughter.

But it had been a thin line.

He had certainly been willing to allow Gunnar to do it if he wanted to.

But Gunnar was strong.

And Gunnar protected what was his.

Now, it seemed that Latika Bakshmi was his, and he would protect her to the end.

On that he was resolved.

CHAPTER FIVE

LATIKA LOOKED TOWARD the back of the room and saw Ragnar, watching the proceedings. For a moment, she wondered what he might do. If he would pull out a weapon and assassinate her there on the spot. But then, her saving grace was the fact that he would never want his name overly sullied. And, that he would not want any physical harm to come to him. It was the biggest reason he would never make a move here. She knew that.

He cared mostly for his own self-preservation, and thanks to that predictability she was insured some level of physical safety.

He was a madman. And he was, in her opinion, nothing less than evil. But he cared for his own skin. For his own money.

And he would do nothing to compromise those things.

And so he simply stood, rendered impotent by the fact that Latika had allied herself with the most powerful man in the room.

That she was now visible.

And that if anything were to happen to her it would create something larger than an international incident.

It would create a wave of global concern.

Because while Gunnar was something of a scorned figure, particularly in his homeland, the world found the Playboy Prince to be captivating and compelling.

He was handsome, and he was roguish, and that was something that won out over respectable every single time.

If you were a man.

Well, thankfully for he was. Because as such, she had been able to use him as her salvation. But she could not escape the feeling that she had jumped from the frying pan and into the fire in many ways.

Although, at least, Gunnar would never harm her. But marriage was marriage. And it was entirely possible that she had gone from one life sentence to another.

You could not just throw yourself onto the altar of marrying a prince and expect that divorce would come easily.

It was possible, certainly. But it would not help Gunnar's reputation. It would not help Astrid's.

Standing there in front of this crowd of people with their eyes on her, putting herself in the exact opposite position to the one she had been attempting to avoid for the past several years, she felt as defeated as she did triumphant.

She had no idea what she was going to do. Not now that she had made herself so vulnerable. Not now that she had cast herself from one jail cell to another.

At least the jail keeper of this one was good-looking.

That was a shameful thought. She despised herself for it.

And even as she did, the enormity of what she had done crashed down around her. Would Gunnar expect that their marriage be real? Would he expect them to have children?

For she would have to marry him. And legally. To be absolutely certain that Ragnar would not simply be able to kidnap her and force her into marriage some other way.

She had to be legally precluded from marriage.

And still, that felt so defeating.

Because she had done all that she could to avoid being in an arranged marriage, and yet, she had gone and arranged one for herself.

Better the devil of your choosing.

Perhaps.

Her lips still burned from Gunnar's kiss. And from the kiss she'd given him earlier.

She had never kissed a man before.

And now she had. Now she had, and in two weeks, was possibly going to be sharing his bed.

And the idea didn't horrify her.

Perhaps there was another solution. Perhaps there was, and you didn't want to. Perhaps it was because you wanted him.

She ignored that voice and attempted to smile.

"Now," Gunnar said quietly to Astrid. "If you'll excuse me. I have to celebrate my engagement with my future bride. In private."

And with that, he looped his arm around her waist and began to walk her toward the door. Once they were out in the corridor, he turned to her. "Not here," she said.

"Then where, Latika? As this is your three-ring circus."

"Your bedroom," she said. "It is protected, and it is private."

"Or are you simply eager to get on with the wedding night? Because I can tell you, there are certain things I'm quite prepared to discuss naked."

"Let us go," she said.

She was trembling as they made their way down the corridor, Gunnar's hand still resting low on her back. And once they arrived in the chamber and he closed the door behind them, he turned to look at her, something cold and vicious in those icy eyes.

"Tell me honestly," he said. "Did you plan this?"

"I told you I didn't. I can take you back to the ballroom and show you the man that I'm running from. Ragnar Stevenson."

Gunnar's lip curled. "I know who he is. He has a... reputation. He has certain sexual interests that I don't approve of. There is little in this world I find distasteful or that I haven't participated in. My line, is consent, and that line is hard. He doesn't seem overly concerned with it."

"Don't you think I know? I heard all about it. I know how much he enjoys pain. Not the kind that both parties agree to enjoy together. He would much prefer to inflict it on women who do not enjoy it."

"How is it that you ended up on his radar?"

"My parents. My parents are very wealthy. They move in elite circles in America. And they wanted his nobility. His connections to Europe. The minute I found out my parents had promised me to a stranger I did as much digging around as I could. In the end it was a friend of mine's father who told me everything. He said I needed to know, and I needed to run. I tried to talk to my parents first. But they didn't believe me when I told them... They didn't believe me. They thought that

I was simply trying to get out of them choosing my husband, something I had always been trying to get out of. They said that I would not have been happy with any of their choices. My friend's father, he encouraged them to sweep my disappearance under the rug. Otherwise he…he threatened to expose them as mercenary enough to marry me to a monster."

"So they did not believe you," he said. "Even when you made it clear that their choice of husband was a sociopath. And they didn't believe your friend's father, yet they swept your disappearance under the rug when threatened with their forcing to wed being exposed?"

"That's the size of it," she said stiffly.

"Where did they tell people you'd gone?"

She rolled her eyes. "To India. To find myself. They couldn't very well tell everyone I'd gone into hiding to lose them."

"How did you find Astrid?"

"She had put out inquiries in my circle about hiring a personal assistant. Of course, a queen does not advertise in the paper. But it made the rounds on the Upper Eastside, and I found out about it. I decided that it would be a fantastic place for me to seek shelter in. I knew a great deal about putting together functions. I had a great many contacts. And I had experience organizing a variety of different events, and schedules. I knew that I could do the job, and whatever I couldn't do I would learn. Because it's really quite amazing what necessity will do for you."

"So Astrid hired you, and did not inquire about your identity?"

Latika shook her head. "I told your sister. I didn't feel right about coming here for shelter without making it very clear that I was running. It wouldn't have been fair."

Some tension drained from his body. "So you have been honest?"

"Yes. Only Astrid knew the truth. But I felt that as long as Astrid *did* know it was fair."

"I can't fault you for that."

"What is it you expect?" Latika asked. As if this had been his idea. As if he were the one who'd flung himself across the ballroom and into her arms. It wasn't fair and she knew it. But she felt slightly helpless just now, and it pained her to feel this way.

"I expect for this to be a marriage," he said. "Because there is little else that will keep him away from you."

"I know," she said, muted. "I did already think that through. An engagement would keep him at bay, and it would certainly give me more visibility. But, when we broke off the relationship I am certain that I would come out looking like the villain."

He chuckled. "How would you come across looking like a villain after the loss of an engagement to a Playboy Prince?"

"There's a very particular appendage you have that makes you much easier to forgive in the eyes of the public."

"True," he said. "I won't pretend that I don't know what you're talking about. Being Astrid's twin has not allowed for me to ignore gender disparity. She has behaved above reproach almost all the years of her life. And still, her ability to rule the country has been questioned, time and time again. I am the one whose competence should be questioned. And regularly. I have never once given the impression that I was overly competent or stable. I am. But I have never demonstrated. Astrid on the other hand has spent a lifetime devoted to Bjornland, and to cultivating a good reputation and yet…it never seems to be enough. It certainly wasn't ever enough for my father, who thought that I would be the superior choice to be on the throne by simple virtue of the fact that I have a penis."

"It is unfair," she said. "But it is true. Additionally, there would be no point in trying to cast you as the villain. The entire point of this ball, the entire point of you getting married in the first place was to improve your reputation. Should we throw up a barrier by deciding to start a rumor that you were unfaithful to me… And infidelity is the only way I could possibly see me coming out the victor… No. I won't do it. I won't do it to Astrid."

"And as you said already, it opens you up to vulnerability. No, legal marriage is likely the only thing that will keep him at bay. And a promise."

"What?"

"We will offer him something. Some sort of diplomatic prize. If he is to set foot in Bjornland again, he will find himself in a jail cell. The fact of the matter is, I have spent a great deal of time running in the circles that he has enjoyed. And I have heard many allegations from women about his behavior. Allegations themselves may not hold up in court, but we have the luxury here in this country of bypassing due process provided the crown sees fit to arrest someone."

"Could you really do that?"

"I could. It would create an incident. Likely a scandal the world over. But, I think that he is conscious enough of his own desire to stay out of prison that it will keep him well away from the borders of this country. Should he set foot over, should he show up in our immigration records, I will have him dealt with. But, that only protects you here. Outside of this place, it would not offer you protection. Only notoriety in marriage would. On that score, he was correct. But he was stupid to tell you. Stupid to think that you, a woman who has been in hiding to escape him for years, would not act in a way that was absolutely necessary to ensure your safety. Clearly, he underestimated you."

"Clearly," Latika agreed. "He underestimates women."

"Likely."

"Can we really have this done in two weeks?" she asked.

"We would be foolish not to. As you said. We must neutralize the threat. Legally tying you to another man, and embroiling you in a media circus so that everyone in the entire world knows your face… It is the easiest way to keep you safe. You must either be invisible or visible to all. And as you have lost your invisibility…"

"How long will the marriage last?" she asked.

"I am sorry, darling, but marriage is forever. At least, from my view it must be."

"But I…"

"If you thought that you could use me as a temporary solution, I'm afraid that you were mistaken. You're very clever, throwing yourself at my mercy and crying sanctuary. But we are a royal family. We cannot subject ourselves to the scandal of divorce."

"Of course not," she said, muted.

"Now, that did not stop my parents from having affairs."

The very thought sent a burst of strange pain through her body. "I have no interest in affairs," she said stiffly.

"Such is your devotion for me?"

"I see no need for it," she said. "It opens us up to pointless censure. The sort of thing we don't need."

"Well then," he said. "Feel free to conduct your business as you see fit."

"And yours?"

"Sadly for you, you are not in a power position."

He was correct. It was the thing that galled her so badly. She had used him. She had used the opportunity presented before her, because how could she not. But Gunnar had only been on his back foot for a few moments, and now it was clear that his was the position of power.

He had been intending to marry anyway, and whether or not it was her or anyone else would hardly matter to him. In fact, all she had done was deliver him an easier bride.

She was the one who would be grafted into a life she had not wanted.

Finding herself potentially shackled to a man she didn't even like.

But you are fascinated by him...

It didn't matter. He was ridiculous. A disreputable playboy.

With a multibillion-dollar company?

That made her wonder if there was more to him.

But she still couldn't... She couldn't fathom sharing a life with him. She could barely share a room with him without wanting to throw something heavy at him.

"I suppose..." She took a breath. This was the only part that would salvage it for her. The one thing that she wanted, above all else. "I suppose there will be children."

"No," he said, firm and decisive.

That shocked her. So much so she couldn't believe he'd said them. "What?"

"I've no desire for children."

The word settled over her skin, a strange, buzzing sensation filling her ears. "You're a prince. Surely you must produce heirs."

"My sister has done so already."

"What if something were to happen to him? God forbid, Gunnar, but it must be considered."

"She will have more children. She and that husband of hers will likely fill the palace. He is Italian."

"That is an incorrigible thing to say."

"I am incorrigible." He shrugged a shoulder. "My father was a tyrant. My time spent in a father-son relationship was unendurable. I have no interest in revisiting it. I have no interest at all in being father to anyone or anything. That word is forever tainted for me. And, as I have no need of producing children…"

"But think of what it would do for your standing in the media."

"Oh, I daresay they will be fine taking photographs of us at various parties. You will be the envy of women the world over."

"Because I'm with you?"

"Obviously." He lifted a shoulder. "I'm rich and handsome. Titled as well. You will be a style icon because you are my wife. Many women would have wanted such an honor. And you have it now."

"But no children."

"Surely your position as one of the top influencers in the world will compensate for that."

Anger vibrated in her core, but she said nothing.

This was worse than she could've possibly imagined. She had not simply trapped herself in a marriage, but she had trapped herself in a childless one. She wanted to be a mother. To fulfill that loneliness inside of her. To repair the distance that she had always felt in her relationship with her own parents, by being a better mother to her children.

And he was not allowing it. He was taking this from her.

It was a thing she could not endure.

But what could she do? She was completely and utterly trapped. Between a madman, and one who had just laid down an edict for her life that she did not know if she can survive. Still, she would have to take Gunnar. Because the alternative may very well actually kill her.

"Well," she said. "If there are to be no children, and you are happy to have affairs. Then I see no point in the two of us having sexual relationships."

Something in his gaze changed. It turned to ice. And then to blue flame. "Is that what you think?"

"As you said. You do not see any reason for a couple in our position to stay faithful, as your parents did not."

"And you think that you can resist me?" he asked.

He was utterly sincere. And she would love to laugh in his face.

Sadly, she wasn't immune to his body, whatever she might want to believe. In fact, his body transfixed her in ways no other man's ever had. Even now, even as he dashed her dreams of the future to dust, she couldn't deny the attraction that flared inside of her.

"It may have escaped your notice, but I have done an admirable job of resisting you for the past three years." That at least was true. She hadn't—as far as she knew—

ever really betrayed her attraction to him. He might suspect, but he didn't know.

"Well, that is because I have never truly tried to seduce you."

She sniffed. "You do have a very high opinion of yourself."

"Well, ask yourself this, Latika. When you needed a port in the storm, where did you look? You looked to me. And I would suggest that that makes me perhaps a bit more than you would like me to be."

"I think perhaps your mind makes you a bit more than you are."

"However you like. Don't think I don't recognize the heat between us. And don't think I don't realize that it is mutual. Whatever I feel for you...you feel it for me."

"How do you know I feel a thing for you?" she asked.

"You were awfully comfortable coming up and kissing me."

Heat stung her face. Shame lashing her like a whip. "When people are in burning buildings, they are awfully comfortable jumping out of five-story windows hoping that they land favorably. I was willing to take my chances with you."

"Call me whatever you like," he said. "A panic button. The fire you jumped to from the frying pan. A last resort. But your mouth doesn't lie when it touches mine. It may when you speak, but you cannot deny chemistry such as ours. Not where it counts."

"I can."

Because he was denying her children. And so, she would deny him her body. There was perhaps no convincing him she didn't want him, but that didn't mean she would weaken in her resolve.

He stared at her, hard. Those blue eyes seeming to look beneath her clothes, beneath her skin. Her heart was thundering, her whole body beginning to tremble. Why did he affect her like this? How?

"You truly expect that we will be married for the rest of our lives and never explore this chemistry between us?" he asked.

She had no defenses left. None but the truth. "It should be no hardship to me. After all, I've reached the age of twenty-four without ever having been with a man. What's twenty-four more years?"

"I did not realize you were so young," he said, his expression strange.

"I don't advertise. Do you think my parents waited until I was very old to try and marry me off? Of course they didn't. They had dynasties to try and make."

"You think we'll only be married twenty-four years? That's not very much time for the rest of your life."

"I was thinking yours," she said, her tone stiff. "After all, your age is much more advanced than mine. And also, I may poison you."

He shrugged. The casual, disaffected gesture such a stereotype she wanted to hit him. "So long as it's in a good whiskey, I may not even mind."

"No commentary on the state of my hymen?"

"I'm not surprised," he said dismissively. "Given how frosty you are, it's little wonder."

Damn. The. Man.

"Well then. It seems that you're not missing anything by being denied my bed and my body. In fact, you should be very happy."

"Consider me overjoyed. I may find a porn star to celebrate our engagement with."

"It's neither here nor there to me, Gunnar. Provided you practice discretion. But then, that's your part. The improving of your reputation. All I need is to be saved."

"I hope you enjoy planning your wedding. We haven't been able to hire you a replacement."

The man was made of ice. She had expected him to protest…to…to something… Act surprised when she threw her virginity down as a gauntlet.

To act disappointed when she said she wouldn't sleep with him, which wounded her feminine pride in ways she would rather not admit. But no. He reacted to nothing.

And he never wanted children.

"Do you care for anyone?" she asked. "Do you even care for your sister really?"

"What does the evidence tell you, darling? For while you may not be able to lie with your body, I can lie with anything I want. I will be much more likely to trust you than me in any situation."

"Well, then I will continue to do so."

She would have to trust herself. She might have used Gunnar, but she couldn't trust him. She would have to remember that. She could trust only herself. And in that regard, while many things felt different in her life at this moment, that one truth remained. She had to rely on herself. And she would. Because she was strong. That truth was the only thing that kept her from slipping completely into despair.

CHAPTER SIX

LATIKA WAS A VIRGIN. Or so she claimed. She was also
intent on denying him access to her body. Clearly the
last-ditch effort of feelings of control in the situation.
Or maybe, an attempt to punish him.

Or maybe... Maybe she truly did not desire him in
the way that he did her.

But, that seemed unlikely.

Twenty-four.

She seemed much older than that.

All these revelations had shocked him to his core.
And yet, he could not allow her to see it. And she had
the nerve to ask him if he even cared for his sister. She
had no idea. No idea of why he lived the way he did.
He had done everything he could to protect Astrid, not
just from his father. But everything he was supposed
to learn in his father's name. What Gunnar's father had
tried to teach was an abomination.

His father had tried to plant the idea in his mind
that women were inferior to men. He'd tried to poison
Gunnar's mind. The cost of his resistance had been
great.

Latika thought she knew who he was, based on the
lies he'd told the world about himself. She was clearly

under the impression that he was every inch the debauched playboy.

It could not stand.

He was going to take her to his office in the States. He would show her what he was.

He couldn't tell her. Not everything. Not about his father. But he could show her that he was more.

But he would wait. He would wait until after their wedding. Because the thing that he wanted more than anything in the world was the chance to prove her wrong using nothing more than her own body.

She thought she was kept at night stewing in her irritation over him, but he knew differently.

She was only a woman. And he was only a man. Neither of them were above the basic biology that demanded their bodies mate.

Of course, thinking of it in terms of biology brought him back to the moment Latika had thrown down her virginity revelation.

It had been when he said they would not have children.

He wondered if that was related strictly to practicality, or if for some sort of emotional attachment to the idea of having children herself.

He supposed it wasn't that surprising, given the fact that many women seemed to want children. Most women, he would have thought, would consider a prince enough of a consolation prize. Though, Latika seemed bound and determined to punish him.

She had been avoiding him since the night of the ball. Throwing herself into the melee of planning the wedding.

Meanwhile, Gunnar had been concentrating on the media component.

"There's the groom to be."

He looked up and saw Astrid standing there. She was dressed immaculately, her red hair pulled back into a tight bun.

"Yes. Here I am."

He had been avoiding her since the announcement. Mostly because he didn't want to get into a discussion. He didn't want her questioning him.

She did so, out of habit. A feeling that she was the oldest, and therefore the protector.

"You've been avoiding me," she pointed out.

"Yes," he agreed. "I have definitely been avoiding you."

"Why?"

"Related to the impending lecture."

"How did you know?" She asked, narrowing her eyes at him.

"Oh, just a feeling I had. I was right, wasn't I?"

"I want to be sure that you don't hurt her."

"Interesting," he said. "A different lecture to the one I expected to receive."

"Oh, you expected me to say that you should be on guard in case Latika hurts you? We both know that is impossible."

And he was left to wonder how the whole world seemed to think of him as heartless. Even by a sister he'd worked so hard to save.

"I've no designs on hurting her. She seems a nice woman."

"You're attracted to her. She's attracted to you. But you need to understand that she's inexperienced and…"

"How do you know?"

"Well, I don't really. But, the things that she said seem to imply as much."

He thought of what Latika had said to him. That she had not been with a man in her whole twenty-four years of life.

That, combined with what Astrid said, made him wonder if it was true. "It may surprise you to learn that Latika has already laid out her ground rules. Which, include staying out of my bed."

Astrid frowned. "Really?"

"We are not a love match, Astrid, as you well know. We can barely tolerate being in the same room as each other."

"But she… Yes. But as you so eloquently put it earlier, you… You're attracted to each other."

"It's obvious, I'd think. But, she would happily slit my throat in bed after. Believe me."

"She turned to you when she needed help."

"A person will take their chances with the pavement below when they're trapped in a high-rise building during a fire." He repeated Latika's words back to his sister.

"Oh."

"I'm sorry, you don't need to interfere. The both of us can handle ourselves."

Astrid sighed. "Yes. My concern is that you won't be able to handle each other."

"Dear sister, I make it my business to handle women."

"But Latika is not like your other women. And you will be stuck with her. So whatever you do, you will have to face the aftermath of it. You're not good with consequences, Gunnar."

Just like that, he heard his father's voice echoing in his head. And he was flooded by memories. Days spent in the dungeon of the palace.

Day after day. Spent in isolation, in starvation.

There will be consequences, Gunnar. If you cannot take on board my lessons.

And there had been. Painful consequences.

"No," he said, grinning. "I'm absolutely terrible with consequences. In that I tend not to acknowledge them"

"What about children?"

A poignant question, considering what was on his mind. "There won't be children."

"Why not?"

"Astrid, you know what our childhood was like. I have no desire to father children."

"I love being a mother," she said.

"We lived different childhoods," he said.

"Yes," Astrid said. "I know. Father distrusted me. Mother supported me. She ignored you. But father…"

"You think that I enjoyed getting attention from a man who despised my sister?"

Astrid blinked. "I didn't… I didn't think that might be a problem."

"Of course it is," he said. "You are like a part of me. You are my twin. We are blood in a way few other people on this earth are. Whatever father wanted from me, he was not going to get it."

"That doesn't mean that you shouldn't have children."

"Oh, there are many reasons I shouldn't have children. That's only one of them."

"That breaks my heart," she said.

"It doesn't break mine. I am perfectly happy watching you with your life. Latika and I have come to an agreement. We will live separate lives. I will protect her, she will enrich my reputation. There is nothing to dislike about it."

"If you say so."

"I do. You might rule the country, Astrid, but in my own life, my word is law."

"Of course. I have never thought differently." What he didn't tell his sister was that he wasn't content with the idea of keeping their lives separate. Not completely.

Because he was not a man given to taking commands. Was not a man who bowed to the will of others.

No.

His father had tried. He had tried and tried to break him. But it had forged Gunnar into the strongest steel imaginable.

As his new bride would soon discover.

Yes. Latika would discover it soon enough.

Latika was carried away on the tide of the farce she was currently engaged in. Completely overwhelmed by her role as bride, and retreating as often as possible into the role of planner. It was easy to make decisions when she divorced herself from the narrative. When she thought of it as planning a royal wedding in the generic sense. Rather than her own.

Not that it mattered what her own personal preference was. Not in the context of this arrangement. What mattered was the spectacle. What mattered, was that she took herself out of harm's way. Whether or not she enjoyed the look of the wedding didn't come into it at all.

But there was one piece of it that she found impossible to divorce her emotions, and indeed her body from. And that was the acquisition of a wedding gown.

She asked Astrid to be there when she made her selection. In part because Astrid was acting as her maid of honor. A farce it might be, but it was a real wedding. And Astrid was her real friend. Much more than Gunnar could ever be considered a real fiancé.

Well, he was real in the sense that she was going to marry him.

She supposed that was the only sense that mattered.

"That one's pretty," Astrid said, but her tone said she did not think it was all that pretty.

Latika looked at herself critically in the mirror. The dress was not to her taste at all, and didn't look particularly flattering on her. For that reason alone, part of her wanted to choose it.

But there would also be pictures, and she was vain enough to not want photographs of her looking anything less than beautiful circulating the world.

But then, maybe she could still find something that didn't feel too personal.

"What I think doesn't matter," Astrid said. "It should be about you."

"It shouldn't be," Latika said. "It is about the spectacle of the royal wedding. It's about putting out into the world what we must."

"And you don't have feelings for my brother," Astrid said, her tone incisive. "Not at all?"

Latika's neck prickled. "It's complicated."

"Is it? It all seems very straightforward to me. Ragnar was at the palace. And I'm very sorry that we failed you in that way."

"Don't apologize to me," Latika said. "The fact of the matter is, I was never going to escape him forever. And I knew it."

"But I said that we would protect you…"

"And you did. You have. And now the crown is protecting me further."

"He told me that you… That you want the marriage to be in name only."

Latika's face flamed. "Why would he tell you that?"

"You may have noticed that my brother doesn't keep secrets."

"Well, it would've been nice of him to keep that to himself," Latika grumbled.

"Why won't you make it a real marriage?"

Latika swallowed. "He doesn't want children. He also said that there was no reason for us to be faithful to one another. If he intends that we sleep with other people, and the two of us don't even have to produce a child, then why bother with each other at all?"

"He *said that* to you?" Astrid asked, incredulous.

"Yes."

"He's an idiot. And I think that he has feelings for you."

Latika laughed. "The only feelings we have for each other are antagonistic. Whatever narrative you've made up in your mind about the two of us… It isn't real. And I appreciate so much that you care about me. About him. You are better than either of us deserve, Astrid. You have been so wonderful to us. But he and I have never had interaction beyond what you've seen. There is nothing secret happening."

"I believe you," Astrid said.

"Your tone says you think I'm telling the truth, but that you don't think I know my own mind."

"I just don't want you to get hurt."

"Believe me. My options are such that I don't fear

any pain from Gunnar." Latika paused for a moment. "You were asking me for advice."

"Well," Astrid said. "I'm married now."

"And I'm still a woman running from overbearing parents and an abusive former fiancé. No offense meant, Astrid, but your relationship with Mauro does not make you an expert on the feelings of every person."

"None taken at all," Astrid said.

But Latika could tell that Astrid still didn't believe her, and she thought it best to say nothing at all. Instead, they continued to rifle through the racks of gowns that had been given to them.

"You should try this," Astrid said, holding up a devastatingly beautiful gown, deceptively simple, and made from the finest white satin. It had long, flowing sleeves and a square neck, a fitted bodice and a skirt that flared out at the bottom.

It was perfect. Sophisticated and sleek, and absolutely something she would've chosen for a wedding to a man she had chosen.

"This one," Astrid said, decisively.

Latika decided she would try it on. But she wasn't certain if she could bring herself to choose it.

The day of the wedding was ominous. Clouds hung thick and low over the mountains, a dramatic effect, the dark green trees piercing through the mist, making it look as if the hills had teeth.

Truly, not an auspicious day for a wedding. But Gunnar did not believe in such things.

He had never been given cause to believe in love at all.

And this was no different. It was not luck that had

brought him here. It was simply a twist of fate, one that he was fine enough to lean into.

He had allowed Latika to continue to evade him up until today. But tonight, tonight he would launch an all-out seduction of her senses.

Why? To prove that you can manipulate her? How does that make you any different than him?

He ignored that inner voice.

He didn't want to manipulate her. He wanted to seduce her. He wanted her. And they were going to be married. The idea that they would only sleep with other people seemed foolish to him, and he had been prepared to offer his wife his fidelity.

He had only said those things to her to get to her, and in many ways, he imagined she had done the same with him. He sincerely doubted that she was actually going to hold to her missish cries anyway. Just as he sincerely doubted she was actually a virgin. The more he thought about it, the more he thought that conversation was designed to give her a power position.

Of course, she would remember that he had said he didn't want a virgin bride. And for whatever reason, she was attempting to prove to him that she was unsuitable in some way.

And again, he felt that had to be about power, rather than any kind of sincere desire to put him off. She needed him to marry her. And given that truth, he didn't actually take any of her nonsense terribly seriously.

He turned and looked in the mirror.

A black suit.

The very thing she told him he didn't require help with for the ball.

He imagined that at that point she had no idea that

the next place she would be seeing him in a suit was their wedding.

He certainly hadn't.

With the decisiveness of a predator, Gunnar turned and walked out of the room, prowling down the halls, making his way to the chapel that was on the grounds of the palace.

Theirs was not a wedding with quite as much fanfare as his sister's. After all, the wedding of the Queen, particularly to someone as famous and outrageous as Mauro, had been an insane spectacle. But, there had been a bit of something as well. The paparazzi was fascinated by her, and of course, a profile had been released about her in the media. Information about her family. They had interviewed her parents, who'd had nothing but good things to say about their daughter.

And he knew that they had contacted the palace and asked for an invitation.

It was a decision that Gunnar had been hard-pressed to make. Because, on the one hand, her parents had clearly tormented her by putting her in the path of Ragnar. But on the other, this marriage solved all of their issues. And keeping her parents away from the wedding might only cause tension, and give Ragnar a foothold.

Indeed, it might also make her parents into problems that he didn't want to deal with. So with regret, he had given them an invite.

He could only hope he didn't regret it. The church was filled already, hundreds of guests in attendance, and millions tuning in on television, and on the computer. And Astrid met him outside the sanctuary.

"Why aren't you already seated?"

"We walk together," she said. She looked up at him,

her green eyes filled with emotion. "I noticed you did not have a best man. Well, I am your twin. And there is no one on this earth who has ever been closer to you than me. So I will walk with you."

His sister's sentimentality hit him hard. At the same time, made great tendrils of acidic emotion churn through his stomach. Because she thought they were close. She thought they shared a bond he wasn't entirely certain they did. She thought she knew him. When he had kept so much back from her. For her own protection.

And yet, she was standing with him. And that mattered. He would let the other things fall from his mind. They walked to the front of the sanctuary together, whispers filling the air, heads turning as they moved. And then he took his position at the head of the altar.

Astrid nodded her head regally, and then went and took her seat by her husband.

Gunnar was very accomplished at not paying attention in church, and he handily tuned out the exhortation given by the priest, and the hymn that went up after. And then, it was time for the bride to walk down the aisle.

The music shifted, swelled, and after a few moments, Latika appeared. Her long black hair was swept up in a bun, her gown made of lace and glimmering beads, the skirt heavy and full, rising and falling elegantly with each step she took. She was an uncommon beauty. And as she walked toward him, his plan became blurry.

Because it was difficult to think straight with Latika there.

Difficult to have a clear-eyed view of his plan. In fact he forgot his plan. Forgot there was anything other than this stark, physical need igniting a fire inside of him. He was in a church, but his thoughts were decidedly less than pure.

In fact, he would not have been surprised to burst into flame at any moment. And when she joined him at the head of the altar, looking all stiff and uncomfortable, he wanted to kiss away those grim lines around her mouth. Wanted to crush her up against his body and kiss her until neither of them could breathe. He already knew how intoxicating a kiss between them could be. How could she deny them? Both of them? They wanted each other, and she was intent on…playing games. Well, it would not stand. She was using him, and he could fully respect that. But that didn't mean she got to be the only one with a say in how their marriage would be conducted.

She turned to face him, wordless. And they both stayed silent until the part came for them to repeat their vows.

It was easy for him, because he had never taken much of anything to heart, or treated anything with reverence, so he didn't know why this should be any different.

Latika, for her part, seemed stilted.

Then she looked over, and he could see the exact moment her eyes came to rest on her parents.

Her face went scarlet, her eyes widening with shock.

She finished out her vows tightlipped.

And when time came for the kiss, he determined that he would do his part in loosening that terse expression.

She might not want to desire him, but the fact of the matter was, she did. And he was going to use that.

He lowered his head, capturing her in his arms and holding her firmly against his body. Then he lowered his head and kissed her.

It was nothing like the other two kisses they had shared. For now, they had an audience, it was true. But he was fully in command of the situation.

And it was Latika who melted beneath the heat between them. He crushed her lips beneath his, and forced them apart, sliding his tongue against hers. She was sweet. She was so very sweet.

A prickly, intoxicating beauty.

One that had resisted him far longer than anyone else ever had. One that made his heart beat faster. Made it feel like his body was on fire, and how long had it been since a woman had interested him in such a way?

He couldn't remember.

His image was a blur of glitter, golden brown and red lips. Latika was the only woman in his memory. The only woman that he wanted. He knew that his kiss was pushing the bonds of propriety for a royal wedding— many royal couples did not engage in physical affection such as this, even during the wedding ceremony.

But he didn't care.

As far as he was concerned, being a married man was more legitimate than he had ever intended to be, and he wouldn't be denied this pleasure. Not now. Not now that he finally had her—Latika—beneath his lips.

And it was only a taste. Only a taste of what was to come later. He wanted her. My God how he wanted this woman. It defied everything. Every basic idea he'd ever had about himself.

The world that he lived in where women were interchangeable and one soft body was as good as the next.

Except, no one would do but her. Not now.

When they parted, he was breathing hard. Latika, for her part, was a blank space.

The priest pronounced them man and wife, and he and Latika held onto each other's arms, and walked down the aisle. Once they were free of the audience, free of the church, she jerked away from him.

"How dare you not tell me my parents would be here?"

"I'm sorry," he said. "I miscalculated your response to that. I did not think it would matter."

"How could you think it wouldn't matter? I haven't seen them in more than three years."

"I thought it wouldn't matter because I thought you were a woman of some intellect. One who understood that sometimes the benefits to something outweigh the potential costs. If your parents feel that this marriage will give them more than what your marriage to Ragnar would give, then they will engage in the protection of it as well. You no longer have anything to fear from them. However, should we have excluded them from the happy event, I fear that they might have retaliated. It is all about ensuring that this gives them more than he could have. You must understand that."

She looked away from him, her throat working. "I understand. But you should have told me."

"Perhaps you should have warned me that we were going to get engaged two weeks ago."

"I didn't know…"

"And I simply made a decision when it came across my desk, Latika. One that I thought was best."

"I can't stand this. *I can't stand this.*" She exploded, all her reserve gone now. And not in the way he'd wanted. "None of my life is in my control. And I fear that it never will be."

"Are any of our lives ever in our control?"

"You're a prince," she sputtered, straightening her hands down at her sides, smacking against her full skirt. "You're a man. You have full control over your life. Control to disobey. Control to do whatever you like."

He grabbed hold of her arm and drew her close, something inside of him snapping. "You have no idea what my life has been like. You have no idea what I have been allowed to do, and not allowed to do. Or why I have made the decisions I've made. Do not speak to me about all the freedom you think I have."

He released his hold on her then, as the doors to the sanctuary opened, and Astrid appeared. Along with Mauro. And their child.

"Is everything all right?"

"Gunnar surprised me with a visit from my parents," Latika said, her tone wooden.

"I thought you knew," Astrid said.

"No."

Astrid treated him to an icy glare.

"I refuse to stand in between the two of you when you do that," Gunnar said. "I'm not a naughty child to be scolded. I made a decision that I thought would best protect my wife, Astrid. I will thank you to not undermine me."

His sister looked shocked, but said nothing.

"We are also not attending the reception," he continued.

Astrid looked doubly shocked at that. "What?"

"We are going away on our honeymoon. My wife clearly doesn't wish to be bothered by her parents. They have been given what they wanted. Access to the palace. I assume, Astrid, that you can make them feel welcome, while Latika gets a reprieve."

"Yes," Astrid said. "I can definitely do that."

"Good. Astrid will see to everything," he said to Latika. "Unless you wish to speak to your parents."

"No. I've made a life for myself, a space for myself where I'm not a pawn. And because of them…well, because of them, here we are. I have nothing to say to them."

"Well, this should handle them once and for all, shouldn't it? In the meantime, I have already taken the liberty of packing your things."

"Why are you doing this?" she asked. "You left the entire planning of the wedding to me, and now you're pulling rank?"

"Because, my dear. You're about to discover exactly how this protection is going to work. If you seek shelter with me, then you must deal with my commands. I'm terribly sorry if that interferes in some way with your preferences. But I am not a boy to be manipulated. You leapt out of the burning building into my arms, Latika. And now you must contend with the consequences."

And that was how Latika found herself thirty thousand feet in the air in Gunnar's lavish private jet. She had been in it before, once, when she had needed to meet Astrid somewhere in Europe, when they had been separated. She had thought it gaudy and extravagant then. She did not think it any better now.

Astrid's was all clean lines and taupe leather. Gunnar's was gold and black, a large bed at the center.

"Well, I see you haven't updated," she said waspishly, sitting down on one of the plush leather chairs, designed for a person to sink into the material. Rather than for lovely, modern form.

"It's comfortable," he said. "I believe in substance over style. When it comes to my furniture. In terms of myself, I obviously go with style. But something has to have substance."

"When did you plan for us to leave directly after the wedding?"

"The moment we were standing there and I saw how upset you were."

She couldn't tell if he was sincere. With Gunnar it was nearly impossible to tell. And yet it did something to her stomach to hear him say that. "Really."

"Yes," he said. "I did not mean to distress you by inviting your parents to the wedding. What I told you is true. I genuinely believed that it was the best thing. But there is no reason you should have to socialize with them. Anyway, I was already planning on taking you to the States for a honeymoon. And so that you could see my company."

"New York?"

"No," he said. "San Diego."

That surprised her. But, she also felt just slightly relieved that she didn't have to return to New York. She hadn't been since she had fled her family. And the idea of leaving her parents behind in his land, only to return to a place that she associated with her stifling upbringing didn't suit her.

"I've never been to California," she said.

"How is that possible?"

"We didn't travel that direction. We went to Europe often. Up and down the eastern seaboard. To India. We never had occasion to go to California."

"You'll like it," he said.

"How can you possibly say that with such certainty?" Like he knew her.

"Because it's different than Bjornland. It will be a nice change of pace. For one thing, the ocean is there."

She did miss the ocean. She had always adored visiting the atmospheric beaches of the Atlantic back home. And she adored Goa on holiday. Being introduced to another beach would be nice.

But she was still feeling angry at him, and determined not to allow him to see that she thought it might be nice at all.

It was sour of her, perhaps. But she still felt so very…

Fragile. And a bit like upon being moved around on a chessboard.

Is that fair? You are the one who went to him for help. For this kind of help. You backed him into a corner, and now you're angry with him.

Well. Yes. She was. She couldn't deny that.

"I still don't understand how you managed to keep that a secret."

"And like I told you, people don't go looking for something reputable when someone is wandering around throwing the disreputable in their face. They assume, of course that what I'd like to hide is my scandalous behavior. No one can quite comprehend the fact that I don't care much about that at all. Who would think to look for success?"

"But you go into the office and…"

"Sometimes. Everyone who works there has signed a gag order."

"You're kidding."

"I'm not. Of course, we will be doing away with all of that now. We will be making our debut at the company as husband and wife, and we will be having a proper show for the media. Where all will be revealed."

"Including why you hid it?"

He shook his head. "No. That's not a story I'll ever tell."

"Will you tell me?" Her question seemed to land in a dead space of air. Changing the feel of the room.

Ice blue eyes rested on hers. "No."

She suddenly felt frustrated. She couldn't get a read on him. It was as if this thing she had thought was a puddle all along had turned out to be a fathomless sea. She couldn't see the bottom. And she could not figure out how she had thought it was a puddle in the first place either.

And all of it left her feeling confused, and for a woman who was already feeling at the end of her tether with not knowing what to do in a situation, it was all a bit much.

"I made the right decision, then," she said.

"And that is what?"

"The decision to not share my body with you."

His gaze sharpened. "You think?"

"Yes. Because if you can't even share with me the story of why you started this company, then I don't know how we could ever share anything else."

"Are you so naïve that you imagine a meeting of bodies must also be a meeting of souls?"

She tilted her chin upward, her heart pounding heavily. "I already told you. I'm a virgin. So I wouldn't really know."

"I don't believe you," he said.

Of all the possible responses to that, this was not what she had imagined. "You don't believe me?"

"No. I think you're telling me that because I told you I didn't want to marry a virgin."

"Not everything is about you," she said. "My virginity certainly isn't."

"I don't believe that. Surely most things are about me."

"No, I hate to disappoint you."

"You don't kiss like a virgin."

Her stomach twisted. "How do I kiss?"

"Well, mostly like an indignant cat who would like to scratch my eyes out, and scratch my back, but isn't sure which she wants more."

"Well, that's close enough to the mark," she said.

"So you do want to leave claw marks down my back. Little virgin, that seems like something you couldn't possibly handle."

"If you're trying to goad me into sex, then you've badly miscalculated."

"I'm not trying to goad you into anything. Goading you is simply the natural way we communicate. I assumed it was our love language."

"I'm tired," she said.

She was. But that wasn't the primary reason she needed to be done with this. Because she felt too wounded, too raw, too fragile to deal with him.

"There's a bed just there."

"I won't share it with you."

"Fine by me. I've no interest in sleeping next to you."

"Why do you want me?" Her frustration boiled over. It made no sense. He made no sense. Why did he want her in particular? Particularly after all this time? Why did it seem to be her specifically? They didn't like each other. They didn't get along. And yet something drew her to him, and she could blame her lack of experience. But he... He could have his pick of women who didn't fight with him. Who didn't irritate him. So why he should want her... She just didn't know.

Suddenly, it was as if a wall dropped between them. "I don't know," he said, his voice rough. "And if I had an answer, perhaps I would not feel so driven to get you underneath me. But I don't know. I don't understand it. I have wanted you with a ferocity that defied logic ever since the first time I saw you. And then you opened your mouth, and I wanted, in equal parts to argue with you. I've never understood either compulsion."

Those eyes were such an intense blue. "People don't compel me, Latika. They don't make me do anything. You... You bring out responses in myself that even I don't understand. I don't like it."

She swallowed hard, her heart hammering. "I don't understand how a person can want to slap someone and kiss them."

"I think you and I have far too much chemistry," he said. "The good and the bad. And there doesn't seem to be very clear reason as to why it's so strong."

The talk of chemistry with that big bed right over there, with no escape, terrified her. Because there really was nothing holding her back from being with him.

Yes, there was her sense of self-preservation. Her desire to control the situation in which she had none. But... But she wanted him. And the question now was if she was truly intent on cutting off his nose and hers, which would spite his face, but hers as well.

The look in those blue eyes nearly undid her. And she nearly went to him. Nearly shamed herself by crawling onto his lap, pressing her mouth to his so that she might get another chance to taste him.

But then it hit her. That he was just another jailer. And the last thing she wanted was to end up with feelings for him. She had loved her parents, but it had not changed the fact that she'd been used by them.

This line of thinking made her head throb, because yes, she had been using Gunnar as well. But she was very afraid that her feelings were vulnerable to changing. That she might find herself caring for him, while he simply saw her as a means to an end. A man who had said his vows in a church, without blinking, while he had already made it very plain to her that he had no intention of keeping them.

"I'm tired," she reiterated. "I'm going to sleep."

CHAPTER SEVEN

WHEN LATIKA WOKE, the plane had touched down in San Diego and when she exited the plane, she was stunned by the brilliant blue. The sea, the sky. The Pacific in all its glory.

The sun on her skin was perfection.

She loved her adopted country, but it was a very cold climate. And even though she was used to the intensity of East Coast winters, she had always preferred blue skies.

She could definitely see why Gunnar had chosen to position his business here.

But, she didn't want to tell him that.

"We can go to my house. And then, we will continue on to take the tour of the business."

"You have a house here?" she asked.

"Of course I do. It would be a very silly thing to have offices here, and no house, don't you think?"

She realized that she had imagined that everything Gunnar did was silly. So, it had truly never occurred to her that there could be such hidden depths to him.

"You don't have to tell me the story," she said as they got into the limo that had met them. "But will you at least tell me why you have gone to such great lengths to play the part of court jester, when you're a prince."

"Court jester? I always thought I was quite like Prince Harry."

"Prince Harry is less shameless."

"You must understand," he said, his voice grave. "My father did not want my sister to rule the country. We were twins, with her born five minutes before me. And he did not feel that was sufficient reason to be denied the male heir that he felt the country deserved. My sister had to work so hard to prove to him that she was capable. And I did everything in my power to make them think that I might not be capable."

"All of this... It was a ruse for your father?"

"Not all. But yes, that certainly played into it."

"And you started the business because..."

"Because I was bored. Because a man of my age cannot be happy bouncing from club to club, and bed to bed of anonymous women endlessly."

"Can't they? It seems to me that a great many men would like you to think that they can."

"Without exception, I find the people with the widest smiles on their faces in establishments like that have the biggest holes inside of them."

"Including you?"

He lifted a shoulder. "I'm not entirely convinced that if you knocked on my chest it wouldn't sound hollow."

And yet, it was increasingly difficult for Latika to believe that. She thought that he wanted the world to believe it, but that he wasn't strictly true. She had called into question his caring about his sister, and she regretted that. She regretted it quite bitterly, because she had

watched him play the role of protector to Astrid, in spite
of the fact that his sister technically inhabited a loftier
position than he did. She had the distinct feeling that
Gunnar would risk his life for her.

"I don't think it's hollow," she said.

"Don't you?"

"You're helping me."

"I'm helping myself," he responded.

"Yes," she said. "I suppose so."

But there was something in the way he said all that
that made her question things. And one of the biggest
was if his heart was truly a hollow place, or if the real
issue was that it was too full of something darker, that
he refused to talk about.

The location of Gunnar's company surprised her. It
wasn't situated in the Gaslamp Quarter, or in the business district of downtown. Rather, it was somewhere
near old town, back up in the hills and overlooking the
ocean. The entire place was built into the side of the
mountain, made from shipping containers, glass cut
into it, running from floor to ceiling. Parts of it were
fashioned with wings from an old Boeing 747, creating
a light, steel roof with strange and interesting curves. It
blended in with the mountain, just the slightest link of
shine, that seemed reflected again in the crystal-clear
waves of the Pacific.

"This isn't what I expected," she said.

"Why would anything I do be expected?" he asked.

"I haven't the faintest idea."

The car wound up beside of the mountain, the wide,
paved road offering a smooth, easy ride.

What surprised her, more than the appearance of the
containers themselves, was that inside it was the epit-

ome of modernity. Neutrals, and incredible natural light filtering in through all the glass and reflecting off the chrome beams that ran the length of the ceiling. The curves, and light metal of the wing that served as the roof offering strange interest to the place, which was more artiste than office.

He smiled when they entered. "Good morning," he said.

There were a great many staff, right there in the room. The building was open, with desks situated all around.

"Good morning," of course came back.

"Is there any news to report?" he asked.

"None," one of the women sitting nearest the door said. She was looking sideways at Gunnar, a questioning expression on her face.

"This is my wife," he said.

"We know that," one of the men toward the back said. "Your wedding was international news. Not that any of us could talk about the fact that we know you."

"I've been avoiding all mentions of it," one of the women said. "I didn't want to let anything slip."

"Well," Gunnar said. "Now you don't have to worry about it. Because the press is going to be here in the next ten minutes. We're going to go on a tour of the facility. This place isn't a secret anymore. The good news is for your trouble, you will all be getting raises."

A cheer erupted from the desks. And Latika couldn't get over just how comfortable everyone seemed to be with him. There was an ease to his interactions with all of these people that she would never have expected to find.

They all spoke to him not even just like he was a normal boss, but like he was a normal person.

Gunnar was neither of those things. Latika couldn't even squint and turn upside down to look at him and pretend it was so.

Latika did a brief circuit of the room, being introduced to everyone here in this portion of the office, and that was when the first reporter arrived.

All told, there were four of them, with cameras and recorders. And they followed Latika and Gunnar around the office, while he made broad, sweeping gestures and talked about the work this company had been doing for years, the strides they had made in both green energy and building.

Innovations that Latika knew about, but that she'd had no idea had been financed by research Gunnar had done.

"Why the secrecy?" One of the reporters asked when they reached the very top shipping crate, that was up two flights of stairs, nestled into a higher part of the mountain. The whole thing served as Gunnar's office, his desk overlooking the pristine ocean.

He was a man that always seemed at ease in his own skin. But here there was something more to it. This was his. The palace in Bjornland was decorated in tradition. And there were updates done now, but they were Astrid's.

This was Gunnar.

Large and at ease. Civilized. But with only a thin veneer between that civility and the wild, raging ocean.

"For a long while I felt it would distract from my efforts. My reputation has never been sterling. And I needed investors. Backers. People who would throw me their best researchers, so that we could make these things happen."

She had a feeling that the words slipping off his tongue were a lie. Very nice lies that everyone around them seemed to be swallowing.

But she didn't.

"And why is this a particular area of interest for you?" one of the reporters asked.

"Bjornland is one of the best examples of the majesty of nature. I grew up surrounded by mountains. Clear sky. I have always loved the outdoors. And I have always felt passionate about preserving it. You may know that I was part of creating a preserve in my home country that left many of the mountains off-limits to development."

He continued. "I was part of that effort in my late teens, and it is something that I found a great deal of satisfaction in. Going out and drinking the night away is fun, but there is little left of that good time in the morning. To be able to invest in something that will last, and to make that investment in the world that we all live in, that is the best thing I can think to do with my money. And it has been a profitable endeavor. Do not imagine that I am entirely altruistic. I assure you that I'm not." He laughed. "But, being with Latika has inspired me to live differently."

"And so the timing of this reveal does coincide with the wedding?" one of the reporters asked.

"How could it not?" Gunnar asked. "It has changed me. This marriage. Being with her. I can make of no better way to mark that, than by laying bare every aspect of who I am. I had to do it with her before we wed. The good and the ugly. I feel that the whole world is fairly apprised of my ugly. For Latika's sake, if nothing else, perhaps more of my good should be out there as well."

He took a few more questions, and then he dismissed them, leaving Gunnar and herself alone in the office.

"Is that all true?" she asked, her voice small in the large space. "About your investment in these projects?"

"Yes," he said. "I blackmailed my father for that preserve. I hope you know."

"You what?"

"I was eighteen, and he was considering an offer from a businessman to build resorts in some of the mountains that surrounded Bjornland. I'm not entirely opposed to development, Latika, you should understand. I'm a businessman in my heart, possibly more than I've ever been a prince. But the proposed plans were grotesque, and the footprint would have been disastrous on the natural wilderness. I went to my father with the proposed plans. That the resorts be put on a side of the country that had mountains already developed, and that we preserve a wilderness area for future generations. He… He did not agree. I reminded him that there were a few skeletons in his closet he would not like to be revealed. He wasn't happy with that. Wasn't happy with the realization that I had ammunition to lobby at him. But there was nothing he could do. So, that's how the preserve came to be. And so it remains. Astrid has expanded those protections. And, it is something that I have made an area of expertise. How we might continue to develop in the world in a smarter, more responsible way. We must live here on this planet. Why should we not live on it more gently?"

"Says a man with a private jet?"

A rueful smile curved his lips. "That was such a predictable statement, Latika, it was nearly boring."

"Then don't be a stereotype," she said.

"I didn't say I was a paragon of any sort of virtue. Simply that I care. And I attempt to affect change in the ways I do care. As humans what else can we do? We can talk about the things that concern us, but if we have the resources to change them and we never do... Better to never even pretend that we care."

She had nothing flippant to say to that. "It's been so long since I've been able to care about anything but myself. It's exhausting."

He frowned. "I have never been given to the impression that you are selfish."

"I am," she said. "The past three years of my life has been entirely devoted to avoiding detection. It doesn't mean that I don't care about Astrid. I always have. But beneath all of it, has been concern for myself. I've had to be wrapped up in the concerns of my own survival all this time. I look forward to being able to care about something else."

She had been so mired in the idea that marrying Gunnar was to submit herself to another version of captivity that she hadn't seen it from that angle. But hearing Gunnar talking about caring for bigger things brought the reality of her own existence sharply to life. It had become closed. It had become small and mean, of necessity and that wasn't the life she wanted.

"Are you hungry?"

She blinked. "My body has no idea what time it is. I think I might be hungry. I might be exhausted. Or ready to run a marathon."

"I find the best thing to do with jet lag is to just start

eating, and keep eating so that you don't fall asleep before you are supposed to. Difficult to go to sleep while chewing steak."

She laughed. "I suppose it would be."

"Come," he said. "And let us return to my house."

CHAPTER EIGHT

GUNNAR KNEW THAT his home was impressive.

A feat of architecture. Made entirely of recycled woods and metals, and constructed into the natural shape of the mountain it was built into. He took for granted the effortless beauty of the place.

But Latika's expression of awe when they pulled up to the house forced him to look at it with new eyes. It created in him a strange sense of pride that was almost entirely unfamiliar.

He had instructed his staff to be absent upon their arrival, and to have dinner laid out and waiting. He was not disappointed, he never was. For he had learned early on that if he surrounded himself with people who thrived on the same level of excellence that he did, then everyone could exist happily.

Every member of his staff had to be almost as type A as he was. Those with less intense personality types would be miserable working for him anyway. And he found, oddly, that surrounding himself with people who had similar levels of intensity created a more serene work environment. Everyone bumped along nicely, no one impeding the progress of anyone else. Gunnar had gone and dressed for dinner, a white shirt and a pair of black pants, and he had asked Latika to do the same. Much like dinner, clothing had been laid out in advance already as well.

Some of her own things had been packed when they had left Bjornland, but he had also taken the liberty of having Astrid's stylist procure some new items.

He had expected the spread set out for them on the expansive terrace that overlooked the ocean to be perfect. And he had expected Latika to look beautiful. She always did. But he had not expected the site of her walking out of the house, wearing a dress that exposed her shapely, brown legs, and showed off her body in a way that would make any man fall to his knees and worship, to leave him utterly breathless.

He had been with some of the most beautiful women in the world. He considered his palate somewhat jaded.

But he had never been with Latika.

And suddenly, that truth felt like too heavy a thing to endure. He wanted her. With ferocity, he wanted her. There was something to her that went beyond beauty. It shimmered across her skin, captured him by the throat, with each shift and slide of that glossy black hair that hung down past her shoulder.

The dress was red. But that didn't matter. Because it *covered* her. Obscured her from his view, and that made it an irritation, rather than anything of note. She seemed oblivious to the fact that she had stunned him completely. That she had reached down inside of him and rearranged things within him so that he could not find his balance.

Like walking into a familiar room and finding the furniture somewhere unexpected.

"This really is quite lovely," she said, crossing the place.

He moved, pulling her chair out for her.

She lifted a brow. "Aren't you the perfect gentleman?"

He chuckled. "I should think a rather imperfect one."

"Perhaps." She pondered that for a moment. "Yes, you do like that story."

"It is isn't a story. It's true. The fact that I put work into a nature preserve, and give a damn about the future of the planet doesn't change these other things about me."

"I suppose not," she said.

"Does it make you feel better to imagine you might be married to someone a bit more decent then you initially thought? After all, ours is not a romantic entanglement. Is it just that you feel the need to have good feelings about partnerships?"

"No," she said. "It's because I find this version of you slightly more interesting."

"Well, I do live to be of interest to you." The words felt true. And he couldn't figure out why, when he'd meant them to be dry.

"I want to know the story," she said. "Because I can't quite piece together all these things I know about you and make one picture. I don't quite understand. I would like to."

"Why?"

"Because from the first moment I met you I... I felt drawn to you. I could not figure out why. I think the answer is in this, and I want the answer."

"Because it damages you so much to think that you want a man you don't like?"

"Maybe," she said. "But I'd like to think it's more complex than that."

"It probably isn't. We people are not overly complex. We want peace. And that's hard to come by, so when we can't find that, we chase oblivion. Through drink. Through drugs. Sex. Our bodies are inclined toward that which is a natural stimulant to us. Oftentimes emotion is separate entirely from that. People will sacrifice whole lives they've built on the offer of being entertained for a few hours. Why should you imagine you're above that?"

"Mostly because I'd like to think I don't even see a carnival ride or a glass of whiskey."

"If you have concerns about that, make it for your own sensibilities, not mine. I for one am completely comfortable being a ride for you."

"Even a ride came into being somehow. Everything was built, Gunnar, even you. And as much as you like to pretend that isn't so, as much as you like to pretend there is no authenticity in you, we both know it isn't true."

"My story is altogether uninteresting. I'm nothing more than a pampered prince, after all."

"If that's what you need me to believe."

It was the boredom in her voice that bothered him. And as they ate their meal, looking out at the ocean beyond, he did his best not to brood on it. It didn't matter whether Latika thought him interesting. He was beyond caring what other people thought, and that included her. They ate in relative silence, and he endeavored to not think overmuch about it.

"It's a strange thing," she said softly. "Growing up in a gilded cage. I understand that better than most. I was nothing but a pawn to my parents. The means by which they could gain some kind of power. I always suspected they weren't able to have more children. Because if they had a son, I think they would have been happy. Except... Maybe not. Because a daughter is an interesting pawn to use to gain greater leverage. Nobility, that was their aim. A daughter is much more useful in that sense."

"I have never thought of it that way, but I imagine so. My own father would have likely been much happier if he could have used me as a ruler, and my sister to consolidate power."

"Of course," Latika said. "My parents' greatest goal was to marry me off to someone like you. They poured every resource into me. Into making me beautiful. Into making me sophisticated. They gave me lessons. I play the piano, you know. And am minorly accomplished in ballet. I learned everything there was to know. Not so much that I would be too smart for whatever man they put me in front of, but just enough that I might be able to carry on a conversation seamlessly. That was very important to them. But none of it was about enriching me. It was all about making me into the prettiest of pets."

Gunnar's lip curled. "Like being sent to obedience training."

The idea of Latika being used in that way appalled him.

She continued. "And I understand that so many people on this earth have it worse. That they must worry about their daily survival. In terms of when they might eat again. How they can find shelter. But for so long I was a creation of my parents, and then I spent all those years in hiding. I understand. I understand that you can be surrounded by the greatest beauty in the world, by all the things that money can buy. But if the people around you only want to use you…it's empty."

"Yes, well," he said, "That is very unusual. A couple of poor little rich kids who feel assaulted by their privileged pasts. Actually, that's most dinner parties that I go to on a given day."

He regretted the words as soon as he spoke them, because Latika had been sincere. Sincerity was not something he had a great deal of experience with and it showed here. It made him deeply uncomfortable, her sharing with him. He had given her nothing and yet, she shared things that had wounded her.

But as far as he could see, it wouldn't benefit anyone for him to get into an in-depth discussion of his past.

On the other hand, there was also no reason not to.

He knew why he didn't tell Astrid. She didn't want his sister bearing any measure of burden over the things their father had done to him. But even more so, he didn't want her wounded by the knowledge of just how drastic the measures her father had been willing to take were. She knew that he had opposed her. But, all that their father had ever let Astrid see was vague disapproval. He had set up a council to obstruct her, and that had been an inconvenience. She had certainly felt the sting, the lack of their father's trust. But she didn't know the more sinister elements of his opposition.

And he never wanted her to.

There was no reason to spare Latika from the truth. And indeed, Gunnar was a resilient man. One who might bear some scars on his body, but was otherwise fine in his soul. Such as it was.

"How much has my sister told you about our father?"

"I know that he was opposed to her being the heir. But also that there was nothing he could do."

"Much of that was due to our mother," Gunnar said. "Our mother was a strong-willed woman. I always wondered why she married him. So, I suppose the title speaks for itself. Our mother made it impossible for him to simply install me onto the throne, as much as he would have liked that. Our mother made it known the world over within ten minutes of our birth that it was my sister who was the rightful heir."

"Would you have wanted to be the heir?"

"I would have done it," Gunnar said. "Anyone who wants such a mantle should not have it in the first place."

"That is probably very true."

"The weight of the crown is heavy. And Astrid's crown twice that of what many people in her position would experience. She had to be absolutely perfect. Perfect in a way that I would not have been expected to be. No, I have never envied her. Neither have I resented her. My father wished that I would. My sister's view of things was that our father favored me, but it could not be further from the truth. I am my father's biggest disappointment. What he wished for, more than anything else was for a son who craved power with the kind of avarice that he did. He wanted a son who could be trained to desire power above all else."

He watched as her face shifted, a softness to her dark eyes that he'd never seen directed at him. "But what my father never understood was the bond that twins share. My sister is a part of me. I would die for her. I would no more betray her than myself. For me, it would be impossible. When he found that he could not simply suggest that to me, he tried to force a change of heart.

He tried with everything in him. There is a dungeon in the palace, if you didn't know. And my father was not above making use of it."

Latika's face contorted. "Gunnar…"

"If I tell you this, you must promise me you will not speak of it to my sister."

"Astrid is my best friend…"

"It doesn't matter," he said. "I'm your husband. And if what you desire is intimate knowledge of my secrets, then you must understand why I have kept them."

"I want to know," she said.

"And if you want to protect Astrid, you will swear to me that she will never know."

"I swear it," Latika said, her voice a hushed whisper.

He knew there was dessert in the kitchen, but he decided to leave that bit of information. No matter how good the Princess cake, it would not be good with this story. It would likely curdle soon.

"My father didn't just doubt my sister's ability to rule. He actively despised that she would. For my father, the monarchy and the patriarchy went hand in hand. He wanted me to be his successor. But he knew that he couldn't simply demand it. First of all, we have a government in Bjornland. A council. And while that council was very loyal to my father, while they would certainly have enforced his rule in normal circumstances, the outright replacement of an heir would have been unprecedented, and indeed, would have likely been impossible without inciting some sort of civil war. When the heir to the throne is born, the military swears their allegiance. Their allegiance to the heir is equal to that of the King. It is the same with the council."

"So…"

"Short of killing my sister there was nothing he could do," Gunnar said.

"He would never have done that," Latika said, the horror laced through her tone so pure it made him feel all manner of soft things for her. He wanted to protect her from this too.

"I don't know," Gunnar responded. "But, he didn't. So, I don't know how much of that was out of the grace and goodness of his heart, and how much of that was a desire to never tarnish his legacy. You see, that was what it was all about. The desire to install me as heir was all about the perfect articulation of his legacy. To be caught murdering his own child…"

"I can't believe it," Latika said.

"Because you didn't know my father. But of course, he knew that I would have just as difficult a time taking the throne by force. But he thought that I might be able to…persuade my sister to step down. He began to educate me, as a boy, about the facts of life. He tried to instill in me an idea that women were weak. That a female ruler could never be as strong as a male counterpart. But I knew my sister. I knew my mother. While my mother wasn't perfect, her strength was unsurpassed. That is not up for debate. I can see all around me evidence that what my father said wasn't true. Astrid surpassed me in patience, and kindness. And to me, those things are a particular form of strength. One that has no sense of being threatened. Astrid is, and always will be, to my mind the rightful ruler of our nation. And nothing my father said could make me turn against her. And that was when he decided to try other methods."

"How could he possibly think he would get away with this? He wouldn't come after your sister… You…"

"Yes, he came for me. He would lock me in the dungeon for days at a time. And he would try to get me to say that I was superior. That the country would be better off with me. And I refused. What he did… It had the opposite effect. The decision that I made down in that dungeon was that I would never be manipulated. I swore my allegiance to my sister over and over again in my head, and out loud when my father came. I refused to allow him space in my head."

Gunnar could no longer look at Latika as he continued. "He didn't deserve it. And if I was truly so strong as he kept insisting I was… Well then. I felt that I should show it. Because if I had any piece of a true leader inside of me, then there should be no man on earth who can tell me what. Ironically, it was in opposing him that I found my sense of strength. And then, eventually I was no longer a boy, but closer to being a man, and my father knew that his ability to harm me, his ability to overpower me had come to an end."

"All of this happened when you were a boy?"

"Yes. That is how…bullies like to behave. Is that not what they say?"

"Gunnar," she said. "How did you survive?"

"I had purpose. My purpose was to protect Astrid."

"And then in order to flaunt your freedom from your father you… That's how you became you."

"I took great joy in forcing him to question all that he thought about who his heir should be, and how the country should be run. I took great joy in proving to him that the fact I was born a boy did not make me more suitable than my sister. Rather than her being the real thorn in his side for the rest of his days, I like to think that it was me. Solidifying to the people of the country that Astrid was the clear and rightful heir. By the time Astrid ascended the throne, I daresay there was not a single person in the entire country that wished I were their King. Do not mistake me. I don't think my sister needed my bad example to shine. But…"

"The world is a harsh and old-fashioned place," Latika said. "You don't have to tell me what it's like, you don't have to."

"So there you have it. My origin story. I'm basically a superhero movie."

Latika took a breath, and then she rose up from her seat at the table. And before Gunnar knew what was happening, she dropped to her knees before him, taking his hands in hers. "I don't know what to say."

"Don't get on your knees before me unless you intend to do something of interest with your mouth," he said, his knee-jerk reaction to seeing her sympathy.

As if taking it up as a calling, Latika stood, bending at the waist and grabbing hold of his chin. Then she closed the distance between them, and kissed him.

CHAPTER NINE

LATIKA THOUGHT THAT she might be crazy. Because this emotion and fire running through her blood was something she had never dealt with before. Because it was something that was foreign to her. Utterly and completely foreign. And yet familiar all at the same time.

Gunnar.

She wanted to touch him. She wanted to reach him. Wanted to pour all of her feelings out into his body.

For that boy that he was. That boy who must've been so terrified. Who resisted every attempt at being indoctrinated.

For the man he'd become. Arrogant and exasperating and so utterly brilliant.

She had known that he was strong, but she had only ever seen it in his irreverence. She saw now that it was his shield. That he had used it to protect himself from a Machiavellian father who had perhaps taken more joy in the attempted manipulation of his children than he cared for the outcome.

And Gunnar had kept it to himself. He had hidden it from Astrid so that she would never know the pain he endured on her behalf.

So she would be spared the full brunt of knowing her father's hatred.

The Playboy Prince was not the disgrace of the royal family of Bjornland. He was the crown jewel.

Latika had disdained him from the moment she had met him, but she had wanted him.

And she had been wrong. So utterly and completely wrong.

The man had been tortured by his father.

She kissed him deeper, allowing her thoughts to fall away. Allowing nothing more than the physical home of desire to exist between them. Gunnar growled, pulling her onto his lap.

His hold was strong, his kiss turning desperate. It was deep and intense, his tongue sliding against hers, his whiskers resting against her cheek.

Her Viking marauder who seemed intent on claiming her. No matter that she was the one who had started the kiss.

But that was all right.

If he needed to be the one to stake the claim, she could allow that. She could be that for him.

What she'd said to him had been true. She had gone without sex for twenty-four years. And in this moment, it became clear that what she had been waiting for was this. Not him specifically, but this feeling. For desire to be tattooed on every beat of her heart. For it to be an undeniable, brilliant force that she could not and did not want to deny.

"I want to see you here," he growled.

"I want to…"

"No," he said. "I have a fantasy of you," he said, standing up from the chair, holding on to her. She wrapped her legs around his waist to keep herself from sliding onto the ground. And then he walked her over to the wall and braced her back against it.

She could see him, his eyes a brilliant blue, the same as the sea behind him. Then he lifted her. Lifted her up and maneuvered her so that her thighs were over his shoulders, the wall bracing her up right.

She gasped.

He chuckled.

Then put his face directly between her thighs, with only a thin scrap of underwear keeping him from seeing everything. He held her fast with his arm, and tilted his head, kissing her inner thigh, and then he pushed her dress upward, the fabric bunching around her hips, first on one side and then the other.

"These," he said, "are very pretty." He dragged the back of his knuckle over her crease, and she squirmed. "Pity." Then he gripped the center of her panties and tugged hard, tearing the fabric. It fell free, exposing her to him, and to the open air.

"The beauty of living up on a hill like this," he said, "is that while we have a great view of all this, no one has a view of us. Latika," he whispered, pressing a kiss even higher to her inner thigh. "Latika." Then he turned his head, his tongue painting a hot stripe of pleasure over her flesh as he tasted her, deep and intense.

She gasped, letting her head fall back. She did not know how they had gotten here. With her comforting him only a moment ago, and now with him licking her in her most intimate place up against a wall. He was so big, his shoulders so broad, one large hand bracing her, holding her ass, and the other teasing her as he continued to lavish attention on her with his mouth. He made her feel small, feminine and delicate.

And most important of all, he made her feel wild.

She hadn't known. Oh, she had realized there was something hot and magical that simmered between them. Something dark and rich and unknowable. But she hadn't known that it would feel like this.

No, she'd had no idea.

She hadn't known that anything could be like this. She arched against him as he continued to lick his way to her center, as he moved his hand, sliding one finger inside of her. She gasped, rolling her hips forward, pleasure crashing over her like a wave. A precursor of something that felt like it would be bigger. Deeper.

She was desperate for something to hold onto. She put one hand on the back of his head, pushing her fingers through his blond hair, and gripped his broad, muscular shoulder with the other.

And he continued to eat her like she was dessert.

Continued to tease and torment her with that finger buried deep inside of her. One that became two, the rhythm becoming so slick and beautiful and perfect that she could barely breathe.

And then it hit. Her pleasure breaking her in half. She squeezed her legs together, rolling her hips forward and pushing his head toward her as she rode out the intense peak pleasure. And then she relaxed, letting her head fall back, releasing her hold on him. Then she realized the only thing keeping her from falling down to the earth was the fact that he was holding onto her. He lifted her easily from his shoulders and pulled her into his arms. "You are beyond anything I could have guessed you might be," he said, his voice rough.

"So are you," she said, feeling dizzy.

"I want you," he said. "More than I can remember wanting anything. When I was down in that dungeon I used to think of things that I like. Cars. Cake. My desires were simple then. Moving into adolescence, I thought an awful lot about women. I would picture things I wanted and couldn't have over and over again."

His words were rough. Compelling. Like he was touching her. Over her body. In her body. She was on fire.

"A study in perfect, torturous deprivation," he continued. "And once I got my freedom I never wanted for anything again. I wouldn't allow it. I indulged in everything. Until you. You... I wanted you from the moment I first saw you. And you made me wait. Oh, Latika you don't even know what a sin that is. To a man like me..."

"Have me," she said, her whole body electric with want.

He could. He could have her. Out here if he wanted to. Against the wall. On the floor. Whatever he wanted, he could have. Whatever he needed, she would become. For him, she would do anything.

He growled, picking her up and sweeping her into his arms, blazing a path into the house. He left the door open behind them, but it was clear that he felt secure and isolated up here in his house on the top of the mountain. He carried her up the stairs, and she barely had the chance to take in the beauty before her.

All the clean lines, warm, honey-colored wood panels and open, sun-drenched vistas provided by the windows that overtook each and every wall.

They went up three flights of stairs, to a bedroom that was positioned higher than the rest of the house, built into the side of the hill, made entirely of windows that looked out over the sea that faded from jade to deepest navy. White-capped waves swelled reaching up toward the sky that was open and like the desire the swelling inside of Latika.

So soon.

So *impossibly* soon after the peak he had just brought her to. The bed itself was large, white and spare, upon a raised platform that put it in line with the view below.

And it loomed larger still, as he carried Latika to it, setting her down on the plush surface.

He laid her down on her back, and she blushed when she realized that her legs had fallen open, and that she was still naked beneath her dress.

"Too late for modesty," he said, pushing his hand against her knee and holding her legs open before she could close them.

Then he moved up her body, reaching around behind her and undoing the zipper on the little red dress that had barely gotten an hour's worth of wear. He pulled down, exposing the bra she was wearing beneath. Lacy and insubstantial, with gaps between the intricate flower design, giving him a clear view of the shape of her nipples.

She knew. Because she had put it on and looked in the mirror and wondered what he might think.

Those eyes became a blue flame, the desire in them so clear, so potent, that she didn't have to wonder.

He wanted her. She had been so focused on wanting to make him feel good that she hadn't fully realized what a wonderful thing it was for her to be wanted by him.

No one had ever wanted her. Not her, as she was.

They wanted her to be the perfect daughter and representation of all that they were. Wanted her to be a perfect prisoner and a slave.

She had been the daughter. A fugitive. An assistant.

Never just a woman. And now, with Gunnar's hungry gaze roaming over her curves, woman was exactly what she became. What she felt, straight down to her soul. He pulled the dress the rest of the way from her body and cast it onto the floor.

Then he moved back to her, unhooking her bra and sending it the same direction as the dress. She still had her shoes on, and it should feel ridiculous, her knees bent, her elbows propping her up, her black hair cascading over her body like a wave.

Like she was a pinup, and not a virgin about to surrender to a man with more experience than she could possibly imagine.

But whether she was Madonna or siren, Gunnar didn't seem to mind. He growled, lowering his head and pressing a kiss to her neck, nibbling his way to her jaw, and to her lips, where he treated her to kiss after drugging kiss, ecstasy making her limbs feel heavy.

Then he tore himself away from her mouth again, making his way down, kissing the delicate skin around her breasts, knee, before moving up to suck her nipple.

She gasped, shocked at the arrow of pleasure that pierced her, so deep and so true she wouldn't have thought that she could feel such pleasure again. Not so close to what he had given her release before.

But still she felt it. And it left her utterly transfixed, in desperate need of more.

"You," she murmured even as he moved over to her

other breast, licking and sucking, bringing her nipple into its heightened point. "I need you."

He stood, and began to unbutton his shirt, letting it fall open, revealing that beautiful body she had admired so many times. Those perfect muscles, dusted with just the right amount of hair.

And then he moved his hands to his belt, and her throat went dry. This was the part of him that remained a mystery to her, and the very idea of seeing him now sent little rivulets of pleasure straight through her.

She wanted him.

Wanted *this*.

He pushed his hands down, along with his underwear, and her breath left her body. He was beautiful. Every inch of him.

And there were a great many inches.

No wonder women lost their minds over this man.

He was everything a man should be. Large and broad and thick all over. The most stunning sight she ever beheld. He was art.

A man seemingly carved from marble and made into hot, delicious flesh.

"See anything you like?" His lips tipped upward, that indolent smile she knew so well curving that wicked mouth.

"Just you," she said, breathless. "That's all."

He growled, coming down onto the bed with her, every inch of his naked body touching every inch of hers. She rolled against him, desperately needy.

He kissed her.

Kissed her until she was slick with her need for him. Kissed her until she felt hollow. Until she thought she might die of the need to have him inside of her. He wrapped his hand around his heavy length, pressing the head to the entrance of her body, then drawing the moisture from inside of her and up the sensitive bundle of nerves at the apex of her thighs.

He teased her like that, teased them both, slowly, sensually, the pleasure like a lightning strike as he did. When he finally placed that thick head back in her entrance, she was trembling. Ready to make him come inside of her.

She might not know if it would hurt, and exactly what it would feel like, but she knew it was what she needed. Knew that only this would bring the fulfillment that she craved.

He rocked his hips forward, and she gasped when he reached the much discussed hymen, but he didn't seem to notice, as he rolled his hips forward, filling her completely.

It hurt, but only for a moment. And then it was nothing but a sense of completion. Of desire deep and real, as her internal muscles gripped him and seemed to pull him deeper inside.

She rocked her hips against his body, and it was like gasoline thrown onto a lit match. They combusted. His thrusts were wild, and seeing him like this, feral and without that urbane wit that he used as a shield between himself and the world, seeing him pure and unguarded, his teeth bared like an animal, his ice blue eyes hot and fierce, his entire body reverberating with a growl every time he claimed her body with his own, was the most intoxicating aphrodisiac that Latika could have ever fathomed. She'd never known how wonderful it could be to be desired by a man.

No. Not by a man.

By *this* man.

This man was everything.

He thrust home, grinding his hips against hers, release bursting overhead like fireworks. And then on a growl, he seemed to give up his control, his big body shook as his length pulsed inside of her, as he spilled himself into her.

And then they lay together, breathing hard, slick with sweat, and all tangled up in each other. Then he moved away from her, with shocking speed and the fluid grace of a panther.

"You were a virgin," he said.

She rolled to the side, revealing a spot of blood, shame filling her. "Yes," she said.

"Then tell me, Latika. You don't happen to be taking the pill, do you?"

And that was when she realized, that she and Gunnar did not use protection.

And given the timing of the month, the risk of her getting pregnant was very real.

Gunnar's pulse was hammering wildly out of control. "Are you on anything?" he repeated.

"No," she answered. The answer that he knew she would give. Rage spiraled through his veins.

"I told you that I never want to have children."

"I wasn't thinking," she said, her face getting pale. "I…"

"I don't believe you," he said, rage an unforgiving, unreasonable monster in his gut.

And when he got down past that bright, burning rage, there was something far worse under it. A sense that he had to escape his skin. That his body, his very essence, had betrayed him and there was no fixing it.

Things had been set into motion that could now not be stopped and the absolute terror he felt over that…

Over the possibility of fatherhood.

He couldn't breathe.

"I don't care what you believe," Latika said. "I didn't think of it. You clearly didn't either, so I don't know why I should be the focus of your rage."

"Is there a pill you can take?" There had to be something. A way to turn back the clock. To stop the mistake.

Her expression contorted. Shock. To pain. To rage. "I refuse," she said. "What will be will be, the mistake was ours, and I'm not going to reverse course and make a decision that I will personally regret."

"Because you want a baby," he said. "And that was your goal along."

She frowned. "No. I do want to have a baby. I always have. But to act as if I was somehow using my feminine wiles to manipulate you…" She stood up, hunting for her dress. "There are easier ways to get sperm, Gunnar. Every single one of them involves not having to put up with you."

"Yet, producing a child with me comes as a very hefty reward, I should think."

"I married you already," she snapped. "Where's the benefit of manipulating you? How would that get me money I don't already have access to?"

He knew that what she was saying was true, and that his response was unreasonable. And yet, he could not stop himself. Panic was overtaking him now, and it was an emotion he was not familiar with.

He had spent days locked in a dungeon in the castle

in Bjornland, and not felt panic. He did not know who he was, and if he despised her for anything, it was this most of all.

He felt like his skin was not his own, and that was something that could not be endured.

"I will have nothing to do with the child," he said.

He expected the words to bring with them a rush of relief. Because it was a decision, if nothing else, and it was the unknown that he could not bear above all else.

But he felt no relief. Instead, all he felt was a sick kind of grim determination that settled low in his stomach and refused to be moved.

"You won't have anything to do with your own child?"

"I already told you how things would be. You are the one who refuses to be reasonable here."

"Fine. Then you may have nothing to do with the child. But if there is a child, and that is your stance, you will have nothing to do with me either. You wanted me. You had me. Understand that it is the last time."

"That's it then? Your first time will be your last?"

She whirled around, her eyes a glittering brown blaze. "It will not be my last. I will go about my life as if I do not have a husband who would deny his own child. I will be discreet, but trust that I will find someone who will share my life with me. And if you seek to cast me out, then the world will know of your cruelty. If Ragnar comes and scoops me up because you deny me your protection, when I have your child, then what will the world think of you? And isn't that why you're doing this? So the world will think better of you. I thought… I thought beneath it all was a good man. But no. You're a bad man, Gunnar. And just because you did something good for your sister doesn't erase that."

Fury rose up inside of him and he reached out, grabbing hold of her arm. "Don't you think I know that? Don't you think I already know that I'm dark beyond the telling of it? It doesn't matter how much light I throw onto myself, doesn't matter how much I pretend to be a man filled with nothing but cares for where his next drink might come from, that I don't know that my soul is a pit."

He released his hold on her.

"Even if there is no child, you will not touch me," she said. "I could never be with a man who would say the things that you have. Who thinks the way that you do. I'm appalled by you. Disgusted. As much as I ever wanted you. I'm going to shower now. I need to wash you off of me."

She turned and went into the shower, and he let her go.

He prowled down the hall, pacing back and forth, and then he went into his office. He looked out over the ocean. He would have liked to stay here longer, but their time here was at an end. He had accomplished what he had come for. They had made a show of his company. Had revealed what a fantastically generous soul he was. But he was more than he had always shown the public.

And he had revealed to Latika just how broken he was.

All the sharp edges that lived inside of him that would only cut those who dared come closest to him.

It was time to leave.

He made a phone call to his pilot. "Ready the plane. We depart first thing in the morning."

CHAPTER TEN

THE TRIP BACK to Bjornland was worse than the trip to
the States. Latika was reeling from the speed at which
they had boomeranged between one continent and another. And if the bed had been uncomfortable and awkward, looming large on the plane on the way over, it
was worse now.

Worse now that she had been with him. Worse now
she knew all the things he could make her feel in a bed
like that.

She felt sick with regret. With sadness.

Because she had felt… For one fleeting moment she
had thought maybe she'd found love.

Oh, she wasn't so foolish to think that Gunnar would
have immediately fallen in love with her, just because
he had bared his soul. But she had felt something for
him. Something that had surpassed anything. As if he
was what her heart had been waiting for all along. And
then it had been for nothing.

Because he had revealed the truth of himself.

He would ignore their child, would hold himself separate. Would sleep with her, and disavow a life they
had created.

And she could not endure that. She could not set a child up for that kind of pain.

Nor herself.

She felt sick with worry. Sick with regret.

When they finally arrived in Bjornland, they did not go to the palace, but to Gunnar's apartments.

She didn't know why that surprised her.

"We will be living here," he said. "Your things have already been moved."

"Of course," she said, feeling like she was floating outside of her body.

On numb feet she walked into the bedroom that he had gestured toward. All her things were there. And it was separate from his.

That was a good thing. Because the only thing she could see happening now was the two of them living separate lives.

In this space that was so much smaller than the palace.

She flung herself down onto the bed, and she couldn't cry. Instead she just lay there with eyes that felt like they had been rubbed with sand.

The next week was a blur, the days leading together like strokes of watercolor on a page.

Except they weren't blurry, no. Latika was all too tied in with what was happening in her life.

And worst of all the things she hadn't fully thought through, she was not Astrid's assistant anymore.

She was robbed of the thing that used to keep her occupied. And robbed of an excuse to spend time with her best friend.

On the fourth day since they returned home, Astrid called her.

"You know, it's quite ridiculous that you're acting as if we can't spend time together simply because you don't work for me anymore."

The truth of the matter was, Latika was partly avoiding Astrid, because she didn't want her friend to notice how sad she was.

She couldn't talk to her about Gunnar's revelations, because she had promised, and because she understood why Gunnar felt that way. She agreed with him. To reveal everything would be to harm Astrid, and Latika didn't want to do that. But she was bored, and she and Gunnar hadn't spoken in days. Her husband came and went like a thief in the night, and otherwise was never home.

She wondered—with a brilliant, burning stab in her chest—if he was already in the beds of other women.

And why shouldn't he be?

Just because he'd been with her a few days earlier wouldn't keep him from seeking another lover. It never had before, not with any other woman, so why would it be different with her? He had made it plain she didn't really matter to him.

So when she had been back a week, she entered the palace for the first time since her marriage and walked slowly into Astrid's personal parlor.

"Hi," Astrid said.

"Hello," Latika responded.

"You don't look good," Astrid said.

"It's fine," Latika said.

"Is being married to my brother such a trial?"

She tried to force a smile. "I knew you would ask me about him."

"Is that why you were avoiding me?"

"No," she said slowly. "Things are strange. Things have changed. And I didn't want to assume…"

"Our friendship is more than you working for me. It's even more than you being married to my brother. I care about you because I care about you. It isn't connected to what you can do for me."

Latika was suddenly so very glad she came, because she had never needed to hear something more in her entire life. It was the thing that she had longed to hear from her parents. The thing she had been hungry for in a relationship all her life.

"Thank you," she said, with deep sincerity. "Thank you. I'm not sure anyone else has ever felt that way."

"Then the other people in your life are fools. And if my brother is one of them, so is he."

They let go of talk of Gunnar, and instead enjoyed lunch, until Astrid's phone rang. She picked it up, her brows shooting upward. "Really? You are sure. You are absolutely certain. Because if this is a hoax of some kind… No. I understand. I'll tell her."

Astrid hung up the phone and leveled her gaze at Latika. "Ragnar is dead."

And just like that, her world, that had seemed right for a moment, turned itself on its head again.

Latika waited. She waited until darkness fell. And Gunnar was still not home. Then she procured the use of his private plane, which was available to her even when she had been Astrid's assistant, and was now unquestionably available to her as his wife.

She flew to Italy. Then requested the jet be sent back home.

From there she got a ticket through a commercial airline and flew to England.

She had money in accounts there. And she knew that if he really wanted to, he could likely find her. But, it would take a little bit of time. Because she had secured her money using an alias, as she had done with her credit cards. Saving them for an emergency. For years, she had no need to spend her earnings as Astrid's assistant that she had socked away, hidden from both her parents and Ragnar.

Ragnar was dead. Something so benign as a heart attack seemed so bizarre given how things had been. But that was what had killed him.

And because Ragnar was dead she did not have to stay with Gunnar.

She booked herself into a hotel room near Piccadilly, cursing the proximity to such insanity, but also grateful for the last-minute availability.

Then she collapsed onto the bed.

And this time tears came.

And when they began to fall, she feared they wouldn't stop.

She was free now. Free from everything. But it didn't feel like freedom. It felt like nothing she would've ever wanted for herself, and for the life of her, she couldn't figure out why.

Gunnar.

She didn't want to believe it.

Didn't want to believe that a man who would say those things to her, who would reject his own child like that, could possibly be the reason she suddenly felt like she didn't want the thing she had been craving all her life.

"I have no obligation to anyone," she said into the empty room. "I am free to go where I want. To do what I want."

She waited for that truth to sink in. Waited for it to make her feel good.

It never did.

When Gunnar arrived back home in the wee hours of the morning, something felt strange in the apartment.

But he had spent the evening working at an office that he owned downtown in the capital city of Bjorn-land—completely unnecessarily, as he could easily work in the palace, or at home—and he was exhausted. He collapsed into bed without investigating the source of the feeling.

He woke the next morning, it persisted.

Typically, he was out until after Latika went to bed, and she was gone by the time he woke up. So the emptiness in the apartment was normal enough. He went to look at her room, and found everything as it should be. Her clothes were hanging in the closet, her shoes lined up.

But then, late that night when he came home again, he checked, and she still hadn't returned.

He called Astrid. "Do you have any idea where my wife is?"

"No," said, her voice filled with concern.

"If that bastard Ragnar..."

"Ragnar is dead," Astrid said.

"What?"

"Latika didn't tell you?"

"No. I haven't seen her. When did you discover this?"

"Early the day before yesterday. You haven't spoken to her since then?"

"I… I haven't seen her."

"Gunnar!" Astrid sounded incredulous. "You haven't seen your wife in two days, your wife has been under threat, and you didn't think to say anything about it?"

"We don't go out of our way to spend much time together," he said, his voice flat.

"I don't know what's going on between the two…"

"Nothing," Gunter said. "Nothing is going on between the two of us."

"That isn't right *when you're married.*"

"You know we didn't marry for conventional reasons."

"Have you tried calling her?" Astrid asked.

"No," he said. "But I will."

He hung up the phone, and dialed Latika's number. She picked up on the second ring.

"Where are you?" he asked, not waiting for her to speak.

"We don't need to be together," she said, sidestepping the question.

"What the hell are you talking about?"

"Ragnar is dead. And the two of us have no reason to continue on with this farce of a marriage. I've taken myself away from you, for a reason."

"What about my reputation?"

"I'll see that it's handled," she said. "I'll see that there is no doubt that the problem was mine. That it's my fault the marriage dissolved. I will be held responsible, and your reputation will be intact. The response that has been given to you owning your corporation has been overwhelmingly positive. I think that you'll find everything will be just fine without me."

"Latika…"

The line went dead, and she didn't speak after.

Each attempt at calling her after that was met with dead air. She refused to answer. And because of that, he couldn't figure out a way to track her phone. He looked for credit cards, and could find nothing.

Any easy paper trail had been erased.

And then, two weeks after his wife had left home, her name popped up in a database. Her real name had been used at a private physician's office.

One specializing in obstetrics.

Gunnar picked up his phone. "We are going to London."

CHAPTER ELEVEN

LATIKA WAS EXHAUSTED by the time she got home. She didn't know whether to laugh or cry. Honestly, she felt like doing both.

She was pregnant.

Pregnant with Gunnar's baby.

The exact thing that would have driven their marriage to the brink anyway.

She owed Ragnar a thank you note for dying of a heart attack with such excellent timing.

She was surprised by the way he had died. Considering it never seemed as though he had a heart.

The thought made her laugh. And then she realized she was a crazy person, standing in her empty apartment, shaking and laughing. The news she had been given today was life altering. She hadn't wanted to be seen out and about purchasing a pregnancy test, nor had she seen the way she could possibly go to a public hospital.

Thankfully, she had so much money squirreled away, that it hadn't been beyond her to get herself into a private clinic.

She had worn a scarf over her head, and large sunglasses, and it felt ridiculous.

But she seemed to have pulled it off. There were no headlines proclaiming that she was in London, after all.

Incognito still was hindering her new sense of freedom. Perhaps that was why she still felt so heavy.

She was resolute in her purpose. She knew exactly what she needed to do. She only needed a few hours to get everything straight.

And a few hours was all it took. With her press release crafted, she was ready to push it out to new sources.

That her marriage to Gunnar was a sham. That she was the villain. That she had married him under false pretenses, and had later found out she was pregnant with a lover's baby.

And that she had decided to dissolve the marriage as a result.

Not him.

Gunnar, she would say, had offered to raise the child as its own.

Because when her child looked back on the news stories surrounding his or her birth, she wanted to have that child feel as if they were wanted by everyone.

Especially their father.

Even if they never knew that Gunnar was their actual father. It was sad to think that would be how it was, but it would have to be. It would be better for everyone.

And everyone would be protected. She wished desperately she could have a glass of wine with this upsetting turn of events, but she couldn't.

Because of the baby.

She smiled, pressing her hand to her stomach.

If nothing else she had purpose now. Maybe it wasn't

wild, giddy freedom. But purpose would be better. Purpose actually made her much, much happier.

She steeled herself, her finger poised to push Send on the press release. And that was when the door to the hotel room opened.

Latika turned, her mouth falling open when she saw him standing there. His expression was grim, an aura of leashed violence around him that she had never before witnessed.

Gunnar excelled in exuding laconic grace.

She had always sensed that there was the potential for danger lurking beneath that exterior. That the way he lounged about the palace in Bjornland was much like a big cat. Watching. Waiting. Incapable of striking with decisive and fatal force in the time that it would take a person to bat an eyelash.

And here it was now. Raw, unvarnished and unconcealed. How had she never seen this before? Gunnar was not a safe space.

Gunnar was lethal.

And she suspected she had crossed him in a way she had not foreseen.

"Feeling relaxed?" he asked.

"I was," she responded, standing up from the computer and stepping in front of the screen. He walked into the room, closing the door behind him.

"How did you get a key?"

He looked at her, one brow raised. He did not answer her question.

"Ragnar is dead," she said. "I had no reason to hide in Bjornland anymore. I saw the opportunity to claim my freedom, and I did it. Don't worry, I will make sure that there is no…"

"You're pregnant," he said.

Everything inside of her went still. Her heart thundered. She felt very much like a field mouse under the watchful eye of the lion. She had no hope of pulling a thorn out of his paw and making it better. For he was looking at her as if she was the one who had put it there.

"You don't want a baby," she said.

"You should've told me."

"Why? Everything is in hand."

"How dare you? How dare you flee in the night and take my heir from me."

His rage was stark. Palpable. And it took all her strength to find a way to speak with that anger, another entity in the room, pressing in on her.

"First of all," she said, "I took myself from you. I claimed my freedom. I didn't know I was pregnant when I left you. It had to do with me, not a baby. Second of all, you said unequivocally that you did not want a child. That you would have nothing to do with a child that we created."

"That is different than allowing my child to be raised away from the palace, and from its birthright."

"What birthright? You're the spare, Gunnar. Every child that Astrid has will be in line before you, and our child would never be in line at all."

"It doesn't matter. All that matters is that my child receive the rights they are entitled to by birth."

"But you don't want them. And I don't want to subject them to such a thing."

"And I will not allow this. You think that you can walk away from me? What about our bargain? You cannot step into this space and use me as a safety net and then leave when it suits you."

"If you're worried for your precious reputation, don't be." She stepped to the side, revealing her computer screen. "I am prepared to absolve you of any wrongdoing. I have prepared a press release, which I'm ready to push the button on. Wherein I declare that this child belongs to a lover that I took before our marriage, and that you offered to give my child your name, and I refused. My reputation will be in tatters, while yours will remain intact. But I don't care. I care nothing for my reputation, I never wanted notoriety. All I have ever wanted is the chance to live my life on my terms. I'm ready to go off in the country and raise this baby alone. I will be happy doing it."

It wasn't sacrifice on her end. It was the pursuit of freedom. The need to cut ties with him utterly and completely. To uphold her end of their bargain so she might walk owing him nothing.

They had married for his reputation, and for her protection.

She no longer needed protection. And if she just lowered herself, her leaving him would allow him to be blameless.

And the slate would be clean between them.

She would finally be free.

"So," he said, his tone soft. Deadly. "You seek to use me as a sperm donor?"

"Why not?" She lifted her chin up, determined to pour every ounce of defiance she possessed onto him. "Astrid sought to do the same."

"It didn't work out for her, did it?"

"Because Mauro has a heart. Because he was willing to cross borders to claim his child. You don't want yours."

"Have I not crossed borders?" he asked, throwing his arms wide. "Is this the demonstration you were hoping to see? I passed your purity test that I might be able to be father to my own flesh and blood?"

"You were the one who disavowed him," she said, advancing on him. "And in so doing, you disavowed *me*. I will not allow my child a relationship with a father that doesn't want them. If I do, how am I any different than your mother? How am I any different at all? And how are you different from your father? He didn't want Astrid. And his desire to be rid of her made him do appalling things to you. Is that what you want? Is that the place you want your child to grow up?"

He went very still. And Latika knew that she had overplayed her hand.

She had been attempting to manipulate, with a knife straight to the heart. But she could see the moment he grabbed the handle of that metaphorical knife, intent on turning it back around.

He closed the space between them, those ice blue eyes cutting her with the chill in them. He stopped when he was a breath away from her, his chest nearly touching her breasts. He leaned in, his mouth set to a grim line. And then he reached past her, grabbing her laptop and wrenching it free of the charger cord.

He threw it down onto the ground and stomped it beneath his shoe.

The screen went fuzzy, then black. Her heart thundered in abject terror, her entire body trembling.

"The child is mine. So are you. If you want to see what I'm capable of, if you want to see the ruthlessness that my father planted into my soul, then you have given yourself a perfect opportunity to do so. My people are descended of Vikings. Do you know what we do when there is something we desire, and it does not belong to us? We take it, and we make it ours. And you, make no mistake, are mine."

He grabbed hold of her, that large, commanding fist buried in her hair as he pulled her forward, his mouth crashing down on hers. She couldn't breathe. Couldn't think. She was melting, the inferno of his rage demolishing each and every one of her defenses.

She could feel it. Like a rally cry inside of her soul. *Surrender.*

She shouldn't want to surrender. It was a foolish thing to do. And it was one she could not afford. And yet, her Viking marauder would accept nothing less, and somehow her body was intent upon allowing it.

Then he picked her up, swept her straight off of her feet, and carried her into the bedroom.

CHAPTER TWELVE

GUNNAR'S RAGE WAS a living thing. Boiling over, spilling out of control.

Latika had said that he was like his father. And he couldn't find it in himself to fight the ways in which that might be true. He was failing. And yet... She was in his arms. She was clinging to him, kissing him back like liquid fire. And he could do nothing to deny himself. With blinding heat, blinding needs, pulsing behind his eyes, and hard, heady desire pulsing through him he could do nothing but stake his claim.

If it was in his blood, if it was inevitable, then he would surrender.

The bedroom in the hotel suite she was occupying had large windows, overlooking the neon and chaos of the city. It was all noise, next to the sophisticated serenity that Latika possessed. She was dressed simply today, and a black dress that hugged her luscious body, cut off just above the knee.

It was demure, really. And yet, it ignited a fire in his veins that would rival the forge of any dwarf king found in the stories his nannies had told him as a boy.

And indeed, his need was honed to a sharpened edge, like an axe. And when it fell, it would be decisive and deadly. He took her to the window, turned her so that she was facing out.

"You know how I got in here," he said. "I was handed a key. Because you are mine, and the world knows it. Everyone down there… They would not lift a finger to take you out of my custody. You are mine. The whole world knows." He gripped the zipper on her dress and pulled it down, letting it fall off of her body, and pool at her feet.

She was wearing black underwear, lace and revealing, highlighting the curves of her delicious ass. He pushed his hand beneath the waistband, grabbing a handful of soft, plump flesh. Before pushing his hand further between her thighs, feeling how wet she was.

"You desire me even now. You ran from me, and you still desire me."

"We all want things that we despise," she said.

"Do we? Or do bodies sometimes know better than our minds?"

"My heart wants nothing to do with you."

"And yet." He leaned in, toying with her between her legs. "Tell me no. If you don't want this. If you don't want me. Tell me no."

"Bastard," she spat.

"Does my touch disgust you?" He drew his fingers across that place where he knew she was most sensitive. She gasped, rolling her hips forward. "Oh, yes," he said. "I can see the way I disgust you. So much that you're on the verge of coming…out of your skin."

"Let me go," she said. "You don't want me. You don't want the baby."

"Don't tell me what I want," he said, stroking her in time with his words. "Don't speak to me like you know. Tell me what you want. Tell me if you want me to stop."

Again, she did. She simply stood, vibrating with fury and need as he stroked her. And he was filled with just enough rage over her abandonment to continue to push. "Are you afraid that if you push me too hard I'll disappear, never to return? Because you can profess to hate me all you want, because you love what I do to your body. I'm sure being a Duchess doesn't hurt."

"I don't give a damn about being your Duchess."

"But you do give a damn about pleasure, don't you? Is it wounding, to discover you're just as base as the rest of us? So many years of abstinence for you, darling Latika, only to be undone so resolutely by my touch. That must be extremely confronting for you."

"Are you going to do something? Are you going to stand there all night with your hands between my legs halfheartedly pleasuring me."

"Oh," he said. "My mistake. Did you want me to put some effort into it?"

He turned around so that she was facing him, and unhooked her bra, throwing it down to the ground, then he dragged her panties down, pressing a kiss to her ankle, her calf, her thigh before standing. Her eyes glittered with rage, her frame shaking.

"One last chance, darling. Tell me no."

Her dark eyes glittered with rage and desire. "Go to hell."

"I'll take that as an enthusiastic *yes*."

He crushed her up against his body, reveling in the feel of all that soft skin beneath his hands, while he remained fully clothed. He kissed her then, pouring all of the fury and outrage that he felt into her body. Into her soul.

If she thought he was a monster, she would get a monster.

He stripped his clothes off quickly, then lifted her up, set her down on the bed. He maneuvered her so that she was on her knees, her thighs thick and luscious, her waist slim. Her breasts heavy. He stroked himself twice, looking at the picture that she made.

"That's more like it," he said. "On your knees, showing a bit of deference to your King. But I should like a bit of praise from your mouth."

She looked up at him, the reluctant hunger on her face an aphrodisiac. He pressed the head of his masculinity to her lips and he saw the moment she surrendered to her need. Her tongue darted out, touching the tip of him and then she opened wide, taking him and as far as she could.

He grabbed hold of her hair, guiding her movements as she pleasured him. And somehow, the game they were playing got lost. Got all tangled up in the dark, deep pleasure threatening to overwhelm him.

Because he could not remember why he was angry anymore. And he could not remember why he had thought allowing her to put her lips on him would give him the power. For she held in her hand the most vulnerable part of him. And he was a slave to the need that she created, with clever fingers and lips and tongue.

He was the one surrendering.

He growled, pulling her away from him and turning her so that she was facing away. Still on her knees. He pressed himself to the entrance of her body, before thrusting deep, holding tightly to her hips as he led the deep, intense pleasure of being inside of her wash over him. She looked over her shoulder, her black hair covering part of her face, her expression one of dazed wonder.

Then, he began to move.

He lost himself in it. In that rhythm, deep and steady. And whatever he had been thinking to put her in this position, to make her so much less Latika that she was, it didn't work. For there was no other woman who felt like her. Who made him feel like this. There was nothing in all the world had ever felt like this.

Pleasure was like an arrow, piercing him, making it difficult to breathe. It was as though it had punched his lung. His heart. He put his hand between her legs and squeezed her, before moving one finger to either side of the center of her need and stroking, until a hoarse cry left her lips and her internal muscles pulsed around him. Only then did he allow the pleasure in him to rage out of control. He pulsed inside of her, pouring himself into her body, spending everything in her.

And when it was done, he collapsed at her side, laying on his back, feeling like a warrior left for dead on the battlefield.

Latika was laying on her stomach, her head turned to one side, the one visible eye appraising him closely.

"Pack your things," he said. "You're coming back to Bjornland with me."

He had embraced all that he was. He had become the conqueror. The marauder.

And yet somehow, as he headed out the door to the hotel, with Latika mutely walking beside him, he felt more the captive than the captor.

Latika could not untangle the events of the past few hours. And even when she was back in the palace in Bjornland, she felt dazed.

Gunnar had made some noise about the fact the two of them needed to be in residence at the palace for a time, but she hadn't fully understood why. For what all the implications might be. He had their things moved into the same bedroom, and Latika knew that everything between them would be different now. And not necessarily for the better. The way that he had broken that laptop so decisively, and then claimed her body with such force replayed in her mind over and over.

He had left impressions on her and in her that were so deep she could still feel them reverberating within her hours later.

She could not pretend that she hadn't been a willing participant. Could not pretend that part of her hadn't been thrilled that he had come for her.

That he had done exactly what Mauro had done for Astrid, for their child. Crossed borders and made demands.

But she still didn't get the sense that Gunnar wanted their child out of a sense other than...she couldn't even fathom what he was doing.

There was a sense of obligation, that she knew, but it didn't come from a place of love. Not remotely. Either way, it didn't matter. She was here. He had given her a great many opportunities to turn him away, and she had not. However she might regret it now, however she might feel weaker for it now, the choice had been hers. A strange realization. She had choice. She had given it to him.

"You're back," Astrid said, walking with great purpose into Gunnar's living quarters.

"Yes," Latika said.

"Why did you leave?"

"Because Ragnar was dead. And I didn't need to stay."

"But you're back," Astrid pointed out.

Latika knew that she couldn't keep any of this from her friend. There was no real point to it. She would find out eventually.

She only wished that there was some way she could sidestep the fact that of course she and Gunnar had ended up in a sexual relationship. Mostly because she didn't want to sit there and have to bear Astrid being right.

She was raw enough without having to admit that she had been wrong about her own desires.

"Gunnar, for his part, did not think that it was a good time to dissolve our marriage," Latika said.

"Did he not?" Astrid's tone sounded light, casual and wholly unsurprised.

"No," she said, knowing that she was being less than forthcoming.

"And why is that?"

"Perhaps because I'm pregnant," she said crisply.

That succeeded in shocking Astrid into silence. But, Latika could scarcely enjoy that.

"Did you know that when you left?" she asked.

"No," she said defensively. Though, it wouldn't have made a difference in her actions. Not after all that he'd said.

"You said my brother didn't want children."

"He doesn't. And he's quite angry with me. But I seem to recall he was involved in forgetting to use protection."

Astrid grimaced. But then, her expression softened. "I seem to recall having to cope with a very angry man who seems to think that a lack of protection was entirely my fault."

"Amazing creatures, men," Latika said. "Are they not?"

"They are something," Astrid agreed.

"So you're staying married?"

"For the time being," Latika said. Then she sighed. "He does not love me."

"Do you love him?"

She thought about it. For good while. All that he told her about his relationship with his father… It made her feel things for him. But then… There was the way he was acting about this child. All the things he had said. But then, the way he behaved as well. It was difficult to sort out what was true. And it was very hard for her to figure out her response.

"He doesn't want our baby. But he also doesn't want to let it go. I find… I don't know how I can love a man who will not love his child."

Astrid nodded gravely. "Give him time. And a chance to change."

"Some men never do," she said, thinking of their father.

"No," she said. "Some men never do."

"And if he doesn't?" Latika asked.

"Then I will be first in line to help set you free. But barring anything egregious… I think the two of you need to work this out for yourselves."

And as much as Latika would like to disagree, she couldn't. Because she might have been forced into the marriage mess, but no one had forced her into his bed. Twice. She was responsible for her own part in this. And she would not pawn that responsibility off. No matter how difficult it was. And right now, it was all pretty damn stiff.

* * *

Women had never made Gunnar nervous. He was a man who had a certain effect on the fairer sex, and he was well aware of that fact. He had always enjoyed the sort of attention he'd received in that regard. But he was walking on uneven ground with Latika. He felt off balance and out of his depth. He disliked that greatly. "Did you have a good day?" he asked.

"Yes," she responded.

"What did you do?"

"I spent some time with Astrid."

"And?"

"And we had a nice time," she said. "But I always do with your sister."

"Good."

She said nothing. Instead, she began to move about the room, ignoring him pointedly as she sifted through drawers in the large, ornate armoire at the back wall.

"What are you looking for?"

"Something to sleep in," she said.

"I certainly don't require that you wear anything to bed."

She looked at him, her expression verging on incredulous. "Do you expect that I'm going to have sex with you?"

He had. He had very much expected that. After all, she had seemed fully and completely into his body when he had encountered her that morning.

It had only been that morning.

It seemed an eternity now.

"It's no secret that you're attracted to me," he said.

"It's no secret that you have rejected our child. That's why I left. No, I didn't know I was pregnant, but I could not abide the idea of being married to a man who would see a child the way that you do."

"Things are different now that it's a reality," he said, believing that the moment the words left his lips.

"In what way?"

"In the sense that I understand deeply that I have an obligation to this child. And I intend to fulfill that obligation."

"A child should be more than an obligation. Just as a child should be more than a means to an end for an avaricious father intent on having his will be done through his descendants. You should love a child."

"I understand loyalty," he said. "I'm not certain that I understand love."

The look on Latika's face was what made him realize that there was something heavy in those words. Something shocking and wrong. He'd always known that to be true about himself. That he didn't understand that kind of depth.

He had been forced to exist in dark, enclosed spaces and he'd grown armor to protect himself. But it had cost. Because all those layers he'd built up had smothered a flame inside of him.

Or maybe…maybe that flame that existed inside other people had never been in him.

"What about Astrid?"

"You are the one who accused me of not caring for my sister, and now you seek to hold her up as an example of how I do?"

"No I… I'm sorry. I never should have implied that you didn't love Astrid. Of course you do."

"I don't know that I do," he said. "I am bonded to her. She is my twin. We are in many ways pieces of one. She is the head of the nation. And I have been her shield. That's different than love."

"What do you think love is?"

For a man convinced of his own rightness in the universe, his own deep sense of knowing who he was, a question like that was confronting.

Because when he dug down to the bottom of himself and searched for the answer, he found it wasn't there. "I don't know."

"Do you think that maybe it could be the way that you protected your sister. At the expense of yourself."

"No," he said.

"You don't think that love sacrifices itself?"

"If that is love, then love is a cruelty visited on the world. As cruel as hatred."

Her throat worked up and down. "Will you be involved with our child?"

"No," he said, something in his gut twisting, repulsion making his skin crawl.

"I don't understand, Gunnar. I don't understand why you would come for me like you did if you are not willing to offer me anything." She frowned. "Why did you come? How did you know I was pregnant?"

"I tracked your name in a database which attached you to that clinic. I knew why you must've gone there."

"You came to me knowing that I was having a child. And even now you can't bring yourself to admit that you might want to be in that child's life?"

"I don't know," he said. "I cannot explain what drives me. I don't like that. Not at all. I am a man who has always known how to stand firm in his convictions. I had to fight for those convictions. I had to fight my own father. I had to withstand torture. And I am not a man given to change, particularly not quickly. What I have always known is that I did not want to bring a child into the world, but now I am. Now we are. And what I know, with equal ferocity is that I cannot abandon the child." The words were like acid on his tongue, like sharp knives in his chest. "I don't know what love is. And I don't know how to be any sort of decent person. But I do know protection. I know I can offer that. And I offer it to you. To our child. I can pledge allegiance to you. To the baby. I don't know what I can give beyond that. But what I always want my child to know is that I will be a protector. Because Astrid and I never had that. Not from our father. I would have our child know he is loved. *I* don't know how to do that," he said, his voice raw. "I will need to count on you for that. For you to show the child that which I cannot."

She looked at him, and the well of pity in her eyes was almost too much for him to bear.

"Gunnar…"

"Forgive me," he said. "For what I said. I was angry, because I was afraid. And it gets me to say that. All of the things my father did to me and I was never afraid. But it's as if it was all stored inside of me for later. For when I was the one with power. Because I do not wish to use mine in the way that he did. And I thought it best… For the longest time, to avoid what I thought made him the monster he was."

"You thought somehow you made him a monster?"

"If I had not been born, then what choice would he have had? He would have had to accept Astrid. Power corrupts. And in me, my father saw the promise of power."

"I think you've proven that you're incorruptible in those stakes," she said, her voice soft.

"I have never trusted it. Why should I be innately better than my father?"

"Because you want to be?"

She sounded so confident and yet he didn't see how she could be. "Do you ever worry?" he asked. "After what your parents did to you, don't you worry that something inside of you might be broken?"

She looked so serene, and he could not understand it. He could not understand how this woman seemed so utterly and completely without fear for the future. For the child that she carried in her body.

"No," she said. "I worry about some things, but not being like my parents. That life didn't make me happy. And their goal was to have more of that life. They cared so deeply about what other people thought. They cared about power and prestige. I lived there, in that life, and it made me miserable. Their pursuit of more made me miserable. I understand that there is no value in treating people like a commodity. Because I understand not only that more things will never make me happy, but that it does unrelenting damage to the person that you put that on. I know everything I don't want to do. I'm sure along the way I will stumble upon more things I shouldn't do, or things I should do more of. I want to be the best mother that I can be. And I know that that begins with not being like my own. I was raised by nannies and teachers. I was raised by everyone but my parents. Their presence only served to make my life miserable. As they brought their expectations down upon me, as they told me all the ways in which I wasn't meeting them. No, I don't worry that I'll be like my parents. And I don't think you should worry you'll be like your father."

"But we have no guide," he said.

"Even if we did, that child will not be you, and it will not be me. It will be different than either of us, its whole own person. We would not be able to plan perfectly even if our parents had been wonderful."

"You won't use nannies?"

"Oh, I imagine we will to a degree. But we will be involved too. Not because we have to be, but because I want to be."

"What if I'm bad at it? What if it would be better if I weren't involved?"

"We can speak of that as the time comes," she said.

And somehow that was more reassuring than if she had simply told him that everything would be fine. Because the fact of the matter was she didn't know. Gunnar was desperately boggled by this uncertainty inside of him. It was nothing like he usually was, and nothing like he wanted to be at all.

That was the root of all that fear he'd felt when they had first made love without a condom.

Like the world had spun out of his control. And control had been his linchpin ever since he had been a boy, attempting to withstand his father's torture.

That deep base he had built inside of himself had been the only secure and certain thing. It was the thing he relied on. That internal compass. He had no idea how he'd come by it, because it certainly hadn't been taught to him by his father. He had no idea how he'd been so fortunate as to have something like that inside of himself. He had often felt like maybe it was part of that connection with Astrid.

At the very least, Astrid had had something more of a connection with their mother.

Their mother hadn't been interested in Gunnar at all, but she had cared deeply for Astrid.

He had always been grateful that his sister had that.

"We can figure it out together," Latika said. "And if something is going wrong, we can change it. We are not made of stone. Our ways aren't set. We can choose who we want to be. I believe that. All I wanted, all my life was my chance to choose my own path. I'll do so now. And so will you. We can do it. We are not bound by this. We don't have to be."

He didn't want to speak anymore. Not now. Instead, he reached out and picked Latika up off of the seat she was on and carried her over to the bed.

He was desperate for oblivion. He craved it. The future was a bright, blaring light of some uncertainty. Of so many things he had not planned. So many things he had always told himself he didn't want. The only thing he was certain of was that he wanted her. With a desperation that bordered on insanity. Yes, that he was certain of.

He stripped her bare, and he spent the rest of the night proving to her that while he might be uncertain about some things, there were others he was infinitely confident in.

For now, that was enough.

The future would have to handle itself.

CHAPTER THIRTEEN

THE NEXT FEW weeks went by smoothly. Latika felt at ease with Gunnar in a way that she hadn't ever before.

They spent their days companionably enough, Gunnar busying himself with work, but often including her in discussions about new projects. She enjoyed that.

It gave her a purpose.

One beyond dwelling on her current morning sickness.

It was really such a terrible thing, and she found that she could barely rise before ten a.m. Which was completely unusual for her. But she was living on unsweetened herbal tea and dry toast and crystallized ginger candies.

After all that settled, she could bring herself to rise.

She was thankful that Gunnar had suggested they come and live at the palace when they returned. Because that put her in proximity with Astrid very often, and, it meant that they had a whole range of staff available at all times, and given that Latika was currently feeling quite down, it was exceedingly helpful.

Physically, she might be diminished, but emotionally things were going better than she could've possibly asked.

She was having a fortunate moment when she went out onto the terrace to sit in a lounger, in the pale sun making a weak appearance in the pale sky.

That was when Gunnar came out to find her there.

"How are you feeling?"

She smiled, a strange, warm sensation flooding her.

Gunnar had told her a few weeks ago that he didn't know what love was.

Latika was beginning to think that she did. She felt that every time she looked at him. Every time she thought about him.

"I just wanted to come and tell you that I will be heading to San Diego tonight."

That startled her. "Why?"

"There's a big project opportunity, but there's been a snag with some of the planning. I need to see to it in person."

"Let me go with you," she said.

"There's no need," he said.

"Why not?"

"You don't feel well," he said. "In any way, you will be well taken care of here in the palace. And you will have Astrid around you. Wouldn't you prefer that?"

"Would I prefer your sister's company to yours?"

"She's your friend, after all," Gunter said.

"And you're my husband," Latika responded. "I'm not sure why you don't think that takes precedence."

"Ours is not a conventional marriage," he said. The way he said it, so casually, hurt her. And she knew that perhaps that wasn't fair. He wasn't wrong.

Theirs was not a conventional marriage. It never had been. She had thrown herself at him in a crowded ball-room and demanded his protection, when he was in a position of such public visibility he had no choice but to go along with what she done.

But over the past weeks their marriage had felt conventional enough. In fact, it had felt more than conventional. They had slept together, shared with each other. Grown together.

He had begun to feel like the most important, defining piece of her life.

With Gunnar, she had found something that she hadn't found with anyone else.

He seemed to accept her for who she was. More than that, he seemed to enjoy all that she was.

He shared his business information with her, and complimented her on the way her mind worked. He valued her mind, he valued her body. Every piece of her seemed important to Gunnar.

How could she feel anything but adoration for him?

He also got angry with her sometimes, and she liked that even better. Because it showed her that he could want her even when their interaction wasn't companionable. That he didn't require her to be perfect in order to want her company. In order to want to kiss her and pleasure her and be inside of her.

Everyone else had only ever wanted her on their terms, with the exception of Astrid, who had been her truest friend.

And in Gunnar, she had found a man who cared for her that way, and she could not understand why he might think that wasn't earth shattering.

"Our marriage might not be conventional," she said softly. "But it's important. I find that I'm not happy when you aren't around, Gunnar. And I should like to go with you to San Diego."

He regarded her, his expression unreadable.

"It would be best if you stayed home," he said.

"I don't understand. Why would you care either way?"

She suddenly felt very silly. Arguing over whether or not he should bring her. Truthfully, it was kind of sad. Because if he didn't want her there then she should just accept it. It was difficult to do, when she wanted him like she did. It was difficult, because she wished more than anything that he would crave her company in the same way she craved his. But if he didn't... Then, even if he agreed to bring her along it was something of an empty victory. No, it was more than an empty victory.

It was a loss, and she a bad loser. But she wasn't sure right then if she cared, mostly because she wanted to know why. Wanted to know why he was avoiding spending time with her.

Maybe he just needs space. And the fact that for you it's a revelation that someone wants your company some of the time is a bit more of a novelty for you than it is for him.

Perhaps.

Except, she knew all he had been through with his father. And she had a feeling that this wasn't an entirely familiar situation for him either.

"If you want to go by yourself, you can. But I'm not sure why you think I might be an impediment," she said slowly. "Unless there's something happening you don't want me to know about."

She truly didn't think that Gunnar would be unfaithful to her. She didn't know why she thought that. He had never once sworn his fidelity to her, beyond when they had taken their wedding vows, and at that time both of them had been lying, since neither of them had had plans to sleep with each other then.

"I'm not going to be manipulated, Latika," he said, his voice suddenly turning to shards of ice. "That was what my father did to me. Manipulation. All the damn time. And you trying to make me feel guilty, trying to make me feel concerned by the questioning of my character is not going to make me change my mind."

"I wasn't manipulating you," she said. She felt horrified that he might think that, but then she looked closely at his face, and she saw he lacked sincerity.

He didn't think that she was manipulating him. Not really. Not deep in his heart. And that meant he was the one doing the manipulating.

"What's going on? That is not a leading question, neither is it manipulative. But you're being strange. We've been close to each other these past weeks."

"We have been sleeping together."

"More than that. You swore to protect me."

"Leaving you in a palace surrounded by guards, and with your best friend is hardly walking back on my promise to protect you."

That was true enough.

"Well, then maybe it's more than that. Maybe I want more. Gunnar... I have always been surrounded by people who wanted to use me in some fashion. And you... It isn't like that with us."

"Latika, it is the very definition of that with us. You needed protection. I needed a way to improve my reputation. And so here we both are."

She couldn't do this. Not with him. She'd been on a quest for freedom, for the life that she would have been destined for if not for...well, if not for her life.

And that was the problem, she realized.

She couldn't be Latika without her past. Without the years she'd spent with her parents, then the years that followed in Bjornland. It had all been her life, and it had made her into the woman she was.

A woman who loved the man she had married.

She was not waiting on this. She wouldn't let him leave without him knowing.

"No. That was true when it first began. What we have now isn't that. It isn't for me. Gunnar… I've fallen in love with you."

He drew back as though she had slapped him. "No," he said, his voice like iron. "You don't love me."

"I do," she said. "I've been thinking a lot about that. What love is. Because you asked the other day. Because you said you didn't know. But I think… Gunnar, I think that you exemplify love more than anyone I've ever known. With no regard to your own safety or comfort you protected your sister. For no glory and no advancement. You shielded me from Ragnar, even though you could have easily acted like I was a crazy person throwing myself at you the way that I did."

"And put your life at risk? How reasonable is that?"

"Let me finish," she said. "And then you came for me. You came for the baby. Even though you didn't know if you could be a good father. Even though it terrified you."

"How can you possibly act as if I exemplified love in any way through those actions. You remember what I said to you. The night that we first made love."

"I do. I remember it well, because it hurt me. It hurt me deeply. But it wasn't the final thing you did. Those were words, Gunnar. You took the appropriate steps, the appropriate action to fix those words, and that matters more."

"But some things cannot be erased."

"No, but they can be forgiven."

"Just like that?"

"It isn't just like anything," she said. "But we've had weeks where you have demonstrated to me that the things you said that night were spoken in anger. Anger that came from a very understandable place of fear. You had a plan for your life, Gunnar, and this was in it. I understand that. And also, when push came to shove, you came for your child. You came for me. And since then, you have demonstrated all of those things I just said. And through it all, you've shown me what I want for my life."

"It's just another cage, Latika. Don't thank me for putting you in another cage."

"What?"

"You are...conditioned to make the best out of a bunch of very bad situations. You chose to be here, you chose to be Astrid's assistant because the alternatives to you were vile. And our marriage is no different. Now you find yourself with child, and you see the benefits to the two of us being married, over the benefits of us being separated. That doesn't mean it's what you would have chosen. With an entire world at your disposal. I was one of two options placed in front of you, and you took the one that would not result in your abuse and torture. And then, I presented you with very few options when I came to London to collect you."

"You didn't threaten me. And you gave me a great many opportunities to tell you no, if you don't remember."

"But I would have threatened you," he said. "If you

had not come with me, I would have threatened to take your baby from you. And I think on some level you knew that. I wasn't going to let you waft off into the distance with my child, disavow all connection of my blood with me. You knew I wouldn't allow it."

"I didn't know any such thing. I did not make the decision to go with you under duress. I left you under duress. I separated myself from you in San Diego under duress. I wanted to be with you. I was upset when you said those things to me because I wanted you to be a different man. Because the man that I saw hints and glimpses of was one that I knew I could fall in love with. And I wanted more of that man. Well, in the past weeks you have given it to me. And I… I would choose you. With the whole world before me. I would choose you."

"You don't know that."

"I do."

"You've never had enough freedom to be confident in that fact."

"By your standards, does anyone? Maybe only you. Except, even then you had your reputation to consider. Who chooses a partner with nothing in their life coming into play? Who chooses a partner with no consideration for anything? Very few people, Gunnar, so if circumstances make it so that my feelings don't count, then I would say that most relationships are invalidated. People find love. They find it in the strangest places. They find it in adversity. They have always done so. Whether it's because our hearts crave companionship, or because fate finds ways to wind our paths together no matter what, I don't know. But I know that love finds us. And it has found me. It has found me here with you."

"I don't believe in love," he said, his face hard like

stone. "And I certainly don't believe in it with the way things have happened between us. How can it be real? These are trying times, the have found us entwined. It's not fate, but a series of choices. Choices made out of desperation. Choices made by evil men. And none of them yours to be made freely."

"I just told you…"

"And I feel it is something you need to tell yourself. Because otherwise, here you are pregnant with my child and in a sense, it's just sadly inevitable. Because you weren't exposed to other men. Because you were never given the chance to marry another. Because a jailer without sadistic tendencies looks alarmingly attractive next to one who enjoys causing pain."

She would not let him win. She would not let him reduce her. She returned volley. "All of my life I've had people telling me what they thought was good for me. I won't let you do it too. You have trusted me. You gave me selection power over your bride in the first place. You showed me your business, and you've been consulting me on certain things. How can you now decide that I'm ignorant and know nothing?"

"All right, Latika, have it your way. You understand your heart. You understand your mind. You love me. But your love is misguided and misdirected. Because I do not love you. I cannot. Love means nothing to me, so if you're seeking to offer it as some kind of gift or prize, then I think you truly misunderstand who I am."

"How can love mean nothing to you? Look at Astrid. Look at how much she cares for you. And surely your mother…"

He cut her off with cold, decisive words.

"My mother knew that I was being tortured," he said,

his voice hard. "She did nothing. My *loving* mother. She didn't care one bit what my father did to me. Because I wasn't the child that mattered to her. I existed to be a pawn in my father's eyes. And I was nothing in my mother's. Do not ask me to cling to some source of love that believe me never existed."

Latika's heart curled in on itself. Pain lancing through her. "Your mother knew?"

"Why do you think…" He stopped himself, paused for a moment, before continuing. "Why do you think I am so certain that there is no part of me who would do well with a child? It doesn't come from nothing. My own family was so very broken, Latika. I have offered what I can offer. And beyond that…there is nothing."

"I don't believe that. I just don't. I believe there's more. I believe that you have more to give. I do. Down in my soul I believe it."

"Because you want to see this as something you can hope for. Because you want to see it as something you weren't trapped in. But you are. You are trapped, as am I. We are trapped with the child between us, and what can be done? You would have lies. You would lie to yourself. You would lie to me. You would try and make all of this something that you could latch onto. But it is just more of life's cruelty. You are a good woman, to be able to possess the power to feel the way that you do after what you have been through. But you have been shackled to a man who cannot. And there is no fixing it."

"Gunnar…"

"No. I'm going to San Diego. And while I am there I will go about my business as if we are not married. Do you understand me? I will be what I am. Pure. Through and through. And when the world sees that, they will not judge you for leaving me. And that is what you will do. You will leave me."

"What about your reputation?"

"I don't care."

"I thought it was for Astrid."

"Have I not pledged to you to protect you? To protect the child? This is how it will be done. I do not recall making it a discussion. Astrid will find her own way. She is resilient. And what I'm doing... It is simply a holdover from when I was a boy, taking on my father's torture in the name of keeping her safe." A sad smile tipped his lips upward. "Perhaps I was never truly protecting her. I sometimes wonder that. Perhaps she never needed me. For she had all the strength that she possesses now, and she had the protection of my mother. I thought that perhaps my mother saw me as a source of protection for her precious daughter. But I think more she accepted that I was a distraction from my father's rage. He decided to try and use me to do his will, and he found me immovable. And I suspect that my mother imagined it was just as well. I was a worthy sacrifice either way."

"So that's what you're doing again? Martyring yourself?"

"It would only be martyring if it was something I didn't want. And I never wanted this life. Not really. So which one is martyrdom?"

She didn't have an answer for that. Not really. All she knew was that in her heart she felt like she and Gunnar had something special. Something important. But he was standing there with his eyes cold telling her that they didn't. So perhaps it was true. Maybe he did not care for her. Not even a little. Not even at all. Maybe there were no feelings between them, and she had been desperate to conjure them up. Because they were together. Because she had shared her body with him. Because he had given her a child.

"I love you," she said, the words broken. "And I don't care about pride."

Suddenly, she was desperate, emotion clawing at her chest. "I don't care about my safety. Please don't give your body to another woman, Gunnar, it's mine. I love it so much. I love you so much. You're mine, and I would choose you every time. Every single time. And I hated you on site because I knew that I could never have you. Because I knew that a man like you was beyond my reach. And maybe I did manipulate the situation asking you to marry me. Asking for your protection. But your protection was the only one I wanted."

She took a deep, sharking breath and continued, "I could have thrown myself at Astrid's feet. I could have simply used my connection to her to keep myself safe. But I didn't. I didn't mean to manipulate you, but I did. And for that I must apologize, because I know how much you hate it. But don't ever underestimate the power of choice. Because I did choose you. I did. We could go on all day about what my options were, and why you were the best one. But I know in my heart why you were the one I chose. Because you're beautiful. And brilliant. Because I was so enraged by your exploits with other women because I was jealous. Because I found your beauty so magnetic and undeniable I couldn't turn off my response to you when we were in the same room, and it terrified me. I want to be with you," she said. "From now and until always.

When we took our vows I didn't know what I wanted. I was confused."

"You told me that you wouldn't sleep with me," he said.

"Because I wanted children. I was afraid. I was afraid that if I slept with you this would happen. And it did. I was trying to protect myself from the inevitable. Because I knew… Gunnar, I knew that part of you not wanting children was you holding back your emotions. Please don't give what we've shared to someone else. Please don't ask me to go."

"Where do you wish to live?" he asked, not responding to her at all. "I will establish your living quarters there."

"With you, you idiot. In your home, in your bed."

"Anywhere else in the world, Latika. It's yours. But not with me. Not here."

He tilted his chin upward. "I swore my protection to you, to the child, and I will give that. But I will give no more. I hope you will have found a new place to reside when I return. You will want for nothing. My word is binding. Because I never use them to manipulate."

"No. You do. You use them to manipulate yourself, Gunnar. And if you can't see that that I don't know how to help you."

But he said nothing to that. Instead, he turned and strode off the terrace, leaving Latika stunned. Because there was no more discussion. And he had simply walked away. From her. From this. From them.

And it all felt too unreal for her to even believe that it had happened.

But the stunning, intense feeling of being cracked from the inside that overtook her when she drew in her next breath told her that it had. She slid off the chair, on her knees on the terrace, gasping for breath. She had never felt like this before. Ever. And she thought she might be dying. She had run away from her parents, parents who had been intent on marrying her off to a madman. Had seen how little value she had to them.

She had hidden away for years, had been through so many things that should have done this to her. Should have immobilized her. Should have left her completely and utterly breathless with pain. And yet none of it had.

But this… This was beyond what she thought she could endure.

Always in her life when she had been backed into a corner, she had known that she had to move. Had known that she needed to take a step away from the threat so that she would be safe. But here she was immobilized. Because the man who had just hurt her far beyond anything she could have ever fathomed, was also the one person she wanted to be with more than any other. And she found she had for self-protection.

Because all of her walls were gone. She had fallen in love, and it had stolen all of her protection.

It had stolen everything.

And she had no idea how she was going to survive this.

But suddenly, she remembered.

She put her hand on her stomach, covering her body. The place where the baby grew.

The baby was why she would survive. Why she would carry on.

And more than that, why she would find ways to be happy.

Because she would never subject her child to an unhappy, bitter upbringing.

Her chance at love was this baby.

And yes, Gunnar had come and found her, and he had given her hope. But the loss of him didn't mean the death of her hope.

If she had learned one lesson through all of this it was that the amount of hope that existed in her was an incredible thing. She had grown up in a cloistered life, but she had hoped for more than what her parents had chosen for her.

She had hoped for more than a marriage without love.

That hope was strong. And it would carry her through, even when she couldn't carry herself.

That she had to rest on the strength of that hope, because more often than not it was the only strength available.

When Gunnar arrived in San Diego, he was something more than jetlagged. Something worse than hung over. He didn't understand the thing that was happening inside of him. He didn't understand why the hell he couldn't seem to think straight.

He'd needed to get away from Latika for a while. Because the days and nights of time spent with her had begun to erode the walls he'd built in his soul to protect himself and he'd begun to feel battle worn.

Not from torture or isolation.

From her soft touch on his skin. From her kisses on his lips.

And so he'd devised a trip to get away from her for a while and then…then it had all gone to hell.

Everything felt like it was wrong.

Muddled and messed up, and like it would never be right again. He had endured a great many things in his life. Things that would have broken many people. Most people. But he had never felt like he lost his purpose. He did now. He felt like he couldn't remember the reason he was supposed to breathe. Or a reason anyone might keep breathing.

The world seemed dark. Beyond dark. The world seemed like a completely and unutterably foreign and dark place. He could find nothing bright or hopeful in it. And in the past, when he had felt that way, he had been reminded that at least there was alcohol. At least there was sex. But the despair that he felt now could not be dealt with alcohol. And he didn't want women. Not any woman other than Latika. Ever. She was everything. And she was gone. He didn't know what in the hell he was supposed to do with that. Or why in the hell he had behaved the way he had.

Except.

Except. The thing she had been offering to him seemed far too good, far too good to be real. That was something he learned in life. That anything that seemed too good to be true was. The one time his mother had ever shown any interest in him was when he had been a boy. He had spent hours being tormented at his father's hands.

He had spent days confined to the dungeon. Kept in an area that was not large enough for him to lay down. He had been cramped and isolated, and when his mother had seen him again she had acted like she was glad to see him. And then it had become abundantly clear that she didn't wish to hold him or comfort him. But that she was only concerned that his father might have made some headway in convincing him to try and overthrow Astrid. To contest her position for the throne.

It had never been about him.

He had only realized later that of course, if it would have benefited her to liberate him from his father's clutches, she would have done so. But it didn't. Because if she had tried to get him over to her side, then it would perhaps inspire his father to use other means to get his way. And if she had exposed him to the public, well then... The entire reputation of the royal family of Bjornland would be at risk. And that was something that of course neither of his parents could ever chance. It was a terrible realization.

To know that his own mother had weighed and calculated that. That his own father had done the same. And given the way that his parents felt about him, he could not fathom that Latika could feel any different.

His chest felt crushed.

Was he really so simple?

Was he really so simple that he could not face her declaration of love because he feared he might be harmed? Because he feared all the weak and vulnerable places in him that it exposed. The kind of husband and father he could not be.

Because he could not expose himself to such pain.

He was a coward. And yet, he did not know if he possessed the strength to fight against his own cowardice. He was going to go out. He had every intention of going out. Of finding a woman and getting caught in a compromising position with her. Of destroying the reputation that he had built up for himself. Of breaking their marriage apart. Latika had begged him not to touch another woman, so logic dictated that the first thing he should do is go out and touch another woman.

Except the very idea turned his stomach.

He prowled through his house, empty.

This house that had always brought him such satisfaction. A place that he had built far away from himself and the legacy of his father. Yes, this house had been important to him. As had the fact he had built a business across the world. But now, it all seemed trivial.

Because for a while Latika had been in this house. And when Latika had been in this house, it had been something magic.

When he had taken her out against the wall in the terrace, and fulfilled the fantasy he'd had of tasting her as he'd done.

When he had taken her up to bed and taken her virginity. When her innocence had acted like a dagger and stabbed him through the heart. Had made him wonder whose blood it was that was on the sheets.

She made him feel things he hadn't thought possible, and he resented her for it.

He had never depended on another person. Not once in his life.

He knew that Latika loved him. Really, love wasn't the issue.

He didn't know how to need.

Because days spent in solitary confinement at the hands of his father had taught him not to. Because living with a mother who had cared so little for him, who had certainly never held him, not once when he had fallen, had informed him that he could not depend on anyone but himself.

But part of him thought he might need Latika.

And he didn't know what to do with that.

And then she would have a child, one that would need him in return.

He could not fathom it. He didn't want to.

It was painful. Utterly and completely to imagine the scenario, and almost worse to imagine the alternative. He needed her.

He didn't want to need her.

They were having a child. He was desperate for that child. He also didn't want to be desperate. And God help him if he knew what the hell he was supposed to do with either feeling.

He had done what he had become proficient in. Running away. Yes, he was very accomplished at that. It was what he had done, after all. The method by which he had handled his father. He had not exposed the old man—and perhaps the excuse that it might damage Astrid's credibility and harm her was valid enough—but there were other factors. Because it had been more satisfying, because it had been easier, to simply walk. To simply cut ties and care for nothing. To wave a red flag at the bowl in that regard. And to give himself reprieve.

He was a man who had made his own destiny, and who was very proud of it.

But a huge portion of that journey had been about twisting the problem to suit him, rather than killing it once and for all. Perhaps that was what he had done here. Perhaps that was what he had done with Astrid.

But he didn't know who he was, at the end of everything. Didn't know what he was actually capable of.

Because all he ever asked of himself was that he protect Astrid. That he survived.

And suddenly, it hit him like a wall of bricks.

He was accusing Latika of reacting because she had no choice. But he was the one who lived in that world. He was the one who had made every decision he had made because the alternative was so undesirable.

Who would he have been without the abuse of his father? If he'd not had to dedicate his whole life to protecting Astrid? Would he have wanted children. Would he have reacted to the news of Astrid's pregnancy with joy rather than with anger? When Latika had come to the palace to be his sister's assistant, would he have immediately allowed himself to fall for her? How different would everything have been? It was impossible to say. It was impossible to say, because they had not been given that opportunity. Because he had not been given that opportunity.

He put his hand in his pocket, felt the sensor that would start his car. He could go out. He could go out and he could make a scandal. He could destroy his marriage to Latika. It was one of his choices.

Choices. Yes, he had them. He could go back to Bjornland, he could confess his undying love, and what then? What then. What would happen when she tired of him. What would happen when he couldn't be what she needed him to be? In his experience, that meant that he was not worth the effort. And as a man who was not worth the effort, he simply could not believe that he was now.

He gritted his teeth, and turned, walking out of the apartment.

Yes, they all had choices.

And sometimes the choices before you were grim.

But he would do what he had to. To set them both free.

CHAPTER FOURTEEN

WHEN LATIKA CAME down to breakfast the next morning, Astrid's face was guarded.

"What?" Latika asked.

"It has to do with my brother."

Latika felt like a knife had stabbed her through the heart. "I assume you mean he's gone out and found himself a lover."

Astrid blinked. "Did you know he was going to?"

"He told me he would."

"Why?"

"Because I told him I was in love with him, and he did not find that to be satisfactory. But I also begged him not to do this. I told him that we…we could be happy together. We could be. I don't know why he is intent upon hurting himself. I feel…" She sank down into the chair, a tear sliding down her cheek. "Give me the paper."

Astrid pulled it toward her chest. "You don't want to see it."

"I should see it. I need to see it. I really do."

"I know. I would feel better if you didn't."

"Well, this isn't about either of us feeling comfortable."

Astrid slid the paper across the table. And there were

photographs. Of Gunnar with a blonde woman. He was only talking to her over drinks, but his hand was rested low on her back, and the headline implied that the two of them had left together. Trouble for the Royal marriage as the Playboy Prince was caught canoodling a California girl.

Latika surprised herself by grabbing the paper and balling it up, throwing it across the dining room.

"I told you," Astrid said.

"I've never been jealous before. It's awful."

"Yes," Astrid agreed. "Of course it's awful."

"I don't want to hurt like this," Latika said.

"Unfortunately," Astrid replied. "It does hurt when they break your heart."

"Like when Mauro broke yours."

"Yes."

"He didn't sleep with another woman."

"Gunnar might not have either."

Latika knew that was true. And in fact, it did make some sense. Because Gunnar wanted to drive a wedge between them, and he wanted to do something that he thought she might find irreversible. In this… Well, this would be that thing. So of course, it made sense that he might go to such great lengths.

"Maybe." She sighed. "He told me to be gone when he got back."

Astrid looked like she was made of steel. "No. That isn't fair. You don't have to leave. He's the one who should leave."

"Well, good luck kicking him out of his own palace."

"It's my palace. I was born first," Astrid said imperiously.

Latika's breath caught. "Yes."

"Why did you say it like that?"

Latika shook her head. "There are things that... There are things that Gunnar will have to tell you someday. But I can't break his confidence."

"Even now?"

"Even now."

Astrid sighed heavily. And then she stood up, both palms on the table. "Well. If you're bound and determined to be that loyal to him, then I suggest you stay. Stay in your bedroom. Keep your things there too. Refuse to leave. Whatever he needs to see... Prove to him that he cannot get rid of you."

"And if he did cheat on me?"

"Only you can answer that question."

Latika knew the answer in her heart. That no matter what, she was committed to him. Committed to loving him. That whatever actions he committed out of a desire to run...she would forgive.

She truly, truly hoped that she didn't have to. But she was willing. Because she loved him.

And she was tired of living a life where she made subpar choices to run from a bad option.

Gunnar was a good option. Even if he wasn't perfect. She didn't need perfect. She needed love.

And in the end, she would see to it that love conquered all. In the end, she would show him just how strong love was. She only wished that she didn't have to demonstrate it with quite so much intensity. But she would.

By the time Gunnar returned to the palace in Bjornland, he was prepared to find an empty bedroom where Latika should be. Because of course he had done what he needed to do.

He had gone out and found himself a woman. That he had betrayed their marriage vows. And why would she think he had done any differently.

Exactly the way he'd promised he would.

Or at least, made it seem as if he had.

In reality, nothing could have enticed him to touch the blonde woman he had spent approximately ten minutes chatting with. He had asked her to step outside with him, and she had complied. Then he had paid her a significant amount of money to walk away and not go back into the bar.

As he had anticipated, opinion pieces on his behavior began pouring in immediately. It was nothing more than he had expected. And nothing more than he deserved. And it would allow Latika to be free. Truly. She would be a paragon of virtue in the eyes of his people, and indeed, the people of the world. His child would know his father, and even if he had to spend a lifetime atoning for the supposed sins he had committed against Latika, the child would not be denied its parentage, and that, was something of absolute importance to Gunnar.

He had solved everything.

And yet, he felt empty.

He stood at the threshold of the palace in victory.

And yet, he felt defeated.

There was nothing to feel overly proud of. Not in this.

He moved through the corridors of the palace, managing to neatly dodge any of the serving staff, but when he went to the staircase that he knew would take him to his room, he was met by his brother-in-law. Mauro was standing on the stairs, his gaze dark, his arms crossed over his chest.

"I didn't expect a welcoming committee," he said.

"You should have. Of course you should know that I would be aware that you had arrived back at the palace. And that we have all seen the headlines."

"Yes. I suppose I should have realized you were monitoring the border."

"Even you can't go undetected when we would like to see you."

"Well, that's good to know. I'll add espionage and surveillance to the long list of my sister's skills."

"How dare you come back here?" Mauro asked.

"I'm sorry, are *you* of royal blood?"

"Not last time I checked. But I am married to your sister. And I am a faithful husband."

"As far as I know, infidelity is as storied a tradition as the grand Christmas ball that our family throws every year. My people have never much concerned ourselves with anything quite so pedestrian as keeping our vows. I'm not sure why I should be the start of that."

"Astrid and I are the start of that. And she thought well enough of you that you might continue it."

"Well, my sister is optimistic. Especially where I'm concerned. I am nothing immensely exceptional. She should not expect it of me."

He began to move past Mauro, and his brother-in-law planted a firm hand on his shoulder. "Explain yourself."

"I do not have to explain myself to a man such as you."

"Explain yourself," Mauro repeated.

"Sometimes the kindest thing a man can do is set a woman free. I would think you of all people would know that."

Morrow's face darkened. "Are you suggesting it would've been kinder for me to set your sister free?"

"No. But I know you thought that one time. And here you are. You are a good father. A good husband. A man that I am happy my sister has found a life with. But for a while you thought that would not be the case. And you did what you had to. I know myself. I know my heart. And what I have done for Latika was the kindest thing that could be done. Trust me on that."

"You were not here to see her distress. I was. You broke her. If you weren't such a coward that you ran to execute your plan, then you could have seen it yourself, and you could've told her that it was for her own good."

Mauro shook his head. "For my part, I cannot see how harming another person in that way could ever be for their own good."

"Why is it that you're speaking to me instead of Astrid?"

"Astrid didn't trust herself around you. She thought she might execute you."

Gunnar laughed, and then pushed past Mauro. In many ways, he would believe that was true of his sister. She was fearsome, and it was one of the things he respected about her. One of the reasons he had always felt it was important that she be the one who took over the throne. That she be protected at all costs.

But what about yourself?

It didn't matter. The choices were made. And they were done.

He had taken up his mother's charge, and even she had not sworn any kind of loyalty to him.

After of a betrayal such as the one he'd committed, there was no reason to believe that Astrid ever would.

As he continued down the corridor, a door opened, and his sister appeared. "We must talk."

"I just shook off your attack dog."

"Yes I know. Because I told him to speak to you so that I wouldn't have to."

"And yet, here you are."

"Because it's important. It's important that we speak. Latika told me that there was something I didn't know about you. And she refused to elaborate. She said she would not break your confidence. She said this to me even after she had seen the news of your betrayal. Because that is the woman that you have behaved so poorly toward. A woman who would protect you when you absolutely did not deserve it."

He shook his head, a grim weight settling in his chest. "Believe me, Astrid, the question was never whether Latika was good enough for me."

"What don't I know?"

"There is no point rehashing this. There is no point at all. Our lives are what they are. You have found happiness with Mauro, and I am glad for you. I don't need to bring my pain at your feet. My life is also established. It is set. I am what I was made to be."

He looked at his sister, who was like gold plated iron, and he realized he was selling her short. Her strength. Her wisdom.

He had always sought to protect her, but in many ways he had underestimated her.

As his father had always done.

And that…that could not stand.

"Then if everything is set in stone, you might as well tell me. If nothing can be changed…"

"You know how badly our father wanted me to be King."

Astrid stared at him, her eyes wide. "Yes."

"He sought to use me as a weapon against you. He wished to turn me against you. And his method of doing that was to attempt isolation. Torture."

The horror in his sister's eyes was everything he had been trying to avoid for the past twenty years. "And you can see now why I didn't want to tell you this. You can see now why I never wanted any of this."

"Why did you not tell me?" she asked, her voice a broken whisper.

"What purpose would it have served? I had to protect you. It was the most important thing I could do. I had to serve you. You are my Queen. You are my sister. And protecting you all this time has meant shielding you from just how corrupt our father was. Because what does it benefit you to know?"

"So that I could know you," she said. "Not everything is about me, Gunnar. And that is a sentence I never thought I would say to you. Because you have lied all this time about who you are. You let everyone believe that you were selfish. And instead, everything you did was for me. How could you let me go my whole life not knowing that?"

"Because I am still broken. And there is no fixing it."

"How are you broken? It was never you. It was them. All this time it was them. Both of them, Gunnar. Mom and Dad. Don't think I don't realize that. But I was the fulfillment of mother's ambition. And that you are clearly the attempted fulfillment of our father's. When we were lost in the middle. But look at how you have loved me. Look at how loyal you were. How loyal you are. Gunnar, you gave me things I did not deserve with your devotion. No one could possibly hope to deserve. Because how can a person deserve to have someone else sacrifice their safety and comfort for them? You can't. Something like that is never about deserving. It's about love. And love is never something any of us could earn. Not love on the level that you gave me. It is a greater love than most could ever hope to receive."

"I have never felt like I possessed any great love inside of me."

"Because you didn't just let it sit inside of you. You poured it out for me. Love is useless as a feeling. It takes on a new shape when it becomes action. And sometimes that action is a sacrifice, and there is nothing comfortable and sacrifice. But it's real."

"I never wanted to hurt you with knowledge of our father's treachery."

Astrid put her hand on her heart, as if it was in pain and she was trying to minimize that pain. "I'm not hurt for me. I hurt for you. For myself... I have never felt so loved, Gunnar. To have a husband who loves me as he does. To know that my brother loves me in such a way. I cannot fathom how I was born so fortunate."

Gunnar had never thought of it that way, and it was as if everything was turned upside down. That what he'd done for Astrid would make her feel not the betrayal of their parents, but the deep love that he felt for her.

And it was love.

He could see it now. The way that she'd spoken of it. Love that fills you up so very much that you had to pour it out. Love that existed somewhat uncomfortably because it demanded things of you that did not feel good or satisfying.

And now he felt he understood something about love. Something that perhaps might have saved his marriage.

Except… Except what he had done to Latika… She would not forgive him.

Though, he had not betrayed her, he had certainly made the world believe he had. And even if he were to try and fix it now, she might not believe him. And the world certainly wouldn't. So she would always have to be the woman who had gone back to a man that had been unfaithful.

He had created for himself an impossible situation and now, it was too late to fix it. She would be gone now. As he had told her to be. Because he had broken her. Mauro had told him that.

"Excuse me," he said.

Because whether or not it was too late, he was going to try.

Choices. These were the choices. He could live forever without Latika, or he could try. Living without her was unacceptable. And so he had to try, no matter how unlikely it was that he would ever earn her love again.

But love was such a very precious thing, and Latika had put her love for him into action. Had laid herself bare. And that kind of love had to be rewarded. Because that kind of love mattered. When he saw it through the same lens that Astrid did, that bravery and that sacrifice… Latika had done all that for him. She had begged, she had put herself before him raw and naked. And he had given her so little in return. He would make it right. He had to make it right.

He pushed his hands through his hair, making his way down the hall and pushing the door open, expecting to find that same sense of emptiness that had been in his San Diego home.

But instead, he saw her.

Latika was sitting on a bench at the foot of their bed, her long dark hair cascading over her shoulders, her expression set into one of seriousness. He could see that she had been crying. That he had made her cry. He had never despised himself more than he did in that moment.

"I thought I told you to leave," he said.

"You did," she responded. "And you did everything you said you would. You are a man of your word, Gunnar, I will give you that. But I didn't agree to leave you. And I won't leave you. I love you, and I want more than anything for this to work. And I know what they'll say about me. How sad I am. That I'm so desperately delusional for thinking that my husband who was unfaithful to me could ever change."

She shook her head. "I don't care. I don't care what anyone thinks of me. I'm not making decisions for other people anymore. I'm making decisions for myself. From my heart. And what's right for me."

"You would... You would stay with me even now?"

She stood. "Yes. I would. Because I fell in love with you, and I fell in love with each and every broken part of you. The broken part that made you feel you had to run. That made you feel you had no other choice but to try and undo this once and for all by sleeping with another woman. If I believe that love can heal, then I must give it time. I won't stay with a man who cannot love me ever. But if you think there is hope, that we can make a marriage work. That we can love each other, then I will stay. I am...devastated that you would give to someone else what we have shared. But I promise that I will do everything in my power to forgive. To never hold it over your head. I believe that you can be better. And if I believe that, then I need to give you the chance to be."

Her words nearly took Gunnar down to his knees. For what had he ever done to deserve such an offer? Such complete and utter loyalty. He had become his father in many ways now. He had tortured her. And yet, she held fast.

And then, he did find himself on his knees in front of her, taking her hands in his. "I don't deserve such an offer," he said, his voice rough.

"Love isn't about what you deserve," she said softly, her words so closely mirroring Astrid's that the truth of them rang through him like a gong.

"My darling, Latika. I don't know why you would choose to believe me. But I did not sleep with her. I didn't even kiss her. I made all the world think that I did, though, and that means that it will follow us. That means that…you will not be free of the insinuations that will come, and the outright, blatant commentary. And that will be my fault. For I have done that to us."

"You weren't unfaithful to me?"

"No. And I'm sorry that I let you keep talking, and keep thinking it. But I wanted you to understand that I wasn't telling you this to manipulate you into staying. If you would stay either way… And you know I have no reason to lie. I swear to you I wouldn't lie. Not about this."

"I believe you," she said softly. "I swear that I do."

"I was afraid. And I was running. And every single thing that I accused you of… I was the one who felt like I was stuck with a series of choices, handed down to me from others. And I realized that I was continuing to let my father manipulate and control my life. That I was allowing my mother to continue to have dominion over what I was."

He pushed his hands through his hair, and saw they were shaking. "I have always fancied myself a man who lived free. A kind of rogue prince who did whatever he wanted, but that isn't true. And it never has been. I let myself wonder…what kind of man would I have been if not for that?"

"A dangerous thing to wonder," she whispered. "We are what we were made."

"It's true, but I think, Latika, I would have chosen you much sooner. I love you. I don't need time to fall in love with you. I simply needed to find a way to rout the fear out of my heart so that I could give that love space to be felt. And more importantly, so that I could allow myself to act on it. I told you I didn't know what love felt like, but I have come to understand that it isn't important to know what it feels like. It is much more important to know what it looks like."

His throat tightened, making his words rough. "Because love that *feels* like much but looks like nothing is useless. You demonstrated deep and real love for me. The way you chose to stand with me, to be steady. When I was not. You offered me faithfulness when I appeared to have given you none, when for all intents and purposes, I had given you none. You demonstrated bravery in the face of rejection when I couldn't. And that, will always be what love is to me. And it is the love that I will endeavor to give back to you. To be brave when I feel afraid. To give when I feel like being selfish. To love when it would be easier to hate. I will make these choices for the two of us. I swear it. I swear it to you."

She threw her arms around him, a sob racking her shoulders. "I was willing to forgive you, but I'm so glad that I don't have to."

"You will still have to forgive me," he said. "Because whether or not the world will believe that I was faithful to you is another story. And our marriage may forever be tainted by the public perception of what I have done."

"I don't care about public perception. That is the only thing my parents ever cared about, and believe me, it never made any of us happy."

"I don't think I will ever elevate the nation. My reputation may be too far gone."

"Whether or not the world ever knows, you did elevate the nation. You protected their Queen. You protected me. I hope someday the world understands the manner of man that you are. But if they don't... I do. And I will ensure that our child knows it too."

Gunnar took her chin in his hand, stared down into her beautiful brown eyes. "I don't need the world to know a damn thing about me. As long as you trust in me, then I will be happy."

"I trust in you."

"Here I give you vows that I mean with all my heart," he said, holding one of her hands clasped in his. "That I will be faithful. That I would lay down my life for you, and our child. But I will reserve the realest parts of me for you. And only you."

"And I will do the same," she said, one small hand covering his. Then Latika stretched up on her toes and kissed him. Pure and sweet and more than he could have ever hoped to deserve.

But the beautiful thing about love, the real love that had surrounded him for longer than he had allowed himself to see it, was that it transcended what a man deserved.

The best things, Gunnar thought as he carried Latika to bed, were free. They were beyond price. They could not be bought, they could not be worked for, they could only be given.

And Latika had given him her love.

The thing that a man who could afford anything, who had been entrenched in a life that involves no denial, and no deprivation, had never known he was missing.

And as they came together, man and wife in every sense of the word, that hole that had always been there in his soul felt filled.

Completed by this woman. Completed by her love.

EPILOGUE

THE KINGDOM HAD rejoiced when Astrid had given birth to her son, the heir to the throne of Bjornland, but there was no less celebration for the birth of Gunnar and Latika's daughter.

The beautiful Princess with jet-black hair and eyes the same color as her mother's.

And when Gunnar and Latika renewed their vows in an intimate ceremony, attended only by Mauro, Astrid and their children, the photos—of the new baby, and of Latika in a wedding dress made of simple, rich satin, that she'd been so afraid to let herself wear to that first wedding—had helped cement the acceptance of the royal couple as one that would last.

A couple worthy of rooting for. Especially in light of the new revelations that had come to light over the past months.

Gunnar and Latika had been willing to figure out a way to address the issues he had created with his headline within their family. To make sure their daughter understood what Latika believed if ever the time came when she stumbled across those stories.

But Astrid had a different plan. Astrid took it upon herself to demolish the secrets and lies that their parents had lived with. The web of deceit and corruption that had surrounded the castle while they had been alive.

Of course, it had dashed her father's reputation. And it created many questions about the long history of their family.

But it had given the world the truth about Gunnar. About his loyalty to the crown. To his sister.

And to why he had contrived to make it look as if he was unfaithful to his wife.

And of course, there would always be people who believed that Gunnar was not a hero, but a villain involved in a desperate PR campaign.

Though Latika knew the truth. And that was all that mattered.

She knew, beyond a shadow of a doubt that she would love this man forever.

Prince Gunnar von Bjornland, her husband, wonderful father and the pride of his nation. A man she loved with every fiber of her being.

It would be her great joy to be his wife, for all the rest of her days.

* * * * *

SHEIKH'S PREGNANT CINDERELLA

MAYA BLAKE

CHAPTER ONE

HIS EARS WERE playing tricks on him. They must be.

Otherwise they wouldn't have relayed the unconscionable message to his brain that—

No.

'Repeat yourself,' Sheikh Zufar al Khalia, current occupant of the throne of Khalia, breathed softly at the short, bespectacled senior aide standing before him.

The man shrank back, very much aware that his King's lowered, even tones were far worse than his bark. Not that Zufar al Khalia, much accomplished, master strategist and all-round frighteningly intelligent head of the exulted royal family, needed to lower himself to such unseemly actions as barking.

Marwan Farhat only managed to withstand his liege's chilling tawny gaze for a handful of seconds before lowering his to the priceless Persian rug beneath his feet.

'Now, Marwan,' Zufar insisted.

'We've been informed that your betrothed has disappeared, Your Highness. She's not in her suite, and her maidservant thinks she's been taken.'

'Thinks? So there's no actual evidence?'

'Uh… I haven't spoken to the servant myself, Your Highness, but—'

'For all you know, my betrothed could be hiding somewhere in the palace, under the pretext of the foolish, pre-wedding nerves that normally afflict women on such a day, correct?'

Marwan exchanged glances with the other aides. 'It is possible, Your Highness.'

Zufar heard the *but* not spoken, loud and clear. 'Where is this maidservant? I wish to speak to her myself.'

The senior aide grimaced. 'Of course, Your Highness, but I've been informed the girl is quite hysterical. I don't think it will be useful—'

'Useful?' The cold disbelief trapped in his chest expanded. 'Do you see what I'm wearing, Marwan?' Zufar drawled in the soft, deadly voice that usually hushed his subordinates into fearful silence, as he rounded the massive teak desk that had previously belonged to his esteemed grandfather.

Marwan's Adam's apple bobbed again as he took in Zufar's heavy burgundy-and-gold military uniform, complete with wide sash, epaulettes, and buttons made of solid gold. Where other men would have looked stiff and pompous, his King looked enviably elegant, his towering six-feet-plus height lending the uniform a regal stature few could emulate.

The accompanying cloak hung on its own specially made frame nearby. Together they formed the King's ceremonial wedding attire, commissioned on his twenty-first birthday for this one momentous occasion. Zufar al Khalia had cut a commanding figure since he hit puberty, but on this day he rose above all men into an exclusive realm of his own.

'Yes, Your Highness,' he responded respectfully.

Zufar tossed the white gloves he'd been about to put on before he was interrupted onto the desk, and advanced towards the men. He had their attention, but he needed to make sure that not a single syllable that fell from his lips would be misconstrued.

'Have you seen the dignitaries and heads of states currently making their way to the Imperial Room? The fifty thousand citizens who've been camping in the capital for the past seven days in anticipation of this ceremony? The three hundred journalists and innumerable cameras waiting on the south lawn to televise this ceremony?'

'Of course, Your Highness.'

Zufar took a deep calming breath, certain that if he didn't he would burst a blood vessel despite his supremely robust health. And that would be terribly unwise considering this was supposed to be his wedding day.

'Tell me again why you think it would not be *useful* to discover the whereabouts of my betrothed as soon as possible?'

Marwan clasped his hands before him, a gesture of supplication that did nothing to appease Zufar's rising temper. 'A thousand pardons, Your Highness,' he said. 'I merely came to inform you that there might be a delay. Perhaps we can postpone the ceremony—'

'No. There will be no postponement. You will find my betrothed immediately and this wedding ceremony will proceed as scheduled.'

'Your Highness, the guards and all the servants have searched everywhere. She is not here.'

A red haze washed across Zufar's vision. His collar began to constrict him, blocking his airway. But he didn't raise his hand to undo a button or in any way indicate his discomfort.

He was the King.

Since birth, streams of instructors and governesses had drummed long-suffering poise and decorum into him, with swift and merciless punishment delivered for stepping out of line. As for rash displays of emotion like the bellow of frustration that bubbled inside him? Those came with a week's banishment to the winter palace on the northernmost part of Khalia with nothing but the frozen mountains and endless reams of Latin recitals for company.

No, unfettered displays of emotion had been his father's eminent domain.

For Zufar and his younger brother and sister, it had been an emotionless existence in the strictest boarding schools in foreign lands. And during the holidays when they were allowed home, they would spend hours being groomed into becoming the perfect ambassadors of the Royal House of Khalia.

On the rare occasion when his temper strained and attempted to get the better of him, like today, people took notice. And fled his presence at the earliest possible moment.

Zufar gathered himself until his spine was a steel column, and fixed his eyes on Marwan. 'You will take me to this maidservant now. I wish to hear what she has to say for myself.'

The senior aide immediately bowed low. 'Of course, Your Highness.'

The palace guards stationed on either side of the door sprang forwards to open the double doors for him.

The moment Zufar stepped into the hallway, he knew something was very, very wrong. The excited buzz that had charged the air during the final preparations for the royal wedding had altered.

Several staff members of the royal palace wore anxious expressions as they rushed back and forth. And while it was respectful to drop one's gaze before the King, he noticed that every single one of the staff was actively avoiding his.

The palpable tension raised the hairs on his nape. Beside him, Marwan also avoided his gaze. In fact, the man was doing everything in his power to extend his short strides in the rush to put self-preserving space between himself and Zufar.

It would've been amusing had Zufar not felt in his very marrow that his impending nuptials were in jeopardy.

Whispers around him grew as he entered the main part of the palace. As with most royal palaces, the women's quarters were separated from the men's by several wings. His own private rooms were to the west of the sprawling palace that sat on top of Mount Jerra.

Quick strides took him across to the east wing. He ignored the bows and scrapes of his palace staff and extended family members as he walked, grim-faced, towards the guest suite that Amira, his fiancée, had occupied since her arrival at the palace three weeks ago.

She was a daughter of his father's oldest friend, and Zufar had been aware of Amira's existence since he was a boy. But she was several years his junior and had clearly found him intimidating to the point of speechlessness at the best of times. He hadn't taken much interest in her until his father had informed him of the agreement he'd made with Feroz Ghalib, Amira's father, for them to marry.

Even then, the wedding had been a distant future event, arranged by others and needing only a handful of meetings for the sake of appearances. Still, he'd taken his duty seriously and ensured during their meetings that she was at ease and not being forced into a union she didn't want. Her assurances had satisfied him enough to accept that she would be his wife when the time was right.

The medical report that had confirmed that she was healthy enough to bear his children had sealed the deal.

Beyond that, he hadn't given her much thought, although she'd been peculiarly distracted during their twice weekly dinners recently.

But Amira was close with his sister and Zufar was confident that Galila would have informed him if there'd been a problem with the upcoming nuptials.

Nevertheless, had he dropped the ball somewhere?

He frowned.

The burden of governing his kingdom was his first and only priority. It had needed to be, considering the chaos it had been left in by his father's sudden abdication.

Tight anger knotted inside him as he strode faster towards the suite of luxury rooms that were reserved for the Queen and other female members of the royal family.

He wouldn't think of his father today, or the fact that the ex-King had banished himself to the summer palace since his wife's death and hadn't spoken to his children in months. Zufar wouldn't think of the sleepless nights and backbreaking work it had taken for him to keep the kingdom that had already been woefully neglected by his father from falling apart.

Today, *this hour*, demanded his complete attention. His people yearned for a royal wedding. That was exactly what he was going to give them.

The footmen stationed outside the Sapphire Suite spotted him and immediately threw open the doors.

Zufar entered, then drew to a stop at the sight of the visibly distressed women in the living room. Two were babbling hysterically, and an older female servant was busy comforting another.

'Which one is she?' he demanded tersely. Eyes swivelled to him, followed predictably by shocked gasps and hurried comportment before the bows and scrapes and averted gazes commenced.

Marwan hushed them, and then uttered a sharp query to the junior aide behind him. The younger man shook his head, throwing a furtive glance at Zufar. Marwan approached the older attendant and questioned her. Clearly nervous, she pointed to the inner chamber.

Zufar strode towards smaller double doors, his temper frothing furiously in his chest. This time he pulled the doors open himself, bitter memories tossing themselves onto the pyre he was trying to contain as he walked into the huge, lavish chamber that had once been his mother's domain.

His gaze didn't linger on the priceless keepsakes, furniture or decoration. He didn't know which items in this room his mother had treasured and which gifts from his father and her secret admirers had been less favoured. He didn't know her favourite book or the preferred flower arrangement for her private sitting room because he had never been allowed in here.

On the rare occasions his mother had tolerated him, they had been in public where her pretended adoration could be captured for the world to see and praise and to provide moments of smugness as she perused the gossip rags. Beyond that, she'd never had a kind word for him or his siblings.

But he wasn't here to dwell on the subject of his mother.

He trained his focus on the figure hunched over near the headboard of the vast bed. She was so slight he almost missed her.

Had it not been for the drab, body-shrouding beige clothes that painfully and distastefully stood out against the gold and cream bed linen, he would've mistaken her for one of the pillows or part of the rich drapery that decorated the four-poster bed.

As he advanced towards her he noticed that her slim shoulders were shaking. Another few steps and the small sniffles of her quiet sobs reached his ears.

Zufar stifled his curse before it ripped free.

He didn't care for weak women. He cared even less for weak, *crying* women.

Behind him, Marwan clicked his tongue sharply.

The figure jumped up, stumbled over her long, shapeless skirt, and immediately tumbled to the floor in a graceless heap at Zufar's feet.

He waited, impatient breath slowly spilling through clenched teeth, for her to rise. But she didn't seem interested in regaining her feet. Instead, she was developing an almost mesmerised interest in his shoes.

He took a step forwards, hoping to dislodge her hypnosis. When that failed to work, he cleared his throat.

'If that is a shoe fetish you're exhibiting, may I suggest you indulge in it another time? When the reputation of my kingdom isn't at stake, perhaps?' Zufar drawled.

A sharp intake of breath, then, finally, she raised her head.

Large, tear-soaked dark eyes rose from his feet, and plotted an excruciatingly slow journey up his body. By the time they reached his face, her expression was creased into abject horror.

Coupled with a face blotched and bloated with tears and a mouth frozen in an unattractive O, she was the most unsightly girl Zufar had ever seen.

'What is your name?' he bit out, praying she could actually string enough words together to answer.

She didn't respond. She simply stared up at him, her horror intensifying by the second.

'Do you not hear your King addressing you, girl?' Marwan demanded sharply.

Her mouth closed. She swallowed noisily, but still uttered no word.

Zufar's fists started to curl. Almost a year's worth of meticulous planning hung in the balance because of one tear-streaked, dumbstruck girl.

About to move, he paused as her gaze darted to his fists and she recoiled.

The sight of her naked fear struck an uncomfortable chord in him. He breathed out and slowly unfurled his fingers. There would be no coherent conversation with her unless he found a way to defuse some of her fear, he realised.

He sensed Marwan moving towards her and held up his hand. 'Leave us,' he instructed.

Marwan made a small sound of surprise. 'Are you sure, Your Highness?'

Zufar's lips tightened. 'Leave. Now.'

The room emptied immediately. He kept his gaze fixed on the girl crouched before him, and slowly extended his hand towards her. Again, her gaze darted between his face and his hand, as if terrified he would do something unpredictable. Like bite. Or strike.

He frowned.

She reminded him of the skittish colts in his stable. The ones that demanded substantial time and patience to respond to his commands.

Except he was in gross negative supply of either today. His marriage ceremony was scheduled to commence in less than two hours.

Zufar leaned down and extended his hand further. 'Stand up,' he instructed, firming his voice.

She placed her hand in his, scrambled upright, and immediately gasped and dropped his hand as if she'd been scalded.

He ignored her reaction, his gaze moving over her, confirming that the drabness indeed extended from the top of the dishevelled tufts of dark hair peeking out of her beige scarf to the soles of her feet.

Except, she wasn't a girl as he'd initially surmised.

She was long past adolescence, if the pronounced swell of her chest and the hint of curves beneath the clothes were any indication. She came up to his chin in her flat, tasteless shoes, her covered arms slender and her jaw holding a delicate strength.

His eyes were drawn to her chest again. It was just her agitated breathing that was snagging his attention. Nothing else. He stepped back, folded his hands behind his back and assumed a gesture of ease that never failed to work on his horses.

'What is your name?' he asked again in a lower voice.

Her gaze dropped to the ground and she mumbled.

'Speak up,' he said.

Her chin jerked up a little, but her gaze remained, once again, on the tips of his shoes.

'Niesha Zalwani, Your Highness,' she repeated.

Her voice was soft, smoky and lyrical, if a little too timid for his dwindling patience. But at least he was getting somewhere. He had a name.

'What is your role here?'

'I—I'm… I was a chambermaid until last week, when I was added to Miss Amira's personal staff.'

'Look at me when I'm addressing you,' Zufar drawled. It

took an interminable age for her head to rise once more. But eventually, her gaze met his, then promptly flitted down to rest on his nose. Zufar prayed for strength and continued, 'Where's your mistress?'

Immediately her lower lip wobbled, her wide eyes grew haunted and her breathing turned agitated again. Zufar forced himself not to stare at the soft globes of her breasts or the pale creaminess of her throat as she trembled before him.

'She…she's gone, Your Highness.'

Zufar's fist threatened to ball again. Resisting the urge was difficult. 'Gone where?' he managed through clenched teeth.

'I don't know, Your Highness.'

'Very well. Let us try another way. Did she leave alone?'

Another frenzied twisting of her fingers, and then she cleared her throat. 'No, Your Highness. She…she left with a man.'

A detached, icy sensation stroked his nape. 'A man? What man?' he asked softly.

'He did not tell me his name, Your Highness.'

'But you are certain she has been taken against her will by an unknown male?' he pressed.

The woman before him bit her lip, drawing his attention to the plump, reddened curve of her mouth as she nodded. 'Yes…well…' Her distress grew.

'Tell me what you know,' he insisted.

'I may be wrong, Your Highness, but she didn't seem… unwilling.'

The possibility that he'd been jilted arrived with ice-cold anger. Except, curiously, Zufar wasn't enraged on his own behalf. Rather, the impending disappointment for his people, the chaos for his kingdom, was what caused his fists to clench behind his back.

'Did she say anything? Did *he* say anything to make you think this?'

'It—it all happened very quickly, Your Highness. But...'
Her hand disappeared into the folds of her skirt and emerged
with a folded piece of paper. 'He...he instructed me to give
this to Princess Galila to hand to you.' She held out the piece
of paper, her slender fingers trembling.

Zufar took it from her, his insides frozen as he unfolded
the sheet he recognised as a torn piece of his own royal
stationery.

He read the message once. Then again.

With a thick curse, he crumpled the heavy, embossed
paper between his fingers, his fist clenched tight until it
shook with the force of his emotions. The red haze of fury
returned, deeper, steeping his lethal mood as he crossed
to the window and pressed his fist against the wide pane.

Before him, the palace grounds sprawled in sun-dappled
splendour. Beyond the windows, the muted buzzing of an
expectant crowd rolled over the horizon. Excited citizens
and eager tourists who'd flown in especially for this occasion were anticipating a fairy-tale royal wedding of their
King to his chosen Queen. The whole kingdom had been
gripped in wedding fever for months.

Only to have his heathen bastard of a half-brother claim
in writing that he'd seduced and stolen his betrothed!

In another life, perhaps, that tiny sliver of emotion piercing through his fury could've been called relief from yet
another responsibility. But Zufar gave it absolutely no room
whatsoever, because he now faced a monumental problem.
Aside from the humiliation of announcing that he was no
longer in possession of his fiancée, this arrangement had
held great economic advantages for Khalia.

He needed to find Amira. Confirm for himself that his
half-brother's claim was the truth.

But how could he, when he had no idea where he'd gone?
The dossier he'd collated on Adir when he'd first made his
unforgettable appearance at his mother's funeral had re-

vealed he had no fixed abode, or, if he did, he'd kept it very well hidden.

Even if Zufar knew his whereabouts, he had no time to go chasing after him. He acknowledged with a bitter laugh how well timed Adir's revenge had been. His half-brother knew that doing this now would cause the most humiliation. The most uproar.

Zufar wasn't about to hand him that victory. Not in this lifetime.

He whirled to face the young chambermaid. 'When did they leave?'

Her throat worked again. But this time she wasn't silent for very long. 'I brought her tea, and left her alone for just ten minutes.' Her voice was wracked with nerves and anguish. She began to wring her hands again. 'I had gone to get the royal jewellery when I heard the commotion.'

'So you saw them leave together?'

Her head moved in a shaky nod. 'Yes.'

'And you're sure he didn't harm her?' Zufar demanded.

'She—she didn't appear in distress, Your Highness. She seemed…willing.'

The tightness in his chest eased a tiny fraction. 'How did they leave?'

She pointed to the very window where he stood.

Zufar's jaw clenched tight. They were on the second floor, with nothing outside the windows but climbing vines. Granted, they were over a century old and sturdy enough to hold a horse, but had his barbarian brother really whisked his betrothed out of a second-floor window?

'Did anyone else see them?'

'Only Her Highness, the Princess, but they were almost on the ground when she came in.'

Zufar frowned. Why hadn't Galila informed him?

Had she tried to stop them and been unsuccessful? Most likely Galila was keeping well out of Zufar's way because she knew how he would take the news.

'How soon after did you raise the alarm?'

Guilt flickered across her face and her lower lip trembled once more.

'Seconds? Minutes?' he snapped.

She paled. 'I—I'm sorry… I thought… I thought it was a prank.'

'It wasn't. And your failure to raise the alarm in time may have aided his getaway.' Zufar was sure of it.

She shrank further into the wall. He whirled away, tension threatening to break his spine.

The scandal just waiting to be triggered by such a revelation struck him stone cold. But under no circumstances was he going to let that happen.

He shoved the piece of paper into his pocket and closed his mind to the burning gross insult against his kingdom and his crown. He would deal with his half-brother later. For now he needed an interim solution to this situation. One that did not involve calling off his wedding.

A quick glance around the room showed the suspended state of preparation.

The gown that should've been adorning his bride-to-be by was draped over a mannequin, the heeled slippers peeking out beneath its hem.

Detachedly, he inspected the rest of the room as he mentally ran through the list of other bridal candidates that had been presented to him when the subject of his nuptials first came up a year ago. Like most royal arranged marriages, although one choice had been favoured above the others, there were always contingencies in case of sudden unsuitability.

Three of those candidates were downstairs, ruled out as potential brides to the King and reduced to honoured guests at his wedding. Could one of them be elevated to the position that would turn out to be a dream come true for them?

Zufar's lips twisted.

There was no way to execute that plan without announcing to the whole world that he'd been jilted. That would only result in frenzied tabloid gossip the media would feed off for years.

Not that any solution he came up with wouldn't cause ripples. But keeping it under wraps until *he* was ready would control the beast.

Which meant he had to keep the circle of trust as tight as possible while he found a quieter, interim solution.

But to mitigate the uproar of impending scandal, he needed a bride; needed to ensure he was married within the next two hours before news that he'd been jilted got out.

His reason for choosing his new bride would need to be explained, of course. That would be a problem for tomorrow.

He turned away from the wedding gown and came face to face with the chambermaid. He'd forgotten about her. To be honest, she was barely breathing, striving to be as unobtrusive as possible. Zufar was surprised she hadn't fled while his back was turned.

Her wide-eyed gaze fixed on him, watchful and wary as she followed his pacing figure.

He slowed to a stop on the next pass, an impossibly ludicrous idea taking root in his brain. 'How long have you been in my palace?' he asked.

'All…um… Most of my life, Y-Your Highness,' she stammered.

He gave a satisfied inner nod. She would know his customs, know the value of discretion.

Sweet desert stars, was he really entertaining this preposterous notion? 'And how old are you?' Zufar growled.

She swallowed, her nostrils quivering delicately as she inhaled. 'Twenty-five, Your Highness.'

He stared at her for a full minute, then nodded briskly. There was neither chagrin nor prevarication in the decision his brain latched onto.

He needed a solution, and he'd found one. His gaze dropped down to her twisting ringless fingers. 'Do you have a husband?' he asked.

A deep blush flamed her cheeks, her gaze flitting away from his again as she shook her head. 'No, Your Highness, I am unmarried.'

Just to be sure, he probed deeper. 'Are you committed to another?'

Her mouth tightened for the briefest second, but she shook her head before she mumbled, 'No.'

He wanted to demand that she repeat that. To look him in the eyes while she did so. But time was slipping through his fingers.

Zufar's chest filled with grim purpose as his gaze sprang from the unsuitable woman before him to the wedding dress, and back again. She was roughly the same size as Amira, if perhaps a little bustier and wider of hip than his...*former* fiancée. Their heights too were similar and so, from what he could see beneath the blotchiness and drabness, was their colouring.

Of course, Amira had held herself with more poise than this maid, years of first-class schooling and a finishing school in Switzerland undertaken for the sole purpose of her future role as Queen. The woman in front of him was nowhere near as polished.

But he didn't need a gem, just a polished stone to pass off as the real thing until he could resolve this situation quietly and on his terms.

'Come here,' he commanded evenly as he strolled to stand next to the wedding dress. Now he'd decided what to do, he couldn't afford any more tears or, heaven forbid, tantrums that would further delay him.

She presented him with that rabbit-caught-in-headlights look again, the pulse fluttering at her throat racing faster.

Zufar bit down his exasperation. 'You're not deaf. I know you can hear me. Come here,' he stated firmly.

She jerked into movement, stumbling to a stop two feet away from him.

He inspected her, noting that her eyes were in fact a

dark amethyst, not the brown he'd thought, and that her eyelashes were far longer than he had initially noticed. Her mouth too was curved in a perfect little bow that, should it ever find its way into a smile, might salvage some of her dreariness.

His gaze dropped, took in the lines of her neck, and again experienced a tiny bolt of surprise at how sleekly it curved to her shoulders, how delicate and flawless were her collarbones and skin.

No, not a diamond, but perhaps a better quality stone than he'd first surmised.

A quality stone, but still rough around the edges, he modified, when he noticed she was still twisting her fingers into an agitated mess. 'Be still, little one,' he commanded.

She made a strangled little sound under her breath but her body stilled and her fingers stopped moving. He suppressed a need to tell her to straighten her spine and look him in the eye when he spoke to her.

Such training was unnecessary for what he had in mind. All that would be required was for her not to collapse into a useless heap before he'd achieved his goal. And he had a way to ensure that happened.

Decision made, he whirled away from her. As if they were in tune with his thoughts, a brief knock sounded on the door before Marwan and the rest of his aides rushed in.

'Your Highness? Have you any news you wish me to relay to the royal guard? A starting point for the search for your intended, perhaps?'

'We are past that, Marwan,' Zufar said coldly, noting absently again that Amira's absconding didn't sting as much as it should. If anything, it was his half-brother's insult that grated harsher.

'Oh? Does that mean the ceremony is off?'

Zufar glanced at the woman standing shell-shocked in the corner of the room.

She looked even worse, as if a fresh bolt of lightning

had hit her. His decision didn't waver as his gaze objectively raked her.

The wedding bouquet would occupy her skittish hands, veils would shroud her face, and heels would elevate her height and hopefully correct her posture.

Beyond that, very little mattered.

'No, it does not. The ceremony is still going ahead.' He slashed his hand through the shocked murmurs echoing through the room. When he achieved silence, he continued, 'I fully intend to be married in two hours' time. Niesha Zalwani is to be my bride and everyone in this room will ensure that my wishes are fulfilled.'

CHAPTER TWO

'*TELL YOUR BROTHER I've not only seduced his precious bride but that she runs away with me willingly. Tell him I'm stealing away his future Queen, just as he stole my birthright.*'

Those were the most scandalous words Niesha had expected to hear today, and possibly for the rest of her days. A day that should've been one of intense joy, but which had taken a wrong turn to hell about an hour ago.

With the Sheikh's appearance in his intended's bedroom, she'd harboured hope that everything would be resolved.

Except King Zufar al Khalia had just spoken words that simply didn't make sense. For a moment Niesha wondered whether the shock of watching Amira Ghalib disappear from right under her nose had dislodged a few million brain cells.

The man in front of her, the formidable, extraordinarily captivating tower of masculinity who prowled through his kingdom with harsh authority and power, commanding and receiving the loyal adulation of his subjects because he was simply that breathtaking, had just said—

No. You did you not hear him right. It was impossible.

Her thoughts were clearly echoed by Marwan, who sprang forwards. 'Your Highness?' His voice was ashen with disbelief.

The King—*her* King, since she too was a subject of the Kingdom of Khalia—moved another step closer, bringing his earth-shaking life force even more dangerously into her space. He stalked so close she could almost see the ice crackling in his eyes, the contained fury vibrating his body.

Niesha shrank away from the elegant folds of the wedding gown, the sheets of icy shock thawing into a cauldron of panic. She glanced around the room, selfishly wishing Princess Galila were still here.

King Zufar's sister barely noticed Niesha most of the time, but her kind smile when she did was far better than the fiercely domineering glower of her brother, and the tableau of horrified expressions spread in panorama before her.

Perversely, those expressions were what hammered home the fact that she'd heard correctly. He'd used her full name. In connection to marriage. *His* marriage. Today. Shock gurgled in her throat.

Her fingers moved then, connected with the soft, warm folds of the most extraordinary wedding gown she'd ever seen in her life. The gown that, finding herself alone in this room three nights ago, she'd secretly indulged in one insane moment's fantasy of wearing herself to marry the ephemeral man of her dreams.

The gown that Zufar al Khalia wanted her to...to—

'I'm sorry, Your Highness...' she whispered, but his voice overrode hers.

'Time is of the essence,' he growled, without raising his deep voice. 'I suggest we begin preparations immediately.'

'Your Highness, this...this will be highly unprecedented,' Marwan said.

'I should hope so, or there would be something seriously disturbing with my reign,' Sheikh Zufar stated without looking the old man's way. 'But make no mistake. This wedding ceremony will happen. She is the one who will take Amira's place,' he uttered with a finality that drove a bolt of fear down Niesha's throat.

Aware that she had to get herself together very quickly or risk being flattened by the force of nature bearing down on her, she straightened her spine and raised her head.

He was watching her with the savage, mesmerising golden eyes of a hawk. Before she could summon any words, Marwan beat her to it. 'Your Highness, perhaps we should discuss this—'

'You are risking insubordination by questioning my command. The subject isn't up for discussion. Get the bridal attendants in here now.'

Niesha realised her head was moving from side to side, a pendulous action she couldn't stop. Shockwaves that hadn't stopped rippling through her since she witnessed Amira and the stranger's extraordinary flight now threatened to drown her. Another sound ripped from her throat.

Dark, tawny eyes zeroed in on her.

'You will not pass out,' Zufar commanded tersely, as if just by issuing the edict, her body would follow. 'Bring her a glass of water,' he tossed over his shoulder.

A cut-crystal glass instantly appeared.

With elegant fingers and an unwavering gaze, he handed it to her.

Niesha took a sip, swallowed it along with the hysterical laughter bubbling up. This wasn't happening. She wanted to go back to an hour ago, when she was the least significant person in the room, no different from the straggly orphan without a past she'd been some twenty odd years ago, the one who'd been absorbed by the state orphanage that bore the royal family's name.

The hand-me-down clothes she wore were two sizes too large, and really should have done their job of hiding her better, she mused dazedly. She'd chosen them out of prudence, not fashion. It had simply meant she wouldn't have to worry about new clothes any time soon.

Except, even covered from head to toe, she felt more naked now than she'd ever felt in her life.

'Drink some more,' he decreed.

Her hands shook wildly, but she managed to take another sip without spilling it. He promptly relieved her of the glass. Still dazed, Niesha watched as it was spirited away.

Then her eyes clashed with his, and the words he'd spoken rose like a horrifying mirage before her eyes. Beyond the space filled out by his broad shoulders and his overwhelming presence, Niesha spotted movement as the bridal attendants entered.

He flicked a wrist, and Halimah, the head attendant of the women's wing, who'd barely tolerated Niesha before today, approached.

Zufar acknowledged her presence with a single glance. 'I do not take your loyalty for granted. But I demand your discretion in this matter.'

'Of course, Your Highness,' Halimah replied.

Zufar nodded. 'My new bride has been selected. You will ensure Niesha is ready at the allotted time. Is that clear?'

Halimah's eyes widened as she stared up at her King.

'Is there a problem?' he demanded.

Her head lowered immediately. 'No, Your Highness.'

Another tremble swept through Niesha as he continued, 'You will dress her and present her to the Grand Hall ready for her royal parade in one hour.' The deep, dark, ruthless timbre of his voice brooked no argument.

No. This wasn't happening.

She was just a maidservant. An orphan with no past. A nobody. She wasn't even worthy of wearing Amira's cast-offs, never mind her wedding gown!

'Please,' she started. The word emerged as a weak, scratchy sound. She cleared her throat and tried again. 'Your Highness, I beg your pardon, but I cannot.'

Pure thunder rumbled across his impressive eyebrows. His eyes, so direct, so hypnotic, drilled right into her bone marrow.

'Yes, you will. Unless you prefer to suffer the consequences of disobeying your King you will go forwards with this.'

Niesha balled her hand and placed it over her racing heart, desperate to calm it before it burst out of her chest. A long time ago, she'd sworn allegiance to him and his family. It had been one of the conditions of inhabiting the palace, and she'd done so willingly. And although he had no inkling who she was or her very small insignificant role his life, she'd done everything asked of her, for him.

In her own way, she'd given him moments of comfort, she liked to tell herself, by making sure that the food she was tasked to serve him in his private dining room was the right temperature, by ensuring his favourite wines were on hand when he returned to his royal apartments after long days away from the palace.

On one occasion, she'd taken it upon herself to purchase a bottle out of her meagre savings when the palace delivery had been delayed.

And when his personal cleaning staff had come down with the flu, she'd volunteered to work in his private quarters. To this day, tucked away in her mind, Niesha had a memory of the scent of his sheets and the unique cologne he wore on his skin.

Those tiny, insignificant but intense moments had made her blush for weeks afterwards on recollection. Still made her blush.

So, yes, like everyone else in this room, she would do anything for Sheikh Zufar al Khalia.

But not this.

The oscillation of her head grew faster as her alarm escalated. 'With respect, Your Highness, you don't want me. I'm nobody. Th-there are others far more suitable for this role. You're making a mistake.' She was a little glad that her voice held firmer than before.

Not so glad when several gasps echoed through the room and his forbidding expression tightened even further.

'I have made my decision. You are my choice. So, do you have any other objections?' he drawled.

Niesha was stunned by his question. Did that mean he would listen if she objected? What further objection could she voice other than telling the King of Khalia that he was utterly, stark raving crazy? The mere thought of doing such a thing made the blood drain from her head.

'By your silence, I assume you do not.'

'Please, you have to reconsider,' was all she could manage.

'This discussion is over,' he declared. 'But, rest assured, you will be adequately compensated for your role.'

He turned away.

Niesha knew she shouldn't trust the tiny burst of relief that spiked through her after being released from the force field of his stare. Her emotions had been on the edge of severe agitation ever since she'd walked in to find Amira and that towering barbarian of a man climbing out of the window.

She'd lost precious minutes frozen in place, unable to believe her eyes. After she'd screamed and sounded the alarm, she was sure she'd been incoherent in the first few minutes. Guilt surged anew beneath her skin.

She should've done more to stop them from leaving. Or raised the alarm quicker, as Zufar had said.

This was her punishment for not acting swiftly enough. If she had, this…*insanity* wouldn't be happening.

Because…marriage? To him?

Sweet heaven, she couldn't do it.

She took a faltering step closer to where he stood issuing clipped instructions. 'Your Highness, please, can we talk about it?' she ventured.

'We don't have time for a discussion,' he stated. His voice was soft and even, but she wasn't fooled. He was seething. 'This is an emergency requiring an interim solution. Any long-term resolutions will be thrashed out later, including whatever concerns you might have.' He went back to issuing instructions.

Heads bobbed up and down, unlike her shaking head and her quivering body, everyone poised to move the moment he finished speaking.

Moments later, firm hands reached for her, fingers tugging insistently at her clothes. She was going to be undressed in front of him? A bolt of rebellion fired through her, and she pushed the attendants away. 'No!'

Everyone in the room froze.

'No?' Halimah whispered in horror. 'You're saying no to your King?'

A row of shocked eyes stared back at her, one in particular lasering her in place. She realised Zufar also awaited her answer. And the expression on his face was telling her everything she needed to know. There would be hell to pay if she didn't obey him. She was the one who had let Amira get away. She was the one who hadn't sounded the alarm in time. When she'd eventually done so, she'd been hysterical and inadvertently alerted the whole palace that the bride-to-be had fled.

She might not have aided his fiancée, but Amira's disappearance might have succeeded partly because of her.

Sheikh Zufar slowly retraced his steps until he towered over her. 'I too am waiting for an answer,' he breathed.

Niesha swallowed, accepting in that moment that she had very little choice. She'd helped cause this state of chaos. It was up to her to fix it.

'No,' she said. 'I... I mean yes,' she amended hurriedly when his face turned to stone. 'I will be your interim...your stand-in bride,' she whispered, her mouth bone-dry.

Niesha wasn't sure why her gaze darted to the window just then.

Sheikh Zufar followed her gaze, and, unbelievably, his face hardened even more.

'If you're thinking of going the same way as my previous bride-to-be, think again. Halimah and her companions will stay with you. They will help you to dress. You will not be left alone until you are by my side at the altar in one hour. Is that understood?'

Her world spinning ever faster on its axis, Niesha barely managed a nod of agreement.

It must've sufficed because he and his aides exited the

room, Sheikh Zufar striding with the regal, animalistic grace infused in his bones since conception. There were sources that said Zufar al Khalia carried the essence of life itself with him when he moved in and out of a room.

The truth of it hit her hard as her breath was expelled in a mighty rush.

At the outer door, he paused, slashing her with golden eyes once more. 'There will be guards placed outside the doors and along every path you take today. Just to ensure that you make it from this room to the wedding ceremony without impediment.'

Niesha wanted to laugh, but she was absolutely certain that she would end up sobbing. And even she couldn't attend her wedding ceremony in tears.

Her *wedding* ceremony!

How on earth was this happening?

She had no time to dwell on it as the women sprang into action, tugging her to the centre of the room before proceeding to disrobe her. Minutes later, she found herself immersed in the rose-scented bath she had drawn for Amira only an hour or so ago.

The water was still warm, luxury gels and shampoos uncovered and ready to be used for the pre-wedding pampering the bride-to-be deserved.

The bride-to-be. *Her.*

Niesha closed her mind to the whispers swirling around her. Her emotional tank was dangerously close to full capacity for further distress. She was fairly sure Halimah and the women were speculating wildly about her. A lowly servant without a past attracted either awkward conversation or derogatory comments, no matter one's age.

Over the years, Niesha had learned to harden herself against the pitying and sometimes callous comments, but somehow the barbs always found their way to her heart. It was why she'd stopped attempting to make friends with her colleagues.

Right now, she was rawer than she'd ever felt in her life. It was almost a relief to sink into the water and let the numbness overtake her. To ignore the awkward silences and the intense loneliness drowning her and pretend this wasn't happening.

She barely felt the hands washing her body or the fingers weaving through her hair as she was cleansed from head to toe. Somewhere in the dark tunnel of despair, she realised she was still shaking, that she couldn't stop trembling even after she was bundled into a thick, luxurious robe and seated at the bridal make-up station. She stared unseeing into the middle distance as her make-up was applied and her hair dried and fussed with.

It was as they nudged her towards the wedding gown that Niesha finally woke up.

'No…' It was a feeble attempt, one a small, wounded animal seeking a last pass for mercy would make.

Of course, there was no reprieve.

'Yes,' Halimah insisted. 'For whatever reason the cosmos sees fit, you have been chosen for this role. You will not dishonour our King by disobeying, and I will not have my head on the block because of you. Now lift up your arms so we can put this exquisite garment on you.'

Interim.

She was just an interim solution. A stand-in for today only.

Tomorrow, Zufar would go into the desert or wherever Amira had been spirited off to and bring her back.

This was temporary.

Remember this.

This time next week, she would be back in her old, familiar clothes, in her rightful place, with this terrifying incident tucked away to retell to her children and grandchildren in years to come.

They would probably not believe her, she mused numbly. She could scarcely believe it herself.

She lifted her arms and let them slide the undergarments over her body before the layers of the specially commissioned wedding gown were added. The skirt was a bit tight at the hip but the snugness wasn't uncomfortable. She held her breath as the zip was tugged up and the delicate buttons fastened.

The sensation of being sealed into her temporary prison threatened to choke her. She hurriedly blinked her prickling eyes before tears fell. Halimah wouldn't welcome her handiwork ruined, and Niesha needed to get herself back under firmer control. The quicker she was done with this, the quicker she could retreat into her shell, and life could go on again.

She placed her feet in the shoes when instructed, angled her head so the magnificent diamond and sapphire tiara could be put in place, and held her hands out for the two dozen bangles that came with the outfit. Precious gems of all shapes and sizes gleamed from her wrists, throat and ears as she was tugged forwards to stand in front of the giant gilded mirror.

Niesha only managed to hold her expression for a split second before her gaze dropped to her feet again. She didn't know the woman in the mirror. And that was a good thing. She could remove herself completely from this situation, retreat to the numb place where she was safest, away from the whispered gossip and the stunned glances. The place where the soft, kind voice lived in her head, the one she didn't recognise but had accepted over the years as her merciful companion, clinging to it the hardest when she felt her lowest.

The carers at the orphanage had offhandedly dismissed the voice she'd unwittingly confessed to as her imaginary friend. Some had ridiculed her, but Niesha had felt no shame in embracing the gentle susurration telling her she would be all right.

You'll get through this.

She was repeating those words to herself as Marwan, his

aides, Halimah, and six ceremonially dressed guards escorted her down a wide private staircase towards the Rolls-Royce Phantom idling in a courtyard at the north wing of the palace. The safety of the three veils shielding her from direct view of everyone else was a welcome presence.

Still, she heard the furtive murmurs as she slowly glided forwards. Behind her, hands fluttered over her train and helped her into the car. Niesha uttered no words as Marwan slid in beside her. The part of her brain that wasn't suspended in disbelief understood his presence.

Amira's father, Feroz Ghalib, had been primed to take this role with his daughter. Even though tongues would wag at Marwan's presence beside her, it would delay the ultimate revelation of exactly what was going on.

Nevertheless, her hands trembled around the stem of the exquisite bouquet made up of diamond-studded cream roses as the car began to roll forwards.

For a wild moment, Niesha contemplated flinging open the door and fleeing as fast as her legs would carry her. She knew every nook and cranny of the royal palace, having spent all her free time exploring it over the years. She could find a hiding place within minutes.

Even as temptation seeped through her, she was dismissing it. The recent death of the Queen had devastated Khalia. The kingdom was still in mourning when its bereaved King dropped the bombshell of his abdication. Though his people had accepted Zufar wholeheartedly, aftershocks still echoed throughout the kingdom.

He'd been right when he'd said that this wedding needed to happen. Galila had said as much last night when she'd voiced her worry over Amira's curious indifference towards her wedding, leading to an exchange of words Niesha had overheard as she'd tidied up Amira's room.

There were larger implications besides a simple marriage between two people who'd known each other since childhood.

The simple truth was that Khalia could ill afford another scandal.

'Wave,' Marwan instructed tersely. 'You need to wave to the people.'

A startled glance out of the window showed they were already on the street outside the palace. She hadn't been privy to the protocol of the ceremony but, from watching other televised royal weddings, she knew there was a brief ride to acknowledge her future subjects and show her gratitude for their goodwill, before the actual wedding ceremony began.

Slowly, she lifted her hand, her movements woefully stilted, and waved.

Screams of joy pierced the thick windows of the car, forcing home the reality that she'd become a symbol of hope to the people. She…the orphan from the poorest part of the capital, the woman with no past and no name save for the one the carers had given her.

Light-headedness clawed at the fringes of her consciousness. A garbled sound echoed from far away but she knew it had come from her throat.

'You will pull yourself together, girl,' Marwan said.

Again hysterical laughter bubbled up. How very easily everyone told her to pull herself together, to rise up to the occasion. To obey. But no one knew the terrifying depths of her emotions. No one knew how she'd secretly watched Zufar move around the palace, on TV, stared at his pictures in magazines for years. No one knew of the secret awe she held for the man who sat on the throne.

For a brief moment in her youth, she had even fancied herself in love with him! She'd grown out of that foolishness, of course, but the unfettered awareness and awe he drew from her had never dissipated.

If she'd been performing this task for any man other than the King of Khalia, she would probably have summoned something other than terror. But he wasn't any other man.

Zufar al Khalia was in a stratosphere of his own, over and above the royal blood that ran through his veins and the crown that sat on his head.

All too soon the ride was over.

Trumpets sounded as the Rolls stopped in front of the Imperial Ceremonial Room where she would be taking her vows before the hour was out. The breath she drew into her lungs did nothing to offer sustenance or clarity, and, even though the senior aide highly disapproved of what was going on, Niesha was grateful for his presence as he alighted and held out his hand to her. She was certain she would've fallen into a wretched heap if he hadn't offered his support just then.

The hand she placed on his arm trembled wildly.

Flower girls she'd never met giggled and danced in front of her, throwing handfuls of scented flowers in her path as she slowly glided up the twenty-one steps to the wide doorway and down a gold-edged, royal blue carpet towards the centre of the exquisite ballroom reserved for the sole purpose of conducting official ceremonies.

Outside, several dozen more trumpets joined the heralding around the kingdom, crowds roaring where they were watching on giant screens across the city.

Inside, Niesha moved towards the man who stood tall, regal, and devastatingly handsome at the altar, her heart firmly wedged in her throat.

When Marwan winced, she realised her fingers had dug into his skin.

An apology tripped on her tongue but was immediately strangled by her nerves.

The murmurs in the congregation escalated, heads beginning to turn as speculation grew as to why Marwan walked next to the bride.

Niesha had no chance to dwell on that. Her sole focus was on Sheikh Zufar as he swivelled on his heel to watch her progress down the aisle.

His face gave nothing away. Years under the spotlight had honed an ability to ruthlessly school his features. But the many interviews that Niesha had watched of the Crown Prince, now turned King of Khalia, had clued her into the nuances of his expressions.

Right now, he bristled with fury, still incandescent at the atrocity that had been perpetrated against him. That fury was ruthlessly caged, the greater calling of duty and responsibility taking priority. He meant to see this through, come hell or high water.

Niesha cursed her senses for choosing that moment to flare back into life. The bright colours of the Imperial Ceremonial Room, the hushed voices of the guests and the laser focus of Zufar's eyes all pierced her consciousness, grounding her mercilessly in that moment.

You will be all right.

How? she railed at the soft voice. She wanted to scream, turn and flee from the room, but there was nowhere to go. They were almost at the altar. Marwan was lowering his arm in preparation to step away.

The moment he did, Galila stepped close. Zufar's sister's face was pale, her mouth pinched as she cast a searching, bewildered glance at Niesha. Unlike the others in the room, she knew why a maidservant stood in Amira's place.

'The bouquet,' she said gently.

Niesha reluctantly handed it over, mourning the tiny support being stripped from her.

Before she could dwell on it, Zufar extended his hand. They were to take that last single step to the altar together.

Niesha stared at the long elegant fingers of her soon-to-be—temporary—husband. Automatically, she lifted her right hand and placed it in his left. She wasn't sure whether to be grateful or frightened by the pressure of the fingers that took hold of hers and nudged her forwards onto that last devastating step.

The cleric began to intone a long string of ancient words. Words that demanded obedience, fidelity, faith, companionship.

Love.

Niesha's insides scrambled over that last word. She'd known none of it in her years. The occasional kindnesses that came her way had been from strangers. In her quiet moments, she'd dreamed of such a feeling, but never in her wildest imagination had she dreamed of it being uttered in such circumstances.

A glance at Zufar showed his face was a stoic mask, the words not having any effect on him save for the façade he'd put up for the public. When it was his turn to repeat his vows he did so in deep assured tones, not hurried, not in any way nervous.

The cleric turned to Niesha. Her heart lurched frantically.

Her fingers began to tremble, then her whole body was seized by vicious little earthquakes that just wouldn't stop.

'Repeat your vows,' Zufar instructed with a grave whisper. 'Repeat them now.'

Niesha swallowed painfully, forcing her dry throat to work. She opened her mouth, and with a sense of wild surrealism said, 'I, Niesha Zalwani, take you, Zufar al Khalia, to be my husband.'

Shock waves rippled through the crowd, echoed outside the palace as the true identity of the bride was revealed. Through it all, Zufar kept his gaze fixed, haughty, regal and straight-ahead.

'Proceed,' he commanded the cloaked cleric.

To his credit, the old man did not hesitate. He recited reams of archaic, binding words.

And a mere half an hour later, Niesha was officially wed to the King of Khalia.

CHAPTER THREE

A THREE-MINUTE STATEMENT was issued by the official press secretary on behalf of Sheikh Zufar al Khalia immediately following the ceremony. That was all it took for the strange tale of the swapped bride to turn the atmosphere from scandalised confusion into roars of elation.

By the time Niesha stood beside Zufar's side on the royal balcony above the Imperial Ceremonial Room, the whole kingdom was in a romantic frenzy. Social media went into meltdown at the idea that the King had followed his heart and married the bride of his choosing rather than the one arranged for him. The media, searching for dissenting views, had only been met with romantic sighs and tales about star-crossed lovers.

The little Niesha managed to catch only added to the surrealism of the whole thing.

A five-minute lesson in wedding protocol instead of the usual weeks of tutoring was all she'd been granted in between leaving the wedding ceremony and arriving on the balcony.

She was to stand to the right of her new husband, not the left. Her arm was never to rise above shoulder level when she waved to the crowd. And while she was allowed to show her teeth when she smiled, her demeanour should not in any way exhibit raucousness. Terse instructions whizzed through her brain, the dos and don'ts of being the new Queen streaking like lightning across her senses.

'Look straight ahead and smile,' Zufar instructed calmly. 'I believe this is the moment when you should go to your happy place and think positive thoughts.'

With everything that had unfolded in the last few hours,

Niesha was terrifyingly close to succumbing to hysteria. Lately, her happy place had been curling up with a book beside the fire in her tiny bedsit on the borders of the palace grounds. Oh, how she wished she were there now. Anywhere but here, where a million eyes gawked shamelessly, and the guests of honour who were no longer bothering to keep their voices down openly speculated as to how *she* had come to be in these particular shoes.

'My happy place?' she murmured. 'I don't think that's a very good idea.'

Even though she'd kept her voice low, he heard her, and cast her a brief but hard glance.

'Why not?' he enquired. 'Isn't that what women do when they wish to escape their troubles?' There was a bitter undertone that pulled her up short but his face displayed the same neutral mask he'd worn since the moment they were announced as husband and wife, and had turned to face their honoured guests.

'I'm not sure I know what you mean,' Niesha said.

'That's not important right now. All I care about is that you do not project anything other than utter bliss to find yourself in this position. Remember, the whole world is watching.'

He probably believed he was helping. This was his way of supporting her through an impossible situation. All Niesha could take in at that moment was the pounding of her heart and the boisterous jubilation of the crowd as they waved their flags and screamed congratulations across the royal park where they were gathered.

'Do your best. That is all I ask,' Zufar muttered. 'It would please me greatly if you did it now, however. The others are joining us.'

That was all the warning she had before the doors behind them parted and the rest of his extended family flooded onto the balcony to join them.

Galila slid into place beside her, while his brother, Malak, took his position next to Zufar. Aunts, uncles, nieces and nephews slotted into their allotted positions and acknowledged the crowd with regal waves and salutes honed into place since childhood.

While each and every one of them cast lingering looks her way.

Niesha felt thankful, for the briefest moment, that Zufar had kept her by his side. One bold relative had attempted to pry out the reason behind his last-minute change in brides. Zufar had responded with a stern rebuke for him to mind his own business.

'I will call a family gathering as soon as I have a moment to spare. But do not hold your breath. I intend to be occupied for a while with my new bride.'

His uncle had retreated with his chastised tail between his legs, while Niesha was left blushing furiously. Word had quickly spread that Sheikh Zufar was not to be questioned on the subject of his bride. Not today at least.

'I suppose congratulations are in order,' Galila murmured.

'Thank you,' Niesha replied.

'I would love to know how this interesting outcome transpired,' Galila continued. 'I mean, I left you a maid-servant. Two hours later, you're my sister-in-law. Not that I don't love a riveting story, but this—'

'Watch it, Galila,' Zufar warned beneath his breath, his hands positioned strategically in front of his face as he waved.

Galila easily maintained her graceful smile as she looked at her brother. 'What?' she asked softly. 'So sue me if I'm dying to know what happened. One minute I was attempting to locate your elusive bride-to-be and the next I seem to have acquired a new sister-in-law altogether. If I didn't know any better, I'd think I'd slipped and fallen into a reality TV show.'

'Enough,' Zufar growled. 'Don't forget there are lip-readers out there. If there's discussion to be had, we will get to it later. For now, remember where you are.'

Beside him, his brother Malak snorted under his breath. 'If you wanted us to behave, brother, you shouldn't have offered us this salacious piece of adventure on your wedding day. If you're trying to get into the history books, then bravo. No one will forget this day in a hurry.'

The only hint that Zufar wasn't in complete control of his emotions was the small tic that throbbed at his temple. He continued to wave and acknowledge the crowd, and even at one point slid his hand around the Niesha's waist as the royal military jets flew overhead.

Niesha was thankful for the deafening roar of the jet engines, as it swallowed the gasp that travelled through her body when his hand settled on the curve of her waist. Besides the moment when he'd helped her off the floor, and the moment he'd slid the wedding ring onto her finger, Zufar hadn't touched her.

She'd been very thankful for that, she told herself, despite the humiliating stone lodged in her stomach when he'd lifted her veils and promptly stepped away without executing the customary newly-wed altar kiss.

But now, with his touch searing through the folds of the wedding gown right into her skin, Niesha couldn't suppress the tingles that swarmed her body. The smile she'd pinned to her face froze as her every sense homed in on the sensation evoked by his touch. It was as if his hand were charged with a unique voltage that zinged through her bloodstream, firing up little explosions of fireworks. A handful of seconds passed, then more, and then all sense of time and space disappeared as Zufar looked down into her eyes.

Tawny-gold eyes seared right into her soul, as if he intended to possess her every thought. Somewhere in the distance the royal jets performed acrobatic loops, and then started their return journey. She knew it was only a matter of moments before millions of confetti pieces would be tossed from the sky and showered upon them.

It was the moment the crowd had been waiting for.

The moment when the King kissed his new Queen.

Never in her wildest dreams had she believed it would be her. Above that, never in her wildest dreams had she believed that a man like Zufar would be staring down at her with that intense look in his eyes.

It was all an act, she repeated to herself. But her hammering heart and the frenzied little cyclones whirling through her veins dared to suggest otherwise. His hand steered her to face him, an insistent move that told her that there was no getting away from this. Zufar, the man she'd harboured silly dreams about in her teenage years, was about to kiss her.

Far above her head, a gigantic burst of blues and golds rained from the sky. Niesha paid little attention. Every single cell in her body was focused on the head slowly lowering towards hers, the hand grasping her waist, and the firm, insistent tug as he pulled her close.

'Relax,' he breathed, his voice holding warning as well as rough reassurance.

But Niesha wasn't reassured. How many women dreamed that their very first kiss would be witnessed by millions, if not billions of people across the world? What if she got it wrong? What if she made a complete fool of herself, more than she had before this whole debacle started? And what if—

'Niesha,' Zufar murmured again, his warning deeper this time.

'I'm trying,' she whispered back fiercely.

'Try harder. You look as if you are heading for the gallows instead of your first kiss with your new husband. Is kissing me such a daunting prospect?' he drawled.

'Maybe it is. Have you considered that it may be the last thing I want?'

His eyes widened a touch with surprise at the spark of defiance in her voice.

Tawny-gold eyes gleamed an instant before the first shower of confetti drifted past her. Another landed on her cheek.

About to brush it away, she froze when he murmured, 'Stop.'

He captured her free hand, the one not holding the bouquet, and laid it gently on his chest. And then, with a suave move, he brushed the tiny gold piece of tinsel from her cheek. Expecting his hand to return to her waist, Niesha gave a little gasp as his fingers stroked her jaw and then drifted to her neck.

This wasn't how it was supposed to go. She'd seen more than a few royal first kisses, had dreamed many years ago of how it would feel to be the recipient of one, just like any other girl her age.

Those embraces had been chaste, the exchanged gazes nowhere near this intense.

Zufar was breaking protocol.

But, of course, she couldn't question his actions. Not without risking her lips being read. So she stood before him, attempting not to tremble out of her skin as sure fingers drew down her neck to rest lightly on her collarbone. His thumb gently tilted her chin upward, causing her shiver to intensify.

'How you tremble so, little one,' Zufar murmured.

She opened her mouth—to say what, she would never know. Because in that moment Zufar closed the gap between them and sealed his lips on hers.

The roar and the call of trumpets were for this staged show, Niesha knew. But every sound intensified the thrill and sizzle in her blood the moment Zufar kissed her. She wasn't sure why she closed her eyes, but it felt like the right thing to do. Perhaps because she was more than a little drugged from the effect of his mouth on hers.

It was like nothing she'd ever experienced in her life. Heat and magic and earth-shaking desire surged through her body, flowing from his lips right through to her very toes. He swallowed her tiny squeak of shocked delight as he deepened the kiss. His hand didn't move from her throat but the one at her waist dug deeper, searing his fingers onto her skin. That tiny moan escaped again. The crowd roared louder. All through it Zufar continued to kiss her, his tongue swiping across her bottom lip, weakening her knees so she sagged against him.

He caught her easily, held onto her as he continued to gently ravage her mouth.

'Enough, you two,' Galila said with a chuckle. 'There are children watching. Let's not turn this into an X-rated show.'

With a muted grunt, Zufar lifted his head. His face reflected a hint of surprise, then irritated bewilderment. Both were quickly masked a moment later.

If it had been anyone else, she would've believed he was experiencing the same sensations cascading through her body, but his eyes studied her with piercing speculation that added apprehension to her already jangled emotions.

What was he thinking?

As if he caught the silent question, his hand dropped from her throat, and he faced the crowd. A smile lifted the corners of his mouth, as if he was acknowledging that he'd just shared a special moment with every citizen in his kingdom, and millions more around the world. A second later, he looked down at her, his eyes telling her that she needed to also acknowledge the crowd.

Blushing fiercely, Niesha faced the crowd again. In unison, they waved, smiled, waved some more. All the while, her senses spun.

Her first kiss.

Was this how everyone felt? She was drowning in sensation, as if the whole world had tilted and taken a different course that would never be the same again. Because how could anything else compare to this?

She wasn't a romantic. Childish, fairy-tale feelings had been beaten out of her by years of hard work and the reality that only a lucky few found their happily-ever-after, most of them in the books she treasured. She was old enough to accept that those foolish daydreams needed to be set aside the moment she closed the book.

So what she was experiencing now was nothing short of a daydream she needed to put behind her as soon as possible.

This was temporary. *She was a stand-in.*

Come tomorrow she'd be back in her beige uniform, fluffing pillows and refilling shampoo bottles in bathrooms in the east wing.

The thought froze the smile on her face, even as she continued to wave to the crowd.

After an excruciating half-hour, with one final wave, Zufar steered her away from the balcony. They re-entered the small anteroom serving as a holding place before, but that was now a path that led to the banqueting hall where the formal wedding reception was being held.

'You did well,' Zufar stated as he tucked her hand into the crook of his elbow.

Despite the tersely murmured statement, a bubble of warmth speared through the sizzling shock that hadn't entirely left her.

'Thank you,' she murmured, pleased that she hadn't completely let him down.

'Of course, you could do with smiling a little bit more,' he added.

The bubble burst. 'I can't smile on command,' she replied.

'You are the Queen now. You have to learn how.'

'But I am not, though, am I?'

'That ring on your finger, my dear, is all the evidence you need.'

'You know what I mean, Your Highness.'

'Do I?' Zufar murmured even as he nodded to a guest bowing as they passed.

'Of course you do,' Niesha muttered fiercely. Why was he pretending he didn't know what she was talking about? 'I'm not your Queen. This was temporary. You said so yourself.'

His body tensed, then a muscle rippled in his jaw. 'We'll talk about this later,' he said.

A spurt of apprehension turned into full-blown alarm. 'What is there to talk about, Your Highness?'

'You calling me Your Highness, for starters. I'm your husband now. You are allowed to address me as Zufar.'

Her footsteps faltered. For as long as she could remember, he'd always been Sheikh Zufar, or Crown Prince Zufar. Not even in her dreams had she addressed him by his given name alone. It felt…huge. As if she were taking a leap into thin air. Niesha started to shake her head.

Somehow, she had to bring this back to reality, back under her control.

'You also need to stop shaking your head at every little disagreement. As my new bride, you're supposed to be glowing and blushing with happiness, not wearing an expression as if you've been led into the devil's own playpen.'

'You know why I am acting this way. I don't know why you're pretending you don't know what I'm talking about. You said this was temporary.'

'Did I?'

Her mouth parted in a stunned O.

'Remember where you are,' he warned. 'Do you really think this is the right time for this discussion?'

She didn't. And she couldn't very well demand an explanation from the King. Not with guests in earshot, and not when they were entering the banqueting hall where attendants lined the walls in their dozens, ready to serve the first course the moment they sat down.

So she walked beside him as Zufar led her to the head of the table.

His white-gloved hand gripped hers tightly where it rested on his arm, as if he was fully intent on preventing her from fleeing.

As if she would. As if she *could*. She wouldn't get very far, even on her own two feet. As he'd warned, there were guards posted everywhere in the palace. Did his warning still apply even now that they'd exchanged their vows? Most likely. But she couldn't think about that. All she wanted at this moment was for everything to be done so she could disappear into her little corner of the world and put this behind her. But he was looking at her in that way again as the guests crowded in.

The way he'd looked at her on the balcony in the moments before he'd kissed her. It was all still an act, Niesha knew. But that tiny fluttering reignited under her skin and grew into huge, wild butterflies demanding freedom.

When the room was half filled, he pulled out her chair and waited until she sat down. He remained standing, his gaze on the crowd who stood as protocol demanded, beside their seats.

Zufar's gaze effortlessly commanded their attention. 'Many of you are wondering about the turn of events today. You will have to keep wondering.' A smattering of laughter echoed through the crowd but eyes slid to where she sat, probing her every expression in the hope of accessing juicy gossip. It took every ounce of composure she didn't know she possessed to maintain a serene expression as Zufar continued, 'All you need to know is that I've made my choice, and I am extremely happy with it.'

Her pulse jumped as he redirected his gaze to her again, his eyes gleaming for a moment before he straightened. 'Now you will do me the honour of acknowledging and accepting Niesha al Khalia as my bride and your Queen.'

Thunderous applause echoed down the banqueting table. Then they took their seats and the formal reception began.

Niesha only managed to pick at a few mouthfuls of the twelve-course dinner. Aside from a few sidelong glances, Zufar didn't question her lack of appetite. She supposed it could all be slotted under the general heading of wedding nerves, even after the fact.

And almost as if he'd instituted an invisible no-fly zone around her, no one approached her even to offer congratulations.

When Galila breached the barrier, Zufar shot her a warning look.

She rolled her eyes but didn't make any more comments except to lean down and brush a kiss across Niesha's cheek. 'You and I will need to have a spa day very soon,' she whispered in Niesha's ear before straightening and walking away.

'What did she say?' Zufar asked.

'She wants a spa day with me, I think,' Niesha responded a little dazedly.

'Hmm, I believe that is code for something else entirely.'

Surprise rounded her eyes. 'What?'

'Curiosity is my sister's middle name. I will caution you to be careful around her. She has a way of prying out information that would make my own intelligence department proud.'

She reached for the crystal water glass, aware that her fingers hadn't stopped shaking. 'Well, you don't need to worry about that, do you? By the time we get around to the possibility of such a day, I'll no longer be your wife.'

For some reason her response made his features tighten. Did he not wish to hear the truth? She opened her mouth to voice the thought but he beat her to it.

'This is our wedding day. Let us endeavour to enjoy at least some of it and not give everything a sour note, shall we?'

She frowned, then quickly smoothed out her features, aware that she was still the cynosure of all eyes. 'It's not our wedding day. Not really. Is it?' she pressed, intent on making him acknowledge the transient nature of what had happened today.

It was that or… The alternative was unthinkable. No, not exactly unthinkable, but impossible for someone like her. A nobody who'd left such foolish dreams beneath the dreary pillows in her lonely orphanage bed.

'Think of it as an elaborate party then, if you must,' he bit out quietly. 'Whatever it is, I wish to enjoy at least some of it for the sake of appearances. Is that okay with you?'

Was he really asking her that when he'd all but dragged her to the altar? But the anger she wanted to summon didn't materialise. Not when she knew the true meaning behind his actions.

He'd done it for his people. So had she. She owed it to the royal family and to every citizen in Khalia not to sustain that anger. She didn't need to be in his shoes to understand it took guts to take such chaos as had been thrown at him only a few hours ago, a situation that would've left other men quaking in their boots, and turn it into a triumph.

Proving once again why he was such an effective, awe-inspiring monarch.

One who had demanded a sacrifice she couldn't in good conscience fault him for. Right in this moment, Niesha couldn't find it in her heart to begrudge the people of Khalia, who had endured the death of their Queen, and seen the kingdom plunged into uncertainty after the abdication of the King.

'Of course, if that's what you wish,' she murmured softly.

His eyes gleamed in that suspicious way again, as if he were divining her thoughts way better than she could. It made her *extremely* nervous. Niesha attempted to look away, but found herself hypnotised by the gold flecks in his tawny eyes.

'That is what I wish,' he reiterated in deep, low tones. 'Now you will smile, and nod, and pretend that this is the happiest day of your life.'

For some insane reason, that command wasn't difficult to obey.

When the corners of his mouth lifted, Niesha found herself following suit. His gaze dropped to her lips, and stayed there for an infinitesimal second, before he lifted his gaze back to hers.

'Much better,' he drawled. 'I will push my luck and request that you eat more than the few mouthfuls you have consumed so far. If the food does not suit, you only need to say and I will instruct a new dish to be brought to you.'

Her eyes widened. What would her peers—the servants—think if she made such a request? She cringed. 'No, that will not be necessary.'

'I do not do it out of necessity. I do it because you are my Queen and what you wish goes.'

What she *wished* right now was for him to stop referring to her as the Queen or *his* Queen. It would be better all round that way. *Safer*, even. The last thing she wanted was to start believing, even for a second that this temporary role was in any way real. She needed to maintain the distance to ensure she left this nightmare with her faculties intact. 'This is fine, I'm sure,' she insisted firmly.

Zufar nodded, and turned to speak to his brother, who sat to his left. The sudden bereft sensation that assailed her took Niesha by complete surprise. It took a few precious seconds to master her composure, after which she lifted her gaze to the guest seated closest by. But that chair was empty, vacated by Galila a few moments ago.

She was about to turn away, but her attention was snagged by Zufar's uncle, the same one who'd attempted to pry information from Zufar earlier. Niesha attempted a smile. He returned it with a speculative gaze, his eyes darting from Zufar and back again.

'You must come to dinner when you return from your honeymoon.'

Honeymoon?

She tried to master the shock that bolted through her.

Of course the King and Queen were expected to go on their honeymoon. She had no clue where Zufar had intended to take Amira. Was she supposed to know of the destination for her own honeymoon?

'I… I…' she stuttered. A moment later, a warm hand covered hers, the gentle but insistent pressure on her fingers applying subtle warning.

'We'll be happy to accept your invitation, Uncle, on our return. Providing of course that our schedules allow,' Zufar slid in smoothly, proving that even though he'd been in conversation with his brother, he had been fully tuned into what was happening with her.

Was he that terrified she would bungle the ruse? A spark of irritation lit up beneath her skin. When she attempted to withdraw her hand from under his, he held on firmly, turning his imperious head to look at her with what everyone else would have assumed was an adoring look from a groom to his new bride. But she saw the warning clear in his eyes. *Behave.*

She lowered her head under the guise of forking another bite of her superb sea bass. But she never lifted it to her lips, because she feared she would choke if she attempted to swallow.

'Where's the honeymoon destination?' the woman seated next to Zufar's uncle asked.

'We will spend a few days in the Emerald Palace, and then I will take my bride on a multi-national tour, ending in the most romantic capital of the world, of course,' Zufar said.

'Oh, you mean Paris, don't you? I love Paris,' his aunt exclaimed, her eyes lighting up. 'I haven't been in months.'

'And there's a reason for that,' his uncle said dryly. 'My

bank account screams in agony whenever you're in the French capital.'

Laughter greeted the response. Amid it all, Niesha noticed Zufar watching her with that same pseudo-adoring, warning look. When his uncle turned away to address another guest, she tried to withdraw her hand once again.

Even though her irritation had faded, a new sensation had taken root at his touch. He no longer wore his gloves, making the sensation even more searing. The burst of relief poured through her when he didn't restrain her. She dropped her hand into her lap, her fingers curling into her palm as her blood sang wildly.

Realising that he was still staring at her, she pinned that smile on her face again, and returned his look. 'You don't need to keep watching me like a hawk, you know. I'm not about to announce to the whole world what is happening here.'

'I'm glad to hear it, but since we did not discuss a honeymoon, I thought it best to step in. Surely you don't have an objection to that?' he murmured testily.

'But what will they say when they find out that it's not true?' she said tightly.

The taut little smile he gave her reproached her for being foolish. 'That will not happen, little one, because it's true. We are going on honeymoon.'

Zafar had never met anyone who blushed with such frequency as his new bride. Or trembled as much. He was stunned she hadn't collapsed into a heap of nerves thus far. His earlier summation that she was as skittish as one of his mares couldn't be more accurate. Even now, as they took their first dance, he sensed she was moments from tugging out of his hold and fleeing across the ballroom.

But just like before, right when he thought she would succumb to her nerves, she straightened her slender spine, raised that delicate little chin, and speared him with a look of such defiance it almost made him smile.

Almost.

Because this was no laughing matter. He had taken a complete stranger as his Queen. Granted, Amira had been little more than an acquaintance despite the arrangement to marry, but this was…unprecedented.

Just like that kiss on the balcony…

He clenched his gut as the memory drew another strange zing through his bloodstream. It had just been a kiss, nothing more. So why was the unique sensation lingering, luring him into wishing to experience it again? He wouldn't, of course.

This whole near disaster had him on edge. The adrenaline high of salvaging a situation that could've exploded in his face was what had blown that kiss out of proportion.

But it was time to wrestle *everything* back under control.

Despite the press release holding at bay the dozens of questions he was sure were coming his way, his people would need definitive answers by morning.

He'd barely been able to stop Amira's father from detonating the whole event even before it'd started. The man was rightly in search of answers for his daughter's whereabouts and bewildered at the news that Amira had jilted the man she was supposed to marry. Only by asserting his full authority had Zufar stopped his father's best friend from causing a scene. Feroz had finally realised Zufar was the wronged party and agreed to return home to await further news.

Zufar resisted the urge to grit his teeth at the thought of his half-brother's actions.

He had set his best investigators on the case to satisfy himself that Amira hadn't been taken against her will, but instinctively he knew she hadn't been abducted. In fact, in hindsight, Amira's lacklustre interaction with him lately was revelatory.

That sliver of relief slid through him again, this time arriving with a cold acceptance that perhaps he'd dodged a bullet that could've seen history repeating itself. Because a wife that could've so easily been seduced by another man, as his mother had been, was one he didn't want. Maybe his half-brother had done him a favour. Had even unwittingly ensured Zufar wasn't distracted from his duty and responsibility the way his father's preoccupation with his mother's infidelity had made him?

His teeth met in jaw-clenching grit. He wasn't so forgiving as to brush away the fact that Adir had done this *today* to extract maximum humiliation—

'Perhaps you should take your own advice, Your Highness,' his new bride stated softly.

He redirected his gaze to hers. 'Excuse me?'

'You want me to smile and not give the game away but you should see your face right now,' she said.

'And what does my face say?'

'That you are terribly displeased by something. Of course, I'm sure I don't need to guess what it is. You think you will find her soon?' she asked.

He pushed his irritation away. 'I don't wish to talk about Amira.' Further thought of his half-brother was not welcome. Moreover, Zufar found he was much more interested in the woman he held in his arms.

For the purposes of keeping in character, of course.

Because Niesha was right. He was at risk of giving the game away. He schooled his features as he continued to look down at her. As he did so, he noticed the changes in her.

The hair he'd believed to be mousy was in fact a lustrous thick chestnut, highlighted with dark gold strands he was sure didn't come out of a tube. Her eyelashes were unbelievably long, fanning almost hypnotically against her cheeks when she lowered them. Lips painted a deep peach drew his eyes consistently to the soft, plump curve of her mouth.

Her eyes were wide and alluring pools edged in kohl that emphasised the amethyst depths.

In her heels, she came up to his chin, bringing him that much closer to the lips he had tasted all too briefly on the balcony outside. Lips that his own thirsted to taste.

The zing threatened to spark into something else, something *more* as his recollection deepened.

She wasn't experienced, that much he could tell by kissing her, but he had sensed an innocent eagerness in her that lit a fire in his belly. The temptation to kiss her, experience that thrill again, fanned his hunger. He curbed it ruthlessly.

He wasn't weak like his father, controlled by his obsessional urges to the ruin of all else around him. Zufar enjoyed sex, and the carefully selected women he'd indulged himself with over the years had more than satisfied his needs. But not a single time had he let his emotions overtake him.

He didn't intend to start now.

Duty had dictated he take a wife and produce heirs. That would be his end goal. And with Amira out of the picture...

He stared at his new Queen. His *temporary* Queen.

His people's reaction to her had been...extraordinary. Surprisingly so. They'd readily accepted her. So why upset the cart?

Why indeed...?

Zufar cautioned himself against revealing to Niesha that, far from thinking that this was only a temporary marriage, she was now bound to him for life. That conversation would need careful strategising.

In the same instance that he accepted his decision, it occurred to him that the idea of binding himself to a near stranger neither disturbed nor displeased him. He'd never intended to marry for anything other than ensuring lasting stability for his people after the turbulence of his father's reign.

He wasn't so weak as to give into ephemeral notions of marrying for love. That emotion was a fairy tale he'd never wasted his time seeking, and especially not once the reality of his position in life had been made clear.

His father had fallen victim to lust and obsession to the detriment of his family and his kingdom. Zufar was well aware of the whispers that had followed his father, the veiled scorn shown towards the weakness that dogged the previous King. He had no intention of falling prey to that absurd sickness.

'I'm in no hurry to locate my former fiancée.'

Her breath caught. 'And why not?'

'Because if she went of her own free will, then she's no longer of any consequence.'

She gasped. 'How can you say that? She was promised to you. You still need a bride! Your people need a queen.'

Zufar continued to look down at her as they glided across the dance floor. Absent-mindedly, he noted the grace with which she swayed in his arms, the way she held herself with careful poise. She wasn't as unpolished as he'd imagined, he mused again. In fact, with a little bit of help, she could become the diamond he sought. The diamond his people deserved.

The more he thought about it, the more the idea settled deeper inside him.

'Your Highness?' Her prompt was tremulous, as if she knew of the monumental decision he'd taken.

Her eyes were growing wide again, her lower lip set to tremble in that alluring quiver that made him want to devour her again.

'I don't need to find her, little one, because I've already found my bride. I've found my Queen. This wedding, and this marriage, will be my first and my last. There hasn't been a divorce in my family in recorded history. In fact, I'm not sure the constitution has allowances for it. So, you see, you and I are bound together for life, Niesha. Accept it.'

CHAPTER FOUR

IF NIESHA HAD been informed only half an hour ago that there was a way for her whole world to be shoved even more off kilter, she wouldn't have believed it. But she was fully installed on that wild, turbulent roller coaster now.

She stared up at Zufar, knowing that this time there was no mistaking what he'd said. Nor was there any doubt that this was an accidental revelation. They were in the middle of the dance floor, surrounded by over three hundred guests. She had nowhere to go, was unable to protest without causing the most horrendous scene.

Zufar al Khalia's diplomatic prowess and mental agility was renowned. He'd won almost every polo match since he was seventeen. The moment he'd entered public office, he'd gained a reputation as a master strategist.

That he'd brought those abilities to bear on this situation was irrefutable. Panic and anger surged in her belly, lending her vocal cords the strength to dig herself out of this hole she was disappearing into.

He shook his head. 'Not here,' he instructed tersely.

'You lied to me,' she whispered, the depth of his trap making her tone husky with shock.

His eyes grew chilly but the smile didn't fade from his face. 'I said, not here,' he emphasised with clear displeasure.

But Niesha was a little too out of her head to heed the warning. 'You planned this all along.'

'If you mean did I plan to speak to you afterwards so we can discuss this like rational human beings, then yes, that was my intention.'

Chilled through by his almost careless dismissal, she took a step back from him, but the arm banding her waist pulled her closer, the fingers curled around hers holding her prisoner. 'You will not cause a scene.'

Her King demanded obedience. But in that moment, Niesha couldn't find the capacity to fall in line like everyone else at his command.

'You keep telling me how to behave, to smile, to breathe. I'm not an object, Your Highness. I'm a human being. I chose to obey you because I thought I was doing the right thing. But you misled me. I will not stand for that.'

His nostrils flared, his whole being tightening against her as his gaze pinned her.

'What is it you're intending to do?' he questioned with a deadly smile.

'I won't cause a scene, if that's what you are worried about.'

A single tic rippled through his jaw before he regained himself. 'That's good to hear. However, I hear a *but* in there.'

'I will remain meekly by your side until this ceremony is over. And then you and I will talk.'

One corner of his mouth lifted in a hint of a smile that promised to be lethal given its full scope. 'My meek little bride seems to have a spine after all,' he mocked.

The bubble of anger in Niesha's belly grew. 'I get that way when I'm misled.'

'Be careful. Don't forget whom you're addressing,' he warned.

A chill went through her body. 'Is that a threat, Your Highness?'

'I am reminding you that we have an audience, and our every move is being watched so if you are going to be disagreeable, I suggest you wait until we are behind closed doors.'

'Disagreeable? You think I'm being—'

Before she could further vent her anger, he leaned close and brushed his lips over hers.

Like on the balcony, this was meant to shut her up. Niesha

knew that. And yet it worked like magic. The high-wattage shiver that went down her spine was so strong she thought she would be lifted right off her feet.

And that was with just a whisper of his lips over hers. She cursed her body's reaction. Continued cursing it as the song ended and she was led off the ballroom floor with suave attentiveness.

As if he knew and meant to capitalise on her reaction to his touch, Zufar didn't release her. Long fingers meshed with hers as they moved from group to group holding brief court with their guests.

For two hours she was subjected to his electrifying touch and blasts from tawny eyes that held her fraying nerves on a tight leash.

The evening culminated with spectacular fireworks on the great lawn of the palace. Across the capital city, individual households joined in, with bursts of fireworks lighting the sky across the city.

Niesha barely acknowledged them. All she wanted to do was to retreat at the earliest opportunity and guarantee her fate wasn't as final as she suspected.

Relief drenched her as her attendants materialised beside her at the stroke of nine p.m. to whisk her off. Moments later, she realised Zufar was not following as she'd expected.

She stopped. They needed to discuss what he'd said now. She couldn't bear to wait another second. 'Wait. I need to—'

He intercepted her as she headed back to where he stood with one of his ministers. 'Go on without me. We will be reunited soon enough, little one,' he said smoothly as he took her hand and brushed his lips over her knuckles.

Dear heaven, he was smooth.

And calculating.

She was struggling to find her breath when the women firmly led her away.

Niesha was so caught up in the conversation she intended to have with him that she didn't notice where they were headed until she realised that they weren't returning to the Queen's private quarters. 'What… Where are you taking me?' she blurted, although she had a fair idea.

Halimah, walking a few steps in front of her, looked over her shoulder and smiled. This time her smile was more tactful, her whole demeanour remarkably altered from this morning.

Of course, Niesha mused, she was now the Queen, and where there'd been whispered speculation and awkwardness before, there were now smiles and an abundance of courtesy and respect.

Even as a tiny spurt of resentment erupted inside her for their about-face, she wanted to blurt out that there was no need for their change of attitude. She was still one of them. She certainly wasn't going to be Queen for very long, not if she had any say in it.

The thought that her wish might not come true sent a fresh bolt of alarm through her. Zufar hadn't misspoken. Niesha didn't know the ins and outs of constitutional law, but she knew the history of the royal family enough to know that there'd been no divorce for generations.

To date, Zufar's own father had been the only one to abdicate the throne and that had sent shock waves through the kingdom.

'Your Highness?'

Niesha whirled around, expecting Zufar to be behind her. When he wasn't, she turned back around, frowning at Halimah.

'Your Highness, which gown do you prefer?' the attendant urged.

She realised that she was the one being addressed, and her heart lurched. 'Please, don't call me that.'

Halimah and the young attendants exchanged apprehensive looks. 'Begging your pardon, but that is your official title. To address you as anything else would be disrespectful, Your Highness.'

'I see,' Niesha replied. Her resentment of moments before dissipated, replaced with the stark notion that, whether she liked it or not, they truly saw her differently now. She might not feel it inside but to them she was now a rarefied species, no longer one of them. Niesha didn't know whether to be sad or to give into more hysteria. She settled for a solemn nod. 'Okay.' She knew how rigorously the rules of the palace were followed. The last thing she wanted to do was cause trouble for the staff. She would be one of them again soon enough.

'I've prepared some tea for Your Highness. Jasmine tea, to calm the nerves before the wedding night,' Halimah offered with a benign smile.

Niesha stopped herself from blurting that it was a waste of time. She didn't intend to sleep in Zufar's private quarters tonight or on any other night.

'Can you help me with my gown, please?'

'Of course, Your Highness,' Halimah sang out.

Gentle hands began undoing her clothing. She wasn't sure why she paid closer attention this time. Perhaps it was the knowledge that she would never be close to such perfect creations again that made her look down at her gown properly for the first time, noticing the precious stones sewn into the skirts swirling around her legs as it was removed, the delicate sleeves and masterful design.

An exquisite diamond and sapphire necklace gleamed against her skin, the gems in her ears and on her wrist adding to the magical quality of the wedding gown that didn't belong to her and never would.

But for one small infinitesimal moment, she allowed herself to believe that this was real.

When she finally met her gaze in the mirror, she dared to dream that when this moment was far behind her, she would one day experience a wedding day of her own.

Smaller and less spectacular, of course, but enchanted all the same.

First, though, she had to get through to Zufar. Had to extricate herself from this web of impossible circumstances closing in on her. She raised her arms as the gown was lifted over her head and spirited away.

Then Halimah was in front of her, gesturing to an array of gorgeous evening gowns hanging from a rail.

Niesha stared at the dresses in surprise. 'Are these new?' They hadn't been there this morning and she hadn't spotted them with the bridal trousseau.

Halimah nodded. 'His Highness ordered these for you himself.'

'Excuse me?' she blurted.

A smile curved Halimah's lips. 'The suddenness of the…new arrangements left you no choice but to wear the only wedding gown available. But I believe your new husband did not wish to see you in another woman's clothes on the night of your wedding. He had the royal couturier provide these for you especially.' There was wistfulness in Halimah's voice that suggested that underneath the sometimes brusque exterior lurked a romantic.

Nevertheless, Niesha was stunned Zufar had arranged all this. Should she really be surprised? If the bombshell he'd dropped on the dance floor was true, then within minutes of entering this room this afternoon he'd made a life-altering decision for her without so much as blinking in her direction.

The formidable calculation behind that staggered her.

'Which one is it to be, Your Highness?' Halimah prompted.

Half dazed, Niesha pointed to the emerald sequinned gown, made of material she was almost too afraid to touch. 'That one,' she murmured.

'A wonderful choice, Your Highness,' Halimah agreed.

That bubble of hysteria threatened again. She swallowed it down, willing herself to remain quiet as the women bustled around her again.

Her hair was rearranged, her make-up touched up, and heels presented to her.

'We thought you would prefer your tea on the terrace, Your Highness. The fireworks are still going on, and you can get the best view from there.'

Niesha trailed after them out onto a stone terrace where an elaborate tea service had been laid out. She'd barely eaten anything at the wedding banquet but Niesha knew she wouldn't be able to eat now either. She contemplated the exquisite offering, wondering whether she shouldn't try anyway to calm her nerves.

But she didn't want her nerves calmed. She'd been too dazed and confused earlier, had meekly stumbled her way through what should've been a firm refusal to succumb to his wishes. She'd gone along with the idea that she would be a stand-in, temporary bride. She intended to make her voice heard this time.

She would scream if she needed to. With a brisk nod to herself, Niesha sat down and held her hands in her lap.

'May I pour you a cup, Your Highness?'

She stopped herself from gritting her teeth at the title. It didn't belong to her and she would never get used to it.

'No, thank you,' she said. 'You may go now. I'll pour it myself when I am ready.'

'But… Your Highness, that is not protocol.'

Niesha swallowed her irritation. 'I'm quite capable of pouring my own tea, Halimah.'

The older woman gave a curt bow, and stepped back. 'As you wish, Your Highness. Will there be anything else?'

Niesha shook her head. But as the women started to re-treat, she turned. 'Do you know when Zu—His Highness will be here?' She heard the nervousness in her own voice but Halimah's gaze only softened.

'You can expect him within the hour, Your Highness.'

Another series of curtsies later, Niesha was alone.

An hour.

She snorted under her breath. The likelihood that she would've gone completely mad by then was very real. The moment she heard the door shut, she jumped to her feet.

There had to be a way out of this, there simply had to be. She paced until her feet began to pinch, and then she kicked the shoes off. Hearing them thud against the wall brought a tiny bit of satisfaction, immediately followed by guilt at the treatment of what had to be thousands of dollars' worth of accessories.

That thought ramped up her agitation. As she turned from her pacing, another burst of fireworks lit through the sky. Niesha lifted her head to watch it, the enormity of why this celebration was happening settling on her. She raised a hand to her throbbing head and caught a spark of her wedding ring. It was unlike any ring she'd ever seen.

From the history of the al Khalia kingdom she'd devoured back in her teens she knew exactly where the ring on her finger had originated. It had belonged to Zufar's grandmother. She'd been married to his grandfather for over seventy years and had worn the ring every day of her married life. The heirloom's historical significance threatened to overwhelm her. Perhaps it was fortunate then that the hard rap on the outer door dragged her from her thoughts.

The bundle of nerves that jumped into her throat suggested perhaps not. On shaky feet, she rushed to where she'd thrown off her shoes and slipped back into the heels. Sucking in a deep breath, she walked through the living room to the doors. With one last slide of her clammy palms over her dress, Niesha opened the doors.

Zufar too had changed. Gone was the magnificent military uniform he'd worn for the ceremony. In its place was an equally captivating tunic that drew her eyes to his broad shoulders and the tapered physique that been honed from his love of polo. Dark curly hair gleamed under the chandelier lights. He'd taken a shower at some point since she'd last seen him.

Despite the emotions raging inside her, Niesha couldn't take her eyes off him. The subtle clearing of his throat embarrassingly long seconds later alerted her to her gawping.

When she met his gaze, his eyes were a touch cool, but as his gaze roved from her head down to her feet a different look replaced it. A look that sent hot tingles surging through her belly to curl low and insistent in her pelvis.

'Are you going to invite me in or do you wish to tackle me where I stand?'

Niesha cursed the blush spreading in her cheeks, and stepped back hastily. He stepped inside and shut the door behind him.

'The gown suits you,' he said with more than a hint of satisfaction.

The thought that he'd chosen it especially for her shouldn't have sent that traitorous bolt of pleasure through her bloodstream, and Niesha immediately wished it away. She didn't want to speak about clothes. Or wonder whether the unbelievably soft and silky gown that clung to her breasts, waist and hips pleased him in any way. She only wanted to talk about her freedom.

'Tell me what you said isn't true,' she blurted heatedly.

He didn't respond but his nostrils flared slightly as he looked around the room. 'Perhaps we should sit down.'

Niesha shook her head. 'No. You said this was an *interim* solution. I want to know why you deceived me,' she demanded, her voice more plaintive than she wished.

'Calm yourself.' His voice was a firm command.

'I'll be calm when you tell me that this marriage will be annulled as soon as possible,' she returned.

He didn't react to the unbecoming screech in her voice or the undeniable accusation she lobbed at him. He merely continued to stride away from her towards the living room, leaving her no choice but to follow.

She watched him lower his impressive frame into the

heavy silk armchair she was sure cost more than two years' salary, and cross one leg over the other.

'I've had you investigated,' he stated baldly. 'You do not have any family, correct?'

A bolt of pain shot through her heart, along with the shock of discovering he was changing tactic yet again.

With balled fists, she stared at him. 'You had me investigated?' she parroted.

He nodded calmly, as if her incredulity was of no consequence to him. Perhaps it wasn't. But the thought that while they'd been exchanging vows he'd been digging into her background made nausea rise in her belly. Knowing what he'd found, knowing that he had evidence that she was a nobody, literally and figuratively, sent another wave of anguish through her.

Nonetheless, she raised her chin. 'Then you'll have your confirmation that I'm unsuitable for this…this…'

'Being my Queen?' he finished softly. So softly she barely heard the words.

Why was he so calm? Why was he not doing everything in his power to be rid of her at the first opportunity?

'Yes,' she hissed, taking a step closer to him even though her instincts warned that it would be wiser to keep a sensible distance between them.

'On the contrary, I believe it is to my advantage.'

'Your advantage?' she echoed blankly.

'Precisely. I have no relatives to appease, no scandals to come out of the woodwork. There is only you to deal with,' he stated with faint satisfaction.

Her heart lurched. 'What exactly do you mean by that?'

His gaze raked over her again, lingering longer this time. As if he had all the time in the world. 'You've had a challenging day, little one. Sit down before you fall down.'

Niesha barely managed to stop herself from stomping her feet. 'I'm not as weak as you think I am. I'm perfectly capable of carrying on a conversation without needing to wilt into the nearest chair.'

'But perhaps it will be more civil that way?' he parried in a mocking tone before flicking one sleekly elegant hand towards the seat next to him.

The suggestion that she was not being civilised cut her to the quick. Niesha brushed it aside. She didn't really care what his opinion was of her. All she cared about was that this evening's conversation ended with her achieving her freedom.

Nevertheless, she made her way to the sofa, acutely aware that he followed her every step until she perched on the corner of it, tucking her legs neatly to one side and folding her hands in her lap. Only then did she lift her head and meet his gaze full on. An expression passed through his eyes, gone too quickly for her to decipher.

'I'm sitting down now, Your Highness. Please explain yourself.'

He gave the barest hint of a smile, but it was gone an instant later.

'The constitution is not as backwards as I allowed you to think. Divorce isn't disallowed, but, were I to divorce, I would be the first in my family's history to do so.'

Relief surged through her, but it was accompanied by an alien, disturbing sensation she couldn't quite pinpoint. 'We can divorce?' she repeated slowly, wondering why the words attempted to stick in her throat.

He remained silent for a long moment, then he gave a brisk nod. 'Yes.' The word was uttered with a single, acrid bite. 'There is a clause that states that divorce can be initiated by either party, but there are specific circumstances under which it will be considered.'

'What circumstances?'

His nostrils flared. 'Infidelity.'

Her eyes widened when he didn't continue. 'That's it?'

'Yes,' he said.

'But—I'm not… This isn't a true marriage…not that I have any intention of doing…being unfaithful…' She shook her head to stem her babbling. 'All this is absurd. What about an annulment?' she tagged on desperately.

He shook his head. 'No history of that in my family either.' An intensely arrogant expression crossed his face. 'No al Khalia has failed to consummate his marriage.'

For some reason that statement sent a bolt of heat surging through her belly. 'But you're going to be the first though?'

Slowly, Zufar uncrossed legs, leaned forwards and rested his elbows on his knees. 'Am I?' he drawled softly, his eyes narrowed like twin lasers on her.

Niesha's fingers trembled. She clenched them tighter. 'Of course you are. That's our only choice.'

'It is not.'

The finality of those three words shook her to her very foundations. The hairs on her nape rose chillingly as he continued to regard her steadily. 'Wh-what do you mean?'

'I mean this marriage can be real.'

'Real?' she echoed as if the word were alien to her. Perhaps it was. None of what he was saying made any sense.

'Real,' he affirmed. 'I will be your husband, and you will be my wife. You will bear my children, and you will be my Queen.'

He'd said those words to her previously. And yet Niesha's jaw still dropped to the floor.

'And…why would I want to do that?'

'Because your reward would be elevation to a position very few women will ever achieve in their lifetime. You will have the respect of a whole kingdom and the adoration of millions.'

Something curled into a tight ball inside her. 'I'm not sure when I gave you the impressive that I wanted any of that. I don't.'

He sent her a disbelieving look as he leaned forwards

even further. 'You wish to remain a chambermaid for the rest of your life?'

The lash of the question was meant to wound. And it did. She didn't need reminding that she was a nobody, with no family or even friends she could count on. That all she had was the deep yearning to leave a mark deeper and more meaningful than the sad and transient childhood that had been thrust upon her.

Despite her shredded emotions, she kicked up her chin, glared down her nose at him. 'No. I have a little bit more ambition than that. But it doesn't involve sitting around basking in the adoration of your subjects.'

He nodded, as if he hadn't all but snorted his disbelief moments before. 'Very well, tell me what it is.'

'Why?' she asked suspiciously.

He levelled a shrug so beautifully arrogant and elegant she blinked a few times before she could concentrate again. 'Perhaps I can help.'

Niesha shook her head. Nothing came for free. She knew that all too well. But his eyes were hypnotising her, the gold depths drilling to the heart of her desires.

She found herself responding before she could stop herself. 'I've always wanted to work with children,' she said softly. 'I've been saving to start a course next year.'

'A tutor will be hired for you,' he declared immediately.

Her breath caught, but the reminder that nothing came for free stuck harder. 'In return for what? You want something, I know you do. Why don't you just tell me?'

His eyes gleamed at her. 'I have already told you.'

She shook her head, shaken beyond belief. 'This cannot possibly be what you want. You…you don't even know me.' Her voice was a perplexed shrill.

He shrugged again. 'Perhaps a blank slate is exactly what I need.' The hardness to his tone sent a cold shiver through her.

'That doesn't make any sense.'

'It may seem that way to you, little one.'

The bolt that went through her this time was all heat and charged electricity. 'Please stop calling me that.'

He stiffened. 'Does it offend you?'

She bit her lip but remained silent because, contrary to offence, every time he used that low, deep-voiced endearment, something decadent churned within her, something she didn't want to fathom, never mind explain.

Everything about this man pushed her severely off kilter. But it was time for her to regain her balance.

Before she could speak, he rose to his full, imperious height.

Long, elegant strides brought him to where she sat, and he lowered himself into the seat next to her.

The virile force of his masculinity hit her square in the face. Niesha attempted to swallow, and realised that even that small action couldn't be achieved with him so close.

'Today my people confirmed what I have known for a while—that they need the stability of a king who is married and stable rather than one who is not. The economic potential of my marriage is immense. To upset that turn of events will be unfortunate and unacceptable. For your part, you have been accepted into their hearts. You, a nobody from nowhere. Even if I wanted to be the first in my family to divorce, which I do not, the reaction to our union has made me rethink my decision. You will stay married to me, and in return I will give you a better life.'

Her insides shook but Niesha forced herself to speak. 'And what life is that, exactly?' She wasn't asking because she was about to accept his ludicrous proposal. She just wanted to buy herself a little time to come up with her own strategy to extricate herself from this situation.

'Any life you wish for yourself.'

'And what about Amira?'

His jaw grew rigid for one second. 'You said she wasn't

coerced into leaving. Unless you were mistaken?' he asked, one eyebrow lifted.

She bit her lip, recalling those moments in the room. As much as she wanted to deny it, the truth had been plain to see. 'No, she wasn't coerced. But don't you want to find her?'

'I know exactly who took her and why. It was meant to cause humiliation and chaos, and I've successfully averted that.'

She frowned. 'But you'll want her back, surely?'

His face shuttered. 'I spoke to her father before the ceremony. Our arrangement is broken.'

'Just like that?'

He gave a cold, firm nod. 'Yes. Besides, I believe I've already said I've made my choice. Right now, I want to discuss us.'

Her heart shuddered once more. *Us.* When had they become us?

'My people have been through enough,' he continued forcefully. 'I will not jeopardise the stability of this kingdom with another emotional spectacle like the one my father exhibited recently.' The heat behind his words shocked her to the core. As if he hadn't intended those words to slip out, his face tightened. 'I need someone with a clear head and a strong work ethic by my side.'

'But…you don't even know me,' she repeated.

'I've seen your file. Spoken to those that matter. Your work in my palace has been exemplary.'

She stared at him, stunned. 'And that's it? That's all it takes?'

'No, that's not all it takes. But it's a good basis on which to start.'

Niesha shook her head, her racing heart seeming to have no intention of slowing down. 'This can't be happening,' she said under her breath.

'Reconcile yourself to it.' The finality to the words frightened her.

'I don't want to,' she whispered heatedly. 'You said this was an interim solution,' she reminded him.

Without warning, he reached out and brushed his knuckle down her cheek. The action, electrifying and unexpected, froze her in her seat.

Several minutes passed in silence. When she chanced a glance at him, his eyes were narrowed, the look in his eyes intently calculating.

Niesha was sure that whatever was going on behind his breathtaking face wouldn't include setting her free.

'My people need us to remain married, Niesha,' he eventually said.

Her heart squeezed painfully. 'I... I don't want to make them unhappy but—'

'But what? You wish to return to a life of single servitude?'

'I want to have a choice in when and who I marry!'

His hand dropped, his expression tightening in offence. 'And I'm so vastly unsuitable?'

'I didn't say that,' she mumbled. On the contrary, he was a little too close to her ideal specification of a husband.

'What will suit you, then?' he asked, but Niesha had a feeling he was just humouring her.

Her chin went up. 'For you to honour your initial agreement, that this was only temporary.'

Again he went silent for several spine-tingling minutes. Then he nodded. 'Very well. Five years,' he murmured deeply and abruptly. 'That is all I ask. Five years.'

'I... What?'

'If a permanent marriage to me is too much for you to handle, then let's revisit our situation in five years. In the meantime, you stay by my side. Bear my heirs. At the end of it, if you still want your freedom, I will grant it to you. In return, you will have the education you want, any position you desire, the title of Queen, and riches beyond your wildest dreams.'

'Can you please stop talking about your wealth? I don't want your money.'

His forefinger tucked under her chin and lifted her gaze up to meet his. 'What about my people? Do you hate them so much that you wish to see them unhappy?'

'That's not fair,' she said.

A grim smile played around his lips. 'Get your head out of the clouds, little one. If life was fair, you would not have ended up in an orphanage.'

There was no malice in his tone, only stark truthfulness. And yet the pain was hard to block out. Although there was no record of her past, the quality of the clothes on her back when she'd been found wandering dangerously close to a ravine had indicated that she might have been cared for at one point. But this was no salve right now. Well off or not, she'd been abandoned, possibly left for dead, the orphanage matron had informed her after endless probing.

Niesha had stopped asking about her past when every query—besides those about what she'd been wearing the day she was found at just five years old—had met with a stern rebuke to look forwards not backwards. She had a roof over her head and food in her belly. She needed to be grateful for that, she was told.

Nevertheless, those questions had never left her. It was what fuelled the burning need to work with children. Especially orphaned children.

If she could at some point in the future reunite one child with their rightful past that would be enough for her. Because the pain lodged in her heart all these years later wasn't something she wanted any child to experience.

The idea that Zufar al Khalia could expedite everything she'd ever dreamed of slowly wove through the waves of pain. The other things he had mentioned—being Queen, bearing his children—sent bolts of anxiety through her. They were so impossibly far-reaching she shook her head. 'You...want me to have your children?'

His lips twisted. 'That is generally the idea when a man takes a wife. But especially so in my case since mine is a hereditary rule.'

She stopped herself from laughing hysterically. Was she even capable?

'If you're wondering if you can bear children, I've also seen your medical file. There's nothing to suggest that you may not be able to carry my children.'

Was there a square inch of her life he hadn't probed? The question was ludicrous, of course. He was the head of the royal family. It stood to reason that he would cover every base. Even though they'd been brought together by a set of bizarre circumstances, it seemed as if Zufar had every intention of making this work.

But did she?

'I need your answer, little one.' He pressed his finger still resting beneath her chin, not allowing any avenue of escape.

'Children,' she echoed, her mind darting to his face, unable to stop her imagination from running wild. Would their offspring look like him? Images bombarded her, filling her with a sudden longing that robbed her of breath.

'Many,' he echoed. 'As many as we can manage in five years.'

The prospect of marriage and children had been abstract thoughts in the daily grind of her work in the palace. It was something she had hoped would happen in the future. The reality that it was happening now, unfolding right before her eyes, was almost too much to take in.

As if he knew he had her on the ropes, that she was reeling from everything he had laid out at her feet, he leaned forwards until his mouth was a scant inch from hers. 'Do you agree?' he breathed.

Marriage. Children. Everything the foolish sixteen-year-old in her had dared to dream about as she'd thumbed through the glossy pages of the royal books in the library. Those daydreams that had followed her into her sleep now wormed their way through the dazed anxiety pressing down on her.

Zufar had spoken no words of love—nor had she expected him to. But looking into the hard contours of his face, she doubted they would be forthcoming in the future. When it came right down to it, they were strangers to one another, thrown together by harsh circumstance.

Still, she couldn't dismiss that image of her sixteen-year-old self, staring after a much younger Zufar as he strode commandingly through the palace.

He'd led a life of integrity, loyalty, absolute dedication to his people; his crown. What better characteristics to look for in a future partner than those?

The notion that she was talking herself into this struck her hard.

She attempted to move, to give herself breathing room.

He stopped her retreat by slipping his hand to her nape, just as he had on the balcony earlier. Eyes sharp with intent gazed deeper into hers. 'You want this,' he murmured. 'Think about all you stand to gain, all the children you can help. Say yes, Niesha,' he pressed deeply. Hypnotically.

Had she yearned to retreat to a life of drudgery only an hour ago? Did she really want to scuttle away to her lonely bedsit and scrimp and save for years until she could make something more of her life?

She knew without a doubt that she would kick herself from here to eternity if she refused to take the chance being offered to her on a silver platter.

His lips moved tantalisingly close, eliciting a deep craving that scandalised her. She wanted to kiss him again, she realised shockingly. Wanted the chance beyond today, beyond tomorrow, as many days as she would be granted.

With Zufar al Khalia, there would never be any doubt that her children would be nobodies like her. They would be princes and princesses, future kings or queens with centuries of history and pedigree at their fingertips. She could set a true path for her children. Perhaps even find an identity for herself that she'd been denied. Maybe that was a little bit wrong. But in that moment, it was a decision Niesha couldn't walk away from.

Her hands twisted in her lap. In the next moment, he grasped them with his free hand. He was taking control of her life, of her whole being, and she didn't even care. Her gaze dropped to the mouth she wanted to kiss so badly, before rising to meet his once again.

And then she breathed the word that seared into her heart. 'Yes.'

For endless heartbeats, he didn't move. Then, without granting her the kiss that she craved, he rose, grasped her elbow and pulled her up with him.

'You have made a wise decision,' he intoned.

'Have I, Your Highness?' she responded dazedly.

Again the corner of his mouth lifted in a barely there smile. 'You really need to stop calling me that.'

A shaky breath moved her. Then her breath stilled completely as he cupped her face in his large, warm hands. 'After all, you can hardly call me *Your Highness* when I am deep inside you,' he said in a low, thick voice.

'I…?' She stopped as heat flamed her face.

'Zufar,' he urged. 'That is my name. Use it.' His thumb caressed her jaw, rendering her speechless.

Numbly, she shook her head.

'Never fear, I will have you screaming it by the time the night is over,' he vowed deeply.

He dropped his hand and captured one wrist. The next moment he was pulling her towards the door.

'Where are you taking me?' she blurted.

'It's our wedding night, little one,' he said without breaking stride. 'Royal tradition is no different from any other. We will consummate our marriage this night. After all, if five years is all we have, then you will need to bear my children sooner rather than later, don't you think?'

The look he threw over his shoulder was filled with rock-hard purpose. There was lust in there, sure—no matter how discreet he'd been, Zufar's liaisons with beautiful women were a known fact—but it was a contained lust, one he seemed determined to keep under lock and key.

As he'd said, tonight was their wedding night. And Zufar fully intended to carry out his duty in the bedroom.

Immediately.

Heart in her throat, she stumbled after him down an endless corridor into his private bedchamber and towards the vast and solid four-poster bed that would be the venue for their wedding night.

The place where she would lose her virginity to the King of Khalia before the night was out.

CHAPTER FIVE

NIESHA BARELY ACKNOWLEDGED the magnificently appointed private suite she'd been so in awe of the handful of times she'd visited the King's bedroom as a chambermaid.

Her every sense was focused on the searing clasp of his fingers against hers. Their palms were glued together, the heat from his branding her, imprinting on her skin the same way the royal crest was embossed on the flags that fluttered along the driveway leading to the palace.

Her heart hammered loud enough to drown out any other sound in her ears, so much so that she was terrified she would hyperventilate if she didn't find a way to calm down. But how could she? How could she remain serene in the face of this earth-shaking set of events unfolding in her life?

This morning she'd woken up believing her day would be ordinary—save for the momentous event of the royal wedding, of course—but here she was on the verge of giving her virginity to the King.

Did she have to tell him? Would he know? What was the etiquette? The flurry of questions reeled through her mind, adding to the turmoil seething inside her.

As if he sensed her unsettling thoughts, Zufar stopped abruptly. 'What's wrong?'

'I… This is going too fast,' she answered truthfully.

She expected another one of his thunderous frowns, but was surprised when he studied her for a moment and then nodded. Without releasing her, he raised his other hand and gently brushed his fingers down her pale cheek. 'Do not fear, little one, I will make this memorable for you. We will endeavour to go as slow as you wish.'

A swell of relief bloomed through her apprehension. In

the next moment, it all evaporated when he cleanly swept her off her feet.

'What are you doing?' she squeaked.

'I believe this is the tradition?' he replied.

He wasn't moving. He stared down steadily, waiting for an answer. Only then did Niesha realise that they were poised outside the doors to his inner bedchamber. Beyond that, the immense emperor-sized bed waited, covered with the exquisite gold and blue coverlet she herself had laid on it only a few days ago. The insane, whirlwind journey from then to now seemed like a hallucination.

A quick swallow later, she redirected her gaze to him. 'If you believe in that sort of thing, I guess,' she murmured.

One eyebrow slowly lifted. 'Do you not believe, Niesha?'

It wasn't the first time he'd said her name, but this time the effect of the deep baritone curling around her given name sent tiny bursts of fireworks from deep in her belly, radiating outwards. She watched him track her blush, a small smile curving his lips, drawing her eyes to the sensual outline of his masculine mouth.

'I believe I have my answer,' he said.

With that, he stepped over the threshold and calmly walked her over to the bed.

Slowly he set her down on her feet, his hands trailing her upper arms to settle on her shoulders. Then his gaze raked her from head to toe, lingering at her breasts and her hips in a very frank, masculine appraisal that sent a flare of awareness over her skin.

Her nipples began to pebble, her breasts growing sensitive as he lifted eyes turned molten gold to her face.

'Beautiful,' he pronounced deeply.

No one had ever called her that. Not even close. She shook her head. 'It's not me. It's the dress and…the make-up.'

'It is also the woman wearing those things,' he declared haughtily.

Recalling that he'd been responsible for the gown she was wearing, she looked down at herself. 'Thank you for this. You didn't have to but—'

He cut her off with a shake of his head. 'You were not given a choice in your wedding gown. The situation needed to be remedied for what followed. I couldn't be so distasteful to ask you to wear another woman's clothes on your wedding night.'

A knot she hadn't even been aware of eased inside her. Consideration where there needn't have been touched a place inside her that sent prickles to the back of her eyes. 'Thank you,' she said again.

'You're welcome, but I'm afraid it's time for the dress to come off.'

Just like that the atmosphere shifted again. The purposeful heat gathering in his eyes sent similar flames surging through her body. His hands slowly drifted up her shoulders to the pulse fluttering in her neck. There he paused, his fingers lazily caressing her skin until a helpless moan drifted from her throat.

'Do you like that?' he demanded, his gaze a little too incisive, as if he was intent on learning her body language.

Molten heat flashed through her. Her tongue darted out to lick dry lips as she contemplated her answer. Would he find her daring if she admitted that she liked his touch? Did she even need to answer? Surely he could see for himself?

'This is part of the "getting to know one another" process, Niesha. There's no need to be shy. I intend to learn your body, the same way I wish you to learn mine.' His elegant fingers caressed again, slightly more insistent, his touch leaving trails of heat on her skin. 'Do you like this?' he demanded again, his imperious voice setting off deep tremors inside her.

'Yes,' she moaned.

'Good.' The satisfied sound rumbled from his throat. Then, with both thumbs resting beneath her chin, he tilted her head up, exposing her face to the golden fire of his gaze. 'I wish to taste your lips again,' he stated.

Before she could stop herself, Niesha swayed towards him. A deeper satisfaction twisted his lips before his face grew taut with a captivating look from which she could not look away.

With a rough sound under his breath, he lowered his head and sealed his mouth to hers. She had no prior experience save for their previous kiss, but even Niesha knew this one was different.

For a start, it seared her to the soul. A deeply carnal, deeply intoxicating experience, it was a statement of subjugation over her that swiftly stripped her of the ability to think.

Her every sense focused on the dark magic being visited upon her, a magic she never wanted to end. The bold probe of his tongue between her lips commanded her to open up for him. With a sigh of need, she parted her lips and experienced an even greater depth of sensation as his tongue brushed hers.

Bold. Fiery. Caught in the grip of fever she'd never imagined possible with a mere kiss, she couldn't stop herself from clinging to his waist as the ground moved beneath her feet. Hungry for more, she parted her lips wider, and moaned low and deep as he explored her with brazen thoroughness. Wave after wave of sensation swept through her, her knees growing weaker with each passing second.

At some point her eyes had drifted shut as she succumbed to the power of touch and scent. She heard his breathing grow heavy to match hers, the hands resting at her throat drifting down her back to cup her buttocks before pulling her closer into his body. No man had ever touched her so boldly. No man had ever done even a fraction of what Zufar was doing to her. It was intoxicating beyond belief.

With another helpless moan, she gave into the temptation and allowed her own hands to roam his body. The silk of his tunic heated beneath her fingers as she slowly circled his waist and tentatively explored his back. Hard muscles flexed beneath her touch, his body tensing and relaxing as she hesitantly caressed him. All sense of time faded away, the only reality in her world the utterly mind-bending sensations carrying her away to an unknown destination.

A harsh hiss issued from his lips. She blinked, then realised her nails were digging into his shoulders. At some point, his fingers had buried in her hair and he used the gentle grip to notch back her head so he could gaze down into her face.

'Do I have a little hellcat on my hands?' he queried lazily.

But there was nothing lazy in his ferocious gaze. It was determined and powerful and intent on conquering.

And she wanted to be conquered. So much.

Her gaze dropped to his lips, eager and unashamed for another taste of his superb kiss.

At her moan, his eyes glittered with an indecipherable edge that escalated her heartbeat. 'You look at me with such unfettered need,' he said. 'It is enough to lead a lesser man into dangerous waters.'

'But not you,' she observed huskily.

Because he was above the weaknesses that plagued mere mortals. Even now, he stood tall and proud and domineering, statue-like evidence that he was extraordinary in every way imaginable. And so very confident in the bold manhood that branded her belly through their clothes.

Maybe it was her imagination, and she certainly had no comparison, but the imprint of his girth was substantial enough to set off a different set of alarm bells through her system.

But alongside it, there was also a thrill, sinful and delicious, temptation at its worst. Between her thighs, liquid heat threatened to melt her into a puddle, even as a terrible hunger tunnelled inside her, demanding fulfilment. She gasped as his hands slowly explored her waist, then drifted up her back once more.

Deft fingers located her zip and pulled it down with steady purpose. The sound filled the whole room a vivid manifestation of what was happening.

The noise that emerged from her this time was less of a moan and more of a whimper.

Before her nerves could eat her alive, he was wreaking havoc again, kissing one corner of her mouth before planting decadent little kisses along her cheek, her jaw and then down her neck to the point where it met her shoulder. Merciless teeth nipped at her skin, dragging a shiver that drew a deep grunt of satisfaction from him.

'You are so responsive. I look forwards to drawing even more reactions from this body.'

The soft breeze that whispered over her skin was her first indication that her dress was undone. Still kissing her neck, he slowly drew the emerald silk down her arms until her breasts were bared to his gaze.

Alarm rushed over Niesha, dampening her desire. Her arms slammed across her chest, covering her breasts as she took a hasty step back.

Zufar froze. A thunderous frown gathered on his brow. 'Something wrong?'

She swallowed hard. 'There is…something you should know.'

A faint wave of displeasure washed over his features. 'Yes?' The prompt was a tight rumble from his chest. Even as he waited for her answer, his gaze moved over her, lingering on her shoulders, the breasts she was desperately shielding from his view, down to where her dress rested low on her hips.

She would never have believed a look from a man's eyes could evoke such cataclysmic feelings inside her. And even though Zufar seemed in complete control of his faculties, the look in his eyes rendered her mute.

But she needed to speak. She had to tell him, despite her insides shrinking at the possibilities of what he would do if he found out that she was untouched. None of them filled her with elation.

Esteemed men like Zufar preferred women who knew how to please a man. The women he'd dated before were all experienced. Sophisticated. The history books she'd scoured in the library had even contained sections on how prospective brides were tutored in the art of pleasing their husbands. She knew nothing except what she'd read in romance books years ago. And even those had sounded unrealistic.

Dejected, Niesha lowered her gaze to his shoes. Zufar had seemed aroused by their kisses, but this was far more than mere kissing. Besides, he'd done all the work and now she was terrified he would find her severely lacking.

'Speak,' he commanded, the directive firm and implacable.

'I don't… I'm not…'

'Niesha.' The dangerous edge to her name sent another skitter of alarm along her nerve endings.

She raised her head, compelled by his voice. His face was a taut, unreadable mask, but she imagined she glimpsed hunger in his eyes. That bolstered her a little.

'Tell me what worries you,' he pressed.

'I'm not…experienced,' she confessed with little more than a whisper.

A wave of decipherable emotion swept across his face. Slowly his eyes narrowed. 'I require a better definition of inexperienced,' he replied.

'Virgin,' she blurted. 'I'm a virgin. And… I don't want to disappoint you.'

For the longest time, he stared at her, his eyes a deep bronze that saw right to her soul. When his eyes conducted a searing scrutiny from her crown to her toes, Niesha was painfully reminded that she was naked from the waist up.

'The only way you will disappoint me is if you fail to tell me how that is possible.'

Another fierce blush swept over her skin.

A sound rumbled from him. Once again he seemed fascinated by her blush, his gaze following the tide of pink as it suffused her skin. When his gaze reached her face, he stared deep into her eyes, waiting for an answer.

'I would have thought it was simple enough. I've never been with a man,' she confessed in a hushed voice.

Niesha was shocked by the naked possessiveness that lit through his eyes. A moment later it was gone, but the searing flame of it remained, heating up her blood as she stared hypnotically at him; as she watched his nostrils slowly flare in a show of frayed control before he sucked in a deep breath.

'You're twenty-five,' he breathed. 'And you've never been with a man?'

Even though she was dying to hide from his all-seeing eyes, Niesha forced herself to maintain eye contact. 'No, I have not.'

His breath punched out. A single clench rippled through his jaw before he cupped her elbows. 'Then you will be mine. Only mine.'

The ruthless, irrefutable possessiveness in those words flattened her lungs. She was struggling to breathe when he drew her arms decisively away from her body, exposing her to his eyes. Caught in a web of sorcery he wove so effortlessly, Niesha let her arms drop, trembling before him as his eyes settled on her breasts.

Another rough sound ripped from his throat. 'You are truly exquisite.'

She couldn't have moved if her life depended on it. With his eyes and his words and his commanding stature, he captivated her. She stood trembling as he firmly tugged the gaping dress over her hips.

It dropped to her ankles. He lifted her effortlessly out

of the tangle of silk and lace. She should have felt vulnerable in just her panties and heels but something about the way he looked at her body sent a thrill of power through her. Maybe he wasn't as unaffected as she'd first thought.

She had very little idea of what making love with him would fully entail, but for now something about her pleased him enough to remain before her, his eyes tracing over her skin as he leisurely explored her body.

Abruptly he swung her around to face her away from him, drawing a gasp from her as his fingers circled her waist and pulled her back into the heated column of his hard, toned body.

They stayed like that for endless seconds before he notched his head into the curve of her neck, his lips tracing over her skin. Slowly, his fingers wove into her bound hair, and began to tug out the diamond pins securing the elaborate knot. One by one he discarded them until her hair cascaded over her shoulders and down her back. 'Incredible,' he breathed again.

Between her thighs, heat built, powering up into unbearable levels as he sifted his fingers through her hair, indolently, as if he had all the time in the world. Only when he was satisfied did his hand drift over her shoulder to the slope of her chest.

Without warning he cupped one breast, his hand a warm bold caress as he gently fondled her.

At her gasp, he grazed her neck with a teasing bite, even as his fingers began to toy with her nipple. Her knees turned liquid but he easily held her up.

'Mine,' he rasped hotly in her ear.

Her soft cry gave way to a helpless whimper as he mercilessly teased her nipple, stoking relentless fire in her belly she knew wouldn't be assuaged until he gave her more, more, *more*. Fully attuned to her need, his other hand cupped her other breast, torturing both peaks with expert tugs.

In that moment, Niesha was convinced she would explode. 'Oh!'

'Does my little hellcat like this?'

Her head dropped forwards as flames of hunger singed her whole being. 'Yes,' she sobbed helplessly.

He gave a soft laugh as he continued to caress her. Behind her, she heard the rustle of clothes but feared that her senses, already overloaded with new, unbelievable sensations, would send her over the edge if she looked at him.

So, letting her imagination run wild, she conjured up what Zufar looked like. But even that fevered imagining left her breathless. Hungry.

The driving need to experience the reality of him brought her head up. But before she could turn, he was touching her again, his fingers sliding beneath the waistband of her panties and firmly pushing them over her hips. Just like her dress, they pooled around her ankles and he lifted her clear of them. Then he turned her around.

Of course, her imagination had fallen far, far short.

Magnificent.

Bronzed from head to toe, there wasn't an ounce of fat on his sleek, muscled body. He could have been hewn from marble blessed by the gods themselves, he couldn't have been more perfect. The hard, hairless planes of his chest were woven into a tight six-pack, before arrowing into defined silky hair that framed an impressive manhood that jutted proudly from his body.

Niesha's jaw dropped. He was beyond impressive. So much so her body flamed with a new, intensely searing hunger as her gaze drifted down his powerful thighs to his feet and back again to that place between his legs that she couldn't pull her fascinated gaze from.

'You like what you see, little one?' he enquired with more than a touch of male arrogance.

Even as the question dropped from his lips, his manhood continued to swell. She watched, her breath completely locked in her lungs. There was no way he could fit inside her.

Accurately deciphering her thoughts, he stepped forwards. 'You needn't worry. I'll take care of you, *habibti.*'

He gave her no time to dwell on what was coming. Powerful arms swept her off her feet, laid her down on the bed and he levered himself over her. Then, excruciatingly slowly, he lowered himself until his hard chest brushed against her sensitive nipples.

At her wild tremor, one corner of his mouth lifted.

The wildness intensified when he dropped down and sealed another kiss on her lips, while his hands roamed freely, possessively over her body, leaving no part of her skin untouched as he explored her thoroughly.

Niesha had no idea how much time passed before he began kissing his way down her body.

Sensual lips trailed from her collarbone to the valley between her breasts, dropping torrid, open-mouthed kisses on her skin before cupping her breasts and fondling her. Hot murmured words she couldn't decipher dripped from his lips before he captured one tight peak in this mouth.

A tiny scream tore free from her throat, her back arching off the bed as sensation like she'd never known rippled through her body. He rolled his tongue over her nipple, sucking her deep into his mouth before releasing her, only to start the torture all over again. He repeated the gesture on the twin peak, leaving her delirious and whimpering when he freed her to trail kisses over the skin above her belly button.

'Be calm,' he ordered thickly. 'You have my promise we will do this again. For now, I must taste what is mine.'

When she fully grasped his meaning, Niesha gasped, and attempted to close her legs. Surely he didn't mean…?

'Yes,' he insisted gruffly.

Powerful hands held her easily captive, clamped on her thighs as he slowly, insistently laid her bare.

His gaze snagged hers for a moment, and then his eyes

dropped to her most intimate place. The fiercest, wildest blush she'd ever experienced threatened to swallow her whole as a deep rumble emitted from Zufar's throat.

'Truly exquisite.'

Niesha was spinning at the power of those two words when his head dropped and he slicked an expert tongue over her needy flesh. A long moan ripped free. She shuddered wildly, even as every cell in her body clamoured for more. Zufar delivered, leisurely exploring her as if he owned every inch of her.

Which he did, she thought dazedly.

At some point, Niesha stopped blushing, the blissful sensation of what he was doing to her overcoming embarrassment as she gave herself over to the magic of his tongue. He teased, nibbled, explored, and then concentrated with single-minded focus on that bundle of nerves at the top of her sex.

Just when she thought there could be no sensation as thrilling as this, he suckled her with steady pressure that detonated a volcano deep in her pelvis.

She cried out, her whole body tightening for one soul-shaking instant before her world erupted in a billion fragments. Convulsions tore through her as bliss blinded her. An eternity passed. Or it might have been one enchanted minute. Niesha had no idea of the passage of time as she was fully engulfed in pure sensation.

Gradually she became aware that her fingers were curled into Zufar's hair, holding on tight as the world slowly began to right itself. She was also aware that his breathing was uneven as he trailed kisses against her skin.

It occurred to her that, far from the tightly controlled man who'd carried her into his bedroom, Zufar's demeanour had altered. He was just as caught up in the fever as she was.

And he'd been that way from the moment she'd mentioned her virginity. Or was she reading too much into it?

She had no time to dwell on it because he was kissing his way back up her body. When they were face to face, he lowered himself onto his elbows, stared deeply into her eyes for a moment before he fused his mouth to hers. The taste of her on his lips should have embarrassed Niesha. But all it produced was a decadent triumph.

She'd done something right. He wasn't pulling away. He didn't look disappointed.

If anything, there was an edge to his kiss, an aggression that spoke to a need that matched the one rekindling inside her.

When the need to replenish their breaths forced them apart, his fevered eyes seized hers. 'Touch me,' he commanded gruffly.

Her hands trembled wildly, from the strength of her release, and from the nerves that were resurfacing. But the need to feel the warmth of his skin beneath her fingers overcame the nerves.

Just as he'd done to her, she drifted her fingers down his neck. Over his Adam's apple. His tight swallow and groan told her he liked it. Emboldened, she continued to touch him, caressing the hard muscle of his pecs before trailing her hands down his stomach to settle on his hips.

Zufar's breathing turned harsh and uneven. With not quite steady hands, he pulled her thighs apart and settled between them. His thick length settled between her folds. Her very wet, very needy folds.

As another wave of embarrassment hit her cheeks, he smiled down at her. 'Do not be embarrassed by your eagerness for me,' he murmured. 'Spread your legs wider,' he commanded.

She complied, her heart pumping like a runaway racehorse. The broad head of his manhood nudged her flesh and Niesha's breath strangled in her throat.

'Be calm,' he instructed again.

She forced herself to breathe even as her fingers bit into the hard muscles of his arms.

Zufar inhaled sharply then pushed inside her.

The sharp pain took her completely by surprise. She cried out.

He kissed her, hard and swift. 'Hush,' he soothed gruffly. He withdrew slowly, then pushed inside her again.

Hot tears welled in her eyes as pain rippled through her again.

Above her, Zufar's jaw clenched tight, his breathing ragged as he stared down at her with dark, ferocious eyes. 'The pain will ease.' It was a directive, as if he had power over her pain too.

For some absurd reason, she believed him. And gave a jerky little nod.

As if that action had triggered something inside him, he gave a rough groan and penetrated her to the hilt. Another shaky cry tore free as tears slid down her temples. And then just as abruptly as it had arrived, the pain disappeared.

'Tell me how you feel,' he rasped.

'I… I'm fine,' she replied softly, and then realised she was.

Above her, he continued to watch her with hawk-like intensity, dark gold eyes scrutinising every expression. After a moment, he drew back, and pushed back in.

Niesha gasped at the new sensations dancing through her bloodstream. With shallow thrusts, Zufar possessed her, his eyes watching her every move as he joined their bodies.

Her moans fusing into one litany of need, she shut her eyes when Zufar lowered himself over her. His breath washed over her face as he lengthened his thrusts, drawing even more exquisite pleasure from her body.

'Wrap your legs around me,' he instructed.

An instant after she obeyed, she gasped as his next thrust drew a sharper, more intense sensation from her. With a grunt of carnal satisfaction, he fused his mouth to hers in a bold mimic of what was happening below.

Dear heaven, she'd had no idea it could be this incredible.

The thought barely registered before another charge lanced through her, sending her spinning even higher.

'Oh... Zufar...'

As if his name on her lips had triggered madness inside him, his thrust grew wilder, pushing her relentlessly towards a pinnacle that far surpassed the one she'd crested only minutes ago.

Her world began to tilt again.

'Niesha, open your eyes,' he demanded.

She pried her eyes open to meet with burnished gold ones. Something about that sizzling connection was enough to send her over the edge.

With a strangled scream, she tumbled from the highest peak of sensation, falling into a never-ending sea of bliss that drew tears to her eyes.

Zufar al Khalia couldn't believe the woman beneath him was the same person he'd met only this morning; the woman he'd dismissed so carelessly. He'd gone into this believing he had his eyes wide open to every angle. Not for one single moment had he believed enjoyment would come into the undertaking. But here he was, unable to deny the surfeit of pleasure rippling through his body. He'd bedded many women in his life, but none came close to the responsiveness of his new wife.

His virgin Queen.

He wondered if it was her complete innocence that added to the thrill of the conquest. More than likely, he concluded. He'd never bedded a virgin, never felt inclined to be the first to stake a claim on a woman. To be honest, the thought of tutoring one to please him had been a deterrent rather than a draw.

But as he thrust into his new wife, Zufar thought of all the ways he could mould her to his liking. How he could teach her to take pleasure in her own body, even as he planted his seed in her womb. They were archaic, primitive thoughts that should have shamed him, but only intensified his pleasure as he let the sounds of her pleasure fill him up. She was his in every way. He stared down at her as her sweet lips parted on another pleasurable gasp, her beautiful eyes glazing over as he crested his own pinnacle.

With a raw shout, he let the sweet taste of nirvana sweep through his body.

It was only as he came down from the unparalleled high that the full effect of his thoughts began to settle in.

Shock ripped through him when he recognised how quickly he'd let temptation sway him from his purpose.

How quickly, like his father, he'd been prepared to set aside his priorities to succumb to desire.

How, for a handful of heartbeats, he'd completely lost sight of just how affairs of the flesh had ripped his family apart.

CHAPTER SIX

So THIS WAS what true desire felt like. This endless cyclone of sensation. This exceptional feeling of touching heaven.

This—

Niesha's thoughts ceased abruptly as Zufar wrenched free from the arms she hadn't even realised were locked around his shoulders, anchoring her to the present.

The thought that she'd been clinging to him like a limpet doused her with a wave of chagrin. Luckily, he wasn't looking at her. In fact, his whole body was turned away from her, and he was getting out of bed.

Heart still racing a little wildly, she watched him walk, gloriously naked and arrogantly assured in his own skin, away from the bed. But there was tension in his broad shoulders and back that chilled her with each step he took away from her. Her heart rate slowed, a little of that magic leaching from her, then fading completely as he firmly shut the bathroom door behind him.

Okay, what had happened?

She hadn't said anything. Had she done something to provoke that reaction? Minutes ago, he'd seemed…into it. Even now, the animalistic roar of his release echoed in her ears, making her blush anew at the memory. Niesha would have felt ashamed at the throb of feminine power she'd experienced in that moment, if she weren't overcome by his masculine beauty.

But that was ten minutes and a lifetime ago. The aftermath was turning out to be a different story.

Her thoughts ceased abruptly when the door opened and he strode back to the bed. She was so busy searching his expression, she didn't read his intent until he scooped her up.

'Wh-what are you doing?' she squeaked.

His eyes had grown remote, if still a touch darker than usual. They met hers for a split second before he strode, set-faced, towards the bathroom.

'Seeing to your comfort. You must be sore.' The matter-of-fact tone of his reply killed any softness the words evoked, although his touch, when he set her down in the shower cubicle and began to wash her, was gentle.

Why?

The question stayed locked in her throat as her breath shuddered out at his disturbingly intimate cleansing of her body. Niesha withstood his touch even though she wanted to sprint back into the bedroom and draw the covers over her head. It would solve nothing. So she stood there, biting her lip as he took his time to perform his task. Maybe it was no big deal. Maybe he did this for all his—

No. Not going there, she concluded fiercely.

Inexorably, her eyes rose to his face. To the tight mask blocking his every expression from her.

'Is…is everything okay?' She hated herself for seeking the reassurance.

His expression didn't change but she saw his shoulders tighten. 'Everything is fine.'

Tell that to your clenched jaw, she wanted to blurt. She bit back the words before they spilled free.

Maybe this was post-coital etiquette? Even as she pondered the question, Niesha knew she was grasping at straws. She wanted to find an excuse for the hollow sensation widening inside her but, really, wasn't it her own foolish whims leading her astray, again?

As the thought struck she noticed his movements had slowed, his hands gliding fluidly over her flesh. Breath snagging, her gaze flew to his face. His lips were parted, his tongue resting on his lip as he glided a soapy palm over her breasts. Between his thighs, his manhood was stirring into life again. Niesha's senses thrilled anew, the foolish notion that she'd got it wrong almost making her laugh with relief.

In the next moment, Zufar turned away. With almost cruel movements, he turned off the shower and stepped out of the cubicle.

No. She wasn't wrong. She'd fooled herself into thinking she'd pleased him. That he would want her again. But as he'd told her in the living room, he needed heirs—and lots of them, quickly—if they were to be married for only five years.

The need to consummate this marriage had been an essential part of that goal. It had had nothing to do with her. The future of the kingdom depended on it. Nothing more, nothing less.

Zufar was a man who placed his duty above all else. He'd performed it and now the act was over.

Despite the warmth of the shower, a chill settled over her. Growing stiffer by the minute, she concentrated on breathing in and out as he wrapped a towel around himself, then one around her, before carrying her back to the bedroom.

Immediately she fled to the far side of the bed. Then, wondering if she was sleeping on his side, she started to reverse position. Then froze in the middle when it occurred to her that they hadn't even discussed sleeping arrangements.

Niesha knew that besides the previous Queen's private suite in the east wing, there was an adjoining suite next to the King's for the Queen's use. Was she supposed to retire there now and await further summons or return to the east wing? Her hands curling in frustration, she started to move to the edge of the bed.

'Where are you going?' he drawled, his imposing figure looming beside her.

A furtive gaze confirmed his demeanour hadn't changed. In fact, he looked even more remote. 'I don't know which side you preferred or…even if I'm supposed to sleep here?'

His brows gathered in a dark frown. 'Where else are you supposed to sleep?'

She licked her lips, her fingers tightening on the sheets bunched between her breasts. 'In the suite next door? Or back in the Qu… Queen's quarters?' She stumbled over the word, was positive she would stumble over it for a long time to come.

His face darkened further, his jaw jutting out as he stared down his patrician nose at her. 'Is that what you would prefer?' he asked with chilling terseness.

Niesha suppressed a shiver. At this moment, she would prefer to be anywhere but here, withstanding his cold, haughty scrutiny, which he managed to pull off superbly despite being completely naked. 'Isn't that what is expected of me?'

'What would make you draw that conclusion?' he bit out.

'It wasn't a secret that your parents did not share the same bed…' Her words withered to nothing when his whole body clenched into terrifying stillness.

'In case the obvious needs pointing out, I'm not my father. And this is not the nineteenth century.' If she'd thought him remote a minute ago, he was positively arctic now.

For some reason, mentioning his parents had hit the wrong nerve. Niesha, like everyone else living within the palace walls, had heard whispers of the strained relationship between the previous King and his wife, despite the King's utter devotion to her. But with no facts to back it up, she'd attributed it to palace gossip. As for the relationship between King Tariq and his children, it had appeared civil if not outwardly warm.

But from Zufar's reaction…could it all have been an act? A series of royal chess moves designed to fool the general public?

Niesha had certainly witnessed how ruthlessly calculating her new husband could be when he desired a specific outcome. Her current position was the living embodiment of that ruthlessness.

She strove to speak despite the unease flaring through her body. 'I know that…but we both know this isn't a real marriage.'

Sensual lips that had kissed hers only a short while ago twisted in faint derision. 'I've just taken your virginity, Niesha. We have agreed to have children. It doesn't get more real than that,' he pointed out, his voice deeply husky and painfully direct.

Her chin dropped, every skin cell flaming. 'You know what I mean.'

'Do I?'

Her head reared up. 'Yes!' She lifted her hand to her slightly throbbing head and pushed back the heavy curtain of hair. 'Look, we both know I wasn't your first choice. I wasn't even in the running.' If Amira hadn't been seduced by another man she would be here right now. The thought lodged a hard knot in her stomach, but she pushed it away. 'So it's completely understandable if you want to maintain your private quarters.'

He took a step closer, braced one knee on the bed. It took everything in her power not to drop her gaze to the impressive manhood between his legs. A part of her felt bitter jealousy for his ability to be so confident in his own skin, especially when she couldn't even control her own stupid blushes.

Her breath stilled as firm hands captured her chin.

'I ask again, is that what you want?' Piercing eyes probed hers.

He seemed to be fishing for something specific. Something she had no clue about. She blinked, glanced at the tousled bed. Unbidden, the image of going to sleep in the same bed as Zufar, surrounded by his unique scent, his magnificent body, the sizzling mastery of his possession, and waking up with him, loomed in her mind.

Did she want that?

Not if each one ended with him staring at her with such remote, almost indifferent eyes. But then how else would she live up to her end of the bargain? Surely it was better to remain here, ensure the deed was done in the shortest possible time?

'As you said, the quicker we ensure that I'm...pregnant, the better for everyone, I think—' The words stuck in her throat, most likely because they were far too clinical, stripped of any emotion, and it wasn't a true reflection of what was happening inside her.

But he was nodding, as if in complete agreement with her.

It drove home the fact that she couldn't afford to let her emotions run free. Or give into foolish dreams of this union being anything but the stark bargain she'd struck. She was only here because another man had stolen the woman he'd chosen.

As for hoping her child was conceived in contentment and warmth, it was really past time she put those fairy-tale notions behind her. Not when she was the epitome of what came *after* conception.

Abandonment. Loneliness. Deprivation.

All things she needed to ensure never happened to her child, no matter how it was conceived.

He dropped her chin and slid into bed. 'I'm glad to hear it. And for the record, this is what I prefer, too. Tomorrow the palace designer will contact your assistant with a view to setting up a meeting.'

'What for?' she asked.

'To discuss what you intend to do with the suite next door. You can turn it into a giant dressing room. Or perhaps a nursery. Entirely up to you.'

Niesha was grappling with that when he pulled the sheets from her with a firm tug and began to rearrange the covers over them.

'You've had a challenging day. Tomorrow will not be any less so. I suggest you get some sleep now.'

On that none-too-reassuring pronouncement, he turned away and doused the bedside lamps.

Niesha awoke to the breath-stealing sensation of a stubbled jaw grazing her cheek. Still lost in a jagged dream of smoke and fire and screams, it was a relief to awaken.

It wasn't the first time she'd had those dreams. Along with the soft voice that echoed reassurance in her mind in times of distress, the disturbing dreams had also been part of her life for as long as she could remember.

It wasn't a stretch to conclude it was her psyche grappling with whatever dark shadows lurked in her past. That the thoughts and fears she pushed to the back of her mind during her waking hours transmitted to nightmares in her sleep.

Despite knowing this, she still woke most mornings with a panicked, racing heart and a sinking sensation that her past would always remain a pitch-black, desolate landscape to her.

Not this morning, though. Before her anxiety could take hold, firm masculine lips moved along her jawline to the corner of hers.

She shuddered, then opened her eyes to meet dark gold ones that burned with single-minded purpose. For the longest moment, Zufar stared at her. He didn't utter a word. Neither did she.

Then one hand dipped between their bodies to settle firmly between her thighs. At her gasp, his nostrils flared, the only sign that he'd registered her response.

The moment he established that she was wet, needy and more than ready for him, he angled the thick column of his erection and thrust, deeply and powerfully, inside her.

Her husky moan was filled with need and awe, her senses ripping apart at the potency of his possession.

Even when she realised that the only sounds filling the

room were coming from her, his silent lovemaking was still electrifying, perhaps even more so than the night before since her body now knew what to expect.

Minutes later, she found out that even in that she was wrong, that there was a new determination in his lovemaking that robbed her of the little breath she'd managed to sustain.

He captured and pinned her arms above her head, and then, with caged intensity, he thrust relentlessly into her, the formidable power of it driving home one purpose—ensuring she took his seed and produced the heir he wanted.

The small part of her that attempted to shrink back from such a complete but detached coupling was soon swept under the traitorous melting that radiated from her core and took control of her own being.

The tiny cry she gave as she crested the pinnacle of pleasure was soon followed by his suppressed groan as he, too, achieved his release.

Moments later, he left the bed. She heard the muted hiss of the shower and sagged onto the pillows, willing her heartbeat and the tumultuous emotions reeling through her to slow.

She really couldn't afford to lose her mind each time he touched her. Every instinct warned that would be reckless in the extreme. Already his brief absence was triggering a craving for another glimpse of him, and somewhere in the back of her mind a tiny clock was counting down the five years she'd agreed with him.

What would happen afterwards?

Banishment from the palace? Niesha jackknifed into sitting position, realising she should have hammered out more than just parting with her freedom for five years. Would she be allowed to take her children with her? Or would she be once again condemned to a life of loneliness and desolation?

She firmed her lips. No, she wouldn't let that happen. No

matter what, the children she produced with Zufar would be part hers.

But then he was the King, with endless resources to fight her if he so wished.

She was grappling with the future threat when he emerged from the bathroom. And just like that every thought evaporated from her head.

His thick black hair was slicked back from his face, glistening damply beneath the low-lit chandeliers. His arms and chest rippled with sleek muscles as he strode towards the bed. But it was the snowy white towel, knotted low on his hips and framing the divine V of his pelvis, that made her mouth water shamefully.

She held her breath, unable to prise her gaze from him as he sauntered over to the bed.

A moment passed, then two. At his continued silent scrutiny, she dragged her head up. 'Good morning,' she said after swallowing hard.

He raised an eyebrow. 'Is it?'

Her fingers bunched in the sheets, her heart lurching wildly. Had the new day triggered a change of mind? Did he wish to renege on the deal he'd struck? Was he going to chase after Amira after all?

Why that thought left a pile of ash in her mouth when she'd all but demanded the very same thing last night floored her.

She lifted a hand in a futile attempt to ease the sudden sharp ache hammering beneath her breastbone.

'I ask because you were having a distressing dream. It was why I woke you up.'

Her hand dropped to her lap, unsettling relief weaving through her. A moment later, her heart dropped too, slowing to a disturbingly dull thud. Was that why he'd made love to her too? To distract her from her nightmare?

'Oh, I see. Thank you,' she murmured, because, really, what did it matter why he'd woken her? She'd agreed, without force or coercion, to be his brood mare. So why was the reality dampening her mood?

His eyes narrowed on her face. 'Are you well?' he asked abruptly.

Did he mean the nightmare? Or what had happened last night and this morning. Or generally? Again, what did it matter? She nodded jerkily. 'I… I'm fine.'

He gave a brisk nod. 'You will join me for breakfast. After that, your time is your own, save for the hour or so you need to select your staff. My chief aide will provide you with a shortlist.'

The briskness with which he walked away towards his dressing room told her she didn't have time to linger on yet another bombshell dropped so neatly at her feet. She would think about what on earth she would do with a staff later, when she was appropriately dressed.

As she rose from the bed, she spotted the telltale signs of her lost virginity on the sheets and her face flamed all over again. Glad Zufar wasn't around to spot her embarrassment, Niesha located her discarded dress and fled the room before he could return.

Her walk of shame wasn't any less cringe-inducing because she was the Sheikh's new bride, because of course the palace was wide awake and the usual bustle of people that went into making the place run like a well-oiled machine were up and about. Her state wasn't helped when her attendants, headed by Halimah, who looked as if they'd been lying in wait for her, descended on her the moment she entered the main wing of the palace.

Within minutes everyone knew she'd spent the night in Zufar's bed.

Niesha managed to hold her head high as she was escorted back to her rooms.

Again, a stunning array of clothes had been hung out for her, this time lighter linens and soft chiffons in pastel colours. Unsure how long she had before her breakfast with

Zufar, she declined having her hair washed and didn't linger in the bath.

Twenty minutes later, dressed in a knee-length ivory and navy block dress with a delicate lace waistline fringe, capped sleeves, and navy platform heels, she retraced her steps back to Zufar's private quarters. An aide led her into the dining room, where he sat at the head of a long antique dining table, reading a newspaper.

Even performing the mundane task of reading while he ate, he was a spectacular sight, dressed in an impeccable suit she knew had been specially imported from Milan.

When she neared him, he deftly folded the paper, inclined his head in a regal nod and watched as she was seated. She kept her hands folded in her lap and her spine straight, tinglingly aware of his direct gaze as her tea was poured and various dishes placed before her.

'You left my bed before I could show you the less…public passage from my room,' he said with a stiffness that spoke of his displeasure the moment the staff retreated.

Niesha fought the blush that threatened. 'Oh… I…didn't know—'

He waved her response away. 'It is done. And since you won't need to leave my bedroom again in the future, we will not speak about your precipitous exit. Eat your breakfast.'

Niesha stared down at her plate, trying to summon an appetite, while curbing a bite of irritation. Slowly she reached for a piece of toast, buttered it and added a dollop of jam made from dates and honey. It melted on her tongue, but, where she would probably have groaned with the delicious taste, she chewed thoughtfully.

'Something wrong?' he queried after a minute.

'You made it sound as if I needed your permission to leave.'

His gaze scoured her face. 'Or perhaps I wished to spare the blushes that come so readily to your cheeks,' he retorted.

It took great effort not to lift her hands to her hot face. 'I'm sorry if my comportment is lacking.'

Something flashed in his eyes before they regained that remoteness again. 'On the contrary, you're the epitome of a blushing bride. Legions of people across the world lap up that sort of thing, I'm told,' he said lazily.

She barely managed to stop herself from asking who'd told him. Did she really want to know who he'd been discussing her with? Or whether he had an opinion on blushes one way or the other?

But even as she thought that, she felt his gaze tracking another rush of heat to her face. One day she would master her flaw. Today she had other matters on her mind.

'What you said yesterday, about the honeymoon... Is it still happening?'

Steady eyes rested on her. 'Of course. Why should it not be?'

Because he'd planned it for another woman. Under the circumstances, the idea shouldn't have lodged a tiny stone beneath her breastbone but she couldn't forestall the ache. She shook her head. 'I was just double-checking.'

'If you're feeling a little...bruised because I'm taking you where I would've taken Amira, don't be. Like you, she and I had an understanding. The continued prosperity and smooth running of the kingdom comes first. Which is why this trip was always going to be partly a business one.'

She wasn't sure whether knowing she was so interchangeable made her feel better or worse. Or that he wasn't bothering to soften where his priorities truly lay. 'When do we leave?' she asked when she'd smothered the growing hurt in her chest.

'In three days. We will stay at the Emerald Palace for two days, then leave for Europe.'

He went on to name the other places they would be visiting, places Niesha had dreamed of exploring once upon a time. But the joy she'd felt then was severely lacking now.

She finished sipping her tea, nodding when expected, all the while feeling the cloak of loneliness and abandonment encroaching once more.

Would she ever be rid of this feeling? She was tied to one of the most powerful men in the world, and yet she felt...hollow.

'I seem to have lost you.' His hard, abrupt observation prised her from her thoughts.

Before she could respond, a knock rapped on the dining-room doors. An instant later, a ping sounded on his phone. He touched the screen as the door opened, and his private secretary strode in.

'Good morning, Your Highnesses,' he greeted, bowing low before turning to Zufar. 'You are needed urgently, sire.' He didn't say more, but whatever lay behind his words was enough to make Zufar's face tighten.

Without further questioning, he rose from the table. 'I'm afraid I need to start my day earlier than planned. Finish your breakfast. Your aide will be here in half an hour.'

With that, he swept out with all the regal authority and purpose of a true king.

Niesha deflated the moment she was alone. After a few minutes of toying with the fresh fruit on her plate, she rose and went to the window. Outside the sun was blazing. On the palace grounds, the remaining signs of the wedding were being removed. In a few hours, it would be a thing of the past.

Desolation crept closer, wrapping tighter around her.

She realised that somewhere between last night and this morning, she'd let the tiniest grain of hope take root, fooled herself into thinking that the bargain she'd struck with Zufar would immediately go towards filling the yawning hole she'd felt all these years.

But it still gaped as wide as ever.

A throat cleared behind her and she steeled herself not to stiffen.

'Your Highness?'

She turned. The woman dressed in a sharp skirt suit was tall, statuesque, with kind brown eyes and an easy, deferential smile. 'My name is Kadira Hamdi and I'm your new aide.'

Niesha had never seen her before but something about her expression eased the knot inside her. For starters, there was none of the judgement in her eyes that she'd witnessed in Halimah's.

And even though the woman before her was stunningly beautiful, Niesha sensed no malice in her.

She nodded and returned the smile. 'I'm Niesha...but of course you know that...' She trailed off, feeling a little out of sorts. She smothered her unsettled emotions. 'What's on my agenda this morning?' she asked brightly.

Kadira stepped forwards, opened a leather-bound folder and ran her finger down a long list of items. 'We will do as much or as little as you desire, Your Highness, but I suggest we get your honeymoon wardrobe squared away. With your permission, I'll have the three stylists I have on standby meet with us now?'

Niesha tried to hide her nervous gulp with a smile. 'That works for me.'

Kadira's smile widened, before she reached for the phone tucked into her folder. Her fingers flew over the surface for a few seconds. 'If you're ready, Your Highness,' she said with a graceful dip of her head.

Niesha left the dining room, thinking she was headed back to the women's quarters. But Kadira turned down a different hallway, one that led past many doors and into Zufar's private suite.

On entering, Niesha realised it was the one that connected the previous Queen's rooms to Zufar's, the one he'd suggested she turn into a dressing room or nursery. She barely had the time to take in the fact that the previously fully furnished room was now empty before Kadira was leading her through a narrow hallway into another room.

This one was just off Zufar's bedroom and was a dressing room similar to his. Within the space large enough to hold an entire new suite, sumptuous sofas had been set up against one wall, with half of the closet space already filled with designer labels and accessories.

'Whose clothes are these?' she asked, a little more sharply than intended.

Kadira looked surprised. 'They're yours, Your Highness. His Highness instructed your belongings to be moved here this morning.'

Niesha hid her surprise at how quickly Zufar had acted, took a seat, then focused as Kadira continued, 'The rest of the space will be filled according to the seasons once the designers have made their presentations.'

'I understand,' Niesha murmured.

Moments later, the stylists arrived, trailing assistants pushing endless clothes rails.

For the next two hours she was bombarded with choices and suggestions until her head started to throb.

The sheer scale of opulence was staggering, and Niesha was glad she was sitting down. She knew another woman in her shoes would have jumped for joy at being so totally immersed in wealth and privilege but, in that moment, she would have given all of it away for a crumb of her past, because she knew that even dressing in the most luxurious clothes and jewels wouldn't dull the persistent ache in her heart.

She was about to ask for a reprieve, or a cup of tea, when a sharply voiced command preceded Zufar's majestic entrance into the room. Everyone stilled for a second, before executing a curtsey, which he acknowledged with a sweep of his hand.

'Leave us.' The command was brusque.

The room emptied in seconds. For a full minute he didn't

speak, just paced in a tight, inflexible line that spoke of his military training.

'Is…is something wrong?' she asked, after watching his jaw clench a few times.

He stopped abruptly and looked at her. 'Yes, we'll have to postpone the honeymoon.' The tightness behind his words drew unease but it was the way he loosened his tie a moment later that caught her attention.

She'd never seen Zufar even a little bit dishevelled, and that included the moment he had found out his betrothed had disappeared through a window only hours before they had been due to wed. Now she watched as he released the first two buttons of his shirt with an angry flick of his elegant hands.

'Oh?'

'Only by a few days, perhaps a week.'

'May I ask why?'

He exhaled harshly. 'It seems one scandal in twenty-four hours isn't enough for my family,' he said by way of explanation. Ice-cold anger bathed his words and she watched, utterly fascinated, as he clawed a hand through his dark hair, upsetting its usually neat order.

He paced to the end of the room and abruptly reversed course.

Was it something to do with Amira? Unable to stand the suspense, she spoke. 'Zufar…'

He froze, his eyes meeting hers across the wide space at her use of his name.

Nervous at the intensity of his gaze and the unsettling need to ease his angst, she slicked her tongue over her upper lip and plunged ahead. 'Can…can I help?'

Surprise flickered over his face even as his gaze lowered to lock on her mouth. After a moment, he lifted his head.

'I'm being blackmailed,' he pronounced icily.

She gasped. 'What? Is it about Amira?' she forced herself to ask.

He frowned, then his jaw rippled. 'No. It looks like her choice was definitive. I've seen security footage of her leaving the palace, which confirms she went of her own free will. I will no longer be wasting time and attention on her.'

The cold dismissal sent tremors through her, probably because of the quiet fury that lingered in his voice when he spoke of her. Perhaps he wouldn't take her back but he wasn't as unaffected as his words suggested.

'Unfortunately, the new set of issues involves my sister.'

Niesha refocused, and frowned. 'Princess Galila? What did she do? Is she okay?'

Zufar exhaled another breath full of ire. 'She's in the middle of what can politely be termed as a hissy fit. One she's blindly refusing to admit is the result of her own actions.' He started pacing again. 'Apparently, she saw fit to get blind drunk at the wedding reception and let loose a few family secrets to a complete stranger,' he snarled as he reached the far wall of the dressing room and reversed direction.

'What secrets?'

Zufar eyed her with narrow-eyed ferocity. About to pre-empt a response to mind her own business, she swallowed her words as he slowly advanced to tower over her. He seemed to be weighing his options. After a moment, his fist unfurled and he lowered his formidable length into the sofa next to her.

'You're part of this family now. If this gets out it will be better that you are armed with a response rather than caught off guard.'

It hurt a little to know the only reason he was confiding in her was because he didn't trust her to react properly in public.

But then she reminded herself that she was barely twenty-four hours into this marriage. To Zufar al Khalia she was little more than a stranger thrust into his life by exceptional circumstances.

Niesha composed a nod, her spine straightening as she returned his gaze. 'Very well.'

She waited.

For several heartbeats he assessed her. Then, 'She revealed that our mother had an affair with Sheikh Karim's father over three decades ago.' He took a deep, hissing breath. 'That the affair bore a son. The same son who took Amira yesterday. So Karim not only knows my family's secrets, but he's been made aware of the existence of his half-brother.'

Niesha's jaw dropped, then her heart dropped lower. 'What?'

He didn't respond, letting the shock waves sink in.

She wasn't aware how protectively she'd held the bubble of a happy-ever-after dream until Zufar callously burst it with his words. The royal family she'd spun her teenage dreams around was nothing more than a broken façade.

But…it was a façade that was affording her a glimpse of the not quite perfect humanity behind the thick veil.

Like her…

Niesha wasn't certain why that thought settled deep inside her. Surely she wasn't comparing herself to them? Her past was broken too, and had plenty of missing chunks. And yet she couldn't dismiss that seed of kinship taking root inside her.

'So your half-brother stole your fiancée?' she murmured, shocked.

Anger darkened his eyes, right before a low, bitter laugh emitted from his throat. 'Because he believes my position in this family should be his.'

'That's what the note meant by *birthright*?' Was that why Zufar had wanted to win the skirmish yesterday at all costs? The thought drew another cold tremor through her.

'Yes. And I believe it was a move I neatly countered and even bettered,' he said with throbbing satisfaction, confirming her suspicion.

Had she, and to some extent Amira, been perfect pawns in their game? Niesha was thankful that too many emotions swirled through her for the statement to pierce any harder. Instead she focused on the reason behind his initial anger. 'So what does this blackmailer want? Money?'

Zufar's head went back as if the reminder greatly vexed him. Which it did, if the harsh breath he expelled was an indication. 'Would that it were so. Sheikh Karim of Zyria has enough of that for it not to be his goal. He's after something else entirely.'

Niesha swallowed a gasp. The kingdom of Zyria was Khalia's direct neighbour, with shared borders and a long history of shared traditions. The magnitude of Zufar's mother's betrayal expanded in Niesha's mind. A few things began to make sense, like the haggard pain she'd glimpsed in King Tariq's face over the years.

'Your father knew, didn't he?' she asked.

After a moment, Zufar nodded. 'Yes.'

The confirmation only further shattered her rose-coloured glasses. But on the flip side, she felt a little closer to Zufar even though she knew such a feeling would only ever be one-sided.

'So if Sheikh Karim doesn't want money, what does he want?'

Zufar's jaw clenched tight until the vibrating muscle turned white. 'He wants my sister's hand in marriage. Immediately.'

Her hand flew to her mouth. 'And are you going to give your blessing?'

He shrugged. 'I have limited options. Scandal must be avoided at all costs. At least if they pull it off, my people will be happy. Two weddings within weeks of one another? Anyone would think heaven itself was smiling down on us,' he mocked bitterly.

Her heart twisted, but she clung to her composure. 'And will Galila agree?'

'She will if she wants what's best for the family,' he said curtly.

Silence descended, and then she cleared her throat. 'Can I do anything?'

Again he seemed surprised by her offer. One corner of his mouth lifted, but any trace of mirth was wiped clean an instant later. 'A guarantee that I'll have peace for at least twenty-four hours would be greatly welcome,' he breathed.

This close, his scent wrapped around her, triggering a yearning to move closer, to feel the heat of his skin against hers. Then she reminded herself exactly why he'd woken her this morning and her spine stiffened.

'I can guarantee that *I* won't be the cause of any unwelcome distraction in that time.'

A strange expression crossed his face before he abruptly stood up, did up his buttons and straightened his tie. When he was done, it was almost as if the brief glimpse behind the wall of royal duty hadn't happened.

Niesha wasn't sure whether to be thrilled or terrified that she'd seen the man behind the mask. And she didn't want to examine why. She watched him stride to the door, and then, unable to stop herself, she followed. 'Zufar?'

He stiffened. Then turned, one eyebrow raised.

'What are you going to do about…your brother?'

A fierce light blazed in his eyes. Then it was gone. 'He intended to disrupt my kingdom with his actions. When the time is right, he'll be dealt with appropriately.'

Meaning what? Revenge? Punishment?

'I will see you tonight.'

He left her shivering where she stood, fairly certain she wouldn't be able to withstand another bombshell.

Infidelity. Betrayal. Revenge. Was this what being an al Khalia was like? To think she'd rhapsodised about and envied them once upon a time!

She was still rubbing her hands down her chilled arms when Kadira knocked and entered.

Moments later they were back to discussing her wardrobe for her now postponed honeymoon.

And then it was time to choose from the list of tutors who would lecture her through her child psychology course.

One filled her with dread. The other with a quiet joy.

Niesha took a deep breath and vowed to cling onto the latter with everything she had.

CHAPTER SEVEN

THE ONE WEEK Zufar had accommodated to broker his sister's marriage while juggling his duties before leaving on his honeymoon turned into two.

It could've been because he received a summons from his father, which he kept postponing simply because he didn't wish to deal with Tariq. Their last meeting had ended with stiff, cold words that still rankled, and the simple truth was Zufar didn't know whether he would ever forgive his father for abdicating.

But his sister's sudden impending marriage needed explanation and whether he liked it or not his father was owed one.

Today was the day he'd made the trip to see Tariq. As he'd suspected, it hadn't been an easy one. Probably because his father hadn't once asked about state affairs or even about Zufar himself. He wore his grief like a cloak and looked even more shrunken than he'd been the last time Zufar had seen him. Or perhaps Zufar's unease was because, despite everything, a small part of him regretted cutting his father out of his wedding. He told himself he'd done it for a good reason—to keep the atmosphere stress-free and his citizens happy on his wedding day.

Out of sight out of mind, after all.

The pat statement rang hollow inside him, driving him from his desk and into a restless pacing of his office. King Tariq might have taken his absence from his son's wedding with pained stoicism but he'd taken the news of Galila's marriage to Sheikh Karim worse. The reminder that his father had once upon a time doted on Galila had further unsettled Zufar. It occurred to him that now his mother was dead, perhaps his father would want to reconnect with the children he'd disregarded for so long.

Zufar hardened his heart against the strange yearning triggered by that notion. There was no room for sentiment. His father had chosen his path, his actions forcing Zufar to choose his.

With the smooth running of the kingdom his priority, he had no space to accommodate might-have-beens.

What was done was done. And for the first time in for ever he had a moment's peace. Even Galila had finally accepted the consequences of her actions.

Zufar didn't know whether to succumb to the silly tradition of touching wood or raise a glass of cognac in honour of that rare peace. As to whether it would last was a debate he wasn't prepared to enter into right in this moment.

He arrived at the window overlooking the rose garden that had once belonged to his mother, and he clenched his teeth as the peace threatened to evaporate.

Many times, he'd toyed with having the rose bushes uprooted.

But he'd kept it as a reminder that loyalty and dedication to duty were far more valuable than the false love his mother had claimed to have for him in front of strangers, and the icy indifference she'd shown to him and his siblings behind closed doors. As for the man who'd occupied this office and this throne before him? Tariq al Khalia had been so locked in his obsession he'd failed to see his children, had forgiven his wife's infidelity, even going as far as to hide the full consequences of her actions right up until the past had crash-landed into their lives in the form of Adir and almost destroyed everything in its path. Until any hope of keeping this family together in the wake of his mother's death was gone for ever.

And then he'd fled, uncaring of the devastation he'd left behind.

Zufar's insides twisted with bitterness and a pain he

wanted to will away with every ounce of his being but had found over the years was near impossible.

That too was a salutary lesson, an abiding reminder to stay away from foolish feelings and keep his trust circle to a party of one.

Those reminders had served him well, would continue to serve him well when it came to the subject of Adir. He would need to be dealt with, of course. Zufar's intelligence chief had pinpointed where Adir had gone into hiding in his desert kingdom but Zufar was in no hurry to pursue his brother. Revenge was a dish best served cold, after all.

Plus, he had a honeymoon to embark upon.

The thought of the woman who was now his Queen, his *wife*, triggered a different sensation in Zufar.

The rose bushes faded from view, his mind's eye conjuring up a vision of shy, quiet strength and surprising beauty that clenched a muscle in his belly.

At every turn his new bride surprised him. He hadn't held much in the way of expectations from the woman he'd plucked from obscurity. Even though her lack of pedigree hadn't bothered him as much as it had his councillors, he'd had reservations about her ability to rise to her position. But she'd taken on the role with an intelligence, poise and dignity that had surprised everyone, including him.

Unlike her predecessor, his mother, Niesha was not filling her diary with appointments with designers, magazine photo shoots and gossip-mongering luncheons. In fact, the occasional demand on her time for anything other than palace duties drew the small press of her lips he was beginning to recognise as signifying her displeasure.

The one thing that made her eyes light up was any activity involving children. And when it was time to take lessons from her tutor.

There were other times when he glimpsed strong emotion in her eyes, too, although after their wedding night she'd attempted to hide those emotions from him. Another earthy sensation shifted through Zufar, his manhood responding to his thought.

Those early-morning hours together were becoming an addictive means of waking her up from her nightmares. They might be sharing a bed in order to produce an heir, but that hour before sunrise was fast becoming a routine he didn't wish to abandon.

He sucked in a breath as his blood sang with fire and the pressure behind his fly thickened. His wife might have been innocent when he took her to bed, but she was swiftly gaining the status of the most memorable bed partner he'd ever had.

He frowned inwardly as the reasons for the need to awaken her each morning sliced through his mind. Niesha claimed not to remember the subject of her nightmares, and he believed her.

Nevertheless it was a problem. One that might need addressing sooner rather than later. As was the subject of her past. All his investigators had been able to dig up so far was that she'd grown up in an orphanage on the outskirts of his capital city.

The last thing he needed was for other skeletons to fall out of his proverbial closet, but it seemed her past was a blank no one could fill.

The knock on his door in that moment was a half-blessing, freeing him from thinking about the enigma surrounding his new bride. Besides, he could do with not inviting problems where there were none, so he turned abruptly from the window.

'Enter,' he called.

Niesha entered, and he couldn't help but stare. He took in her slender form, his eyes lingering on the shadow of her cleavage, the neat little waist he'd gripped to hold her steady as he lost himself in her body, and the curve of her hips that could even now be cradling his child.

For the first time since his clinical discussions of heirs

and legacies, Zufar allowed himself to wonder what their child would look like.

He frowned, pulling himself from the brink of useless daydream as she drew closer. Dressed in a burnt-orange dress that complemented her colour superbly, with her hair pulled up into some elaborate knot, she more than held her own as a queen.

And even though he'd availed himself of every inch of her body only a handful of hours ago, a gnawing hunger began to beat a restless, relentless beat through him.

She stopped before his desk, spine straight, head angled as if she'd spent a lifetime learning comportment rather than a scant two weeks, and looked him straight in the eye, sending the rush in his blood higher.

'I was told you wanted to see me?' she asked.

Zufar forced himself to focus. 'Yes.' He indicated the chair before his desk and waited for her to sit. 'I wanted to inform you that we leave for our honeymoon tomorrow. But before we do, there's one engagement today that needs to be filled.' The reason why that engagement had now fallen on Niesha made his mouth tighten. 'I need you.'

Her eyes widened a touch before they swept to the window, avoiding his gaze. He found himself wanting to capture her chin and redirect her attention to him. He blunted the need.

He couldn't afford to indulge in carnal pleasures when he had a kingdom to run.

You have a fifteen-minute window of free time, a voice whispered insidiously in his ear.

He pushed it away, striding to his desk and settling himself behind it. 'Galila's departure has left a few engagements unfulfilled. I've delegated most of them, but I need you to handle this one,' he said briskly.

'Oh, I see. How can I help?' There was a briskness to her tone that drew a frown from him despite his own effort to display the same demeanour. He liked her softer, Zufar realised.

She caught his frown, and a moment later her face was the serene mask she'd been presenting to the adoring public since she first stepped out in her role as his Queen two weeks ago. That his people had taken to her was an understatement. Everywhere she went she was met with bunches of flowers and adoring crowds. But that mask was for the public. Zufar was a little irritated that she was maintaining it when they were alone.

'Your schedule is free for the next few hours, I believe?' he enquired.

She nodded. 'Yes. It is.'

'Good. This is an opening ceremony at a local children's hospital. Galila was supposed to have attended but of course circumstances have changed.' His sister was currently in Zyria, Sheikh Karim having wasted no time in whisking her away the moment Zufar had given his agreement.

Niesha picked up the sheet he slid across the desk, scrutinising the page before setting it back down. This time when she looked at him, a genuine smile was in place. She was pleased, as he'd known she would be when the suggestion of being surrounded by children came up.

Again, he found himself wondering about his own future offspring, whether his son or daughter would be cherished by Niesha the way he'd never been by his parents. Zufar was a little taken aback to realise that hidden behind the gratification of certainty that his own child wouldn't be neglected or visited with indifference was a thread of jealousy.

Was he really jealous of his own unborn child?

'I'd be honoured to attend. I'll try not to let you down,' she said with a small smile that drifted away all too quickly.

He looked closer and saw the faint shadows beneath her eyes. 'They were expecting a princess. They're getting a queen. The honour will be theirs, I am sure of it.'

Her lips parted, as if she was going to respond, then she pressed them firmly together again.

Zufar wasn't entirely sure why his unease deepened. Rounding his desk, he drew a finger down her cheek. 'Are you well?' He noted that his tone was abrupt and felt a little irritated with himself.

She drew away under the pretext of rising to her feet. 'Of course. I had better go and get ready for this.'

He frowned as she started to walk away. 'Wait.'

'Yes?'

He strode towards her, the soft and alluring scent of her perfume tugging at him. 'I've had to add a few more appointments to the schedule on our honeymoon. It seems the lure of my Queen is too much for dignitaries to resist. I'd advise you therefore not to overtire yourself. We have a busy couple of weeks ahead of us.'

Her lashes swept down, the long silky length brushing her cheek. 'I'm glad I can be useful. It is my role here after all, isn't it?' she enquired softly with a smile that didn't quite reach her eyes and a note in her voice that further grated.

His eyes narrowed on her face but for the life of him, Zufar couldn't dig beneath her serene demeanour. The realisation that he wanted to know what was bothering her jarred him hard.

He was the King. He didn't deal in emotions.

'Yes,' he affirmed. 'It is.'

'Then I'll be ready.'

He went with her to the outer door, waved away the guard and opened the door himself. Then he stood watching her walk down the wide hallway, again struck by the dignity and grace in her stature and the smiles and reverence she commanded in her wake. He had no doubt she wouldn't let him down.

The first speech she'd given had been so in tune with his own vision that he'd wondered whether she'd conscripted his private secretary as her speechwriter. The discovery that she'd written the speech to his army veterans on her own had been a stunning surprise.

All of that though didn't explain the withdrawal he glimpsed frequently in her eyes.

Zufar returned to his desk, unable to shake off his frown or unease. For the first time in his life, he had a problem whose solution was eluding him and the reality of it jarred.

He had a wife who was shining in areas his own mother had severely lacked. At the thought of his mother, his mood plummeted. But try as he did to dismiss her from his thoughts, he found himself circling back to the woman who had given birth to him and then treated him as if he was an inconvenience.

Sure, there had been times now fading from memory when she'd bestowed a kind smile and a gentle touch. But that had been a long time ago, possibly even figments of his imagination. As he'd been prone to wondering lately, had those moments of brief affection been because she couldn't be with Adir, the child she'd truly loved?

His fingers tightened on the edge of his desk.

Was that it? Adir had spoken about the letters his mother had written to him in his youth. Letters declaring her love for him. That revelation had driven home the grating fact that all her devotion had been reserved for the child she'd never been able to claim as her own, with nothing left for her remaining children.

The unpalatable thought pierced him but it wasn't so easily dismissed on recollection of Adir's fury at their mother's funeral. Had their mother's love for her bastard son eventually faded too, usurped by the wealth and prestige she'd craved more than anything else?

Enough!

It was no use dwelling on his mother and a fruitless past he needed to move on from. Zufar planted his elbows on his desk and attempted to dig into the mountain of work awaiting his attention. But concentration was at a premium. Perhaps he should've touched wood after all, he mused bitterly.

When his private secretary knocked, Zufar tossed down his pen.

'Your Highness, your next appointment has been cancelled. The foreign minister's daughter was taken ill suddenly. I have sent flowers.'

Zufar's mouth twisted at his relief.

His foreign minister was an obsequious man, prone to rambling for an hour on an issue that required ten minutes. Reluctant to return to his sour thoughts, he rose from the desk.

'Free up my appointments for the next three hours,' he said, even before he'd fully made up his mind.

'Immediately, Your Highness. Can I arrange anything else for that time?'

'Inform my wife's motorcade not to leave without me. I'm attending the ceremony with her.'

His private secretary hid his surprise well, made a quick note on his tablet, bowed and hurried away to do his bidding.

Ten minutes later, Zufar waited in the limo as her bodyguards escorted Niesha to the car. For the several seconds it took for her reach him, he stared, once again arrested and a little stunned that he'd ever imagined her plain.

Sunlight glinted on her thick, luxurious hair, which had been rearranged into another attractive knot. The sea-green dress she'd changed into hugged her slim torso before flaring at the waist, the skirt showing off shapely long legs balanced on designer heels. A pulse of satisfaction went through him as he spotted the emerald necklace he'd given to her two days ago circling her neck.

It was part of a larger collection of jewellery that had belonged to his grandmother, and, even though the emerald was the smallest of the lot, it was eye-catching on Niesha and suited her outfit perfectly.

She was truly exquisite, he observed with a curious catch in his chest and a slowly elevating heartbeat.

When his gaze rose again to trace her delicate cheekbones and wide, generous mouth, renewed hunger punched through him.

He hurried to adjust himself or risk embarrassing both of them as the driver held the door open for her.

She slid in and froze, her eyes widening in surprise and then suspicion. 'What are you doing here?'

'I found myself free of obligations.'

'So you decided to come to a ribbon-cutting ceremony?'

He shrugged and reached out to secure her seat belt. 'I'm in danger of losing my position as the most popular figure in Khalia,' he mused dryly.

She didn't return his smile. 'There's no danger of that, and even if there was, you're not vain, so there must be another reason for your presence,' she said, her eyes growing wary as the motorcade left the palace grounds.

'A compliment slapped away by suspicion. I don't know whether to be pleased or wounded, Niesha.'

Her face remained set in lines that suggested she wasn't too pleased by his appearance.

'What's really going on, Zufar? Do you not think I can execute my duty properly?' she asked with a trace of hurt in her voice.

'I wouldn't have given you this responsibility if I didn't think you could handle it,' he stated, a little put out by the need to explain himself.

'Then why? Don't forget I saw your itinerary in your office.'

He'd kept his schedule free to spend time with his wife. It was that simple. And that complicated, Zufar realised.

'There may be questions about Galila.'

'Questions you don't think I can handle.' It wasn't a question but a flat statement.

For a moment, he wished he'd stayed in his office after

all. It was certainly an odd feeling to know his presence wasn't required. Unsettling still to acknowledge that he wasn't wanted. That brought back memories he'd dwelt on for far too long already today.

'I don't believe I owe you an explanation of how I use my time,' he added, his voice emerging a touch more tersely than he'd intended.

He caught her wince and her pinched face, and suppressed a growl.

For several minutes they travelled in silence. Then she reached into her handbag and pulled out a sheet of paper. 'Well, I'd intended to read through my speech in the car, so if you don't mind…?'

'You may practise it on me, if you wish.'

Her breath caught faintly before a wave of colour flowed into her cheeks. It took every ounce of control he could muster not to touch her in that moment. 'Are…are you sure?'

'Of course,' he replied.

She stared at him for endless moments, then gave a small nod. After straightening the sheet, she cleared her throat. And then she began to speak.

Zufar listened. Watched her. Struggled not to get lost in her husky, melodious voice. Not to get lost in the powerful message of support, the strong empathy and even the self-deprecating jokes she managed to slot in so effortlessly.

It took a few beats to realise she was done, and staring at him, eyes wide and wary.

'You wrote that by yourself in three hours?'

She immediately averted her gaze, looked down at the paper. 'Is it that bad?' Her voice was a little unsteady.

Before he could stop himself, he reached across and captured her hand. 'It's that good.'

She gasped. 'Really? Are you sure? I always worry that I'm gushing a little too hard. Or not enough.'

His thumb stroked back and forth across her hand, a strange need that had nothing to do with sex mounting higher inside him. 'There's a perfect amount of gush. But I would nix that last joke at your own expense. You can keep that one private.' *For me.*

She nodded, then began to rummage in her handbag. He reached into the sleek compartment next to him and offered her a pen.

The smallest smile curved her lips as she took it. 'Thank you.'

A yearning to see a wider, longer-lasting smile hit him hard, but he settled for watching her amend her speech. When she was done, he took her hand again. She made no move to withdraw it, and, finding that he liked touching her silk-smooth skin far too much, he kept his hand where it was right up until they arrived at the hospital.

An excited hum of surprise went through the sizeable crowd as he stepped out. Then it turned into shouts of adoration when Niesha joined him on the bright blue carpet. 'I believe my assessment is proving accurate,' he murmured.

Her smile as she waved to the crowd was warm and open. 'I'm just a passing fancy. You'll regain their total devotion before the month's out, I'm sure.'

He wasn't sure why that transitory statement rubbed him the wrong way. Perhaps it was the reminder that he'd placed a ticking-clock clause on their marriage, one that was already chiming much too loudly for his liking.

He shrugged the thought away and accompanied Niesha as she approached the crowd. As with her smile, her greeting was warm and engaging, although Zufar noticed that she gravitated towards children and mothers with small babies, taking time to draw a smile or laugh before she moved on.

Almost automatically, because such occasions were bred into his bones, Zufar expertly navigated the crowd until it was time to go inside.

They were given the tour, the hospital staff beside themselves to be graced by two royals. Again Niesha lingered with the children, especially the disadvantaged ones, listening to them and reading them stories that drew smiles even from the sickest children.

When the time came for her speech, she delivered it with grace and eloquence, drawing immediate and enthusiastic applause when it was over.

But even as he experienced a satisfying swell of pride, he couldn't shake the niggling thought that, though his wife seemed to be settling into her role as his Queen, perhaps she was also counting down the time until the five years were up.

'You're frowning,' observed the deep voice.

Niesha looked up from the medical webpage she'd been reading, a little startled by Zufar's sudden appearance.

From the moment they'd taken off four hours ago, he'd been ensconced with his advisers at the front section of the stunning royal plane, leaving her with her own smaller staff. Her meeting to go over her itinerary had lasted barely an hour, after which she'd dismissed her staff and found a quieter area towards the back of the plane.

She'd needed a moment or three with her thoughts but had declined Kadira's suggestion that she head upstairs to the master bedroom to rest.

The thought of sliding into bed, with Zufar in such close proximity, sent several traitorous tingles through her body, a state she couldn't seem to block no matter how much she tried.

Besides that, there was also the fact that last night she'd noticed a little spotting when she'd taken a shower. But this morning there'd been no trace of it. She'd debated whether to tell Zufar and decided to keep it to herself for now in case it was a false alarm.

Deep down though, Niesha knew the reason she was keeping quiet was because of the possibility that if she was pregnant, Zufar, with his duty done, might instigate separate bedrooms after all. Since that first time they'd made love, that remoteness had remained, even though he managed to skilfully draw sensations from her she'd never thought possible. He was an undeniable expert in the bedroom, and a huge part of her was terrified that she'd already grown addicted to her husband's touch.

Very quickly their time in bed, especially in the dawn hours when he drew her from a restless sleep, had become the highlight of her day. And try as she might she couldn't find the strength to give it up just yet.

So she closed her tablet and the page that gave dire predictions for spotting during pregnancy, uncrossed her legs and attempted to school her features. Thankfully, when she raised her gaze, his was on her legs. A moment later, probing eyes met hers, and his eyebrow quirked as he awaited a response.

She grimaced. 'I unwittingly clicked on a link while I was reviewing a list of charities. I told you not everyone was enamoured of me.'

It was a smaller, safer truth in a greater list of things on her mind.

He sank onto his haunches, surprising her a little, and then set her heartbeat soaring by bringing his masculine perfection even closer. His clean, musky aftershave drifted over her, sending vivid images of how shamelessly she lost herself in it when they made love.

'Do yourself a favour and ignore them,' he dismissed offhandedly. 'You don't need the headache, and I don't want an overwrought wife on our honeymoon.'

'I like to think I'm made of sterner stuff than that.'

'Then why do you have shadows beneath your eyes?'

She stiffened. 'Is that your way of telling me I look a mess?'

'It's my way of saying you should've taken your secretary's advice and gone upstairs to bed.'

She wasn't even going to ask how he knew that. 'Are you

here to order me to bed?' she retorted, cringingly noting the huskiness in her voice.

His eyes blazed for a moment before they cleared. Rising gracefully to his feet, he held out his hand. 'That is precisely what I'm doing. We don't land for another three hours. I'll make sure you're woken before then.'

Disappointment followed hard on the heels of the breathlessness that seized her. She was so busy trying to hide it she let herself be pulled up and tugged up the stairs.

The bedroom took up the whole smaller top deck of the plane, and was so dreamily, jaw-droppingly beautiful, Niesha would've been completely lost in it had Zufar's riveting presence beside her not commanded her attention.

She barely heard the door snick shut behind her, but she was intensely aware of his overwhelming presence, the dizzyingly broad width of his shoulders as he drew her towards the bed. Her heart began thundering as he plucked the tablet from her hand and deftly tossed back the coverlet on the king-sized bed.

The jacket of the stylish navy trouser suit she'd worn for the flight came off neatly under his ministrations, leaving a cream silk camisole that suddenly felt too hot against her skin. Her nipples were beginning to pebble and that dragging sensation had started low in her belly.

Niesha shook her head when his hands went to her hair, intent on removing the diamond clip holding it up. 'I really don't need help undressing. Nor do I need to rest at all. I'm f—'

'You're not fine,' he interrupted. 'You spent the night tossing and turning.' The grim set to his face told her he wasn't pleased. 'Another nightmare?'

It was easier to nod to that than admit that her suspicion of her new condition was what had disturbed her sleep. 'I'm sorry if I bothered you.'

He dismissed her apology with a wave of his hand, and stepped forwards with renewed intention of freeing her hair. This time he succeeded. 'How long have you had them?'

She steeled herself against the clutch of pain confessing the truth brought. 'For as long as I can remember. I think the only thing that will stop them is a full account of the years I lost before I ended up in the orphanage.' She wasn't sure why she let that slip but once it was out there, she couldn't take it back.

He stilled. 'Perhaps you should consider reconciling yourself to the possibility that you might never know,' he suggested after a moment.

Hurt lanced through her. Her heart thundered louder as she took in his grim expression. Would this flaw in her lineage reap consequences down the line? Make her a damaged queen? 'You think I haven't tried? That I want my subconscious to keep dredging it up every night?'

His eyes narrowed. 'Calm yourself—'

Hurt built up higher. 'That's easy for you to say, isn't it? You've had your whole life documented a few hundred different ways from the moment you drew breath. All you need to do is pluck a book off a shelf and you can refresh your memory on even the tiniest detail. Well, I'm glad you can be so glib about me forgetting my past but you'll excuse me if I don't feel the same!'

'Enough, Niesha. I won't have you distressing yourself,' he commanded with a bite to his deep, masterful voice.

But she wasn't in the mood to heed this warning. 'And I won't have you ordering me about, telling me when to go to bed or telling me how to feel!'

Perhaps it was the reality that she might be pregnant that sent her emotions into free fall. Or the dire predictions for her spotting she'd foolishly looked up on the Internet. She'd done it as a means of alleviating her worry but had ended up even more distressed.

Because thinking about the child she would possibly be having nine months from now, she'd been confronted with the fact that one day her son or daughter would ask about her past. And she wouldn't have an answer for them. One side of their family tree would be full to brimming with generations of history, and the other side, *hers*, would be woefully empty.

Zufar started to raise his hand.

She shook her head wildly, knocking his hand away. 'I don't want your sympathy. Or your directives. I want... I want you to leave me alone!'

He completely disregarded her request, strong hands gripping her shoulders to pull her into his hard, brick-wall body.

One hand was splayed on her back while the other captured her nape, trapping her against his impressive length. Before she could protest, both hands began a languorous kneading, digging with gentle pressure into muscles knotted tight with tension.

She parted her lips on a gasp that never made it because he was kissing her, his tongue delving between her lips to boldly stroke her tongue.

The resulting effect of the outer caress and the inner melting was so wonderfully divine, she moaned helplessly. Then kept moaning as he deepened both caresses, rending her mindless as her knees weakened and she sagged against him.

The floating effect continued even after he'd laid her on the bed and levered himself over her without breaking the kiss. His thighs bracketed hers as he continued to hold her tight against his body, ravaging her lips, flooding her whole being and especially her sex with warmth and desire and so, so much hunger.

This.

This was the addiction she already feared she would never be free of.

With a strangled cry, she spiked her fingers into his

hair and threw herself into the kiss, her body writhing against his.

She was fairly sure he didn't remain as removed or as silent this time. Or perhaps the muted growl she heard might have been the hum of jet engines.

Niesha didn't really care.

All she wanted, all she *craved* was for him to keep wrecking her with his potent kiss, his magic hands. He cupped her breast, moulded her flesh before mercilessly teasing its tight peak.

'Zufar…' She gasped.

The plane hit a pocket of deep turbulence, rudely jarring them apart.

For an eternity Zufar stared down at her, his breathing harsh, his face a tight mask of unbridled hunger. Hunger he mastered before her stunned eyes seconds before launching himself off her to stride several steps away.

'Zufar…'

He rounded on her, his face under even tighter control. 'My apologies,' he bit out thickly. 'I didn't mean for things to get so carried away. It won't happen again.'

She wasn't sure whether the chill that descended on her was because he was apologising for touching her or for the hint of self-loathing she caught in his voice. Both, she suspected.

The reality that their lovemaking was really only about duty for Zufar lanced like forked lightning through her. Every anguished cell in her body wanted to curl up in a ball. But she forced herself to remain contained, to rise and force her weak legs towards the door she hoped led to the bathroom. 'No need to apologise. You were looking for a way to calm your hysterical wife. Don't worry,' she threw over her shoulder, 'I'll be the picture of composure by the time we land.'

With that she thrust the door open, glimpsed the porcelain sink and shower stall, and rushed inside, locking the door behind her.

She avoided her gaze in mirror as she splashed water over her wrists and face. Then, knowing she couldn't go out and face him, not just yet, she braced her back against the door, wrapping her arms around her middle as she fought the tears that were determined to fall.

Niesha wasn't sure how long she spent in the bathroom, but by the time she emerged he was gone. Yet relief was nowhere in sight. Not when the dawning suspicion that, far from being a thing of the past, her childhood crush on Zufar seemed to have resurfaced, and, much stronger this time, now loomed like a spectre on her horizon.

CHAPTER EIGHT

TRUE TO HIS WORD, the incident on the plane didn't happen again. Nor did Zufar make any attempt to touch her either during the night or in the early hours of the morning as he'd previously done.

By the sixth day of their honeymoon tour, Niesha was beginning to think she was one of the unfortunate few women who wouldn't experience the most intimate part of her honeymoon. And while a greater part of her desperately struggled with the loss of his touch, a tiny, self-preserving part of her urged her to count her blessings.

She hadn't been able to completely expel the niggling voice that whispered she was much more invested emotionally than she was willing to admit. Because it couldn't be true. Not so soon. Not so foolishly.

So she pushed the voice away, joined Zufar for breakfast each morning before they made whatever appearance in whatever museum or charity or luncheon they were supposed to attend, where she gazed adoringly at him, waved at the crowd and pinned the smile on her face until the photographers had their money shots.

After that he had her driven back to whatever splendid hotel or villa or mansion they were staying at while he went off to conduct business, and she was supposed to spend endless hours getting ready for another evening function.

Tonight, it was a ball being thrown in their honour by the Khalian Ambassador to Italy. They'd arrived in Venice last night and visited all the main sights this morning. After Dubai, Prague and London, the magnificent sights were beginning to blur into one. But Venice had been truly breathtaking, something she wasn't going to forget in a hurry.

But as she dressed in a sweeping, strapless dove-grey silk gown, overlaid with soft chiffon mesh, into which delicate butterflies had been sewn, Niesha's heartbeat began to thud faster.

Her period still hadn't arrived.

And she really couldn't hold back from telling Zufar any longer. For all she knew, he had the exact dates of her monthly cycle memorised. Was that another reason for his sudden lack of interest?

She tried to breathe through the heavy, unbearable weight that pressed on her chest as Halimah settled the small diamond tiara on her head. Apparently it was customary headwear for all overseas Khalian-hosted functions.

After the second day, she'd given up keeping track of protocol when it came to her attire and jewels and let Halimah take over.

Like now, she tuned out a little as she was primped and made up. But her smile of thanks was genuine, as were the butterflies fluttering wildly in her stomach as she left the suite and headed to the living room.

Zufar stood at the glass window of their villa, his gaze hovering in the middle distance as he nursed a cognac. For a moment she was struck genuinely dumb at the magnificent figure he cut in his tuxedo.

Truly, no man had the right to look this good, this powerful, this rawly masculine. And yet the evidence was right there before her eyes. Irrefutable. Dangerous to her senses.

She inhaled shakily and audibly, enough to drag him from wherever he was. He swivelled to face her, and Niesha wanted to groan with the indecency of his breathtaking face.

She swallowed the sound, curled her fingers around her minuscule clutch to keep from doing something foolish like reaching out for him as he approached.

He didn't speak. Not immediately. Instead, his gaze rested for a long time on the tiara, then conducted a lazy inspection of her from head to toe. 'You look exceptionally beautiful,' he breathed.

The faintest hint of cognac and mint wafted over her face and she wanted to close her eyes, taste him from the source. Instead she locked her knees. 'You don't look so bad yourself.'

Her words sounded stilted, even to her own ears. He didn't react, merely inclined his head before handing off his glass to a hovering attendant and holding out his arm. 'Shall we?'

The sleek speedboat they boarded took them smoothly down the Grand Canal and beneath the Rialto Bridge before traversing a series of smaller canals. Their destination was another architectural masterpiece that took her breath away.

The Chiesa Palace was owned by Zufar but loaned to the embassy for its residence. She knew from absorbing royal history that it had been painstakingly restored from a crumbling heap to its former glory, including the stunning cathedral windows, the priceless paintings that had almost perished during wars and floods, and the chandeliers made of crystal and Murano glass.

Everything in sight glittered and gleamed as they stepped onto the red carpet and greeted the long line of guests awaiting their arrival.

Halfway down the line, her heel caught in the carpet and Niesha stumbled. Zufar immediately caught her, righting her with a sharp look.

'Are you all right?' he murmured, ignoring the guest in front of them waiting to be greeted.

'Yes, I'm fine,' she said, somehow managing to keep the smile pinned on her face.

A moment later, Zufar's hand settled on her back. The branding heat of his hand and the act itself was so unsettling, warmth flushed through her.

She wanted to lean into him, absorb even more of him.

Which resulted in holding herself stiffly until they were in the stunning reception room of the palazzo.

'You…you can let go of me now.'

Tawny eyes scoured her face, as if he was searching for something. A moment later, his hand dropped.

Immediately she wanted his touch back. Cursing her traitorous body, she slid into diplomatic mode, smiling and conversing, and even managing to waltz with Zufar without letting her emotions slip.

But it was a drain on her senses. So the moment they returned to their villa, and had a moment of privacy, she gathered her courage and faced him. 'Zufar, we need to talk.'

His face tightened, and he stiffened as if bracing himself for a blow. 'To my knowledge those words either herald catastrophe or something…different. I've yet to experience the latter but do go on,' he rasped.

'It's up to you how you view the news that I think I'm pregnant.'

As Niesha was beginning to recognise, the wheels of royalty and privilege were programmed to turn so smoothly and efficiently, she barely noticed their motion.

Since becoming Queen, in her every waking moment, she only had to lift a finger for her tiniest request to be put into action. And sometimes even that wasn't necessary, a seemingly telepathic connection of the staff accurately deciphering her desires before she knew about them herself.

So she shouldn't have been surprised when a team of physicians trailed into their living room suite moments after their arrival in Paris the next day.

She was sure that had it not been after midnight when she'd voiced the possibility that she might be pregnant, he would have summoned them to the palazzo in Venice.

The sensation that her world was spinning out of control wouldn't abate. Heart racing, she pulled the lapels of her elegant silk lounging wrap more firmly around her as a suited

Zufar approached where she stood on the terrace, trying in vain to distract herself with the view of the Eiffel Tower.

'The doctors are here,' he said.

'Do we need to do this now?' she hedged, unable to stop the scenarios that reeled through her head, all ending with the unassailable fact that if she was confirmed pregnant, her honeymoon would be over.

True, her supposed honeymoon had been filled with accompanying Zufar to endless engagements and smiling through luncheons and state dinners when she would rather be curled up with a book in one of the quieter rooms of their royal suite.

But during those events, she had a front-row seat to the daily life and work of the man she'd married. No longer did she have to watch him on a TV screen or gaze at glossy, still pictures in a magazine.

She'd watched in real life as he'd negotiated a trade deal over pre-dinner cocktails with little more than a handful of sentences. She'd listened, stunned, as he'd given his frank opinion on a decades-long border dispute between bitter enemies, only to see it implemented days later. Last night she'd looked on, her heart melting, as he'd charmed the eight-year-old daughter of his ambassador.

Who cared that he barely said more than a handful of words to her throughout their engagements? Fine, she cared. No one liked being ignored.

But still, those times she spent with him, secretly hoping she would absorb even a little of his effortless ability to govern and charm? Niesha…liked it, she admitted reluctantly. Watching him navigate the sometimes choppy waters of diplomacy was a sight she wasn't ready to be rid of despite the dangerous waters her heart waded into.

She didn't need to be a genius to know that the moment her pregnancy was confirmed she would be whisked back to Khalia. If he wasn't touching her on their honeymoon she could guarantee they would resort to separate beds, like his parents, on their return. On the other hand, if her pregnancy wasn't confirmed then…

The idea that she was hoping she wasn't pregnant just for a chance to stay in Zufar's bed for a little longer struck her in equal parts with shame—for being so weak—and with a hunger she couldn't dismiss.

'It needs to be done, according to royal protocol,' he pronounced, in answer to her question. There was no gentleness to his tone, only a firm recital of purpose and duty. 'I'm assured it won't take long.' At her continued hesitation, he beckoned with a commanding hand. 'Come.'

Little one.

He hadn't used the endearment since their wedding night and even as she mocked herself for the absurdity of missing it, she couldn't deny that its absence left a small hollow inside her.

Firmly, she pushed that sensation away, then forced herself not to dwell on the fact that his hand dropped to his side when she approached him, instead of reaching for hers as he did when they were out in public.

Those moments were for show, she reminded herself. Zufar and Niesha al Khalia had been hailed as the world's most photogenic and romantic royal couple. She barely managed to stop her lips from twisting.

If only they knew.

So, as she'd trained herself to do, she went to his side, making sure to keep a small distance between them as they re-entered the living room.

There were three physicians in total, two male and one female, all of middle age, and a younger male intern who bowed as they approached.

'I'm Dr Wadya. We will not keep you very long, Your Highness,' the female doctor promised with a smile.

A little more at ease, Niesha acknowledged other introductions and took a seat on the sofa. Zufar took his place behind her, one hand resting lightly on the seat a hair's breadth from her shoulder. When she was instructed to, she removed her wrap, handed it to an attendant hovering nearby, then resisted the urge to run her sweaty palms down the thighs of her silk slip dress.

Try as she might, she couldn't stop her racing heart. Not when she, and everyone in the room, were holding their collective breaths at the possibility that she could be carrying Zufar's heir.

The drumming in her ears precluded her from hearing what was being discussed. In a way it was a blessing because she could temporarily forget that her life was being planned and plotted around her.

Still, she heard the sharp inhalation from the older male doctor, Dr Basim.

'What is it?' Zufar enquired sharply.

The man's pale-faced gaze was fixed on the birthmark on her forearm. He gave a slight shake of his head, but remained silent, his focus on the pink starfish mark that resided on the inside of her arm just below her inner elbow.

She frowned, her heart lurching as she looked at the faces of the doctors.

'Is something wrong?' she asked.

As if dragged from a stupor, Dr Basim's rose gaze from her arm. 'I'm sure it's just a coincidence,' he said.

'What is a coincidence?' Zufar bit out. 'Explain yourself, if you please.' The statement was less request, more directive.

'I don't wish to jump to conclusions, Your Highness,' the doctor said. 'I merely thought I recognised the mark on Her Highness's arm.'

Tense silence descended on the room. Niesha's breath strangled in her throat as everyone remained frozen in place.

Zufar moved, his elegant hand flicking in a subtle command that got everyone moving. The young intern approached with the equipment and swiftly set it up.

Niesha barely acknowledged the process, her heart racing now for a completely different reason. The moment they were done, Zufar dismissed everyone save for Dr Basim.

'How do you recognise it?' she blurted, unable to keep the question inside.

Dr Basim shook his head. 'It's nothing. I don't wish to alarm you, Your Highness. My apologies.'

She wanted to protest that it wasn't nothing, not when his reaction had been so strong. But one look at Zufar's closed expression and she held her tongue. Numbly, she watched Dr Basim prepare to leave.

She wasn't sure why she jumped up and trailed him as he left the living room. But as they approached the door, she knew she couldn't let it go. Something was wrong. 'So, what now?' she asked, watching the doctor.

Dr Basim paused and turned around. 'Your Highness?'

'How long before we know whether my wife is pregnant or not?' Zufar slid in.

It wasn't what she had meant to ask, but she held her breath all the same. 'The blood tests will reveal if there's a pregnancy within a matter of hours, Your Highness.'

Zufar nodded.

She watched the doctor reach for the doorknob. 'Wait.'

Beside her Zufar stiffened. 'Niesha? What is it?' he enquired softly, even though the set of his jaw showed that he was as puzzled by her reaction as she was herself.

'I have some questions,' she addressed Dr Basim. 'Can you please stay for a few more minutes?'

As the royal doctor, he couldn't very well refuse, and she was selfishly counting on that.

Acutely aware that Zufar followed closely behind, she returned to the living room. Then before she could lose her courage, she faced the two men. 'What do you know about me?' she asked Dr Basim boldly.

The doctor's eyes widened, and he slid a quick glance at Zufar. But Zufar's narrow-eyed glance was on her face. It remained there for a long time before he turned to the doctor. 'Answer my wife's question.'

Dr Basim hesitated. 'Your Highness...'

Niesha shook her head. 'You have my word that you won't be in any trouble. I only wish to know what you thought when you saw the mark on my arm. You recognised something about it. Am I right?'

Zufar tensed even harder, then he redirected his gaze to the doctor. 'Did you?' he demanded.

Dr Basim's unease grew.

'Please... I need to know.'

She stared down at the starfish mark on her arm, which had started to throb and burn as if yearning for its secret to be set free. Something inside her told her to push the doctor. Something unstoppable.

Zufar turned to the older man. 'Is she right? Do you know something?'

Dr Basim took a deep steadying breath and then slowly nodded. 'Perhaps I do.'

She lunged forwards before she could stop myself. 'What?'

'Before I emigrated to Khalia, I was a citizen of Rumadah.' He named the small country nestled in the most southerly point between the Middle East and Africa, known to many as a desert paradise, rich in oil. The only other facts she knew about the small kingdom were those she'd read in glossy magazines.

'Go on,' she urged with a voice that croaked a little.

'I had the honour of being the royal physician, right up until...' He paused, a wave of anguish unfurling over his face.

'Yes?' Zufar prodded impatiently.

Dr Basim cleared his throat. 'The royal family were on a private family holiday when tragedy struck.'

Zufar stilled, his whole body assuming the appearance of a granite statue. His eyes darted to Niesha before returning to the doctor. 'You were the royal family's personal doctor?' he pressed.

'What were their names? What happened to them?' she cried, unable to keep her emotions bottled.

Eyes reflecting pain met hers. 'As far as I am aware, Your Highness, a tyre exploded and their vehicle veered off a bridge while they were visiting a resort in Zyria. It burst into flames on impact and the whole family perished.'

She staggered backwards, swaying on her feet. The next moment Zufar was in front of her, taking her by the elbows and placing her in the seat. 'Stay there,' he instructed firmly under his breath.

Turning around, he faced the doctor again. 'I vaguely recall the incident but what has it got to do with my wife?'

The older man's gaze dropped to where she was still absently rubbing at the birthmark. 'The King's five-year-old daughter had the exact same birthmark as Her Highness. It was what made me think that there could be a connection...' He stopped, realising the enormity of his words. 'Or it could just be a coincidence.'

'You don't think so, otherwise you wouldn't have reacted so strongly,' Zufar countered.

Dr Basim spread his hands in apology.

The rock that lodged itself in Niesha's chest threatened to choke her, cutting off the air to her lungs and any possibility that she'd, *at last*, found some answers.

The hope she'd wildly entertained turned to ash in her mouth.

She dropped her head and fought the tears that stung her eyes. Words had lost meaning the moment he'd mentioned the bridge. The accident he spoke of had happened in Zyria. According to the matrons, she'd been found wandering in a ravine in Khalia.

Nowhere near a bridge or a resort.

Besides, the thought that she could be associated with royalty was absurd. Because surely if that was the case, other members of her family or *someone* would've come looking for her?

'When exactly did the accident happen?' Zufar probed.

Dr Basim's gaze grew thoughtful. 'Twenty years ago.'

Her heart lurched again, but she shook her head. It wasn't her. It couldn't be. The truth was, she would never know her real family. She needed to accept it, especially now that she was possibly pregnant with her own child. She needed to look ahead, forge a future for her children without clinging to the past.

She summoned a smile at Dr Basim. 'Thank you for your time. That's all I wanted to know.'

She caught Zufar's frown, but he dismissed the doctor with a casual wave of his hand. She remained frozen in the seat as they walked away. Once again her hopes had been dashed. She would never really know who she was, where she came from or if she belonged to anyone.

Even now, despite her title and the ring on her finger, she didn't belong. She was just a vessel to carry al Khalia heirs.

It should be enough.

It is enough, she affirmed to herself. But the reassurance rang hollow, the pain in her heart not letting it take root. The anguish of knowing she would never find answers wrapped itself around her heart, squeezing every last bit of her hope out of her.

She attempted to straighten her face as Zufar returned, and swallowed when he placed himself directly in front of her. The look in his eyes was intently speculative, drawing a small shiver across her skin. 'What?' she asked.

'You may be carrying my child. The need to discover your past burns strongly but it would please me greatly if you didn't distress yourself unduly over it.'

A laugh scraped its way out of her throat. 'You heard what the doctor said. These…people perished in Zyria. I was found in Khalia. There's no connection.'

His eyes darkened a touch and his mouth pulled in a firm line. His whole body thrummed with tension. 'Nevertheless you are disappointed. And emotional. I may not have experienced what you're going through but that doesn't mean I don't empathise.'

Her eyes began to prickle all over again. 'Thank you.'

He nodded. 'And while you may not believe there's a connection, I will instruct my investigators to dig a little deeper with the new information we have. When Dr Basim returns, he'll provide the additional information we need.'

She inhaled sharply, astonishment bursting through her. 'You want to help me?'

'Why does that surprise you when my investigators already attempted once?'

Her shrug didn't quite hit the mark. 'I don't know,' she floundered, 'maybe because you said you preferred me to be a blank slate?'

His face closed, and then he nodded. 'I don't want any surprises, but I also don't want you to distress yourself over the question of your past.' His eyes dropped to where she was rubbing her birthmark. 'It's a matter that needs to be resolved one way or the other. I wish it to be sooner.'

Because of the baby.

Her heart thudded dully inside her. Everything needed to be smooth so nothing disturbed any pregnancy, now or in the future. She wasn't sure why the offer bruised her. She should be glad he was putting his considerable resources and authority behind the quest to find her past.

Still she shook her head. 'There's nothing to find,' she said flatly, unable to rouse any enthusiasm for the task. 'I asked the matrons at the orphanage for years and they had no clue what happened to me before I was found near that ravine. I was miles away from civilisation and no one came forwards then or afterwards. It's a waste of time.'

His lips compressed. 'With respect, I have a little more clout than your matrons.'

She nodded. 'I know, but I still don't want you to waste your time.'

'Because you are afraid of further disappointment?'

A burst of anger propelled her to her feet. 'What's that supposed to mean?'

'Calm yourself, Niesha,' he warned silkily.

'You're doing it again,' she snapped.

His eyes narrowed. 'And you're getting agitated. It's not good for your condition.'

She laughed. 'What condition? We haven't even verified that I'm pregnant yet,' she exclaimed wildly.

'But you know. Don't you, Niesha?' His voice was like the softest, most potent magic, weaving its way through her as he caught her by the shoulders. 'You know you're carrying my child.'

Helplessly, she swayed against him. 'Our child. It's *ours*.' She had no past to claim, but this…*this* she would claim.

He captured her chin, propelled her gaze to his. The stark possessiveness that gleamed in his eyes stopped her breath. A heartbeat later, his hand dropped to splay over her flat belly, and his chest expanded in a long inhalation. 'Indeed, it is ours. And we will *both* make its well-being our priority.'

There was something so final in those words that she shifted on her feet.

'Enough fretting,' he commanded thickly without raising his voice. 'Stay.'

Perhaps it was the electrifying effect of this touch, or the deep timbre of his voice. But she stilled, unable to look away from the gold depths as he gazed down at her.

His eyes raked her face a moment before he swung her up in his arms. With quick, sure strides he went down the wide hallway into the master suite. She thought he would leave her there, and her pulse rocketed wildly as he drew back the sheets and joined her in bed.

But all Zufar did was press a kiss to her forehead before

drawing her into his arms. 'I've cancelled our appointments for the day. You will rest until Dr Basim returns.'

A part of her wanted to protest at his high-handedness. But really what was the use? He was the King. And she… she was cocooned in warm, powerful arms, her thoughts already beginning to drift away, as if reacting to his directive. With a sigh, she snuck her arm around his waist, rested her head on his shoulder and let her senses succumb to nothingness.

She would need her strength for when Dr Basim returned with further disappointment and heartache. Until then…

She was pregnant. Of course she was.

Zufar's seed had most likely taken root on their wedding night. Her heart sang wildly with a mixture of joy and apprehension as she listened to the doctors' instructions on how to take care of the royal baby in her womb.

She glanced at Zufar as the doctors rattled on about vitamins and healthy eating. Besides the initial gleam that lit his eyes, his face was an inscrutable mask. As for her, she couldn't stop her gaze from darting to the briefcase Dr Basim had brought with him.

It stood beside his chair, offering dangerous hope she couldn't stem.

A noise echoed through the room. When Zufar's eyes narrowed on her, she realised it'd come from her.

'That will be all,' he said abruptly. 'Thank you. Dr Basim, you will remain.'

The others bowed and filed out. Sensing suspense wouldn't be tolerated, the doctor reached for his briefcase. 'Your Highness, I've consulted my old notes. We'll need to do further tests, of course, but the blood type I have on file matches yours. And I've gathered pictures of all royal skin markings including the Princess and your…um… King Nazir's. The one of the Princess is an identical match to yours.'

King Nazir. Her father. Maybe.

A jagged whimper left her throat. Zufar's warm hand enfolded hers, lending her much-needed strength. 'What… what was his…their full names?'

Zufar answered, 'Your father's name is…was… King Nazir Al-Bakar, Sheikh of Rumadah, and your mother was Queen Ayeesha. If the records are correct you also had an older brother, Jamil, who perished in the crash. Your own name is Princess Nazira Fatima Al-Bakar, named after your father.'

Nazira not Niesha.

She had a name. A history. But she was still all alone.

Her cracked heart broke into further pieces at the thought of the parents and brother she would never meet, never share a smile or a joke with. Never confess her worries to or share theirs. 'How did you know?' she croaked.

'I did some research of my own while you were asleep.'

'A-and?' Her voice shook horribly but she was past caring.

'And you are the exact likeness of your mother,' Zufar delivered with a deep, low voice. 'In hindsight, it's astonishing how the similarities could've been missed.'

Shock continued to reel through her. In some distant corner of her mind, she knew she was crying but she couldn't help her tears. 'Because no one was looking for a pr-princess in an orphanage. Or in a chambermaid's uniform.'

Silence throbbed as her words seeped into their very bones. A moment later, Zufar handed her a handkerchief.

She dabbed her eyes, then refocused on the doctor. 'You said you'll need to do further tests?'

'Your blood type is rare. So was your father's. Because of that we kept samples in storage in case they were needed for surgery. Comparing yours to his won't be a problem.'

'But how can they still be in storage twenty years later?'

'The laws of your kingdom prohibit the destruction or disposal of a king's property for twenty-five years in case of his sudden death and no heir apparent. But besides the blood, there are other forms of DNA we can test. With your permission, of course, Your Highness.'

Niesha nodded numbly, shock holding her prisoner. 'I… Of course. You have my permission.' She bit her lip, unable to contain what was happening to her. 'But…how is it that I ended up in Khalia and not Zyria with my family?'

Zufar's hand tightened on hers. 'The place where the tragedy happened was very close to the border with Khalia, separated by a deep ravine. I think you were thrown clear when the accident happened and you wandered off.'

'What? But I was only five years old.'

'I only met you a few times, Your Highness, but you struck me as very determined, even at such a young age. You may have gone to seek help and got lost. Or you may just have been disorientated, the trauma wiped from your memory by the time you were discovered,' Dr Basim said.

Niesha realised then that she would never truly have all the answers she sought. But there was one deep, burning curiosity she could satisfy. She licked her dry lips and nodded to the sleek tablet lying on the coffee table. 'Can I see… Do you have pictures of my family?'

'Of course,' Zufar said, reaching for the tablet.

Seconds later, she found herself staring into eyes that looked so much like her own, further tears welled. Her mother was delicately beautiful, like a rare flower. Her father stood tall, broad-shouldered in traditional clothes. His eyes were darker than hers but, within the depths, Niesha recognised herself. Her soul.

She moved to another picture. In this one, a candid shot probably taken in between more scripted ones, her parents were staring at each other with such utter devotion that the camera was an intrusion. Her gaze moved to her brother and her heart began to break all over again.

Jamil.

Eight at the time of his death, he bore all the hallmarks of turning out just like their father.

Lastly, she located a picture of herself as a child. She wore a deep lavender dress with a white ribbon tied at the waist. The ribbons were replicated in her hair and she was beaming at the camera, leaning forwards with the eagerness and impatience of a five-year-old. Her hands were propped on her knees, and there, clear as day, was the starfish imprinted on her skin.

At the sight of the birthmark, another sob escaped.

'Niesha.' Zufar's voice held a throb of concern, but she waved him away.

'I'm fine, I promise.'

She scrolled through until she found a video interview of her parents. They were about to celebrate some event and had given a few minutes to a reporter. Fingers shaking, Niesha hit the play button. Her father was speaking, his deep, baritone voice authoritative but warm.

And then her mother spoke.

Niesha gasped, a deep trembling seizing her body as she listened to her mother's voice. The voice she carried in her head. The voice that soothed her in times of distress…was her mother's voice.

'Mother…'

She didn't feel the tablet slipping from her fingers.

Or the tight curse from Zufar before he caught her in his arms.

All she felt was blessed darkness.

CHAPTER NINE

SHE WOKE UP propped against soft pillows, the thick coverlet pulled up to her chest.

'What happened?'

Zufar's mouth tightened and his darkened eyes scoured her face. 'You fainted after hearing your mother's voice.'

Memories rushed back, buffeting her with profound sadness. But beside that emotion there was a curious warmth, a lessening of the hollowness that had been part of her life for so long.

Her mother's voice.

It had stayed with her all these years, assuring her that she wasn't truly alone. That she was loved.

Tears began to well again, but she blinked them back, if for no other reason than because she was sure any more tears would make Zufar confine her to bed indefinitely. She couldn't allow that, not when there was so much more to learn about her family. About herself.

Absently, she noticed her wrist being tugged and turned her head to see Dr Basim taking her pulse. She held her breath as he finished up.

'Well?' Zufar demanded.

'She's fine, Your Highness.' Dr Basim smiled at her. 'As long as you take it easy, the episode shouldn't happen again.'

'It shouldn't have happened at all,' Zufar stated with a near growl.

'I'm fine. Really.'

'So you keep telling me. And yet the evidence tells a different story.'

Dr Basim tucked his stethoscope away. 'I'll leave you to rest.'

'Wait,' Niesha rose off the bed, only to be firmly tucked back in by Zufar. Her glare merely bounced off him. She redirected her gaze to Dr Basim.

'Can we... Can we keep this confidential? I don't want anything to get out until...in case it's a false alarm.'

The doctor smiled. 'I'm almost certain it won't be, Your Highness—'

'Nevertheless, I want your word that nothing about this will get out until we have an answer one way or the other. Zufar... I mean, Khalia can do without the upheaval right now.'

Beside her, she saw her husband's imperceptible stiffening. 'You're thinking about me? My people? In this moment?' There was a trace of astonishment in his voice.

'They're my people too, aren't they? They deserve better than to have another bombshell thrown in their laps.'

An emotion shifted across his face, gone before she could read it properly. 'You forget that our marriage ended up being less of a bombshell and more of a welcome celebration.'

'And I'd like to keep it that way for as long as I can, if you don't mind,' she said.

Again something gleamed in his eyes, arresting her focus, not that she needed much to take her focus from Zufar's face. Everything he did, every breath he took seemed to captivate her in some way.

In all ways.

She wasn't sure how long they stared at each other.

A discreet cough reminded her the doctor was still in the room.

Zufar was the first to regain himself by standing and sliding his hands into his pockets. 'You will do as my wife says. Keep the circle of trust small and tight. Report directly to us once you've done your tests.'

The doctor executed an elegant bow. 'Of course. It will be exactly as you wish.'

'A private jet will be chartered to fly you to Rumadah today. We're returning to Khalia tonight. You have forty-eight hours to present us with your findings there.'

The doctor bowed again and left. Zufar crossed the suite to the phone and picked it up.

Unable to lie still, Niesha rose and padded to the window. Through the window of their presidential suite in the heart of Paris, the Seine glistened sinuously in the sunshine and the spear of the Eiffel Tower looked almost close enough to touch.

But this time the view didn't hold as much appeal. Alternate waves of heat and cold surged through her as she wrapped her hands around herself.

'I suspect I'll have a fight on my hands if I suggest you return to bed but I have ordered an early lunch for you and you will eat something.'

She rounded on him, her heart pounding. 'What if I'm not this…this person? What if all of this is a wild coincidence?'

'It's not,' he replied. 'The pictures alone prove your connection. Besides, you were the only one unaccounted for following the accident. You were most likely presumed dead because no one expected a five-year-old to survive such an incident.'

Another shiver danced down her spine. A moment later, warm hands cupped her shoulders, then drew down her arms.

'You are the Princess. It's time you start believing it,' Zufar commanded, his deep voice sending a different sort of shiver through her.

The small laugh she gave held a touch of hysteria. 'I don't know that I can. It all feels so…overwhelming. And so messy for you.' She gave a pained laugh. 'Perhaps you would've been better off going after Amira, after all.'

His hands tightened fractionally. 'I've found that it's useless dwelling on things we cannot change.'

Her insides shrank a little that he didn't issue a firm denial of any desire for his ex-fiancée. Because deep down it was what she'd been selfishly, hungrily angling for.

'As for things being overwhelming, you proved that you can handle overwhelming when you married me three weeks ago.' That odd note she'd heard a little while ago pulsed through his voice, but, scrutinising his face, Niesha couldn't decipher his thoughts.

'If my name really isn't Niesha, do I have to change it?'

'I expect you can do whatever you please. You are the Queen of Khalia. And soon to be confirmed as the rightful heiress to the throne of Rumadah.'

She gasped. 'But…how will that work?'

For a single moment, his jaw clenched tight, and Niesha was reminded that whatever happened to her would also cause Zufar, and more importantly Khalia, huge upheaval.

The very thing he'd striven to avoid by marrying her.

'With very careful strategising,' was all he said before he released her.

Before she could speak, a member of his staff wheeled a trolley onto the grand terrace, where a table had been set for two.

Despite her inner turmoil, Niesha forced herself to finish the vichyssoise starter. She was eating for two, after all.

She saw the gleam of approval in Zufar's eyes as she tucked away a good portion of pasta with rich creamy sauce and French bread. When she was done eating, she placed her napkin on the table and attempted to enjoy the view.

'Would you like to go out?' Zufar asked abruptly.

She returned her gaze to him and watched the sunlight dance over his glossy hair. 'Where?' she asked warily.

He shrugged. 'Wherever you please.'

'I thought you'd cancelled all our engagements.'

'I did. But I won't have you cooped up in the suite, climbing the walls. We're not scheduled to fly for another few hours. If you wish to go out, we will.'

She wanted to point out that they were in a fifteen-room

suite, hardly a space that evoked a coop. But her eyes lit on the tower again, and she nodded. 'I'd like that. Thank you.'

He rose and held his hand out to her. Pulse jumping into her throat, she placed her hand in his, absorbing the tingles that raced up her arm as she let him help her up from the table.

In their bedroom, he walked her to the dressing room. 'I'll summon your attendants.'

She grimaced. 'Can you not? I'd like to dress myself for once without all the fussing.'

He hesitated, then gave a regal nod before heading for his own dressing room.

The off-shoulder design of the maroon jumpsuit came with wide palazzo pants that made it look like an elegant day dress. The outfit was a little more casual than she'd worn for any occasion during her honeymoon but even before she slipped it on, Niesha knew she would love its easy comfort.

She'd watched Halimah and her attendants closely enough to expertly apply light make-up and twist her hair into a stylish bun in minutes. Deciding on simple diamond earrings, she slipped them on. Then she slid her feet into blood-red heels that matched her belt, scooped up oversized sunglasses and a clutch and left the suite.

As always, Zufar was waiting for her in the living room. He'd swapped his suit for a softer pair of grey trousers coupled with a light blue shirt over which he'd worn a jacket two shades darker than his trousers. His tie was gone, in its place a silk scarf tucked neatly into his collar. Handmade loafers completed his outfit and she stared, thinking he could easily have stepped off a magazine cover. As he drew nearer, she saw the House of al Khalia monogram embroidered on his jacket pocket. She wanted to say that he didn't need it.

Every inch of him shouted his regal status.

In the lift down, he drew a pair of sunglasses from his pocket and slid them on. The moment they stepped out into the sunny reception, Niesha knew what she wanted to do.

'Can we walk for a while?'

'Not unless you want to be mobbed.' The ever-present paparazzi loitered outside.

She grimaced. 'Then I'd like to just drive around, if you don't mind?'

He nodded. 'It will be as you wish.'

They set off in a smaller convoy.

From the back of the limo, she tried to forget her turmoil and just bask in the sights. But it proved impossible.

Strong hands captured her twisting fingers. 'It will be all right.'

Different words, said by a different voice but both owned by people she knew she was emotionally heavily invested in.

She would never get to meet her mother or hear the real-life version of the sweet words she'd whispered in her ear.

But Zufar was right here, a temptation she'd told herself to resist the moment she'd set eyes on him as a romantic teenager with her head in the clouds. Temptation she knew could decimate her when she took his name and accepted him into her body.

His tempting words were the ones she needed to be wary of because Zufar would never see her as anything other than a replacement for another woman. A woman he hadn't cared about enough to go after. If he'd found it so easy to discard Amira, what hope did she have of ever finding anything deeper with him?

When her feelings grew too much to contain she tried to prise her hands away. He held on tight. 'Tell me what troubles you.'

'I'm scared,' she blurted before she could stop herself. But self-preservation stopped her from expounding.

To her surprise, he nodded. 'I know. You'll recall I, too, have been in your shoes.'

'You've been pregnant?'

He looked startled for a moment, before his mouth curved

in a smile. It was the first genuine full smile she'd seen on his face. And it floored Niesha completely.

'No, that is a privilege you will enjoy on your own.'
Smooth.

So smooth, she felt a little of her agitation drift away. And when he meshed his fingers with hers and drew her head onto his shoulder, she went with her insides melting, her heart pounding and her head telling her she was just ten kinds of fool for leaving herself wide open for further heartache.

'Niesha. Wake up.'

The low, deeply voiced command tickled the shell of her ear.

With a small shiver, she blinked awake, and realised she was draped all over Zufar.

She jumped but didn't get very far as the arm clamped around her tightened. She raised her gaze, about to murmur an apology for falling asleep on him, when she noticed where they were. 'We're at the airport?'

'Yes. You fell asleep in the car. After we drove around Paris for two hours I thought it best to come straight to the airport.'

'I've been asleep for two hours?'

Tawny eyes gleamed at her. 'Clearly you needed the rest.'

The thought that he'd driven around with her even though she'd fallen asleep shouldn't have touched her, not after the stern warning her head had issued her heart.

And yet, she found herself softening against him, the decadent desire to melt into his warmth sucking at her. She told herself she would only give in for a minute. Or two.

When his gaze dropped to her mouth, she added one more.

But the kiss she yearned for never came.

Without taking his eyes from her, he gave a casual flick

of his wrist, and the door was thrown open, ending the private moment that only she had wanted more of, it seemed.

Zufar stepped out, and held out a courteous hand for her.

Niesha placed her hand in his, struggling to reconcile the man who'd driven around the streets of Paris just so she could take a nap with the man who had clearly seen her invitation and declined it.

The baby.

Of course, it was all to do with the baby. How could she have forgotten?

At the first opportunity, she drew her hand from his, vowing never to repeat her mistake. Besides, with her future in turmoil, the earlier she learned to stand on her own two feet, the better.

She ignored the sharp look he sent her and hurried to board the plane.

For the duration of the flight, she stayed in the bedroom with her tablet for company. By the time they landed in Khalia, she'd devoured everything she could find on her family. And shed a few tears along the way.

Zufar scrutinised her face as they stepped out of the plane but didn't comment. The ride to the palace was also conducted in silence, but when they approached their bedroom, she couldn't hold back any more.

'So what happens now?'

'Once we have irrefutable confirmation, my special council will meet with yours and we'll take it from there.'

It wasn't what she'd wanted to know, but discussing their bedroom arrangements when two kingdoms stood to be plunged into uncertainty felt trivial.

'What do you mean, take it from there?'

He shrugged. 'You will appreciate that this is a unique situation for both of us. We'll need to strategise the best way forwards.'

'You're speaking but not really saying much.'

He dragged a hand through his hair, the first sign that the

circumstances they found themselves in weren't straightforward. 'I can't give you an answer I don't have. Not without further investigation.'

'Investigation?' she echoed.

'All signs point to the fact that Rumadah needs its rightful ruler back on the throne. It hasn't had one for two decades.'

'Because a new one couldn't be crowned for twenty-five years,' she added, recalling what she'd read about her country's constitution on the plane. According to the laws, a missing heir to the throne couldn't be ruled out until twenty-five years had passed. In that time a twelve-member council, the same that had served the last King, would rule the kingdom.

In another five years, she would've lost her birthright.

But was it one she wanted, if it meant what she was beginning to fear? Because how could she claim her Rumadian birthright and still remain Queen of Khalia? Zufar's wife?

Her insides shook at the mere thought of walking away from him. It seemed more impossible now than ever. Because the loss of her family wasn't the only reason she'd cried on the plane. She'd also cried because she'd finally accepted that she was in love with Zufar. And painfully accepted that that love would never be reciprocated.

'Perhaps we shouldn't jump the gun just yet. This could all be an elaborate hoax,' she said, more in hope than expectation.

The look in Zufar's eyes told her the same. 'A few days ago I urged you to reconcile yourself to never discovering your past. That landscape has changed and delivered everything you hoped for. Perhaps you should reconcile yourself to this blessing?'

She flinched at the trace of censure in his voice. Before she could respond, he turned from her. 'I need to catch up on a few engagements. Don't wait up for me.'

The last statement was both a blessing and a curse. He

intended to find her in their bed when he deigned to return but he didn't care whether she was awake or asleep now that she was pregnant?

Niesha was rubbing at that agonising spot in her chest when the doors opened again and Halimah and the rest of her retinue descended on her.

She forced herself to respond that, yes, she was happy to be back, and that, yes, her honeymoon had been everything she'd dreamed about as they helped her undress and ran a bath for her. She withstood their attention for as long as she could, until she felt as if her face would break if she smiled one more time.

They respectfully retreated when she asked for privacy. With a sigh, she sank into her lavender and jasmine-scented bath. Immediately, a few dozen questions crowded her mind.

Zufar had suggested she be grateful to have her birthright back. But would everyone else feel the same? Would her people even want her once the inevitable announcement was made?

With no definitive answers in hand, she ate a light dinner and went to bed early.

If Zufar came to bed at all, he was gone when she woke, and when Kadira arrived, she was told His Highness had instructed her workload be kept light until further notice.

If he wanted to set tongues wagging about a possible pregnancy, he couldn't have done a better job, she thought with a bite of irritation. All day, Kadira slid smiling, speculative glances at her. And Halimah and her attendants joined in as they helped her prepare for bed.

Again, she didn't see Zufar, even when she woke in the middle of the night.

When she next woke, it was with a heavy, pounding heart.

Today was the day.

Dr Basim had been given forty-eight hours. Whatever happened, she would have a choice to make.

* * *

His wife, his Queen, who carried his heir, was herself an heiress to another kingdom. Even though Zufar had known it was inevitable the moment he'd clapped eyes on the pictures of Niesha's parents, he wasn't ashamed to admit a small part of him had hoped that the information would be proved wrong.

Dr Basim and a team of doctors in Rumadah had proved conclusively that Niesha, or Nazira, as she was being addressed in his conference room, was the rightful heiress to the Rumadian throne.

Not that he'd wished for her past to remain a closed chapter to her, but this situation was not at all what he'd anticipated or remotely wanted.

With their reports, however, another bombshell had been dumped into his lap. One that demanded immediate remedy.

He watched the councillors who had accompanied Dr Basim bow and scrape before Niesha. Watched her shy, smiling acknowledgement, and the eagerness with which she absorbed every morsel of information they delivered to her.

For the most part, her seeming return from the dead was very welcome news indeed. And with each moment that passed, he could see the wheels turning in the councillors' minds regarding how to swiftly reclaim their Queen.

A few cast furtive glances towards him, wary of his silence.

The simple truth was that to vocalise his true feelings would've shocked them all. The churning in his chest that had begun long before Niesha's past had been revealed, and which had grown considerably since the revelation, exploded into gut-clenching proportions as he watched them slowly sink their claws into the woman he had claimed for himself.

Or attempted to claim.

Behind his back, his fists curled, his whole body tensed

up in battle mode. The thundering of his blood hissed that, regardless of his acceptance of her birthright, he wasn't about to let her go that easily.

You may not have a choice.

He ignored the voice that had been growing louder. By his own bargain, he'd placed an exit clause on their marriage. Whether he chose to accept it or not, a termination date could very well be on its way back to bite him.

He noticed his own councillors sending him questioning looks, but for the first time in his life, he didn't have ready answers available. He hadn't had them back in Paris when the thought had first occurred to him that he might lose Niesha.

'Your Serene Highness, we will need to make an announcement soon. When can we expect you to return to Rumadah?'

This came from the chief councillor, a cunning old man who'd been eyeing Zufar since they entered his conference room.

'Return?' Niesha echoed.

'Of course. Once the announcement is made, your people will wish to see you, to reassure themselves that you are well.'

'She is well, as you can very well see.' Zufar attempted to modulate his voice, but knew he hadn't succeeded when more eyes turned wary.

'Of course, Your Highness, and we will be grateful to you and to your people for ever for taking such good care of our Queen.'

'But…?' he trailed softly. There was a *but*. It was written on all their faces.

'But…with a thousand pardons, her rightful place is back in Rumadah. Her people need her.'

Simple words.

Heavy, life-altering words, as he very well knew.

Not too long in the recent past his own councillors had

pleaded with him in the same manner, urging him to save Khalia after his father's abdication.

Even now, his people needed him. Khalia might have regained her rightful position as a powerful state to be reckoned with but Rumadah had merely trundled along, no one stepping up to make the bold decisions that would take it from a game player to a shot caller.

Without a bold leader to ensure its considerable power was harnessed in the right way, it risked falling into apathy or, worse, into enemy hands. From the research he'd done himself, Zufar knew that the oil-rich country had only stayed on an even course because of its substantial deposits.

A glance around the room of ageing councillors delivered the hard truth that it was only a matter of time before the situation altered for the worse. They needed a true leader, a visionary, who would rule with a firm but compassionate hand.

Someone like Niesha.

His wife.

His Queen.

The mother of his unborn child.

It was impossible.

It was also inevitable that a decision needed to be taken. And soon.

He turned and looked at the two dozen people in the room.

Niesha sat at the head of the table, nodding and making comments where necessary, but he knew her head wasn't in the game. How could it be, when they were all speaking at once?

Over their heads, her gaze snapped up. Wide amethyst eyes met and locked on his, and something deep and profound moved in his chest. *That* sensation had also been escalating, confounding him at the oddest moments.

But far too soon, her gaze dropped away from his as she turned to address the man seated to her right. Whatever he was saying to her wasn't good because after a few minutes she paled a little, even as she nodded.

Enough.

Realising he hadn't vocalised the word, he spoke again. 'Enough.' When he had their attention, he went to Niesha, placed his hand at the back of her chair. 'Give us the room,' he ordered, stamping his tone with implacable authority. 'I wish to speak to my wife in private.'

The councillors looked a little surprised, but one by one they filed out.

'Thank you. I needed a break,' Niesha murmured.

'Then you should've asked for one.' Realising his voice was still brusque, he modified it. 'This must be overwhelming for you.'

'Despite their collective age, they're like a pack of over-zealous wolf pups, all with sharp teeth they don't know can hurt.'

Her description couldn't have been more accurate. He also remembered that pups grew into adulthood, some into alphas who relished a challenge. 'The trick is to train them early, show them who's in charge. Yours doesn't need to be the loudest voice in the room, but it needs to be the final authority.'

The look she gave him was filled with gratitude. As much as he welcomed it, Zufar yearned for another look. One whose absence made the band around his chest tighter by the day.

'I need to write these things down, don't I? To remember them for later.'

'You won't need to. You're their Queen. Leadership was bred into you from birth.' And soon, if her councillors succeeded, she would take it and herself away from him.

She sighed and lifted a hand to rub her temple. A moment later, she straightened her spine, a resolute look settling on her face.

How could he not have spotted signs of her breeding from

the moment they met? Royalty was stamped into every fibre of her being, every drop of her blood.

'You wanted to talk to me?'

Words eluded him for a moment as the combination of delicate jaw, sensual mouth and alluring eyes flattened him. But he forced himself to focus. He'd cleared the room to give her breathing space but there was another subject that needed discussing. 'Dr Basim hasn't told them you're pregnant. Is he planning on telling them?'

It would be one way to force her quicker return to Rumadah. A risen-from-the-dead queen would please her people. One expecting a royal heir would be euphoric.

He wondered whether it was a card she intended to play.

She laughed. 'I've barely managed to get their names right.'

Her self-effacing response didn't please him. 'It's customary to keep news of pregnancy under wraps for the first trimester,' he pressed.

She blinked, then rose and went to stand before the floor-to-ceiling windows. Framed against it, she looked almost delicate. But her spine was straight, her resolve absolute. 'I'll tell them when I'm ready.'

Relief and the breath he hadn't realised he held burst through him. She burst it a fraction of a second later.

'Half of the advisers are returning tomorrow. The other half leave on Friday. They want me to accompany them when they return to Rumadah.'

When had these arrangements been made? While he'd been tuned out, feeling sorry for himself? 'Friday is three days away,' he growled. 'We just returned from our honeymoon. I can't leave again so soon.' Especially when he didn't have an answer on how to stop the freight train he could sense heading his way.

Her lashes swept down, veiling her expression. 'I understand. I'm sure I'll be fine on my own,' she said.

That vice threatened to squeeze every last breath out of him. 'I see. And how long will you be gone?'

'Three days. Maybe four.'

The prompt answer froze the blood in his veins. 'Was that the plan all along?'

Her eyelashes lifted. 'I beg your pardon?'

'Use my duty to my people against me?'

She gasped. 'Zufar, I don't know what you're talking—'

He stared down at her, the inevitability of loss continuing to suffocate him. 'And what happens after that?'

Her eyes widen. 'What do you mean?'

'Do you intend to commute back and forth between your kingdom and mine?'

Her forehead gathered in a delicate frown. Then she shrugged. 'This is all new. I don't have the answers, Zufar. But I think you know that I owe it to my people to at least let them know who I am.'

A part of him felt shame for her hurt, but it wasn't enough to overcome the terrible anguish scything its way through him. He despised the feeling. Enough for him to approach her, despite his vow to refrain from touching her.

She had enough on her plate without his ever-growing hunger for her saturating the atmosphere between them. It was a decision he'd made in Prague after watching her sleep, seeing the shadows beneath her eyes, and knowing that he was partly to blame for it.

For the first two weeks of their marriage, he'd never let a night pass without making love to her, his need so great it had confounded him even then. That need had grown into unbearable proportions by the time they'd arrived in Prague.

When the demands of his duties had kept him way from the marriage bed for that first night, he'd watched her for signs that she'd missed him the next morning. There had been none.

The idea that the carnal weakness was on his part alone had brought him up short. And when, night after night, Niesha had made no attempts to reach for him, he'd had his answer. He'd roped her into a bargain to provide him with an heir, but was that all it was for her? Was that the only reason for her welcoming him into her body?

Perhaps that was the reason she could speak so freely of leaving him behind for four days.

'If that's the plan, you'll need to rethink it because it won't be sustainable,' he bit out.

She paled a little, but continued to hold his gaze boldly. 'What are you saying, Zufar?'

'I'm saying that even the shortest of separations has a habit of growing. It's not healthy for any marriage. My parents led separate lives, my mother lived in the east wing and my father lived in the west. Even under the same roof, their marriage was a sham. I do not wish this for myself.'

'I agree, but—'

'I know what I want and it certainly did not involve living in separate countries.'

'So you wish me to renounce my birthright?' she demanded with a hint of tears in her eyes.

Ice gripped his nape hard. 'I'm saying that hard choices need to be made.'

'And you want me to be the one to make them?' Her eyes brimmed, her mouth trembling for one second before she pursed it.

He wanted to lift his hand to her face, brush away her tears, but that would be giving in. For as long as he could remember his father had given in to his mother's every whim, making himself deeply miserable at every turn. Zufar had vowed never to leave himself that vulnerable. But…was it already too late?

'We had an agreement,' he threw at her.

She took in a heavy, shaky breath. 'And I am not reneging on it. I'm only trying to find a way—'

'A way to do what?' He knew he was being unreasonable, but for the life of him, he couldn't stop. He was floundering, hurting her, hurting himself in the process but there didn't seem to be a life raft in sight, and with every moment that passed his anguish strangled him, making him hold tight to the one thing that he knew he couldn't hold onto.

Niesha.

'You promised me five years,' he repeated, as if that would make her fall at his feet, and give him everything he wanted. When really, a greater part of him wanted it to be the other way round. But how could he, without leaving himself desperately exposed?

Slowly her regal head lifted, her eyes condemning him, challenging him to remain obstinate, to keep standing in her way. 'I don't recall signing any piece of paper saying you owned me for five years.'

He wasn't sure why that statement both shocked and made him proud. He had already admitted his flaw in striking that bargain. A part of him applauded her for jumping through that wide loophole.

'I'm aware that all we had was a verbal agreement,' he stated. 'But I still wish you to stand by it.'

Her shoulders sagged a little, but in the next moment she pulled herself back up. 'Don't push me, Zufar. You might not like the consequences.' After a moment, her gaze softened. 'But if you let me work this out on my own, perhaps we can find a solution that works for both of us.'

The only solution he wanted was her here under his roof, in his bed, at his side, bearing his children, loving them the way his mother had never loved him.

'Three days. That's all I ask. Surely you can give me that?'

Could he? Already he felt emptier than he'd ever felt in his life, and she was standing right there in front of him.

Zufar didn't know where he found the strength to nod. 'Of course. Go with my blessing.'

The realisation terrified him that despite everything he'd said he meant it. Because wasn't that something his father would have done? Ripped out his organs if his mother had asked?

'Thank you,' his Queen said, her gaze searching his.

For signs of his obsession, perhaps?

He clenched his jaw, attempting to neutralise his expression. 'You'll let me know of your travel plans once they're finalised?'

She nodded.

He left her in the conference room, calmly walked out even though he wanted to bellow to the skies; to rip himself inside out just so he could reach the pain inside that was decimating him. The walk to his office was the longest he'd ever taken.

Once he was there, he strode to his desk and sank into the chair.

He couldn't even take three days of separation. How would he take a lifetime? Because he knew that was coming too. Unless something changed drastically, Niesha would be out of his reach even before their child was born.

He slammed his fist on the desk, his thoughts churning a thousand miles an hour. Sunset came and went and still he had no solution. When the door to his office opened without announcement from his private secretary, he nearly snarled.

He managed to bite it back when he saw Malak framed in the doorway.

'I'm hearing all sorts of juicy gossip about you and your new bride, brother,' Malak drawled.

'You know very well what's happening. Your private secretary received the same memo I sent to Galila and Father.'

Malak shrugged as he strolled over to the drinks cabinet and poured two fingers of cognac into crystal glasses. Returning to Zufar's desk, he slid one across the smooth surface. Then he sprawled himself in the chair across the desk.

'I have to say, your new wife is turning out to be quite the surprise, isn't she? I admit, I wasn't very impressed in the beginning, but—'

'Watch yourself, brother,' Zufar warned.

Malak held up one hand as he sipped his drink. 'No disrespect meant, brother. But I'm not the one who harped on about wanting some peace and quiet around here, only to turn around and start tossing dynamite like it was a party favour.'

'Did you come here to make a specific point or are you just here to annoy me? If it's the latter, then bravo, you are succeeding.'

Malak laughed. 'I came to offer you whatever help you need. I may be the selfish playboy the tabloids like to portray me as, but underneath this handsome exterior lives a semi-decent heart that's bleeding for you right now.'

The words were laced with so much amusement, Zufar's irritation mounted. 'You claim you want to help, but all I see is you sitting there drinking my cognac.'

Malak waved a gracious hand. 'Tell me what you need and I will do my best to give you a simple yay or nay.'

Zufar stared into the amber shadows of his drink, two words ticking over and over in his head. *Three days.* He'd agreed to three days. Would she come back? What would he do if she didn't?

'Or I can leave you to brood into your drink?' Malak suggested.

Zufar stood and paced to the window, that feeling of being turned inside out surging to breaking point. He tossed back his drink, then his gaze dropped to the rose garden below his window. He stared at the perfect flowers, his thoughts churning.

After several minutes, his brother joined him, his gaze zeroing in on the same place. 'Why didn't she love us?' Malak asked in a thick, heavy voice.

Zufar was unprepared for the question, just as he was unprepared for the canon of the pain that shot through him. He'd thought he was over that, or at least had suppressed it enough not to feel the agony of his mother's indifference any more.

He shrugged. 'Because she was incapable of it. Ultimately, she couldn't love anyone but herself.' Perhaps it was a flaw he needed to come to terms with, and move on.

Niesha wasn't like that though.

She loved children. She would love their child with the same passion with which she loved his people. The same devotion with which she loved her people enough to threaten to walk away from him and his crown to serve them again. That kind of selflessness was humbling. Inspiring.

How could he stop her from pursuing that, from giving to people who would love her back, and welcome her with open arms the way his people had done?

Malak sighed. 'I wish he'd done something.'

'Who?'

'Father. I wish he'd made a decision one way or the other. Demanded that she love him and us, or leave her. Instead of trailing after her all those years. Instead of making us live each dreadful moment with him.'

'I don't think it was that simple,' Zufar found himself explaining. 'Maybe he was left with very little choice.'

His brother sneered, turned and started walking away. 'Whatever. I'm over it. Anyway, it's been a good talk. If you decide you need me after all, you know where to find me.'

Zufar barely heard him leave. And as he stared into the bottom of his glass, he found his thoughts veering in another direction.

To his father.

CHAPTER TEN

NIESHA STOOD IN front of the plane door, waiting for the attendant to open it. Unlike the flight to Europe, this one had been short and nerve-shredding, her emotions swinging between what awaited her in Rumadah and what she'd left behind.

The last three days had been alternately perfect and horrendous. The coordinated news of her real identity had been greeted with another wave of happy frenzy across the world, the short interview she'd given to explain her unfortunate absence accessed over a billion times online. That had been her public life.

In private, she'd remained in turmoil.

Even though he'd given her his blessing, Zufar had stayed away from her, and in the rare moments when they'd met, his gaze had chilled her. He still came to their bed, but it was only to sleep, with his back to her and a mile between them. When they needed to communicate, they did so via their private secretaries.

That was how she'd found out he'd granted her access to his royal jet to make this trip. That was how she'd found out he'd gone on a whistle-stop tour of his kingdom and wasn't expected back before her departure.

Their conversation in the conference room had left her bruised and hollow and heart-wrenchingly convinced that her days with Zufar were numbered. It was why she'd thrown herself into this visit.

When he was out of her life, at least she would have this, her new life, to fall back on. The more she'd absorbed about her heritage, the more she was certain she wanted to claim her birthright. Her parents had loved this kingdom and dedicated their lives to it. How could she walk away?

In a way it was easier that Zufar had laid down an ultimatum.

No. It wasn't.

She would have preferred a different ultimatum. One that made loving and dedicating herself to both kingdoms possible. But she knew it was another dream she needed to let go of. Just as she knew she would need to reconcile herself to letting Zufar go.

Divorce.

That was what one of her advisers had cautiously suggested during their meeting in Khalia.

Divorce the man who hadn't meant to be her husband in the first place so she could be free to fully embrace her destiny.

Such an easy suggestion. With such catastrophic consequences for her heart, her soul, every breath she took from here on out.

'We're ready, Your Serene Highness,' the Rumadian attendant said softly, with a blinding smile and shining eyes that hinted of tears. 'And if you'll permit me to say, I'm so happy you're here,' she gushed.

Niesha returned her smile, then her heart lurched wildly as the door slid soundlessly open and sunshine poured into the doorway.

Momentarily blinded, she blinked a few times, smoothing her hands over her royal blue wrap dress before stepping forwards. Immediately, a deafening roar went up over the sound of the still-whirling jet engines.

The lump of emotion wedged firmly in her throat grew as she caught sight of the crowd beyond the barricades set up on either side of the plane.

She paused for one full minute to wave before she slowly descended the stairs.

She'd been briefed on the protocol.

Her council of elders would be the first lined up on either side of the red carpet. Beyond that the senior members of the military...*her* military, would be next in line. Then a few prominent ministers and dignitaries.

So she was startled when a figure broke away from the line and approached the bottom of the steps.

Niesha gasped as the unmistakeable figure of her husband materialised in front of her. 'Zufar...what are you doing here?' she whispered as he stepped forwards and took her hand.

'It is my right as your husband to be at your side, is it not?' he returned.

She kept a smile pinned to her face as he raised her hand and kissed the back of it. Peripherally, she heard the crowd go wild.

'Welcome home, Your Highness,' he intoned deeply.

She took another step down, their height disparity forcing her to look up at him. His face was a perfectly neutral picture of regal discipline, his eyes giving away none of his feelings.

'I don't understand...'

'You don't need to. You're perfectly capable of doing this on your own. But I'm here nevertheless.'

For how long? she wanted to demand. But she'd already broken protocol, albeit through no fault of her own. He took a single step to the side and stood tall and proud and royal, but out of her way.

With a nod, she stepped onto the carpet, widening her smile as the chief adviser held out his hand.

'We are so very fortunate and honoured that you have returned to us, Your Serene Highness. Welcome home.'

All through the greeting of her statesmen and military, she was acutely aware of Zufar's presence one step beside her.

How had he got here before her?
Why was he here?

Was he staying?

The questions tumbled through her mind over the next few hours. At some point it struck her that she'd become an expert at compartmentalising because she managed to talk and walk and respond easily to conversation, even while her insides churned.

But everything fell away the moment they left the State House and approached Nazir Palace, the home she'd lived in so very briefly before losing it all.

Unlike Zufar's hilltop palace, Nazir Palace sat in the centre of the city, right on the doorstep of the people. In fact, hundreds of citizens and tourists were strolling through the public grounds as her motorcade entered the gates and drove through secured gates to the private front door.

Niesha struggled to remember any aspect of her home during the grand tour. Nothing came to mind, not even the toys left in the same position as the day she'd left and never returned. When she said as much, she received sympathetic murmurings.

'You will make new memories, I'm certain, Your Serene Highness,' her chief adviser said with a gentle smile.

Niesha wasn't unaware of the gentle pressure coming her way. Or the way Zufar stiffened each time the subject of her return was casually dropped into conversation.

When they reached her parents' bedroom it all grew too much. 'May I have a moment alone, please?'

'Of course.'

The room emptied immediately, save for Zufar. He walked by her side as she walked through the bedroom suite, touching her father's discarded tiepin, inhaling her mother's silk scarf that still faintly held her scent.

In their dressing room, she picked up her mother's hairbrush, gasping when the faintest memory materialised.

'I remember her...this room. She would sit me on her lap and comb my hair with this brush.' The last of the words dissolved into a sob.

Beside her, Zufar held out his handkerchief.

She took it, her gaze snagging his for a moment. 'Thank you.'

He gave a stiff nod. 'You are strong. You can do this.'

A moment later she was alone. As alone as she'd been from the beginning. As alone as she would be when Zufar left as abruptly as he'd appeared.

You will be all right.

She wanted to laugh. She wanted to cry and scream and throw things. But she bottled it all up because she was a queen. *Twice over.* And queens didn't break down into uncontrollable hysteria.

She reminded herself of that as she gave another interview and expressed her joy to be back home. It came in handy when she danced in Zufar's arms and he held her courteously but stiffly that night at a ball thrown in her honour.

And she reminded herself *many times* of that, the next morning, at the breakfast meeting with her chief adviser.

'As I have said, I will give you an answer in due course once I've given the matter more thought.' She picked up the tea and sipped it, her heart alternately joyful to be sitting in her mother's favourite breakfast chair, drinking from her favourite tea set, and heavy because once again Zufar had made himself scarce the moment they were alone.

'If it is a matter of pride, Your Serene Highness, please be assured it is not necessary. No one will judge you. We are simply thrilled that you are back. But we want you back permanently and as soon as possible. Your kingdom needs you. And the only way to extricate yourself from all things Khalia, we strongly feel, is by divorce.'

Icy water drenched her veins. But a numb part of her had already seen this coming. Wasn't that what Zufar himself had suggested in his own way a few days ago? He'd spoken of hard choices needing to be made. And when it came down to it, wasn't a dissolution of a marriage that was doomed to failure anyway the only option?

'You want me to divorce my husband in order to assume my birthright?'

'At the moment, it seems to be the only course open to us, Your Serene Highness.'

The boulder-sized pain that lodged itself in her chest made it hard to breathe. The joy of being back among her parents' things faded, her hands trembling as she set her teacup down.

'Very well.' She stopped, those two words birthing a thick sob she had to swallow to keep down. 'I understand—'

She froze as Zufar stepped onto the balcony. The look on his face chilled her to the bone.

'I'm guessing I'm no longer needed here, in that case,' he said, his voice edged with soft deadliness. 'Perhaps you wish for me to make myself scarce?'

'Zufar—'

He batted her words away in that unique way of his. 'You can save your words. I came to say goodbye. You have saved me the tedium of saying a more permanent one at a later date.' His gaze dropped to her stomach before rising to her face again. 'But be assured, Your Highness, that what is mine will remain *mine*.'

The shock of his words rooted her to her chair. Her world turned grey as he executed the perfect military turn and disappeared from view.

From her life.

Another sob threatened to escape. With every cell in her body, she wanted to let it rip free. She contained it as she'd never contained anything else in her life.

She was a *queen*. Queens didn't break.

'Wait! You're what?'

Zufar stared at his brother. 'Which part of it do you need repeated?'

Malak stared at him, shock and apprehension written all over his face. 'All of it. Better yet, let's just pretend everything you said was a joke. I can appreciate the odd joke when—'

'It's not a joke, brother. You said you wanted to help. This is what I need from you.'

Malak snorted. '*Help* means handling a difficult meeting in your stead, or picking out a gift for your wife when you run out of ideas. *Help* doesn't mean tossing your throne in my lap, telling me you're abdicating and expecting me to take your place.'

'Not expecting. Requesting. And the throne is too heavy to toss so you'll just have to settle for sitting on it.'

His brother exhaled noisily. 'I'm glad you're okay with cracking jokes. That means you're not that far gone. That you still have time to—'

'My mind is made up, Malak.' He injected the conviction of his decision into his words.

Once he'd come to the realisation that it was his only option, it had been surprisingly easy. The greater battle of winning his wife's heart was yet to come.

'You really mean it,' Malak observed with a stunned look. At Zufar's nod, he threw out his hands. 'What the hell? I don't want it either.'

'But you will take it because this kingdom is important to both of us. And our people need you too much for you to walk away.'

Malak opened his mouth to protest. But a full minute passed in silence as he breathed in and out, his gaze locked with Zufar's.

Zufar saw the moment duty overcame individualism, when the mantle of responsibility settled firmly on his brother's shoulders. It had been exactly like that for him.

'Okay. I accept.'

He rounded his desk and held out his hand. 'Godspeed.'

Malak pulled him into a hug. 'Same to you, brother.'

* * *

Five hours later, Zufar stood looking at his father, wondering for the umpteenth time if the visit had been wise. He didn't know. In fact, he wasn't sure about a lot of things any more.

But one thing he saw—and recognised—was the pain of loss on his father's face. It was similar to the one currently clawing deeper roots into his heart.

Was this what it felt like to have something right in front of you and lose it so completely, leaving only a gaping wound?

Because he'd lost Niesha. His foolish attempt to join her in Rumadah to mitigate the looming loss had failed miserably.

'Why have you come here, son?'

Son.

Another wrench of agony joined the endless symphony of pain slashing his heart. Zufar couldn't remember the last time his father had called him that. If ever. Or perhaps he had called him that but Zufar, too wrapped up in his own bitter loneliness, hadn't noticed?

He tried to shake off the feelings but they wouldn't leave him. What else had he missed while he'd been busy feeling wronged and aggrieved? Looking into his father's eyes now, he thought he saw a plea that looked like his own. Even a wry understanding.

As if he saw something Zufar didn't.

For some reason that observation both soothed and terrified him. For so long he'd harshly denounced anything to do with his father. But what if the wrongs he'd condemned his parent for were imprinted in his own DNA after all? What if he'd been predestined to repeat the same sins?

Or…what if they weren't wrong at all? Just an extremely misguided obsession but one that could have been mitigated with the right partner by his father's side?

Again he tried to shake off the disturbing thoughts. They

persisted until he realised he hadn't answered his father's question.

'Father, I have some news to share with you.'

Niesha walked into Zufar's library, her heartbeat drumming madly in her ears. She'd come straight from the airport to the palace, the urge to speak to him after an excruciating twenty-four hours without him, paramount.

He was sitting elegantly cross-legged on a large, stripped antique sofa, a book on Khalian history balanced on his knee.

As usual, the sight of him arrested her, slowing her steps as she absorbed his virile essence. He was in one of her favourite rooms of the palace but the books might as well have been candlesticks for all the attention she paid to them.

He looked up, his gaze slowly raking her from head to toe before reconnecting with hers.

'You have returned.' The observation was deep, husky, lethal to her senses.

She gave a jerky nod, then ploughed ahead before she lost her nerve. 'We need to talk.'

He tossed the heavy book to one side and stood. 'I agree,' he said. 'But first I need you to take a look at this.' He picked up a bound document from the coffee table as he came towards her.

She went cold, her heart shredding into smaller pieces. Surely he hadn't drawn up divorce papers that quickly?

'What is it?' Her hands shook as she took the papers he held out to her.

'Take a look,' he commanded softly.

She gathered the nerve to look down at the document. Then her heart dropped to her toes. 'This is… No, it can't be,' she said, although a terrified part of her just *knew*.

'It is exactly as you see, little one,' he murmured.

Niesha gasped, that small endearment she had missed

so much momentarily overcoming the momentous, life-changing document she held in her hands.

She searched his face, desperately wanting to know if any of this was a cruel joke that would further pulverise her bleeding heart. But as usual, Zufar's expression was an enigma that challenged and thrilled her at the same time.

But it didn't stay that way for long. As she searched deeper, his eyes grew lighter, his expression clearing to leave ferocious resolution. 'Read the document, Niesha,' he urged again.

Her gaze dropped to the weighty document. At the top of the first page, the heading blared loud and clear—*Petition For Abdication.*

'No,' she breathed again. 'You can't do this.' Her whole body shook as chills went down her spine. 'You can't!' she repeated fiercely.

'I can, and I have,' Zufar replied.

She shook her head. 'No, I won't let you do this.'

He reached forwards and brushed his knuckles down her cheek. 'My fierce Niesha. You cannot change what is already done.'

She flung herself away from him. 'You cannot abdicate. You should've checked with me, Zufar.' Her hand trembled as she waved the paper at him. 'This is unacceptable.'

He merely smiled. 'You will reconcile yourself to this too, *habibti*, because there's no going back.'

'But your people. Your kingdom—'

'Will always be my people and my kingdom. But I will not be their King.'

'Just like that? But why?'

'Because I realised that no amount of power or privilege is worth losing you. My place is with you. By your side. I'd give up a thousand kingdoms for the chance to spend a lifetime beside you.'

Hope flared wide and bright through her heart. 'I… I don't know what to say.'

'Say you're not still considering divorcing me,' he implored, his jaw clenching tight as he waited for her answer.

'Saying that would imply I considered it in the first place.'

The grim smile tugged at his mouth. 'I heard you, Niesha. I'm not ashamed to say it was the worst moment of my life.'

'Then I wish you'd stayed a moment longer because you would've heard me decline the suggestion. I admit it did cross my mind, but only because I thought you wanted it.'

'When did I give you that impression?'

'When you said there were hard choices to be made. I thought you meant going our separate ways.' Her eyes fell to the paper. 'But you meant this, didn't you?'

He gave a single, solemn nod. 'Yes.'

She swallowed, unable to fully accept the enormity of what he'd done. 'We should've talked about this. Your people will hate me for driving you to this.'

He leaned forwards, brushed his lips over hers. 'They will not. They will throw themselves wholeheartedly at their new King.'

She frowned. 'Their new King?'

He nodded. 'Malak will take my place. The council has already met with him. They're preparing his coronation speech as we speak.'

The progress he'd made without her having any inkling staggered her. She dropped to the sofa, her hand going to her head. 'Zufar…'

He was with her before she'd finished saying his name. He dropped down onto his haunches, his hands settling on her thighs. 'Whether you accept me or not, I will not retake my throne. That is now in my past. I aim to dedicate myself to the future.'

A desperate sob broke free. 'Your future is here with your people.'

'No, my future is with you, by your side, the only position I will accept.'

'But you'll lose everything, Zufar. Your title, your—'

'The only title I wish to assume is that of husband. Lover. Father. If you'll have me.'

'I can't believe—'

'Believe it, little one. For so long I've lived in misery and bitterness. You shone a light into my life where there was only darkness. When I realised my feelings for you had deepened I fought it. I believed, based on what I'd witnessed from my father, that loving you would make me weak. But I watched you loving everyone you came into contact with, watched them fall under your spell and grow stronger because of it.' He reached for her hand, bringing it up to his lips to kiss her knuckles. 'I'm a stronger person today than I was yesterday and that is because of you. How can I resist craving more of that? More of you?'

'Oh, Zufar, you have no idea how much that means to me.'

'I have a fair idea. I want to be a father to our children. I want to grow old with you.' His jaw tightened for a second. 'But before that I want to strike a new bargain with you.'

'A bargain,' she echoed faintly.

'Yes. If you'll have me, if you'll stay my wife, I promise a lifetime of loving you.'

She gasped, then launched herself at him. His arms immediately folded around her, wrapping her tight against him as she fell off the sofa and into his embrace. She didn't care that they both knelt on the carpet. And she definitely didn't care that she was sobbing.

'Is that a yes?' he demanded, his mouth dropping tiny kisses against hers.

'It's a yes. It's an absolute definite yes. But on one condition.'

He tensed slightly, leaning back to look down into her face. Then he gave one of those very regal nods she adored so much. 'Whatever it is, I agree.'

'Promise me you'll never make such life-altering decisions without discussing it with me first?'

'Niesha, you stepped up to be my Queen when I demanded it. It was my turn to return the favour. Rumadah needs her Queen.'

Her happiness dimmed a little. 'Are you sure, Zufar? Absolutely, irrevocably sure? Is there a cooling-off period for abdication? Can we take it back?'

'Hush, little one,' he said, then dropped a longer kiss on her lips. 'There's no going back. There is only going forwards.' One warm, bold hand splayed on her stomach, gently cradling their baby. 'Besides, this project is going to be a full-time one, I suspect.'

She sighed. 'You will be a great father, Zufar, but I don't want you to be just a father. Our coming together may have been a little unorthodox, but without you I would never have found my family, or claimed my birthright. You've helped me in ways that you can never imagine. I don't want you to give up your life here for me, and I came back to tell you just that—that I'll stay in Khalia and be your Queen if that is the only way to hold onto you. I selfishly want a lifetime with you too. But if you think you'll be happy in Rumadah with me, then I want more for you.'

'It shall be as you wish.'

She shook her head. 'You don't understand. I don't want you to just be my husband. I want you to be my King.'

Shock flared through his eyes. 'Niesha, you don't have to.'

'I want to. Just as you wanted me by your side as your Queen, I want you by mine as my husband and my King. That's another non-negotiable condition.'

A wider smile curved his mouth. 'I get the impression there will be a few conditions along our journey through life.'

'You drove a hard bargain when we met. I learned from the best.'

His hands framed her face, his thumbs caressing her cheekbones as he stared deeply into her eyes. 'Even back then, without knowing why, I knew I couldn't let you go. You were in my heart, in my blood, and I didn't even know it.'

'But you know it now?'

'Without doubt or regret.'

'You're in every fibre of my being too. And I wouldn't want it any other way. I love you, Zufar.'

'And I love and adore you, my magnificent Queen.'

EPILOGUE

'Is HER SERENE HIGHNESS ready for her next present?' The words were whispered against her nape, right before warm kisses rained on her bare skin.

Niesha—or Nazira, as she'd reverted to calling herself—laughed. 'You can't keep showering me with gifts, Zufar. One was enough. Twenty is beyond excessive.'

'I have no idea where you got the impression that I have twenty gifts for you.'

She chuckled. 'I'm sorry to inform you that your private secretary caved under pressure from mine.'

Zufar's head dropped onto her back and he groaned.

She laughed harder. 'In his defence, I think he has a crush on her.'

'Well, if my secret is out, then you'll have no choice but to accept.'

He rolled her over and tugged her into his arms. Nazira draped herself over his wide chest, deliriously happy to watch as he reached beneath his pillow, and brought out a small square box tied with ribbons. It was the sixth one he'd given her today and it was barely morning. He'd woken her with deep, intoxicating kissing, and proceeded to take her to heaven and back. As a start to her twenty-sixth birthday, it had been second to none.

And then the presents had started. That Zufar intended to keep to his promise to deliver twenty presents for all the ones she'd missed was evident.

While she was happy to let him because it pleased him, she was content just counting her blessings.

Just a few short months ago, she'd been drowning in loneliness and despair.

Now, she had regained her past, been crowned a queen and, best of all, was tied for life to the husband of her soul.

She accepted the box, and gasped. The diamond pendant was a replica of her birthmark, the starfish the same size as the mark on her arm. And on the back were the names of her family, etched into the white platinum. 'Oh, it's gorgeous.' Tears brimmed in her eyes as he nudged her upright and fastened the necklace.

'I thought you might want a symbol of how you found yourself,' he murmured. 'And the inscription will keep your family with you, always.'

'Oh, Zufar, just when I think I can't love you any more.'

He drew her back into his arms, then demonstrated that there was another way she could love him more.

After they caught their breath, she reached for the folded piece of paper on her beside table. 'I have something for you, too.' She handed it over and watched him open it.

'This is the guest list for my coronation.'

She held her breath. 'Yes.'

His gaze dropped to the sheet. She knew the moment he spotted the addition. 'You want him there? Are you sure?'

She nodded. 'I reached out to him a few days ago. He responded yesterday with an acceptance.'

Zufar remained silent for a moment and then he nodded. 'If you're happy to have him here, then I will welcome Adir and attempt to put the past behind us.'

She smiled, her heart bursting because she knew it had taken a great effort for him to say that. 'And you're not sore because he stole your intended?' she teased.

'*You* were my intended. The one my heart truly wanted. If Adir is happy with Amira, then I'm happy for them both.'

'I love you, Zufar.'

He kissed her long and deep, until her insides melted. 'Keep saying that to me and I will be your slave in this life and the next.'

They stopped talking for a long time after that.

An hour later, as Zufar watched his wife dress for the start of her birthday celebrations, his breath caught all over again.

He couldn't believe how life-changing loving her had been for him. Gone was the bitterness and misery that had clung to him before he met her. He'd accepted her proposal to make him King mostly to honour her, not because he wanted the position.

For the privilege of loving her and being loved by her in return, he would have happily lived in her shadow for the rest of his life. His acceptance had made her happy.

His upcoming coronation in two weeks wrung happy smiles from her each time she spoke about it. Who was he to deny her any of that? His heart grew to bursting as she dropped the towel on her way to the dressing room and he caught the small swell of her stomach. His cup had truly run over, and he couldn't wait to hold their son in his arms.

He'd foolishly thought he wanted a polished stone to pass off to his people. What he'd been blessed with was a gem that shone brighter than the brightest star in the sky.

For as long as he lived, he vowed to ensure that radiance never dimmed.

* * * * *

SHEIKH'S PRINCESS
OF CONVENIENCE

DANI COLLINS

To my fellow authors, without whom the romance genre wouldn't exist. You have given me hope and tears and guidance and passion, and best of all a belief in happily-ever-after. Also a special shout out to my fellow authors in this quartet— Tara Pammi, Maya Blake and Caitlin Crews. I'm privileged to have met each of you in person and you are all wonderful in every way.

CHAPTER ONE

DO I LOOK PRETTY, Mama?

The reflexive question, one she had learned to suppress, still jammed in Galila's throat along with her heart when she turned and caught sight of an apparition.

She held herself motionless on the tiled platform in the center of the reflecting pool, staring at the woman who appeared against the window to her mother's lounge. With the subtle golden glow cast by the lights around the courtyard, it seemed as though her mother looked out at her, watchful and unsmiling.

As usual.

Galila wore a stunning tangerine gown, strapless and with a skirt of abundant shimmering silk. A long-sleeved tulle overlay was embroidered and bedecked with silver and glittering jewels—as suited a member of the royal family on the new king's wedding day. Her hair cascaded from beneath a tiara that only ever came out on special occasions, and until now, only on her mother's head.

The dress was too young for her mother, but those were definitely her mother's eyes, scrupulously emphasized with greens and gold, liquid eyeliner ending in a cat's tail. At one time, those doe-like eyes would have swept over Galila with indulgence. Affection.

So pretty, my pet. Her painted lips would have smiled with tender love as she stroked Galila's hair.

Tonight, Galila's mouth—as sensuously curved as her mother's had been and wearing her mother's signature glossy red—tightened. Her elegantly arched brows drew themselves together as she critically sought flaws, exactly as her mother would have done if she had still been alive.

Your skin looks sallow, Galila.

It was the yellow light and her imagination, but the reproach still had the power to sting. To make her yearn to correct the flaw and recapture the love that had dried up and blown away like sand across the desert.

She ought to be glad her mother wasn't here; ought to be grieving properly for a life lost. Instead, it was her secret shame that she was mostly grieving her chance to win back her mother's love. Or perhaps just to understand how she'd lost it.

What had she done that was so terrible—except to grow up looking exactly as beautiful as her mother had been? Was that her great crime?

Could she finally bloom freely now that she wouldn't overshadow her mother?

She lifted the glass she held, leaving another kiss print on the rim.

Not champagne, either, Mother. She directed that baleful thought to her image and received a dispassionate glance in return.

The brandy she had learned to drink at boarding school seared with blessed heat through her arteries, promising the numbing effect Galila sought.

In a perfect world, she would drink herself unconscious and possibly drown here in an inch of water, escaping the chaos raging around her.

Don't make a spectacle of yourself, Galila. That's Malak's purview.

"Your dress is getting wet."

The male voice, so deep and velvety it matched the caress of the warm night air, had her turning to peer into the shadows, expecting—well, she didn't know who she expected. A man, yes, but not *such* a man.

He leaned against the edge of an archway, features sharpened by the low light and framed by the drape of his *ghutra*. He was dangerous and handsome at once. Dangerously handsome with those dark, deeply set eyes and strong jaw beneath a short, black beard. Breath-stealing, in fact, in his gold-trimmed *bisht* that might have been the color of a good merlot. It hung open across wide shoulders to reveal his embroidered *thobe*, tailored to his muscled chest, collar closed at his throat and decorated by a yellow sapphire the size of her fist.

She told herself it was the alcohol that made her sway, but she suspected it was the impact of his virility.

He straightened and held out a hand. "Come. Before you ruin perfection."

He sounded indifferent, perhaps a little impatient, but her confused, bruised-up heart reached like a flower toward the sunshine of his compliment. She used her free hand to lift her skirt and carefully placed her feet on each round tile. She was a little too drunk for stepping stones and appreciated when he took the drink from her hand and clasped her forearm, balancing her until she was completely away from the water.

His touch undermined her equilibrium as much as

the brandy, though. More, perhaps. Brandy didn't make her chest feel tight and her eyes dampen with longing. Her ears picked up the distant sound of the wedding music, but all her senses were trained on him. Something in her flowed toward him. Sought...*something*.

He was tall, radiating magnetism while a force field seemed to surround him, one that made him seem untouchable. It cracked fissures through her that she couldn't begin to understand.

Maybe it was the brandy causing this overwhelming reaction.

He smelled the glass and his mouth curled with disdain. He set the glass aside.

"You don't approve of alcohol?"

"I don't approve of drunkenness."

It should have sounded too uptight for words, but she was ever so sensitive to censure. His condemnation cut surprisingly deep. Why? He was nothing to her.

But he was also like nothing she'd ever experienced—and she'd seen a lot these last few years, living in Europe. He wasn't like any of the urbane aristocrats or earnest artists she'd met. He didn't even match what she expected here, in her home country of Khalia. He was almost too iconic in his arrogant sheikh demeanor. She had long decided that if she ever did marry, it would be to a progressive, cultured man from abroad. Not one of these throwback barbarians from five centuries ago.

Yet he was utterly fascinating. A tendril of desire to impress him wormed through her. She wanted to stand here and hold his attention and earn his regard.

Quit being so needy, she heard Malak say in her head. He had learned to live without love or anyone's good opinion. Why did she think it was necessary?

She didn't, she told herself and reached for the glass. "It's my brother's special day. I'm celebrating."

"People do stupid things when they're drunk." Sheikh Karim of Zyria didn't raise his hand or his voice. He didn't even tell her not to drink.

Nevertheless, his deep tone carried the quiet command instilled by his station. It was evidently enough to make her falter and reassess him, perhaps understanding she would ignore him at her own peril.

He returned her scrutiny, taking advantage of the chance to do so up close. That's what he told himself he was doing, in any case.

He had watched the royal family all day and evening—the ones who were here, at least. Princess Galila, with her stark resemblance to her deceased mother, fascinated him the most. She flitted like a bird from perch to perch, joining this group and that, welcomed by all and animated as she spoke, flirtatious and not above rolling her eyes at anyone, including her brother, the groom and newly crowned King of Khalia.

Had her mother possessed that same sparkling energy? Was that how she had so ensnared his father? He had seen photos of all of them over the years, but in person, Princess Galila was not merely beautiful. She was potent and enthralling, pulling at him in a way he resisted out of principle.

Out of self-preservation, a voice whispered deep in the back of his mind.

Not that he was in danger of infatuation, he assured himself. She struck him as far too superficial, thriving on being the center of attention. The way she smiled and bantered told him she was fully aware of the power in her beauty and sex appeal. She used it without shame to steal the spotlight from every other woman in the room.

That's why it had surprised him when she'd slipped into the garden and walked away from the party into the family's private courtyard. He had followed because he wanted to understand how this woman's mother had destroyed and reshaped his entire life, not because he had been compelled to keep her in his sights.

Had her mother, Queen Namani, been this vain? He'd watched Galila preen in front of her own reflection like a lovebird, so deeply enamored with herself that she hadn't been aware of his presence.

He wasn't a stalker, lurking in shadows, spying on pretty maidens. He was a king, one with questions he had never been able to answer. Besides, he wanted to see her up close. Discover the secret of her allure.

He'd called her out of the pool—which was when he'd realized she was drunk.

Disappointing. He abstained, never wanting to be so far into his cups that he thought a leap off a balcony would solve his problems.

When he'd told her drinking was unwise, he'd thought for a moment that despair clouded her eyes, but she'd quickly switched to using her stunning looks to distract and mesmerize.

"What's stupid about enjoying myself?" she challenged lightly. She lifted her hair off her neck and let it flow carelessly off her forearm, watching to see if he followed the movement.

There was a man inside this royal casing. He felt desire the same as any other, but he knew when he was being invited to lose focus by ogling a breast. Much as he longed to eye the weight of her curves, he kept his gaze locked with hers.

"Exhibit A. You're on a tear of self-destruction." Locking horns with him was a grave mistake, he silently warned.

She was disconcerted by his unaffected response. She might even have been burned by it. Her brow flinched. She quickly lifted her chin in a rally of spirit, though.

"Perhaps I have reason. Did you think of that?" Her long lashes blinked in big, innocent sweeps.

"I'm sure your life is very fraught," he said drily.

"I lost my mother three months ago," she threw back at him with quiet anguish. "I'm entitled to grieve."

"You are." He dipped his head, but that was as much condolence as he was willing to offer. He hadn't been allowed any self-pity after his father's death. The circumstances had been far more disturbing and he'd been a child of six. "Drinking yourself blind will only make things worse."

"How is *that* possible?" she cried softly. "My father is so grief-stricken, he's like a shell. I can't reach him. No one can." She looked to the huge window where her own reflection had stood. "He misses my mother terribly."

Karim understood that affliction, too. No matter what he did, he had never been able to ease his mother's heartbreak over her loss, either. Protecting her from the fact that his father's death had been a suicide was the best he'd ever been able to do.

"She had an affair," Galila whispered. "He loved her anyway, but now we all know about it, which seems to have tripled his agony."

Karim's heart stopped. Even the breath in his lungs stilled.

As if she noted his jolt of alarm, she nodded to confirm her shocking statement, eyes wide and tortured.

"Your father knew but kept it from you?" Karim's mind raced. He had never confided in a single soul, no matter how long and heavily the truth had weighed on him—and it had. Endlessly. With the death of Queen Namani, he had thought that at least the secret of the affair would die when he did.

"He's known for years!" Her tone rang with outraged astonishment. "He helped her cover it up when she became pregnant. They sent away our half brother the day he was *born*."

Karim had to concentrate on keeping his face expressionless, his feet rooted to the marble tiles so he didn't fall over. His ears rang as though the soft words had been a cannon next to his head.

Galila gave a choking half laugh of near hysteria. "Explain to me how one processes *that* sort of news except to get roaring drunk?"

"You have a third brother? A half brother?" *He* had a half brother? His carefully balanced world wasn't just tilting on its axis. It was reaching such a sharp angle everything was sliding into a jumbled mess at his feet.

"Yes!" She didn't seem to notice his deep shock, too caught up in layers of emotional turmoil within herself. "My brothers and I should have been supporting each other, comforting our father, but *he* showed up at the funeral. Told us how our mother had been writing to him for *years*. How she regretted sending him away because she *loved him best*." Her eyes gleamed with a thick sheen of tears. "Because he was her only link to the man she truly loved."

Her fist went to the spot over her breast where she seemed to stem the cracks in a bleeding heart.

"Our father had a complete breakdown. Who wouldn't? We nearly all did! Zufar had to step in and take over... And now that's where Zufar's intended bride is, with *our half brother*." She spoke with livid bewilderment, arm flinging out to some unknown location. "Zufar wasn't supposed to marry Niesha. Amira's been promised to him since she was born, but Adir came back this morning and talked Amira into running away with him. I watched her go through the window. Adir said it was his revenge for being denied his birthright."

"Adir," Karim repeated faintly. That was the name of his brother? He barely heard the rest of what poured out of her.

"Zufar is so single-minded, he married our *maid* rather than admit there was anything wrong. Malak has quit the palace entirely, gone gambling or to work his way through a harem, I imagine. Where does that leave me? With *no one*. So excuse me if I take some comfort in a bottle of brandy."

When she started to drink, he stole it and tipped the alcohol onto the tiles. He had to. This news was utterly explosive.

"Who else have you told?" he demanded.

"No one," she muttered, giving a *tsk* of annoyance at the brandy puddle. "Now I have to walk all the way back for a fresh one."

"Who is Adir's father?" He kept his voice level but held the empty glass in such a tight grip he expected it to shatter in his hand, leaving him dripping blood onto the evaporating alcohol.

"No one knows." She gave her hair a flip. "Mother took *one* secret to her grave, it seems. Although, I have half a mind to ask around that crowd." She jerked her chin toward the balcony across the darkened expanse of the garden, where light poured out the open doors to the palace ballroom. "He must be there."

The elite from all the neighboring kingdoms mingled in a kaleidoscope of colored gowns and robes. Voices competed with the music in a din that suddenly grated on him more than he could bear.

"Why do you think that?" he asked, forcing a tone of mild curiosity while his blood prickled in his veins.

"My mother wouldn't take up with a servant. It had to have been someone of her stature, very likely one of those men congratulating my brother on his mismatched marriage."

She was right, of course. His father had been exactly at her mother's level, not that Karim would confirm it. Maybe the affair had started at an event like this, he imagined. His father and her mother would have been about his and Galila's age when they met, in their prime and bursting with biological readiness. Perhaps they had slipped away into the shadows to indulge their passion, as other couples were doing even now.

He was far too practical to wish, but he had an uncharacteristic longing to be one of those carefree couples with Galila. If only he could enjoy a simple dalliance, like other people, rather than listening to her sing his personal scandal to the night sky while racking his brain on how to most quickly prevent it going further than his own ears.

She was inordinately desirable, he noted with determined detachment. He almost understood his father's desolation at being rejected by such a woman. Of course, his father had been married and never should have started the affair in the first place, but Karim had no such restrictions.

In fact, remaining close to this pretty bird was exactly what he ought to do. He had devoted his life to ensuring his mother never learned the truth about his father's death. He wasn't about to watch it all come apart through one woman's brandy-lubricated tongue. In fact, he had to ensure the entire family's silence on the matter.

Hmm.

"We should get back to the party," the mysterious stranger said.

Through her haze of growing infatuation, Galila distantly realized she shouldn't be loitering alone with a man, let alone spilling family secrets in his ear, but there was something exhilarating about holding his attention. For weeks, in many ways *years*, she'd been an afterthought. Female, and therefore less than her male brothers. Princess, not queen.

"Mmm, yes, I'd love to fetch a fresh brandy," she said with a cheeky slant of her lashes at him.

No smile of answering flirtation, only a circumspect look that made her heart sink under the feeling she had disappointed him.

"I don't need your permission," she pointed out, but her confidence was a stuttering thing in her chest.

"We'll see," he said cryptically and took her arm to steer her around the pool.

His touch sent a shock of electricity through her. She

jolted and nearly turned her ankle. It was disconcerting, made even worse by his disapproving frown.

I'm not that drunk, she wanted to claim, but all coherent thoughts seemed to have left her brain.

Her entire being was realigning its magnetic poles with something in him. She wasn't just aware of him. His presence beside her seemed to surround her in a glow that tingled her skin and warmed her blood. It compressed her breaths while making her feel each one come into her like scent, except it was his aura she was taking into herself.

In a daze, she let him guide her toward the path that would lead them into the garden and back to the wedding reception.

"You don't drink at all?" she asked, trying desperately to ground herself in reality.

"Never."

"Oh, please," she teased, leaning into his firm grip on her elbow. "Let me be the one to initiate you."

Some dim instinct for self-preservation warned her that provoking him was a terrible idea. Something deeper, even. A sense that her gentle mockery not only failed to impact him but was misplaced. He wasn't weak at any level. Nor innocent. He was worldly to the point of cynical, and inimitably strong because he allowed no one to influence him.

Looking up at him as they entered the garden, she noted that his mouth was a work of art. Despite how very serious it was, his lips were full and sensual. How would they feel, crushed against hers?

The flush that went through her at that thought was pure lust, hitting in all her erogenous zones and making her feet tangle into themselves again.

He stopped and steadied her, frowning. "Do I have to carry you?"

She laughed at the thought of it. She was worldly enough to have fooled around with men, but she knew who she was. She had kept her reputation intact along with her virginity for the sake of her family. Maybe even to avoid one more harsh criticism from her mother. The deep-down truth, however, was that she'd never been overcome with enough desire to give her body to anyone.

The compulsion to throw herself into the arms of this man, tonight, was intense enough to unnerve her. A drunk and stupid idea, indeed, but exciting. She didn't even know his name!

"What were you doing over here? Following me?"

"Same as you." A muscle in his cheek ticked. "Reflecting."

"On?"

"Responsibility."

"How boring. I'm surprised I didn't find *you* drunk and facedown in that pool."

The severity in his expression didn't ease. His hold on her arm sent glittering sensations through her bloodstream. She ought to shake him off. What would people think if they returned together? Nothing good, that was certain.

Such a remarkable man, though. One she really didn't want to share with a party full of beautiful women. She wanted him to be hers. To look on her with adoration and desire.

His expression in the moonlight was cool and decidedly intent. Ruthless, even. But there was hunger buried deep beneath his layers of control. Avid male need that she had seen often enough to recognize it. His narrowed eyes focused on her mouth, telling her his speculation was along the same lines as her own.

"Don't you want to throw caution to the wind sometimes? I do." She flipped her hair behind her shoulder again. *Look at me. Want me.* "Malak gets away with it all the time. I'm tired of being the good girl."

"Are you?" Something in his silky tone and the way he flicked his gaze down her front wound around her like ribbons, exciting and wicked. Tightening and binding, compressing her breasts, yet making her feel free.

"Am I tired? Or a good girl? I'm both." She thought of her charity work, her carefully cultivated image of kindness and purity, her endless striving to earn her mother's approval and her stalwart presence beside the men in her life as they took their own self-destructive paths.

All her life, she had tried to be like her mother. They had all thought Queen Namani so perfect, but she hadn't been. Why should Galila live up to something that was an illusion? Live up to the expectations of a woman who not only hadn't held herself to such high standards after all but was also *dead*.

"I'm ready to do what I want." She pressed herself to his front and lifted her mouth.

"I don't take advantage of inebriated women," he said, but with a glance toward the light of the party. His cheeks hollowed, giving his profile a chillingly ruthless appearance. His hands on her arms tightened in some internal struggle.

"I'm not that drunk," she dismissed in a sultry voice. She was low on inhibition, certainly, but more intoxicated by the excitement he made her feel.

They were in a faraway, unlit corner of the garden, where the scent of roses and herbs, orange blossom and frangipani coated the air, making it feel thick as a blanket around her.

"Kiss me," she demanded when he hesitated.

His hands almost began to push her away, but he only held her like that, staring into her uplifted face. For three heartbeats that shook the entire world, they stood like that, as he debated and came to a decision.

With a muttered imprecation, he circled his arms around her. His fingers dove into her hair, tilting back her head as his mouth came down to cover hers.

For another pulse of time, that was all it was. One mouth against another while the universe seemed to open itself, leaving her utterly vulnerable yet transfixed by the vast beauty of it.

With a harsh noise in his throat, he dragged his lips across hers. Instantly they were engulfed in a kiss that was beyond anything she had ever experienced. Intimate and passionate. Hot and damp and demanding. A statement of possession but with a quality that swept her into abandoning herself willingly. Joyfully.

The texture of his tongue met her own, boldly erotic. She reacted with a moan and mashed herself into him so hard her breasts hurt, but it felt good, too. The contact assuaged the tips that stung like bites. When he started to ease back, she whimpered and pressed her hand to the cloth covering his head, urging him to continue kissing her with this mad passion. She wanted to feel his hair, taste his skin, strip naked and know the weight of him over her.

She wanted to know how that hard flesh that was pressing against her belly would feel stroking inside her.

With an abrupt move and a ragged hiss of indrawn air, he pulled back. "Not here."

Had he read her mind? Her body?

"My room," she whispered, already plotting their discreet path through the halls of the palace.

"Mine," he stated. She couldn't tell if it was a preference of location or if he was staking a claim on her. Either way, she let him take her hand and drag her from the garden toward the stairs that led up to the balcony outside the ballroom.

She balked in the shadows at the bottom of the steps. "My lipstick. People will know."

"I thought you were ready to take control of your own life?"

In the slant of light, she saw a mercilessness curl at the corner of his mouth. He pivoted them a few steps into the shadows beside the wall of the steps.

She was more than ready to give herself to him, but this was her home. Her brother's wedding. She was the Princess of Khalia. She was sober enough to know that she had to be discreet about having an affair, not parade it through the middle of a state ceremony.

But as her would-be lover pressed her to the stones that had barely cooled in the hours since sundown, she forgot her misgivings. Her hands found the heat of his neck and she parted her lips, moaning as he kissed her again.

He transported her to that place of magic they seemed to create between them.

As she lost herself to his kiss again, he stroked her hip and thigh, urging her to pick up her knee and make space for him between her legs. Cool air grazed her skin as he shifted her skirt up, up and out of the way, touching—

She gasped at the first contact of fingertips against the back of her thigh. Arrows of pleasure shot into her core, making her yearn so badly her eyes grew damp along with her underthings. She arched her neck as he trailed his mouth down her throat.

It was exquisite and joyful and…

Wait.

He was hard where he pressed between her legs, but something was off.

She touched the side of his face, urging him to lift his head. There was heat in his glittering eyes, but it was banked behind a cooler emotion. Something deliberate. His skin might have been flushed with arousal, but his expression was dispassionate.

He wasn't as involved as she was.

Hurt and unease began to worm through her, but before she could fully react, she heard a gasp and a giggle above them. Someone said a pithy, "Get a room."

"That's the princess!" a female voice hissed.

"With who?" She knew that demanding masculine voice. She looked up to see several faces peering down at them over the wall of the balcony, one of them her brother's. He did *not* look pleased.

Did her lover release her leg to find a modicum of decorum? Not right away. Not before she caught a dark look of satisfaction in his hard features.

Gaze solely on her, he very slowly eased his hold on her leg so his touch branded into her skin as she lowered her thigh. Humiliation pulsed in her throat, made all the more painful by the way he had gone from passionately excited to…this. Remote. Unaffected. Perhaps even satisfied by her public set down.

Angry and embarrassed as she was, her abdomen

still tightened in sensual loss as he drew away from their full-frontal contact, which only added to her mortification.

"You were right," he said. "We should have gone to your room."

She had no choice but to take refuge there. Alone and *fast*.

CHAPTER TWO

GALILA WOKE TO a dull headache, some low-level nausea that was more chagrin than hangover and a demand that she present herself to her brother *immediately*.

Despite what she would have hoped was a fulfilling wedding night, Zufar was in a foul mood and fifteen minutes in, didn't seem to be tiring of tearing strips off her.

"You can't bring that sort of shame down on the palace and think it doesn't matter."

"What shame?" she cried, finally allowed a word in edgewise. "A few people saw us kissing. Malak behaves far worse *all the time*."

"And you hate it when he gets the attention! You couldn't put your own silly need to be in the spotlight on hold for one night? The night of my wedding? Is anyone talking about our ceremony or my bride? No. The buzz is all about the fact you were seen behaving like a tart."

"You're welcome," she said with a glance at her manicure. "Because the things they were saying about your marriage to the maid weren't all that flattering."

"Mind how you talk to your king, little sister," he said in a tone that should have terrified, but she refused to take him seriously. It was just the two of them in here and he was behaving like a Neanderthal.

"I don't know what you want me to do," she said, throwing up her arms. "I can't undo it."

"You could start by promising you'll show more decorum in future. This shouldn't even be happening. Why Mother let you go this long without marrying you off to someone who can control you, I will never understand."

"Can't you?" she bit out sharply.

"What is that supposed to mean?"

"She saw me as competition, Zufar." It was plain as day.

"Get over yourself, Galila. *You* are the one who sees everyone as competition. Take heed now. I won't have you upstaging my queen. You will learn to take a back seat."

"I wouldn't—"

They were interrupted by a servant. He entered after a brief but urgent knock and hurried to lean into Zufar's ear. All Galila caught was "...very insistent..."

Zufar's expression hardened. "Show him in." As she turned, Zufar added, "Where do you think you're going?" He glared at Galila's attempt to exit.

"I assumed we were done."

"You wish. No, I have no idea why he insists on speaking to me, but I imagine it concerns you, so you'll stand here while he does."

"Who?" She looked to the door the servant had left through.

"Sheikh Karim of Zyria."

"Is that his name?" She had imagined he was one of their more illustrious guests but hadn't realized—

Zufar slammed his hand onto his desktop, making her jump. "Do not tell me you didn't even know the name of the man who had his hand up your skirt."

She looked to the corner of the ceiling, biting the insides of her cheeks.

"Do you honestly think my life has room for your childish antics?" Zufar demanded.

She started to scowl at him, but *he* came in. Sheikh Karim of Zyria. He had exchanged his ceremonial garb of last night for a Western-style bespoke suit in slate gray sans headdress.

If possible, he was even more knee-weakeningly handsome. The crisp white of his shirt and blood-red tie suggested a man who commanded any world he occupied. He stole the breath from her body in a psychic punch, utterly overwhelming her.

His gaze spiked into hers as though he'd been waiting to see her again, but before her heart fully absorbed that sensation, he offered a terse nod and turned his attention to her brother, leaving her feeling promptly dismissed and inexplicably bereft.

After ensuring Princess Galila had indeed retired for the night, Karim had gone to his own guest apartment, somewhat disgusted with himself. He had been telling the truth when he'd claimed not to take advantage of women in a weakened state. He considered himself an honorable man.

But he hadn't been able to take the chances that she would leak his secret to someone else after her next sip of brandy.

He had been wrestling with his conscience over whether he should seduce this tipsy woman to his room, where he could at least contain her, when she had thrown herself against him in the darkest corner of the garden.

Their kiss had been the most potent drug imaginable, jamming into his veins and bringing him throbbingly alive at the first taste of her. As if he'd been dead for three decades. Existing, yet not seeing or tasting or smelling. Not *feeling*.

Then, for heart-stopping minutes, he had been resurrected. Sunlight had dawned upon him, shaking him awake from a long freeze. Everything in him had wanted to plunge into that world and never leave it.

Somehow, he had pulled back, much the way any sane man would catch himself before teetering like a crazed addict into a hallucinogenic abyss.

That shockingly intense reaction had been a lesson. One he would heed. Now he knew *exactly* how dangerous she was. It meant he was now prepared to withstand the power of her effect on him.

He kept telling himself his abominable actions were for honorable ends. He was protecting her family as much as his own. His deliberately public display had worked beautifully to put an end to any inquiries she might have made about the man who had impregnated her mother.

Temporarily.

The rest of his strategy would play out now.

With one brief glance, he took in her suitably demure dove-gray skirt and jacket with a flash of passion-pink blouse beneath. Her hair was rolled into a knot behind her head, but she was every bit as beautiful as she'd been last night, if looking a little haunted around the eyes and pouty around the mouth.

He didn't allow his gaze to linger, even though the flush on her skin was a sensual reminder of her reaction to him last night. She had worn a similar color when their kisses had sent the pulse in her neck racing against the stroke of his tongue. That response of hers had been as beguiling as the rest, and not something he could allow himself to recollect or he'd embarrass himself.

For the most part, Karim kept his emotions behind a containment wall of indifference. It wasn't usually so difficult. He'd been doing it his whole life.

Last night, however, this woman had put more than one fracture in his composure. Those tiny cracks had to be sealed before they spread. His reaction to her would be controlled. His command of this situation would be logical and deliberate. Effectual—as all his actions and decisions were throughout his life.

He started by refusing to react with any degree of emotion when her brother offered a blistering, opening attack.

"I expected better of a man in your position, Karim." Zufar didn't even rise, lifting only one sneering corner of his mouth. "You should have had the grace to be gone by now."

"Allow me to make reparation for any harm to your family's reputation," Karim said smoothly. "I'll marry her."

Galila gasped. "What? I'm not going to marry *you*."

Karim flicked a glance to her outraged expression. "Do not tell me you are promised elsewhere." He had to fight to control his reaction, never having experienced such a punch of possessiveness in his life. He would shed blood.

"No." She scowled. "But I'm not ready to marry anyone. Certainly not a stranger. Not just because I kissed you. It's ridiculous!"

"It's highly practical and a good match." He had spent much of the night reasoning that out, determined emotions wouldn't enter into this arrangement. "You'll see," he assured her. Her flair of passion could wait for the bedroom.

"I will not see!"

"Quiet." Zufar held up a hand, rising to his feet.

Galila rushed forward and brushed it down.

"Don't tell me to be quiet," she hissed. "I will decide whom I marry. And while it's a kind offer—" she said in a scathing tone that suggested she found Karim's proposal anything but, she stared Karim right in the eye as she said emphatically, *"No."*

Her crackling heat reached toward him, licking at the walls he forced himself to keep firmly in place.

"Clearly your sister has a mind of her own." She was the kind of handful he would normally avoid, but greater things were at risk than his preference for a drama-free existence. "Was that the problem with your first bride?" Karim asked Zufar with a blithe kick below the belt. "Is that why she ran off with your brother?"

"What?" Zufar's voice cracked like a whip, but Karim kept his gaze on his intended bride, watching her flush of temper pale to horror.

"Half brother, I mean," he corrected himself very casually, despite feeling nothing of the sort. This was high-stakes gambling with a pair of twos he was bluffing into a straight flush.

"Galila." Zufar's tone was deadly enough that Karim shifted his attention—and the position of his body— to easily insert himself between the two if necessary.

Incensed as her brother looked, he didn't look violent. And culpable as Galila grew, she didn't look scared. She was glaring blame at Karim.

"Why are you doing this?" Her voice was tight and quiet.

"I am in need of a wife. Or so my government takes every opportunity to inform me." It wasn't a lie. "You are of suitable… What was the word you used when describing your mother's lover? Station? Stature. That was it."

"This goes beyond even your usual nonsense," Zufar said in a tone graveled with fury. "A moment ago, you didn't even know his name, yet you talked to him about our family's most intimate business?"

"I was drunk." She looked away, cheeks glowing with guilt and shame. "That's not an excuse, but it's been a very trying time, Zufar. You know it has. For all of us."

Zufar's eyes narrowed on her and his cheeks hollowed, almost as if he might accept that as reason enough for her imprudent behavior.

"Allow me to assure you," Karim said with scalpel like precision, "that if you agree to our marriage, your family's secrets will stay between us."

The siblings stood in thunderous astonishment for a few moments.

"And if I don't agree to the marriage?" Zufar asked, but Karim could see they both already knew the answer.

"Blackmail?" Galila asked with quiet outrage. "Why would you stoop so low? Why do you *have* to?" she challenged sharply.

He didn't. He hadn't made marriage a priority for a

number of reasons, most of them superficial and convenience-related. He was a workaholic who barely had time for his mother, who still very much needed him. Women expected things. Displays of emotion. Intimacy that went beyond the physical.

"I'm not going to hurt you, if that's what you're suggesting," Karim scoffed. "I'll treat you as gently and carefully as the pretty little bird you are."

"In a gilded cage? You know, you could ask me to marry you, not trap me into it."

"Will you marry me?"

"*No*. I would never have anything to do with someone as calculating and ruthless as you are."

"You already know me so well, Princess, you're practically made for me. It certainly seemed that way last night."

Zufar made a noise of outrage while Galila stomped her foot, blushing deep into her open collar.

"Stop talking about that! There are other women," Galila insisted. "Pick one."

"I want you."

"I won't do it."

Karim only swung his attention back toward her brother. "I've made it clear what I'm prepared to do to get her."

"Why? What else do you want?" Zufar flared his nostrils in fury.

Above all, Karim wanted to forestall any speculation about who might be the mysterious man their mother had fallen for. If it became known that Queen Namani's lover had been his father, King Jamil, the news would not only destroy his mother, but it would rock both kingdoms right down to their foundations. Not to mention what this newly discovered half brother might do with the knowledge.

So Karim only asked, "Is it so remarkable I might want her?"

"You didn't even introduce yourself. Last night was a setup," Zufar said.

"Oh, thank you very much," Galila interjected hotly, but hurt and accusation lingered behind her glossy eyes as she glared at Karim. "I don't care what you threaten. I'm not some camel you're trading."

Karim had given his explanation some thought as he had lain awake last night, having anticipated that Zufar would be a man of intelligence, capable of seeing his sister was being used for reasons that went beyond her obvious charms.

"I'm not the only man who noticed last night that the princess is very beautiful," he said to Zufar. "She's unmarried and much is changing in Khalia with you taking your father's place. An alliance with the sister of the new king could only be an advantage to me."

"And you think I want to form an alliance with a man of your methods?" Zufar scoffed.

"If I'm married to your sister, yes. I think we will both work toward aligning our countries' goals. And I believe, in the long run, you'll appreciate my methods. I'm saving you months of fielding offers from lesser men and having to play politics in refusing them."

"Such magnanimity," Zufar said with venom-like sarcasm, adding darkly, "But I can't refute the logic."

"Try harder, Zufar," Galila said scathingly. "Because I won't marry him and you can't make me."

"I'm your king, Galila." He said it flatly, but not unkindly.

As she tried to stare down her brother, her cross expression slowly faded into something disconcerted. She clearly began to realize what she was up against and grew pale.

"Zufar, you can't."

"I am not Mommy and Daddy whom you can manipulate with your crocodile tears. You have stepped way over the line this time. I can't put this back in the box for you."

It was tough love in action, something Karim would normally subscribe to, but he sensed genuine distress in the way she reached for a tone of reason, though her voice trembled.

"This isn't like our parents' time when everything was arranged and Mommy was promised to Daddy from when she was a girl. We are allowed to marry for love—"

"Did *I* get the bride I wanted?" Zufar interjected. "The time we are in, Galila, is one where we all have to make sacrifices for the crown of Khalia. You made this bed you're already half in." He sent a dark look at Karim. "Whether you were seduced into it or tricked or went there of your own volition."

Karim didn't bother explaining that as far as that side of it went, she had been a willing partner. He might not be a man who indulged his passions, but he and Galila certainly hadn't lacked any. That was the one thing that made him cautious about this arrangement, but that was a worry for a later time, after he got what he wanted.

Which was *her*.

Even though she looked shattered by his demand for her hand. She visibly shook but found the courage to turn and confront him. "I refuse. Do you understand me?"

"Come," Karim responded, holding out his hand, almost moved to pity by her anxiety but not enough to change his mind. "It is done."

"It is not," she insisted. "I'm going to talk to my father."

"You should inform him," Karim agreed. "Do that while I negotiate our marriage contract with your king."

Her father offered no help whatsoever. He gave her a halfhearted pat on her cheek, eyes red and weary.

"It's past time you married. Listen to your brother. He knows what is best for you."

No, he doesn't!

Malak didn't even answer her text. Her friend Amira was gone—seduced into running away with Adir. Galila was jealous of her friend. Amira's escape might have been dramatic, but at least she wasn't forced into a marriage she didn't want.

Galila felt as though she was being kidnapped in slow motion. Even her one trusted ally within the palace, Niesha, had gone from being someone who might cover for her long enough for a getaway to being her *queen*. Galila wasn't allowed to see her without an appointment and didn't have time to make one. A travel case had already been packed for her and Karim was knocking on the door to her apartment while she flittered back and forth in a panic.

"Ready?" The detached question made her long to dismiss him as a robot, but there was something deeply alive about him. He was a lion—all-powerful and predatory, completely unfeeling in what he pursued or how much pain he caused, so long as he could feast on whatever it was he desired.

"I will never forgive you for this," she said in reply.

"Let's save our vows for our wedding day."

"There won't be one." She used a glare that unfailingly set a man in his place, but he was impervious, meeting her icy gaze without flinching.

Much to her chagrin, as she maintained the eye contact, she felt the tug of desire all over again. His eyes were such a dark brown they were almost black, velvety and holding far more depth than she initially gave credit for.

The whole time he had been blackmailing her brother and admitting that he had manipulated her last night to capture her hand before anyone else could, she had been thinking about how delicious he had made her feel.

She had thought about him *all* night, mostly feeling disappointed that they'd been caught and interrupted, not nearly as mortified as her brother had wanted her to feel when he had criticized her behavior.

But the enigmatic stranger who had kissed her was gone. He had turned into this disinterested man who had used her. His complete lack of reaction toward her, his utter indifference, reminded her that all the feelings and attraction had been on her side. That thought carved a hole right next to the ones already leaving a hollow feeling inside her.

Even if it was about time she married, even if she absolutely had to succumb to marriage, it should be to a man who wanted *her*. Not Zufar's sister. Not the Princess of Khalia. Not the politically expedient ally. *Her*.

He ought to at least offer her the adoration her mother

had had from their father. No one should expect her to accept *this*.

And yet, as they walked outside to the cars, a polite round of applause went up.

For appearance's sake, her brother had announced that their engagement had been kept secret for weeks, so as not to overshadow the coming wedding. If Zufar thought the departing wedding guests believed that, there were several bridges in America he could purchase at an excellent price.

Repulsed as she was by the lie, she didn't make a scene. Far too late for that. She accepted congratulations with a warm, delighted smile. Let them all think this was as grand a romance as her brother tried to package it.

The better to humiliate Karim when she left him in the dust.

"Are you really a sheikh?"

Oh, had his fiancée finally chosen to speak to him? He glanced up from his productive hour on his laptop.

She hadn't cried or begged as they left the palace, which he had half expected. She had thrown waves of cold, silent resentment at him, making it clear that if he hadn't personally escorted her into the car and then his helicopter, she wouldn't be here.

As a man highly in demand and averse to theatrics, Karim told himself that receiving the silent treatment was a gift. At the same time, he had to acknowledge her strength of will was more than he had bargained for. He wasn't someone who thrived on challenge and overcoming conflict. He didn't shy away from it, either. He met obstacles head on and expected them to get out of his way.

This woman, however, with her royal blood seething with passion, wasn't cowed by the mere timbre of his voice. On the surface, she appeared soft and delicate, but he was beginning to see the length of steel in her spine.

He hoped like hell that didn't portend clashes. He had no time for tantrums.

"I am," he answered mildly.

Her skeptical gaze left the window to scan the interior of the helicopter cabin, then dropped to the clothes he'd changed into for travel. He'd worn a suit for his high-stakes meeting with her brother but wore typical Arab attire as often as possible. Not for religious or political reasons, but because he found it the most comfortable.

"I was not expecting company when I left Zyria," he explained of his helicopter and its lack of attendant. It only seated four in the cabin, but very comfortably. "This aircraft is the fastest and most flexible." He could fly it if he had to and regularly did, to keep up his skills. He would be doing so now, if she wasn't here, not that she seemed to want his company.

Her brows lifted in brief disdain as her attention went back out the window. Her frown increased and he almost smiled, realizing why she was skeptical.

The metropolis of his country's capital, Nabata, was not appearing beneath the descending helicopter. Instead, all she would see out there was a speck of a palace in the rugged desert.

"My mother is looking forward to meeting you. She spends much of her time at the palace my father built for her away from the city." She liked to escape grim memories.

It almost felt an insult to bring the daughter of his father's lover to meet his mother, the Queen Mother Tahirah. She had no idea of her husband's infidelity, of course. Keeping the knowledge from her was why Karim had orchestrated to marry Galila, but *he* knew. It grated against his conscience along with the rest of the secrets he kept.

Galila noted his expression and asked, "What?" with a small frown. She looked hurt as she touched the scarf she had tucked beneath her popped collar, then glanced down to ensure her skirt and jacket were straight. "Is my hair mussed?"

He cleared whatever shadows had invaded his expression. "No. You're beautiful. Perfect."

Her thick lashes swept down and she showed him her profile, but he knew she was eyeing him, suspicious of his compliment.

"You are and you know it," he chided. "Don't expect me to pander to your vanity."

Her painted mouth tightened. "Because I'm not a person whose feelings you care about or even an object you desire. I'm a rung on a ladder."

He pursed his lips, weighing her words and the scorn beneath them.

"Our marriage is expedient, yes. That doesn't mean it can't be successful. Many arranged marriages are."

"When both parties agree to said marriage, I'm sure they are."

They landed and disembarked, forestalling further debate—which was unproductive at this point. She was going to marry him and that was that.

"This is very beautiful," Galila said, gazing on the pink marble and intricately carved teak doors.

While Karim agreed, he found the extravagance of the palace disturbing. Clearly his father had been eager to please his wife with it. This wasn't a guilty conscience. He had built it before Queen Namani had come into the picture. Sadly, whatever he had felt for Karim's mother had been overshadowed by what he had felt for the other woman. And Karim and his mother hadn't been enough to live for, once Queen Namani ended their affair.

What, then, must his father have felt for Queen Namani if his first—and supposedly lesser—infatuation had produced this sort of monument? It was a depth of passion—of possession—Karim couldn't wrap his head around. He instinctively shied away from examining it too closely, maintaining a safe distance the way he would a conflagration or other life-threatening force.

As Galila started up the steps, he touched her arm, halting her.

She stilled and seemed to catch her breath. A soft blush rose under her skin.

Her reaction caused an echoing thrill inside him, one that warned him that he was tying himself to a ticking bomb and had to be very careful. On the surface, this physical compatibility might be exciting and promise a successful union, but he knew what indulged passion could do to a man.

He yanked the reins on his own response, hard, especially as he realized he was taking advantage of every opportunity to touch her and still had his palm on her arm. He dropped his hand to his side with self-disgust.

She was looking right at him and whatever she read

in his expression made a tiny flinch cross her features. It was gone so fast, he could have been mistaken, but it slid an invisible wall between them, one that niggled at him.

She lifted her chin to a haughty angle. "Yes?"

"You'll be kind to my mother."

Her spine grew tall with offense. "I'm always kind." She flipped her hair. "I was being kind last night when I let you kiss me."

It took him a full second to understand that the unfamiliar sensation in his throat was an urge to laugh. He couldn't recall the last time he'd loosened up enough for *that*, and fought it out of instinct.

At the same time, a deeper reaction—not ego, but definitely something that had roots in his masculinity—was affronted at her dismissal of their kisses last night. He knew exactly how potent they had been and didn't care for her trying to dismiss that inferno as "kindness."

The impulse to *show* her... But no. He refused to allow her to disarm him in any way. He waved her forward. "I'll look forward to your next act of kindness, then."

She narrowed her eyes.

"Come." He broke the eye contact. He could not, under any circumstances, become enamored with her. He had seen with his own eyes what falling for her mother had done to his father. He would not be another casualty to a Khalia temptress.

Despite its compact size and remote location, expense had not been spared on the desert palace. Galila was no stranger to wealth, but even she had to appreciate the effort of transporting marble and teak doors.

Inside, a fountain provided a musical ripple of noise and cooled the air. Columns rose three stories to a stained-glass dome. Mosaics in green and blue covered the walls to eye height before switching to delicate patterns in golds and blues and tangerines. Wrought iron marked the second-and third-floor walkways that encircled this grand foyer.

"I don't know what this is. A genie's lamp?" She was in love. "It's too beautiful for words."

Karim drew her up some stairs so thickly carpeted their shoes made no sound. They entered his mother's parlor where he introduced her to the Queen Mother Tahirah.

The older woman rose to greet them, her face holding deeply etched marks of grief that reminded Galila of the ones her father wore.

"It's like Queen Namani has come to visit me. Her beauty survives, if not my dear friend herself," she said, taking Galila's hands as she studied her features. "I'm so sorry for your loss."

"Thank you," Galila murmured, returning Tahirah's kisses against her cheeks, genuinely touched by her condolence. "I didn't realize you knew my mother, but of course you must have met her at some point through the years."

Was it her imagination that Karim stiffened? She glanced at him, but only saw the aloof expression she couldn't read. The one that stung because it felt like a condemnation for reasons she didn't understand.

"When we were young, yes," his mother said, drawing her attention back to her. "We often met up after we were both married, but lost touch after my husband passed. My fault. I ceased most of my royal duties and

rarely went on social visits. I couldn't face the respon-
sibilities without my soul, Jamil. Thankfully Karim's
uncle was able to manage things until Karim was old
enough to take his rightful position. And now my son
has found happiness." Her faint smile was a weak ray
of light in her otherwise anguished expression.

Oh, yes, they were both quite giddy and could hardly
contain themselves, Galila thought, but she *was* kind
to the less fortunate. Tahirah might be surrounded by
extravagance, but she was the living embodiment of
money not buying happiness. Her heart was clearly broken and had been for a long time.

"I expect we will both be very content as we go into
the future," Galila prevaricated, adding a silent, *sepa-
rately*. Read the news, gentlemen. Times had changed.

"And the wedding?" Tahirah asked.

"Within the month," Karim said firmly. "As soon as
it can be arranged."

Galila stiffened, wondering if he had been planning
to ask her about the timeline, but kept her pique to herself as Tahirah drew her across to the satin-covered
loveseat.

"There's time for you to wear my engagement ring,
then. I had it brought out of the safe."

"I...don't know what to say." Galila looked from the
velvet box that Tahirah presented to her, then looked up
to Karim, completely taken aback.

He nodded slightly, urging her to accept it.

She opened it and caught her breath.

An enormous pink diamond was surrounded by
white baguettes. The wide band was scrolled with tendrils of smaller diamonds, making it as ostentatious as
anything could be, but it was also such a work of art,

it had to be admired. Coveted and adored, as every woman would want to be by her fiancé as she anticipated joining with him for a lifetime.

Her heart panged at the love that shone from such a piece, something she would never have if she married this man. She swallowed, searching for a steady voice.

"This is stunning. Obviously very special. I'm beyond honored." And filled with anguish that this was such a farce of a marriage when this ring was clearly from a marriage of total devotion. "Are you quite sure?" She looked again to Karim, helplessly in love with it but not wanting to accept something so precious when she was quite determined to abandon him at the first opportunity. She couldn't be kind *and* lie to this poor woman.

"I am," Tahirah said with a husk in her voice. "I haven't worn it in years, but it is beautiful, isn't it? Karim's father loved me so much. Spoiled me outrageously. Built me this palace..." She blinked nostalgia-laden eyes. "Losing him still feels as raw today." She squeezed Galila's hand. "And I'm quite sure Karim is as enamored with you. He has always told me he was waiting for the right woman. I'm delighted he finally found you."

Galila conjured a feeble smile that she hoped his mother interpreted as overwhelming gratitude. She felt very little conscience in defying her brother or even Karim, but misrepresenting herself to Tahirah was disrespectful and hurtful. She was genuinely sorry that she was going to disappoint her.

Karim took the ring from the box and held out his hand for Galila to offer hers.

His warm touch on her cool fingers made her draw

in her navel and hold her breath, but it didn't stop the trickle of heat that wound through her, touching like fairy dust to secretive places, leaving glittering heat and a yearning she didn't completely understand.

Yet again, she experienced a moment of wishing there could be something more between them, something real, but he was being entirely too heavy-handed. She was a modern woman, not someone who would succumb to a man because she'd been ordered to by another.

At the same time, she reacted to Karim as he bent to kiss her cheek. The corners of her mouth stopped cooperating and went every direction. She thought he drew a deliberate inhale, drinking in the scent of her skin when his face was that close, but he straightened away and she was lost at sea again.

She looked to her hands in her lap, pulse throbbing in her throat and tried to focus on the ring. When she finally saw it clearly, she was utterly taken with it—as she was by all sparkly, pretty things. But it was legitimately loose on her, not even staying on her middle finger without dropping right off.

"I would feel horrible if anything happened to it," she said truthfully to Karim. "Would you please take custody of it until it can be resized?"

"If you prefer."

"Do you mind?" she asked Tahirah before she removed it. "I would be devastated if I lost it. It's so beautiful and means so much to you."

Tahirah looked saddened but nodded. "Of course. It's even loose on me these days. It fit me perfectly through my pregnancy and Karim's childhood, but I haven't had a proper appetite since losing his father. Once I took it off, I couldn't bear to wear it again. It reminded me too starkly of what I'd lost. Everything does."

This was why Karim was marrying Galila, this anguish that his mother still carried three decades after her loss. How could he take the grief she attributed to a tragic accident and reveal that her husband had deliberately left her? That he had thrown himself off a balcony, rather than face life without the *real* object of his love?

Fortunately, Galila asked about the palace and other things, not letting his mother dwell too far in the darkness of the past. Karim had been worried when the topic of her mother had come up as they arrived, but now they were moving on to a recap of her brother's wedding and other harmless gossip.

At a light knock, his mother said, "I've had a luncheon prepared. Shall we go through to my private dining room?"

Galila excused herself to freshen up.

"She seems lovely," his mother said as Galila disappeared.

"She is," Karim said, relieved to discover Galila was so skillful at small talk. Their marriage was expedient, and he had spent a restless night thinking that having her as a wife would be a sexually gratifying, if dangerous, game, but he was seeing potential in her to be the sort of partner who fit into his world as if made for it.

She was royal herself. Of course she understood the niceties and other social finesses that were required, especially with women and the older generation. He wasn't sure he wanted to like her for it, though. He needed his guard up at all times.

A servant started to come in, saw they were still in the parlor and quickly made apologies for interrupting them, turning to exit just as quickly.

He noticed what the girl held and waved her to come in and attend to her task.

"Haboob?" he asked his mother as the maid crouched to set the seals in place around the door onto the balcony. He'd been too distracted this morning to check the weather, but the dust storms came up very suddenly, which was probably why his pilot hadn't said anything.

"I'll have rooms prepared for you," his mother said, taking his arm as he led her into her private dining room. It overlooked the oasis next to which the palace was built. The wind was already tugging at the fronds of the palms and whirling sand into small devils.

"I need to return to Nabata this afternoon. Perhaps we'll skip the meal—" He glanced up as a different servant appeared, wide-eyed and anxiously wringing her hands. Thankfully, she stood behind his mother so his mother didn't see her.

Karim knew instantly what the trouble was. Galila should have rejoined them by now. He scratched his cheek, not revealing his instantaneous fury.

"You'll have to excuse us, Mother. We'll stay ahead of the storm. I hope you'll join us in Nabata very soon and have a proper chance to get to know Galila before the wedding."

"Of course," she said with disappointment. "Be careful. I should say goodbye."

"No need." He kissed her cheek and strode from the

room, taking the maid into the hall with him. He asked which car Galila had taken, then hurried outside the palace to snap his fingers at his pilot.

They had to catch his runaway princess before she was caught in the coming storm.

CHAPTER THREE

GALILA'S GETAWAY WAS an exhilarating race down a straight stretch of paved road through the desert. If the sun seemed to dim, she blamed the tinted windows, not her mood. She didn't have any gloomy feelings about leaving Karim. Zero. She couldn't do it fast enough.

Then the light pouring through the sunroof really did change. It became a strobing flash as a helicopter hovered over the car, casting its shadow on the hood. The *rat-a-tat* chop of the blades cut into the otherwise luxuriously silent interior.

"So what?" she shouted. "I have a full tank and an open road."

She would get herself to the border into Khalia and once there, she would be her own person again. She would fly to Europe and stay there. Pull a Malak and quit the family. Do whatever the hell she wanted.

She jammed her foot even harder onto the accelerator. The road was straight and clear, not another car in sight.

He raced ahead, staying low, then stopped and landed in the middle of the road.

"Bastard!"

She had half a mind to ram the car straight into him.

With a muted scream of frustration through gritted teeth, she lifted her foot from the accelerator.

As her speed dropped off, she searched for a way around the helicopter, but it blocked both lanes. This car wouldn't get very far off-road, unfortunately. The soil might look hard-packed, but pockets of loose sand could swallow a tire in a heartbeat. This was the sort of sedan built for a paved highway, not scrubby desert. It would spin in the dirt until it ran out of fuel.

Turn around? The only place to go was back to his mother's palace.

Oh, she was frustrated as she braked! She came to a reluctant stop as she reached the helicopter while its blades were still rotating.

She flung herself from the car. The wash off the rotors caught at her hair. She used a finger to drag it out of her eyes.

"I *will not* marry you," she shouted in single-syllable blurts when Karim came out of the helicopter, expression thunderous.

"Look," he said with a stabbing point to her left.

That was when she realized why the sky had been growing darker. A red-brown cloud rose like a tsunami against the sky. *Haboob.*

She didn't normally swear out loud, so she swallowed the words threatening to fall from her lips.

"We'll outrun it. I want to be in Nabata when it hits." Karim threw his arm around her, using his body to shield her as best he could while he more or less dragged her toward the helicopter.

Much as she wanted to fight him, windstorms could be deadly.

"What about the car?" she shouted.

His pilot was already leaping out of his seat. Galila presumed he would take the vehicle back to the palace and allowed Karim to push her into the copilot's seat.

"This isn't an agreement to marry you," she told him as she buckled in and accepted the headphones he handed her.

He ignored her statement as he quickly buckled in himself and put on his own headset. Maybe he didn't hear her. He lifted off in seconds, perfectly adept as a pilot, which was kind of sexy, not that she wanted to notice.

Within moments, they were racing toward the rocky hills in the distance.

She eyed him, trying to gauge how angry he was. It was difficult to tell when his body seemed to move with natural precision and that stern mouth of his had probably never smiled. She hadn't expected to get caught so she hadn't worried too much about his reaction to her escape, but he wasn't her father and her brothers.

Until this morning, she had been confident she could cajole nearly anything out of anyone—schooling in Europe, Thoroughbred horses, designer clothing. When it came to her charity work, she was a money-raising machine, squeezing record donations out of men and women alike. With very few exceptions, she always got what she wanted.

Things had changed, however. Her stupid brother had put her at the mercy of this wretched man and Karim didn't strike her as the indulgent sort, his mother's remarks notwithstanding. In fact, the longer she watched him, the more her uneasiness grew.

He swore, sudden and sharp as a gunshot, loud enough to make her jump because it came into her head through the earmuffs, crystal clear. For one second, she thought the curse had been aimed at her, then he made a sudden veering motion that tilted them as he avoided something.

She looked forward where visibility had become severely reduced. Despite his efforts, the storm was wrapping around them, buffeting the helicopter. They were running out of time. And options.

He went lower, searching for a safe place to land, but the rotor wash kicked up more dust, making it nearly impossible to see what was on the ground.

"There!" she said as she saw a flash of blue and green, black and yellow—colors and symmetries that didn't belong in the rust-red of the desert. It was a Bedouin camp, men running around securing tents and corralling the camels.

Karim set down on the nearest flat piece of land and turned off the engine, but the rotors continued to turn and whine.

"I have to tie down. Wait here." He leaped from the helicopter.

One of the Bedouins clutched his head-covering and ran to greet him. She saw the shock and flash of a wide smile of recognition before the man hurried to help, shouting at one of his fellow tribesmen that their sheikh was among them.

"Tell the women," she heard him shout. To prepare food and suitable lodging, Galila surmised.

She pulled off her headphones and drew the scarf from around her neck to drape it over her head and prepare to wrap it across her face. Zyria wasn't a country where face covering was demanded, but she would have to protect herself from the blast of dust.

That was when she realized her purse was in the car and she didn't have her sunglasses. Her toothbrush was with her luggage, though.

She went through to the passenger cabin, having to catch her balance twice because the wind was trying so hard to knock the helicopter off its footings. The luggage compartment was easily accessed and she quickly retrieved her necessities along with stealing the shaving kit out of Karim's case. Such things were always the last into the luggage so it was right on top.

Then she shamelessly dumped his laptop bag onto an empty seat. She began filling it with the contents of the onboard pantry—coffee and tea, fresh oranges and bananas, nuts and dried figs, cheese and crackers, chocolates and Turkish delight. Caviar? Sure. Why not?

"What the hell are you doing?" he bit out as he came through from the cockpit.

"Food." She showed him the bag, swollen with his travel larder. "Our toothbrushes are in here, too. Time to run?" She buttoned her jacket and drew her scarf across her face.

He clearly hadn't expected this. He glanced at her heeled shoes. Yes, well, she hadn't made a priority of digging out her pool sandals. She'd been too busy making herself useful.

The helicopter jerked again. They couldn't stay here. The very thing that kept this bird aloft was liable to topple it in the wind. The Bedouins had spent centuries learning how to wait out these types of storms, however. She and Karim would be safer in one of their tents.

Karim leaped out the side door, not bothering with the steps. He reached back to take her by the hips and lift her to the ground while one of the Bedouins stood by and slammed the door behind her.

She dragged her scarf up to peer through the layer of silk, relying more on Karim's hard arms around her to guide her than the ability to actually see. She had only ever watched a storm through a window. It was terrifying to be in it, making her anxious when Karim pressed her into a tent and left her there.

A handful of women were moving around inside it, efficiently smoothing bright blue sheets and plumping cushions on a low bed, setting out a battery-operated lantern on a small dining rug and urging her to sit at a washing basin.

The walls and roof of the tent fluttered while the wind howled and sand peppered the exterior. She removed her scarf and jacket, grateful to wipe away the worst of the dust with a damp cloth. She wound up changing into the silk nightgown she had thrown into the bag since all of her clothes felt so gritty. It wasn't cold in here, not with the sunbaked earth still radiating heat and so many warm bodies in here, but she accepted the delicate shawl one woman handed her.

The entire camp had been informed that the sheikh's intended bride, the Princess of Khalia, was among them. They were pulling out all the stops, eager to praise her choice of husband.

Choice? Ha!

But they wanted to make her comfortable so Galila bit her tongue. She had done enough work with the underprivileged to understand that her problems were not the sort that most people identified with. These women had chapped hands and tired smiles. Everything they owned, they carried.

She let them fuss over her, rather appreciating the motherly kindness of the old woman who wanted to brush her hair. After she had washed her face and hands, she gave her moisturizer to the old woman. The woman laughed and said nothing could erase her wrinkles, but she was pleased all the same.

The other women were excited by the fresh fruit and other treats, insisting on adding a selection from the bag to Galila's meal of stew and lentils.

That was when Galila realized the dining mat was set for two.

What had Karim told them? They couldn't share this tent! They weren't married.

Karim was their sheikh, however. When he entered the tent, the women scattered with gasps and giggles, not a single protest for Galila's honor.

It was fully dark outside by then, despite the still early hour. The tent was lit only by the small lantern over the meal they would share. The wind howled so loudly, she couldn't hear any voices in the neighboring tents.

Now she realized why the women had been so admiring of this silly nightgown, intent on ensuring her hair was shiny and tangle-free as it flowed around her bare shoulders and fell just so across the lace on her back. That was why they had praised him and called him lucky and said she would make him a good and dutiful wife.

They thought she was consummating her wedding night!

She hugged the delicate shawl more closely around her. Her pulse throbbed in the pit of her belly. She curled her toes into the silk nap of the rug beneath her feet, clammy and hot at the same time. Her mind trailed to the way he'd made her feel last night, kissing her so passionately, while the rest of her fluttered with nerves.

He took a long, leisurely perusal from her loose hair to the hem of her ivory nightgown.

Without a word, he removed his robe and scraped his headwear off, tossing the dust-covered garments aside without regard. He wore a white tunic beneath that he also peeled off, leaving him bare-chested in loose white pants that hung low across his hips. He stepped out of his sandals.

She swallowed.

His mouth might have twitched, but he only turned and knelt with splayed thighs on the bathing mat, using the same cloth she had run down her throat and under her breasts to wash his face and behind his neck.

She shouldn't be watching him. Her pulse raced with a taboo excitement as she gazed on the burnished skin that flexed across his shoulders. Her ears picked up the sound of water being wrung from the cloth, and his quiet sigh of relief. Those sounds did things to her. Her skin tightened and her intimate regions throbbed.

She imagined replacing that cloth with her hands, smoothing soap along the strong arm he raised, running slippery palms up his biceps, over his broad shoulders, down to his chest and rib cage. If she snaked her touch beneath his arm to his navel, would she be able to trace the narrow line of hair she had glimpsed, the one that disappeared into the waistband of his trousers?

What would he look like completely naked? What would he *feel* like?

As wildness threatened to take her over completely,

she tried to forestall it by blurting, "You shouldn't be in here."

"Worried about your reputation? We're married." He stayed on the mat with his back to her, continuing to stroke the cloth along his upraised arms and across his chest.

"I don't know how to say this more clearly, but—"

"They have already given up one much-needed tent for me," he interjected, pausing in his bath to speak over her. "I won't ask them to prepare one for you as well. We share this one. Therefore, we must be married. We are."

"Just like that?" she choked. "The sheikh has spoken and thus it is so?"

"Exactly."

She didn't even have words for the weakness that went through her. She told herself it was the deflation of watching her childhood dreams of a royal wedding disappear in a poof, but it was the way her life had changed in the time it took for him to make a declaration.

"You can't." She spoke so faintly she was surprised he heard her.

"It is done, Galila. Accept it." He rinsed the cloth and gave it a hard wring.

"I can't."

She had avoided marriage for many reasons, one of the biggest ones being that she wanted a choice in how she lived her life. At no time had she been satisfied with the idea of putting her fate into the hands of any man—particularly one who didn't love her and didn't seem to even *like* her. She barely knew him!

What she did know was that he was strong and powerful in every way. No one would come to her aid here even if they heard her scream over the wailing wind.

In a matter of a few words, he had stripped away all the shields she possessed—her family name, her station as Khalia's only princess, even the composure she had taken years to construct. There was no affection or admiration or infatuation to leverage here. This was all about expediency. About what *he* wanted.

She tightened her fists at her sides, throat aching while the backs of her eyes grew hot, but she refused to let him see she was terrified.

"You are an educated man with intelligence and—I would hope—a shred of honor." Perhaps that wasn't true, considering he'd used her at the wedding and seemed to have no conscience about behaving like a barbarian from centuries ago. Realizing that made her tremble even harder. "You can't just declare us married and force yourself on me."

"I'm not going to attack you," he said sardonically. "Quit sounding like a terrified virgin."

"I *am* a virgin." She spat it out with as much angst as anger.

He froze, then dropped the cloth and rose, pivoting so neatly on the ball of his foot, the rug gathered beneath him into a knot.

"How?" he asked, sounding very casual with his inquiry, but the intensity that seemed to grip him caused the hot coil in her belly to tighten and glow while her heart teetered and shifted. It thumped in wavering beats, unsure whether to feel threatened or excited under his laser-sharp regard.

"What do you mean, 'how'?" She grew prickly with self-consciousness, face scorched even though virginity was nothing to be ashamed of. "The usual way. By not having sex."

"You're twenty-*five*."

"Six."

He gave his head a small shake, as if he didn't understand the words passing between them.

"How have you not been with a man?"

"I've dated. Had boyfriends. I'm not…completely inexperienced." None of her relationships had lasted, though, because she didn't put out. Not much, anyway. She confined things to kissing and a bit of petting. She knew what happened between the sheets. Girlfriends had described the process in profound detail over the years, which truth be told, hadn't always been a selling feature. The process sounded both incredibly intimate and kind of ridiculous.

"Weren't you curious?"

"Sure." She shrugged, trying to appear offhand when this conversation was equally intimate and awkward. "But not enough to sleep with a man just to know what happens. It's not a book where you can skip to the end and make sure it will satisfy before you wade through all the exposition."

He made a noise that might have been a choke of amusement, but his face remained a mask of astonishment.

"What?" she demanded. She had wanted more. So much more than the tepid feelings that most men inspired in her. Even when her suitors had been adoring and dazzled by her, it hadn't been enough. She hadn't trusted their infatuation to last. She needed *more*.

Karim hung his hands off his hips. "You were going to take me to your room last night," he reminded.

"I was drunk," she claimed, even though with him, it had been different. She had felt the "more" that she'd been craving. At least, she'd thought she had. Now she was so confused, she didn't know what she felt.

He barked out a single harsh, "Ha!" and came toward her.

She stumbled backward in alarm only to have him catch at her arms and steady her.

"You're about to step into our dinner."

She shrugged off his touch, disturbed by the way her whole body was now tingling, and lowered to the rug with him, the food between them.

He stretched out on his side, propped on an elbow. His stern face relaxed a smidge. Maybe. She watched him closely, but wasn't sure.

"Are you laughing at me?"

"No." He reached for an olive in a dish. "Us, maybe. I don't care for lies," he stated. "Tell me now if it's not true. You're really a virgin?"

In the low light, his eyes were more black pupil than brown iris as his gaze came up to take hold of her own, refusing to let it go.

"I am," she said, wondering why her voice had retreated behind a veil and came out shy and wispy. She cleared her throat, searching for the confident woman who usually occupied her skin. "Are you?"

"No." Flat and unapologetic.

She managed to break their stare by rolling her eyes. She had fully expected that answer, but a pang struck in her chest all the same. Jealous? That would be a ridiculous response when she kind of hated him.

Didn't she?

He ate another olive, still watching her. "Be thankful I'm familiar with writing compelling exposition."

"Don't be smug." The pang went through her again.

She wanted to splay her hand over his face and give him a firm shove.

His mouth twitched. "You've been living in Europe for years. I would have thought you would have been drunk before last night."

She had, but she ignored the dig inside his comment and asked, "How do you know where I've been living?"

He shrugged. His gaze lowered to scan the food, but it seemed like a subterfuge.

"Big fan of gossip sites, are you?" she prompted.

"My advisors have kept you on my list of prospects for years. Ours has always been seen as an advantageous match. I would have thought it had been viewed that way in Khalia as well. Your father never suggested me when discussing your own marriage plans? Frankly, I'm surprised you're still single, never mind a virgin."

"Names came up, yours among them," she admitted. "I wasn't interested in marrying so I never bothered to look at photos or read any of the advisements I was sent. Being in Europe, I didn't attend many events to meet any bachelors, either. My mother always sided with me that I didn't have to hurry into marriage."

"That seems odd. Why not?"

Galila shrugged, curling her knees under her, trying to get comfortable but feeling as though she sat on sharp stones. It wasn't the ground beneath the floor of the tent, however. It was the rocky relationship with her mother that was poking at her.

Karim reached a long arm to the bed and handed her a cushion.

"Thank you," she murmured and shoved it under her hip.

"Your mother didn't encourage any match? Or just

not ours?" He seemed to watch her with hawk-like attention.

"It wasn't personal." She told herself she was reading more intense interest from him than the topic warranted because she was feeling so sensitive. She took her time arranging her nightgown so it covered her feet, not wanting him to read the layers of mixed feelings she carried when it came to her mother. They were far too close to the bone to share with a stranger. She wasn't drunk tonight, and she had learned the hard way that he used every weakness for his own gain. "She was sensitive to the signs of age. Preferred to put off being called Grandmother as long as possible."

It hadn't been about her daughter's well-being, but it had suited Galila to avoid the shackles so she had been grateful.

He made a noncommittal noise and accepted the bowl of stew she served him.

"Karim," she said, boldly using his name and finding it a caress in her throat. "I am a modern woman with a liberal education. You cannot expect me to give you my virginity simply because you declare us married."

"Galila." Somehow, he sounded as if he mocked her solemnity, yet turned her own name into an endearment. "You caught fire in my arms when your senses were dulled by alcohol. Your sober brain is now regretting your impulsiveness, but I expect we'll be even more combustible when we lie together. You will give me your virginity because you want to."

She couldn't move, felt caught in amber, her whole being suffused with thick honey that suffocated with the aim of creating something eternal.

"I had hoped that would be tonight," he added in a

voice that seemed to roll into her ears from far away, barely discernible over the noise outside the swaying walls of this tent. "But your inexperience changes things. We'll wait for your trust in me to grow. I've given my staff two weeks to arrange a wedding ceremony and reception at the palace. We can wait until then."

She choked. A whole two weeks? Wow.

"How am I *ever* supposed to trust you when you tricked me into this?" she asked, voice cracking with emotion. "How am I supposed to feel confident—proud—to be your queen when I'm only a strategic political move?"

That was his cue to profess a deeper interest in her as a woman. It wouldn't be a lie to say he was intrigued by the facets she kept revealing. He had thought her impulsive and spoiled, not given to thinking of others. That was certainly the impression she had left last night. Her brother's disparagement of her actions this morning had more or less confirmed it.

But she had put his mother at ease and it didn't escape him that she had ensured the family ring stayed in his possession while she plotted her foiled escape.

He had been prepared to let loose with his riled temper when he confronted her on the highway, but she hadn't kicked up a fuss at their emergency takeoff. She had evacuated with as much awareness of their danger as required. She wasn't balking at camping with the Bedouins, either. Instead of acting like she was above these rough conditions, she had ensured they contributed to the community food supply, guaranteeing she reflected well on him and the union he had made and knowing full well it would affect his country in subtle, unalterable ways.

The worst complaint he had so far was that she had cost him a favored laptop bag, since he wouldn't dream of asking for its return. Even her escape had worked to his advantage, providing him a reason to shift their marriage from intended to a *fait accompli*. He had been on fire since he had spoken the words.

Now he had discovered she was a virgin? He had neither expected nor particularly wanted an untouched bride, but having one was an inordinate thrill. A primal possessiveness gripped him, chest and belly and groin. He would be the only man to stroke and taste and mate with her. She was *his*.

His inner barbarian howled with triumph, recalling the way she had ignited in his arms, demanding to stoke that blaze into an all-consuming inferno *now*.

The very fact he hovered so close to losing his rational brain to the primal one, however, told him he had to slow things down. For her sake and his own.

So he was careful to keep his tone even, not betraying how craven desire licked like flames inside him. "You're very beautiful, Galila. Of course I desire you."

Every man she had ever come into contact with must have desired her. It defied comprehension that she had never physically shared herself with one of them. He wasn't in the habit of disbelieving people, but he genuinely couldn't understand how a woman of her naturally sensual nature hadn't indulged her passion to its fullest extent. *He* had.

Or rather, he had always believed he had. She might have already reset the bar—which was yet another disturbing layer to this thing between them.

All of these thoughts he held to himself behind an impervious mask.

She studied him, picking apart his words and seeming to grow more and more skeptical of them as the seconds passed.

"My beauty has nothing to do with this. You don't care if I'm beautiful. You're beautiful. Do you want me to believe you chose me so we can make beautiful babies?"

He felt his eyebrows jump. The topic of an heir hadn't entered his mind beyond the abstract, but now she had brought it up...

"We should talk about that."

"How beautiful you are?"

"Children."

She scowled and shifted to hug her knees. "Politically expedient broodmare. Is that what I am? How romantic. A thousand times yes, I wish to be your wife, Karim."

He ought to curtail that sarcasm. No one else in their right mind would speak with such casual disrespect toward him, but he found her temper revealing. She probably didn't realize how much of her genuine thoughts and emotions she betrayed with that barbed tongue of hers.

"You had other plans for your life? Tell me how I've derailed them. Perhaps there's a compromise."

"Yes, you strike me as a man who compromises all the time."

Ah. That was what she was afraid of.

"I rarely have to," he admitted. "From the time I was old enough to grasp an adult conversation, I sat with my father in his meetings. He died when I was six and my uncle continued to include me in every decision he made on my behalf, explaining his reasoning. By the time I was fourteen, I was effectively running the country with his guidance and support. *He* carried out *my* wishes until I was officially crowned."

She blinked wide eyes at him. "Zufar is barely ready for that level of responsibility at thirty-three."

"He has the luxury of a father who still lives."

She cocked her head with curiosity. "What happened to your father? It was an accident, wasn't it? I don't recall exactly."

"He fell from a balcony at the palace." He repeated the lie by rote, even though it grated on him to this day that he was forced to carry such a dark secret. He hated lies, probably because his father had burdened him with such earth-shattering ones. "He'd been drinking."

"Ah," she said with soft compassion. "That's why you were so disparaging. I see now why you resent anyone who fails to appreciate the destructive power of alcohol."

He resented a lot of things—his father's affair with her mother, her mother for leaving his father and causing his father to pursue a desperate act. Now Karim learned there had been a child? It wasn't as though he hadn't considered that possibility over the years—and again in the last twenty-four hours specifically where Galila was concerned. She had been born long after his father had died, however. There was no chance they were related, which was quite possibly the only bright spot in this otherwise three-act tragedy.

"Do you want to tell me about him?" she invited gently.

"No." He didn't regret his abrupt response. He rarely spoke about his father, but the way she closed up like a flower, showing him her stony profile, caused him to sigh internally.

Women. They were as delicate as thin-skinned fruit, bruising at the least thing.

"Your father left you without a choice," she summed up, still not looking at him. "So you're comfortable imposing a lack of choice on others."

He wasn't so soft he felt stung by that remark, but he did feel it, maybe because the fact she was striking out that hard told him how deeply her own resentment ran at what he was demanding of her.

"You weren't planning to avoid marriage forever, were you?" People in their position couldn't.

"I was waiting to fall in love."

Ah. Something like regret moved in him, but he wanted there to be no false hopes between them.

"It's true that I will never expect or offer you love," he agreed. "That particular emotion is as treacherous and devastating as alcohol."

"You've been in love?" Her pupils exploded as though she'd taken a punch.

"No. Like alcohol, I don't need to imbibe to see the inherent risks and have the sense to avoid it."

A small flinch and her lashes swept down, mouth pouted.

"It doesn't mean we can't have a successful marriage. In fact, going into this union with realistic expectations ensures we won't be disappointed in the long run."

"Is that what you think?" She took a cube of cheese. "Because the problem isn't whether you can grow to love me. It's that I expected to choose my own husband, not have one forced upon me. I *expected* to make a family when it felt right, because I wanted to see something of my husband in the children I made. If you give me sons and daughters, I'm sure I'll love them, but I don't desire your children."

That one did land in a previously unknown vulnerability. Why?

"Meanwhile, you expect me to give up my freedom so you won't have to go through the inconvenience of renegotiating a few trade agreements with the new Sheikh of Khalia. The two most important decisions any woman will make are whom she will marry and whether she will have children. You expect to make both of those decisions for me. That's not fair."

"As I said, we can talk about children." He wasn't a monster. He had already said they could curtail the sex, hadn't he?

"You still expect me to breed with you eventually," she said with a sharp angst. "You gain on every level with this marriage and I gain nothing. In fact, I lose everything. And I'm not even allowed to feel disappointed? *Your* expectations are the ones that are too high, Karim."

CHAPTER FOUR

"I CAN GIVE you pleasure."

The wind had died down, the light was off, and the sound of a gently plucked string on a *rababeh* carried from one of the other tents. They weren't expected to appear before morning so they had turned in early. Galila had formed a dam down the center of the mattress with a rolled mat and a few cushions before asking Karim which side he wanted.

"Everything that happens in bed between us will be your choice," was his response.

She had sat there stunned by what sounded like a vow, trying to understand why she felt both moved and overwhelmed. It felt like too much responsibility for a woman who knew so little about the things she might want from her marriage bed.

And now, in the darkest dark, he was telling her he could teach her.

She wanted to say something cynical but couldn't find any words, let alone form them with her dry mouth and even drier throat.

"Are you awake?" he asked in a quieter voice.

"Yes." She probably should have stayed silent and let him think she had missed hearing what he said, but she revealed her wakefulness and died a little inside. She threw her wrist across her eyes, wanting to go back thirty hours or so and never take a single sip of brandy at her brother's wedding.

The silence between them grew with expectation.

"I can give myself pleasure," she pointed out, glad for the dark so he wouldn't see her blush at the admission she was making.

Silence was his answer, but she swore she could hear him smiling.

"Don't even pretend you don't…" She couldn't finish the sentence.

"Read the footnotes?" he suggested.

"Oh, yes, you're a delight in bed. So glad I can share this one with you." She turned her back on him and clenched her eyes shut. Her fist knotted in the edge of the blanket and nestled it tight under her chin.

After a pensive few minutes, he said, "I had to take advantage of the opportunity you presented me, Galila."

"Yes, well, I'm not presenting one now. Perhaps give me some quiet so I can get my beauty sleep."

"For various reasons, I never thought you and I would be a good fit, despite the fact my advisors consistently brought you to my attention. You seemed young, wayward and superficial."

"Are you sure you're not a virgin? Because you're offering very little pleasure with remarks like that."

"No one else appealed to me, though." He sounded almost as if this was a surprise revelation only occurring to him now, one that dismayed him. He sounded disturbed, even.

She sighed. "Please don't make this about my looks,

Karim. That's no better than using me for political gain."

"I didn't come to the wedding intending to make an offer for you. I wouldn't have kissed you if you hadn't kissed me first. But when we did…"

"Karim." She was glad for the dark because she was wincing with mortified agony. "I know you weren't as involved as I was. I felt your…" She swallowed. "Distance. Before we were seen."

"That only proves how attuned we are to one another. Physically."

"No! It proves you can manipulate me with my body while I have no such power over you."

He shifted abruptly, voice now coming from the space above and behind her shoulder, telling her he was propped on an elbow. "Did you want me to lose myself and make love to you against the wall where everyone could see us?"

"I wanted you not to use me!"

"I'm offering you a chance to use me."

"You're not that simplistic. Or generous. You're going to get me all worked up, then say, 'Why don't we go all the way?' Not my first rodeo, cowboy."

"Am I?"

"What?"

"Going to get you all worked up? Because I know how to settle myself down. You have no fear I'll prevail on you to provide *my* happy ending."

"Oh!" She buried her cry of frustration into her pillow. "Fine," she declared with the impulsiveness that had earned her a reputation for being exactly as spoiled and wayward as everyone thought her. "Go ahead and prove there's something in this marriage for me. Give me all this pleasure you're so convinced you can provide."

Nothing. No compliments or commands. He didn't move.

She suspected he still hovered over her, but it was too dark to tell. She turned to face him, one hand inching just enough to feel the silk tassel on the cushion still between them.

He drew the rolled mat out of the way and his hand bumped hers when he sought the cushion. He kept hold of her hand.

She didn't know what to do. Pull away? Let her hand rest in his? She was nervous. Curious. Furious. Frustrated in more ways than one.

He lifted her hand and rubbed his lips against her knuckle. The short whiskers of his closely trimmed beard were silky soft where the backs of her fingers brushed against them.

"This isn't about how you look, Galila," he breathed across her skin. "I can't see you. It's about how we make each other feel."

"How do you feel?"

His humid breath bathed her palm before he spoke into it. "I'll let you know when you get there."

The light play of his mouth exploring her skin, the dampness when he opened his lips, sent heady tingles through her entire body. When he pressed a kiss into her palm and set his blazingly hot mouth against the inside of her wrist, tongue swirling against her pulse, she gasped at the wave of arousal that throbbed through her. It sent heaviness into her loins, stinging tightness to the tips of her breasts, and a helpless sob to catch in her throat.

"How are you doing this to me?" He was touching her *hand*.

"What am I doing? Tell me. I can't see you."

"You're—" She didn't want to admit he was seducing her. "I can't breathe. My heart feels like I've run miles."

He moved her hand to his neck, setting the heel of her palm against his smooth throat, next to where his Adam's apple moved as he swallowed. The artery there held a powerful pulse, one that was quick and hard.

"You're excited?" she asked.

"Of course."

No. He was tricking her again. But she found herself doing what she had last night, acting out of instinct, but this time her fingers were in his thick, silky hair. She urged him down and somehow their mouths found each other despite the blinding darkness.

The lack of light amplified the acuteness of her senses. Such a rush of heat went into her lips, her mouth stung under his, assuaged by the lazy way he settled into the kiss, easing her lips to part. She was the one to seek a deeper kiss by searching for his tongue with her own and moaned as their kiss grew fully involved.

His arm snaked around her and he tucked her half beneath him, weight settling more heavily on her. Then he lifted his head just enough to say, "Say yes," against her lips.

He wanted this to be her choice and it was. His bare chest pressed where the straps of her nightgown left her upper chest bare and she had never felt anything like that specific heat and texture. It was intoxicating.

"Yes," she whispered, arching to pull her hair out from beneath her.

It brushed against his skin, and he made a noise that suggested he had to reach for restraint.

"This might become my obsession," he said, gathering the long waves and burying his face in it. When he turned his head, his mouth was against her nape. He licked into the hollow beneath her ear and sucked on her earlobe, making her whimper in delight.

His touch moved to play his barely there fingertips against the silk of her nightgown, following the band of lace beneath her breasts where it hid her navel, coming back to climb the slippery silk alongside the swell of her breast. By the time his touch met where his lips had strayed, and he began to ease the narrow strap down her shoulder, her breasts were swollen and aching. She was so needy, she was feeling wild. Her own hands were moving restlessly across his shoulders, excited but apprehensive.

"I'm going to make love to you with my mouth," he said in a voice that barely penetrated the rush of blood in her ears. "That's not a pleasure you can give yourself."

Was that what she wanted? She didn't know, but she was too caught up in the sensation of his beard across the top of her breast. He bared it and she stopped being able to think straight. The heat of his breath warned her just before his mouth engulfed her nipple, but nothing could have prepared her for the way electricity seemed to shoot through her, stabbing into her heart so she thought it would burst. Sexual need raced in sharp lines to her loins, making her tingle and tremble as he pulled and laved and cupped the swell in his big hand and flicked his tongue against the turgid tip.

She could feel herself growing damp and slick. Heard wanton noises escaping her throat. She wanted him to keep sucking her nipples, but wanted to kiss him, too. It was the sweetest torture and she actually lifted and offered herself when he eased the other strap down, desperate for the delicious torture on her other breast.

Oh, he was making her crazy. She swirled her hands through his hair, over his damp neck, across his shoulders. The dip of his spine was an intriguing place and she even wickedly slipped her hand down to touch his chest, finding his own nipples sharp as shards of glass.

He rose to kiss her mouth again, hard and thorough. She moaned her approval, body rolling into his of its own volition, knee crooking.

When he ran his hand down her hip, he pushed the blankets away at the same time. Then he gathered the skirt of her nightgown, drawing it up so her legs felt the cool night air. It was erotic and almost a relief, she was so hot, but it was a moment of truth. Was this really what she wanted?

The darkness was a wonderful place, allowing her to hide and somehow protect her modesty as his touch strayed inward and brushed the damp hair between her thighs. He caressed her swollen lips, more of tease, so entrancing she allowed her thighs to relax open.

He didn't get the message and continued being so gentle, she wanted to sob with frustration. She was nothing but an agony of anticipation, waiting, longing, yearning for a firmer touch.

He shifted and slid down, pressed her legs wider, beard brushing the sensitive skin of her inner thigh, sweeping in brush strokes that made her gasp and quiver with need. When he turned his face against one thigh and the other, refusing to make contact where she pulsed with molten heat, she sobbed, "Karim."

"You want my mouth here?" His wide palm settled on her mound, the pressure not nearly firm enough.

He wanted her full surrender. She instinctively knew this wasn't compromise. It was his way of forcing her to accept his will, but it was such a wickedly delicious way. Seductive. Impossible to resist.

"I do," she admitted, feeling as though she gave herself up to him with the words, binding herself irrevocably to him. "I do, I do."

Openmouthed kisses edged closer. He parted her with delicate care, then wet heat slid along her most intimate flesh. Glittering pleasure suffused her, waves of growing arousal that rose as his attentions deepened. In fact, her level of involvement skyrocketed so fast and high, she didn't know how to handle it.

He paused, causing her to open her mouth in a silent scream of agony. Only his hot breath caressed her as he spoke in a graveled tone.

"Use your words, my pretty bird. I can't tell if you're struggling because you don't like it or you like it too much."

"Too much," she gasped. "So much. Please. Keep going."

He held her thighs open with firm hands, muting the buck of her hips as he took his time, seeming to recognize when she was on the brink of climax, then slowing to hold her on that plateau, forcing her to languish in that place of mindlessly unbearable perfection.

She stroked her fingers into his hair again, thinking this was ridiculous and far too personal, but she didn't care. She only wanted him to keep doing this forever, yet she could barely withstand the intensity of this pleasure. Not much longer. Couldn't. Absolutely couldn't bear it.

He pressed his mouth over her with firm possession, causing her to hit the crest of her wave with a cry of loss and triumph. Her entire body shuddered as the climax rolled through her in powerful waves.

He remained attentive, ensuring every last pulse was teased to its fullest degree, until she was spent and splayed, panting in the dark. She felt the dampness on her lashes against the arm she threw over her eyes. Yes, that had been so good, she had wept from the power of it.

He lifted away from her but remained between her legs so she couldn't close them. She was aware of his rapid movements, heard his shaken breath, then his long, jagged, relieved sigh.

She dropped her arm and blinked, trying to see him in the absolute dark.

"Did you—?"

"Yes." He stretched out beside her.

She felt a little cheated. Her hands itched to explore him.

He only turned her so she was spooned into his front. Her nightgown was still up around her hips, but he stopped her from trying to pull it down between them.

"Let me feel you against me." His hand smoothed up her hip, then down to settle on her abdomen. His lips touched her shoulder. "Think about how good it will be when I'm inside you and we come together."

When? Did he really want to wait until after their formal ceremony?

The naked contact with him was delicious. In fact, latent desire made the flesh of her mound tingle at the proximity of his hand. He might have given himself release, but he was still firm against her bare buttocks and she was already wondering how it would feel to have him moving inside her while she shattered. She didn't know if she wanted to wait until tomorrow morning, let alone two weeks from now.

Which had no doubt been his plan all along. Ruthless, vexing man.

His arm around her grew heavy as he relaxed into sleep, but she continued to blink into the darkness. She was starting to realize the power she had handed him by letting him take her to such heights. He was in her head now, making her eager to feel exactly what he had suggested. Him, moving inside her while they shattered in unison. He was making her want what he willed.

How would she take herself back from that?

Karim left his wife sleeping soundly beneath the light blanket. He was hard as titanium, more than primed to fully consummate his marriage, but *he* was master of himself. Not her. Not this need he had stoked by pleasuring her last night.

It was a toss-up as to which of them had enjoyed that more, much to his consternation. Had it been self-indulgent to offer himself like that? Absolutely. When he had settled beside her, he had had no intention of touching her.

But he did want this marriage to work. He did expect progeny from her. And yes, maybe his ego had been stinging from that remark she'd made about not desiring his children. He had definitely wanted to remind her that she desired *him*. That there was something he offered her that no one else could.

Maybe he had needed to prove it to himself, a dark voice whispered. Maybe he had wanted to prove he could pleasure her without losing command of himself—which he very nearly had. If she had invited him to deflower her, he would have been lost completely.

No, all he had proved last night was that the sexual connection between them was so potent, he couldn't entirely trust himself to be alone with her. It was exactly the depth of irrational passion he refused to succumb to the way his father had.

He *would* wait until they were formally married, if only to prove he could.

To that end, he steeled himself and stepped out to the cool morning air, found clean clothes for both of them in the helicopter, then did his preflight check while tribesmen brushed the sand off the blades and footings. He was drinking coffee with the men on the far side of the camp when Galila emerged from their tent in the linen pants and T-shirt the women had taken in to her.

Her gaze scanned the encampment until she found him. Pink stained her cheeks and sensual memory softened her expression. Her tentative smile invited him to smile back.

It took everything in him to stay rooted where he was and not cross to touch her. A nearly overwhelming pull urged him to move forward and press her back into their tent for the kind of lovemaking that drummed like a beat in his groin. A kiss, at least.

He confined himself to a cool nod of acknowledgment.

He was already glancing away when he saw her expression stiffen. He glanced back and her lashes had swept down. She quickly gave her attention to some children who approached, but her cheer seemed forced. She didn't look his way again as she was drawn into the circle of women and children.

His blood stayed hot with memory as he watched her. Her response to him had been exquisite. Explosive. Everything he could want in a wife—if he wasn't a man who knew there was a high cost to high passion. Seducing her had been a pleasure and a strategic move, but it had also been something that could all too easily take him over if he wasn't careful.

He watched her charm that side of the encampment as he continued his discussion with the elders in this tribe.

Karim might not have known Adir al-Zabah was his half brother, but he had heard the name through the years. Adir was renowned in the desert for his toughness and strong leadership, very much revered among the nomads. They couldn't tell Karim what family Adir had come from, however. His parents were unknown.

They asked why he was inquiring, but he brushed aside his questions as idle curiosity. The burden of secrets was his alone to carry.

The way the women and children adulated her was a much-needed balm to Galila's ego after Karim had barely acknowledged her this morning. She knew it was pathetic that she drank up this sort of starstruck wonder like water, but it filled a hollow spot her mother had carved with the hot-cold sway of her affections.

Sometimes Galila wondered if her desire for validation and appreciation ran deeper than that, and was a shared character flaw she had inherited from her mother. Perhaps it wasn't just an enjoyment of being recognized, but an expectation of glorification. Her mother had always acted as if the way her husband doted on her was natural and something to which she was entitled.

That certainly wasn't something Galila could anticipate from *her* husband, she acknowledged with a clench of hurt when he sent a young boy over to relay the message that it was time to leave.

She made promises to the women of supplies and aid as she said goodbye, enjoying the way they blessed her and touched her arms, asked her to kiss a baby and pray for a good marriage for the unmarried girls among them.

Karim waited until they were airborne and waving down at the Bedouins before speaking to her. They were connected via the microphone on the headsets again, making the communication feel almost more like a phone call. "You don't have to send anything. I asked the men. They don't need anything."

She heard something like her brothers' disparaging cynicism in his tone. *They* didn't buy regard with magnanimous acts the way she seemed to try to.

"It is a mark of pride among them, I'm sure, to insist that they meet the needs of their women without help," she responded. "It's little things. Teething gel for the boy who was crying. Feminine supplies for the young girl who is too embarrassed to ask for it. Things that aren't easy to come by out here. If you don't want to pay for it, I will." She had ample funds that had been set aside for her as part of her marriage contract.

"Of course, I'll pay for it," Karim said impatiently.

She curled the corner of her mouth. All men were

created equal when it came to impugning their pride, apparently.

He didn't realize how happy she was to spend other people's money on the needs of the less fortunate, however.

She quickly accepted his offer, adding, "I would appreciate very much if I could say you underwrote the things I send, since I also want to include some books for the girls. There seems to be controversy as to whether education is for all the children. It would go a long way if you made it clear you expect everyone to learn to read, not just the boys."

"I do." He wore a scowl as they approached the outskirts of Nabata, as if the remark struck a nerve.

Someone hailed him and he relayed an expected time of arrival, then returned to speaking to her.

"I realize we've fallen behind our neighbors in some ways. When my father was alive, my mother spearheaded women and children initiatives, but she has largely been not much more than a figurehead since his death. Without strong leadership, things have stagnated, rather than continuing to progress. Would you take up that mantle?"

Her first instinct was to leap on the opportunity. In Khalia, she had been her mother's envoy, often earning the credit but not receiving it. There were many times when she hadn't agreed with her mother's decisions, but had had to go along with her because she was a loyal subject of the queen and a dutiful daughter.

"Would I have to run everything by you?" she asked.

"Is that so unreasonable? I'm all for advancements, Galila, but at a pace people can adapt to."

She supposed that was fair, but: "Are you just offering me this role because you know I like it? As a way to persuade me into accepting our marriage?"

"What I offered last night wasn't enough?" he asked in a silky tone that caused a shiver to trickle down her spine.

She refused to look at him.

A moment later, he clicked a button and spoke again to the voice she presumed was at the landing pad. The palace appeared and captured all her attention.

It was clearly the product of centuries of additions. The highest dome dominated the center structure while annexes stretched in four directions, each with a variety of smaller domes, flat roofs, solar panels and even an arch of solarium windows over a great hall of some kind. From each of these four legs grew smaller additions, apartments perhaps—there were a number of small pools and courtyards with palms and fountains.

He landed in a circle on one of the highest rooftops where three other helicopters of various sizes were already tethered. They were hanging their headphones on the hooks above the windscreen when he spoke again.

"How you come to terms with our marriage is up to you, but it is a fact. You may weigh in on the details of our celebration as you see fit, but my staff is perfectly capable of making it happen without your input. As for representing the women of my country—*our* country—I would like you to be their voice, if you're willing. Is that something you would enjoy or not?"

She hesitated, drew a breath and admitted, "Each time I say yes to you, I feel a piece of me fall away. It's not the same for you, though, is it?"

People were approaching to tether the helicopter, but he didn't look away from her, only said a quiet, "No."

It hurt a lot more than she had braced herself for, pushing a thickness into her throat and a pressure behind her eyes.

"Is this still about love, Galila? Look at my mother. You don't want that. Be practical and accept this marriage for the beneficial partnership it can be."

To whom? Everyone *but* her.

She was being offered the chance to elevate the living conditions of a country full of women for the low price of her own freedom and the loving marriage she had always promised herself.

"I've never understood how people live without love." Her brothers did, maybe because they hadn't been loved in the first place. She had, though, and maybe that was proof that Karim was right. She had grown addicted to being seen as special and valuable and wanted. Losing her mother's love was still a deep and agonizing wound.

She knew better than to fall into another situation where she was yearning for feelings that weren't there, yet here she was, distantly hoping he would come around and feel something toward her.

"It's not that difficult," Karim replied drily, essentially driving a coffin nail into her heart. "Come. Let me show you our home."

"Well, I guess I don't have a choice, do I? Not unless I want to throw myself off the edge of this roof and end things right now."

"Why would you say that?" His voice lashed at her, quick and snapping sharp as a whip. "Don't ever say anything like that. *Ever.*"

His vehemence had her recoiling in her seat, heart hammering. She recalled with chagrin that his father had fallen from a balcony here. "I didn't mean—"

He cut her off with a chop of his hand through the air between them and disembarked, then impatiently demanded she come out behind him, picking her up and releasing her with abrupt motions.

He exchanged a few words with someone, then hurried her out of the heat and into the relief of air conditioning where a handful of personnel awaited them, all wearing attentive expressions.

"Cantara." He introduced a middle-aged woman in traditional dress with heavily made-up eyes, a wide smile and a tablet and stylus at the ready. "My mother's assistant, when she's here at the palace. Cantara will show you around and help you hire the staff you need. I'm required elsewhere."

He strode away. The rest of the staff flowed into position behind him like birds in a flock, making him seem to disappear.

She waited, but he didn't look back. Last night's intimacy was forgotten. It certainly hadn't changed anything in *his* agenda.

"I've had tea prepared in your chamber. May I show you there?"

Galila found a polite smile and dutifully followed where she was led.

Karim forced himself not to look back, but he still saw Galila. Heard her.

How did each word she spoke have such power over him? She loaded a single glance with a thousand emotions, saying, *I've never understood how people live without love*, while a kaleidoscope of despair and confusion, yearning and wistfulness took their turn across her angelic face. Somehow, she caused those feelings to be reflected in him, twisting his conscience at the same time, which was distinctly uncomfortable.

And when he tried to move her past her melancholy, she thrust a knife from a completely unexpected direction, flippantly suggesting she throw herself to her death the way his father had done.

Whatever pangs of guilt had reverberated through him had been slapped out by that statement, sparking his temper with the power of a lightning strike.

That slam of energy had had its roots in a white-hot fear. He would never wish his experience on anyone, certainly could never face witnessing something so traumatic again, but somehow knew it would be especially devastating if she did it.

He'd smacked a hard lid on that sort of talk, seeing how wary his outburst made her, but he didn't even want her to dare think of doing something so horrific, let alone threaten it.

The entire five-minute conversation had left her limpid eyed and looking abandoned as a child when he left her with an assistant and turned away.

Perhaps she was entitled to some bewilderment. Their lovemaking had been so powerful, he had stooped to reminding her of it himself, unable to dismiss it from his mind. He wanted her to recall every twitch and sigh and caress. It was all he could think about.

But it was completely reckless to let himself be so distracted and preoccupied by carnal desires. He had married her to keep a secret that could rattle swords in both their countries—upend the entire region, even. Not to mention the personal cost to all of them. Her mother's affair was already a sore topic with her and her siblings.

He didn't want to force painful discussions on them any more than he wanted them himself.

No. She might open herself to him and offer a type of pleasure he had never experienced, lure him like a bee to a nectar-laden flower, but he had to remain stoic and indifferent. And after the way she had behaved at the wedding? Getting drunk and spilling what she had to *him*? There was no way he could entrust her with the rest. Too much depended on him keeping their parents' affair a secret.

To do that, he had to keep her contained, yet at a distance. In his palace, in his apartment, but not in his bed. It was best for all their sakes.

CHAPTER FIVE

TEN DAYS LATER, Galila was fed up with being ignored.

Not that she was ever left alone. Rather, maids and clerks and advisors hovered constantly, asking for her preference on *everything*, right down to which side of the gold-plated bathroom tap her cut-crystal toothbrush cup should sit.

She was changed at least four times a day, from silk pajamas to comfortable breakfast wear, then to casually elegant midday wear, then sophisticated evening wear and finally back to pajamas. If she and Karim were entertaining, there might be poolside wraps while amusing the wife of a visiting diplomat, cocktail attire before dressing for dinner or something ceremonial for an official photograph.

They were always entertaining. Or meeting with some dignitary over a luncheon. Even breakfasts were business meetings, where she and Karim ate across from each other, but staff hovered with tablets and questions, asking for replies on emails and finalizing their schedules for the rest of the day.

The strange part was, she didn't mind the demands. She found it invigorating. There was something both thrilling and satisfying in making seating arrangements or setting a menu or suggesting a blue rug would look better in this room, and seeing her wishes carried out promptly and without question.

As a princess in Khalia, she had had influence, but even Malak's disinterested male opinions had held more sway than her own. She had nearly always been contradicted by her mother, which Galila had sometimes thought was purely a desire on her mother's part to reinforce her own position, not a genuine partiality to whatever suggestion of Galila's she had decided to overrule.

Now, as Queen of Zyria—and that title made her choke on hysterical laughter because she had yet to properly sleep with her husband, the king—Galila discovered the power of her position. At first, she'd been tentative, expecting to hear that the Queen Mother Tahirah ought to be consulted or had always preferred this or that.

To her amazement, Galila was assured that such courtesies as consulting the Queen Mother were at her discretion. The only voice that might veto her own was her husband's. What a heady thought!

So she tested the extent of her privilege. She sought out her husband unannounced and said she would wait for the king in his anteroom.

She was not turned away. She was offered refreshments. His highest-ranking assistant offered to interrupt the king's conference call if it was an urgent matter.

"It's not. Merely a private discussion I'd like to have before our guests arrive. I'll ring if I require anything."

She was left alone to explore the private library. It was a retreat, a place for Zyria's ruler to freshen up between meetings, since there was a very luxurious bathroom and a small walk-in closet with a spare of everything.

It ought to smell like Karim in here, she thought, as she lifted the sleeve of a robe to her nose.

She was actually craving the scent of him, some lingering evidence of their intimacy. Her nights were agony as she relived the way he had pleasured her in the tent, then fantasized all the other things they might do to one another if he came to her. Why hadn't she at least pleasured him the same way when she had had the chance?

In the darkest hours, when she was sweaty and aching with desire, she rose and walked to the closed door between their apartments but couldn't bring herself to knock.

Was he being honorable? Giving her time to adjust to their marriage as he had promised he would? Or had he completely lost interest in her?

She always went back to bed bereft, wondering what she had done to turn him off.

As brutal as the nights were, the days were far worse. Each time she was in his presence, she fought lust. His lips on the rim of a coffee cup made her shake with desire. His voice stroked across her skin, causing her pulse to race. If she caught his scent, she had to close her eyes and take control of herself.

Even now, anticipating being alone with him, her intimate regions were tingling with anticipation. Her one-track mind turned to fantasies of making love on the floor of his very closet, his naked weight upon her. His thick shaft piercing—

Flushed and impatient with herself, she went back into the main area.

The only thing worse than suffering this constant yearning would be his discovering how deeply she felt it and feeling nothing in return.

She shook herself out of her mental whirl by taking a more thorough look around the main room. Did he even come in here? There wasn't a speck of dust in sight, but she had the sense he spent very little time in here.

A sofa and chairs were arranged to face a television, should there be breaking news he needed to watch, but the cushions were undented. The liquor cabinet held nothing, not even nonalcoholic choices.

When she looked at the books, they were also dust free and arranged with precision, but who read actual books anymore? Especially dry nonfiction. Give her a romance and she would sneeze her way through the most yellowed pages, but biographies and history? No, thanks.

She couldn't help touching the mane of the gold lion that lounged on an ebony bookend. His one front paw was relaxed and dangling off the edge. His tail appeared about to swish. It was an eye-catching piece, one that looked vaguely familiar, making her think she'd seen something like it, perhaps by the same artist. She would have remembered if she'd seen this one. It was not only startlingly lifelike, with the animal's musculature lovingly recreated, it emanated power along with the innate playfulness of cats. The lion peered around the edge of the upright slab of ebony that he lounged against, as if waiting on his mate. Inviting her to come to his side of the books.

Galila looked for the match, but there was only the one. Strange. Bookends came in pairs, didn't they? That was why there was an expression about things being "bookended."

She looked on the desk for it, then realized the heavy curtains behind the desk hid a pair of tall doors that led onto a balcony. She pulled them open.

Was this where his father had fallen?

She wasn't a morbid person, but something drew her to open the doors and step onto the shaded balcony. The heat crushed like a wall, but the view of the sea was stunning. There was a broader balcony on the other side of the palace that was used for ceremonies. It overlooked a public square and had been a means of addressing the masses before television.

This one, like the room behind her, was a place for reflection.

With an unforgiving courtyard a fatal distance below.

"No," Karim said, startling her into gasping and spinning. She clutched her chest where her heart leaped.

Mouth tight, Karim pointed her back into the center of the room.

"I didn't—I was just—"

He closed and locked the doors, then drew the drapes across with a yank on the cord. The room became cooler and darker, but she was still hot and flustered.

"Karim." She had come in here on a wave of temper, determined to confront him, but found herself in the middle of the carpet with her hands linked before her, apologies on her tongue.

"It's not up for discussion," he stated.

She didn't have to ask him if that was where the accident had happened. She could see the truth in his severe expression. He'd been six. How was it such a painful, visceral memory for him?

As she searched his expression, her infernal attraction to him began to take root and flourish through her. She noted how handsome he was in his business attire of pants and a button shirt. Nothing special, but it was tailored to his strong shoulders and framed his hips just so. He was as sexy and casually powerful as the lion she had admired.

He also had a thorn in his paw. She yearned to be the one who pulled it, she realized. The one he cherished for healing him.

"The ambassador and his wife will arrive soon. You should change."

It was a dismissal.

They were alone for the first time since the tent and he didn't have any use for her. Just like that, her temper flared. She remembered why she had been so infuriated, why she had hiked the distance across the massive palace to confront him.

"I need to talk to you." She folded her arms, chin set.

"It can't wait?"

"Until when? Do you propose I discuss my doctor's appointment over the dessert course so our guests can weigh in?"

His whole body tightened, as if bracing himself. His brows slammed together and his gaze swept her up and down. "What's wrong?"

"Nothing," she admitted, realizing she had alarmed him, which was a tiny bit gratifying since he hadn't given her any indication of even a mild passing concern for her health and well-being since he'd poured out her brandy the night they met. "I mean, it's not a health problem, if that's what you're thinking."

He made an impatient noise and flicked his hand

at her. "That's exactly what I thought. But if you're healthy, then what?"

"I want to know why you told the doctor I could go on whatever birth control I would prefer."

His head went back with surprise. "You said you didn't want children right away."

How was it possible for him to become *more* inscrutable? He pushed his fists into his pockets. The motion drew the fabric of his trousers tight across his fly, which revealed the hint of his masculine flesh.

She had been spending way too much time wondering about that part of him and her guilty conscience pushed heat into her cheeks. She forced herself not to stare and looked instead to the hardness in his jaw. Something in his stance made her think he'd been offended when she had told him she didn't have a particular desire to have his children, which had been true-ish at the time.

Now, she folded her arms, defensive because she was so—oh, she was going to have to own it. She was frustrated. Sexually.

"Aside from the fact it is not *your* decision what I put in *my* body," she declared hotly and for all womankind, "I don't understand why you think birth control is necessary when you seem to have decided on abstinence."

He blinked. His face relaxed with a hint of satisfaction that made her think of the lion swishing his tail, pleased he wouldn't have to run her to ground because she was edging close enough he wouldn't have to make any effort to chase her at all.

Oh, he read her agitation like it was a neon sign, she could tell. She blushed even harder.

"Hot and bothered, are you? We agreed to wait until after the wedding ceremony next week."

"Is that what we agreed? I thought you stated it and I have been given no opportunity to discuss it. What happened to it being my choice what happened between us in bed?"

His eye ticked, then his jaw hardened.

"If you can't wait for our wedding night…" His hands came out of his pockets and he waved them slowly at himself in offering. "Help yourself."

As bluffs went, it almost worked. She was still a virgin and already feeling very scorned by him. This was daylight, not the safety of a pitch-black tent. Years of reading sexy romance novels, a rich fantasy life and curiosity were all a far cry from the reality of staring down a fully dressed man whose mouth was curling with smug knowledge that he was getting the better of her.

Because he thought she was some trembling wallflower who wouldn't make advances.

Well, he thought wrong. She was sick of feeling like his dalliance. A flame of fury glowed hot within her, refusing to be at the mercy of his whims. She would not be the only one obsessing about how they would feel together. *She* could give *him* pleasure.

She was determined to prove it.

When she walked up to him, however, and he loomed over her despite the heels she wore, her heart began to beat fast with apprehension. This was a dangerous game.

He didn't lower his head to cover her offered mouth. He made her set a hand behind his head and draw him down into *her* kiss. Then he had the gall not to respond to her first uncertain advances. *All* men wanted to kiss her. Didn't he realize that?

She forced her tongue between his lips and pressed

harder, rocking her mouth under his as she pulled his tongue into her own mouth.

He made a growling, primal noise and encircled her with hard arms as he took over the kiss with passionate roughness. It lasted for a few uncontrolled, thrilling heartbeats before he caught her arms in a firm grip and set them apart from each other.

His gaze clashed into hers with accusation, as if she'd forced him to react in a way he didn't care for.

But that brief crack in his control only fueled her resolve. She brushed his hands off her arms and pressed his wrists behind his back, meeting his fierce glare with a scolding one.

"You just gave yourself to me, didn't you? Are you going back on that? What are you afraid of?"

Her breasts grazed his chest and their thighs brushed through the fabric of her skirt and his pants. She could feel he was aroused and that bolstered her confidence even more.

"I'm not afraid of anything." His voice was gritty, his words pushed through clenched teeth. "But what are you planning to do? Lose your virginity here on my desk?"

"I'm going to make love to you with my mouth," she dared to say, and felt the jolt that went through him. The muscled wrists in her hands became rock-hard, strained tendons as he bunched his hands into tight fists.

She smiled under a rush of feminine power.

"Do you like that idea?" She drew back a little and brought one hand to his fly. She caressed his hard flesh through the fabric. "I think you do." *She* did. Her hand was trembling.

His nostrils flared, but he held himself very still. She couldn't tell if he was trying to act unaffected or if they were playing a game of chicken and he was waiting for her to lose her nerve first.

She might. She'd never done anything so boldly wicked.

With two shaking hands, she unbuttoned his shirt and spread it wide, indulging herself by splaying her hands across his hot skin and the light sprinkle of hair. She turned her face back and forth against the contours of his pecs, played her touch over his rib cage before she licked at his nipples to see if he reacted.

He did. He made a harsh noise and his fist went into her hair, but he didn't force her to stop. When she offered her mouth this time, he took it like a starving man, without hesitation, greedy and rapacious.

She almost lost herself to that kiss. Her blood was running like wildfire, her oxygen all but eaten up. She longed to let him take control, but she also needed to prove to both of them that she wasn't alone in this sea of lust.

She ran her hands over his buttocks, then traced her fingers beneath the waistband of his pants until she came to the front.

She unbuckled and unzipped, stepped back enough to open his pants and push them down his hips. Then she eased the black line of his shorts down, exposing the thick flesh that had been keeping her up nights. Her breaths were coming in deep pants, like she'd been running for an hour, breasts rising and falling.

"You've taken this far enough," he said grimly, catching her hand before she touched him.

"You don't want me to?" She looked up at him with craving nearly blinding her.

Whatever he saw in her expression caused his own

pupils to expand. The heat between them was like flames, licking back and forth, scorching. Shadows of struggle fought with a glaze of desperate hunger in his eyes.

"I want to," she assured him in a husky whisper, sinking to her knees before him.

She didn't know exactly what to do, but there didn't seem to be a wrong move as she lightly caressed and explored, getting to know his shape. Her first touch had him sucking in a breath. His flesh seemed to welcome her grasp with pulses of enjoyment. He muttered imprecations between ragged breaths, but didn't stop her.

He watched her with a fierce, avid gaze that only encouraged her to steady him for the first dab of her tongue.

Then he tipped back his head and groaned loudly at the ceiling, like it was pain and pleasure combined. She lost herself then, did everything she could to pleasure him with exactly as much devotion as he had shown her in the Bedouin tent. And when he was reaching the peak of his endurance, when his hand was in her hair and he was warning her he couldn't last, she was so aroused, she couldn't resist touching herself and finding release at the same time he did.

Karim left his stained, sweat-damp clothing on the floor of the closet and dressed in fresh pants and a shirt, shaken and stunned—utterly stunned—by what his wife had just done to him.

He came back into the main room and she was already gone from the bathroom where she had retreated moments after taking him to such heights of ecstasy that he had thought he was dying.

What a way to go.

He looked around the room he passionately hated and knew his regard for it had been completely rewritten. He would always think of her now, when he was in here. Galila on her knees before him, hair a silk rope that bound both his fists to the back of her head. Her mouth working over his tip, her slender fingers a vice of pleasure around his shaft. And then, when his fantasy-turned-reality could not possibly have become more erotic, she had burrowed her hand beneath her skirt and pleasure had hummed in her throat as they found satisfaction together.

How could any man withstand such a thing?

He ran his hand down his face, trying to put his melted features into some semblance of control before he had to rejoin his staff, let alone ambassadors from around the world.

He had been avoiding her, it was true. The more he wanted her, the more he fought against going to her. Making himself wait until their "wedding night" had seemed a suitable, if arbitrary way of proving he could control his lust and resist her.

Like hell. He had lost the battle the second he'd been told she was waiting for him, never mind when she had sidled up to him and kissed him.

This had been a defeat, one he already regretted, even as his blood purred in his veins and every bit of tension in his body had left him.

With regret, he squatted and swept his hand across the nap of the carpet, erasing where his own footprints faced the impression of her knees.

As he squatted there, from this vantage, he was the height he had been when his father had sat at that

desk, rambling about things Karim hadn't even com-
prehended.

*I love her. Do you understand? Your mother can
never know. She doesn't know. Doesn't understand what
this kind of love is like. Pray you never experience it, my
son. It destroys your soul. And now she says it's over.
How do I go on? I can't. Do you understand, Karim? I
cannot live without her. I'm sorry, but I can't.*

Karim hadn't understood. But the memory was a
timely reminder as to why he had been trying to avoid
giving in to his desire for Galila. Such intense passion
could very easily become addictive. Obsessive and soul-
destroying.

As he straightened, he pulled on the cloak of control
he'd been wearing since bringing her here, determined
to set her at a distance and keep her there. Permanently
this time.

It wasn't easy. An hour later, she arrived at his side
wearing a hijab, since the ambassador and his wife
were Muslim. Somehow her conservative gown and
face framed in closely draped indigo were more pro-
vocative than one of her knee-length skirts with a fitted jacket.

Galila was beautiful no matter what she wore, but
he could barely keep his gaze off the lips that had left a
stain of pink on his flesh, or the lashes that had framed
the wide eyes that had looked up at him.

He quickly made a remark about a political situation
and drew the ambassador aside so he wouldn't embarrass himself by becoming freshly aroused.

This constant flow of dinners and entertaining had
been partly a series of prescheduled meetings, but also
a necessary means of introducing his wife to key dig-

nitaries before the celebration that would cement her as his wife and queen. Their marriage had been surprise enough. With all the rumblings of concern at lower levels, he had to ensure she was accepted.

Galila, he had to acknowledge, had a particular gift for charming people onto her side. She flowed effortlessly from small talk over the best shoe designer in Milan to a policy discussion. If she had a question, she asked it in a way that never seemed impertinent. If she had an opinion, she always managed to voice it in a way that was nonconfrontational but made her point.

As for the reports he received daily on the various decisions she was making as queen, well, he was grateful to have fewer things to worry about so he could concentrate on the ones that had broader impact.

"Oh, you know my father?" she asked with surprise now, voice drawing Karim back to the dinner and the conversation.

"That's an overstatement," the ambassador said with an embarrassed wave of his hand. "I met him, well, it must have been thirty years ago? I was quite young, just starting my first career as a translator. He came to our country as part of a diplomatic tour. He has such a sharp mind. I very much admired him and only wanted to express my concern for his health, given he stepped aside recently. I hope he's well?"

"Grieving my mother." Galila stiffened slightly, just enough for Karim to notice, but this was another area where she seemed to finesse her way without a misstep.

"I expect he was quite heartbroken. I'm sure you all are, but, well, it was obvious to me, even back then, how much he loved her. He cut short his tour to be with her. I remember it so clearly because I couldn't imagine having a woman in my life whom I couldn't bear to be apart from. Then I met one." He smiled at his wife.

She blushed and told him not to embarrass them.

Galila offered a smile, but it didn't reach her eyes. She stared off into the middle distance a moment, murmuring, "I didn't realize he had ever been apart from her for any length of time. It certainly never happened in my memory, but that would have been before I was born."

If she did the math and realized Karim's father had killed himself roughly thirty years ago...

"We need to add a discussion on your country's foreign banking regulations to tomorrow's agenda," Karim cut in, changing the subject.

Moments later, the women had moved on to an innocuous topic and the rest of the evening passed without incident. He realized, however, that this was another angle of vulnerability he had to protect himself against. His marriage of expedience was a minefield of potential disaster.

Galila excused herself the moment their guests were gone. She had a lot to think about. Deep down, she was still reeling from her experience with Karim, feeling self-conscious about the way she had behaved.

When she saw him at dinner with the ambassador, he had once again been the remote man who revealed only the barest hint of regard toward her. His indifference crushed her soul into the dust, but she hadn't allowed herself to look him in the eye or her gaze to linger on his expression. She had fought all evening to hide her aching soul, asking mindless questions and pretending an interest in the wife's dog-breeding techniques.

Then the ambassador had made that remark about her father's trip thirty years ago.

She had enough going on with her new marriage that she shouldn't have room for obsessing over her mother's lover, but she couldn't help but wonder. She couldn't ask her father about his trip, but she sent an email to both her brothers, keeping her inquiry very vague, asking if they knew anything about that particular trip their father had taken. She doubted they would. Malak hadn't been born and Zufar had been a toddler.

Still, she sighed with disappointment when she received their blunt "No" replies the next morning.

"What's wrong?" Karim asked as he nodded to accept more coffee.

"Nothing. I asked my brothers if they knew anything about that diplomatic tour my father went on, the one the ambassador mentioned. They don't."

"Why?"

She looked at him, conveying with a flick of her lashes that it probably wasn't a topic that should be raised in front of the servants. "I'm curious about it."

He knew exactly what she was telegraphing and said dismissively, "I don't see that it matters."

"With all due respect," she said in a carefully level tone, "it wouldn't seem important to you because it doesn't concern your parent. I have questions, however."

The listening ears would think she was still talking about her father, but she meant her mother and Adir. Perhaps Karim took offense at her remark despite her attempt to maintain a suitable amount of deference. His fingers tightened on the handle of his coffee mug.

"Surely you have more important things to do with your time. How are the reception plans coming?"

She knew when she was being patronized and flipped her hair. "Perfectly. Your excellent staff would provide nothing less." She smiled at the hovering assistants.

The party was only days away, and much as she enjoyed being the center of attention, she was quite nervous. Everything would be exquisite, she had no doubt at all, but Karim intended for them to consummate their marriage that night and she was having mixed feelings about that.

She had wanted to prove something to him yesterday, but she wasn't sure what. That she was brave? That she would be a lover who would satisfy him? That he couldn't resist her?

What she had discovered was that even when she took the initiative, she had no control over her reaction. No modesty or inhibition.

In fact, the more she thought about their encounter, the more anxious she became. She kept seeing herself as besotted as her father was with her mother. Loyal as a hound, he'd loved his spouse into her death despite the fact she had committed adultery and never gave more than passing consideration to the children she had made with him.

Even more of a fearful thought was that she might become as dependent on Karim's regard as she had been on her mother's. For a time, she might be his sexual pet. There was a certain novelty within a new marriage, she was sure. They might both indulge themselves, but he had already demonstrated that his desire was fickle. He could turn his emotions on and off on a whim.

She couldn't bear to invest herself in him, grow to care for him, only to have that rug pulled. How would she withstand years of his casual indifference?

At least as a daughter, she'd been able to escape to Europe and distract herself with schooling. But charity work and its accompanying accolades only went so far in filling up the void inside her. She needed more.

Karim, however, would never offer the "more" she sought.

Why? What was wrong with her? What was her great flaw? She had convinced herself that her mother's fading beauty had caused her to grow jealous as Galila's allure ripened, but Karim was behaving with the same ambivalence toward her.

Perhaps that meant there was a deeper shortcoming inside her that kept people from truly loving her?

She was a kind person, an obedient daughter. She was trying to be a loyal wife, but Karim didn't even seem to value that much in her. It was agonizing.

She had no choice as far as attending the reception went, but she didn't know if she could become his wife in every sense of the word afterward. He would surely break her heart.

CHAPTER SIX

CORONATIONS WERE NOT a lavish affair in this part of the world. Galila knew that from her own country and had been told that Karim had a cousin appointed as his successor should he fail to produce one. That designation and the allegiance of all his cousins and other dignitaries had been handled with public, verbal pledges witnessed by the rest.

Recognizing Galila as his queen had been a matter of Karim stating that he had chosen her that night in the Bedouin encampment. It was all the people of Zyria had needed to accept and recognize her as their monarch, but they would feel cheated of a party if he didn't host one.

That was all that this day was—a formal celebration here in the palace, but one followed by all. Festivities were extended across the country, providing the entire population a reason to take a day to enjoy themselves.

Galila was nothing if not scrupulously adept at planning this sort of event. Along with charity work abroad and at home, she had always led the charge on family events—to a point. Her mother had liked Galila to do all the work of choosing menus and decor, then always swooped in at the last minute to change the color scheme or the order of the speeches, putting her own stamp on it.

This time, every single detail was Galila's own.

As part of that, she had carefully considered the message the event would send. Obviously, she had to convey that she was pleased to be Karim's wife and that she embraced her new country. She needed to highlight the advantage of a union with Khalia, too. It was a celebration and needed to be lavish enough to reflect their position, but she didn't want to pin *spendthrift* to her lapel and require years to remove it. She wanted it known that she was eager to begin charity work, but didn't want to appear critical and suggest Zyria was failing to meet the needs of its people.

The guest list had been its own Gordian knot to unravel and there had also been kosher meals and other diverse religious observances that had to be considered.

In the end, Galila pulled a small cheat by adding some well-respected professionals to the mix. She seated doctors and teachers next to ministers and other dignitaries with appropriate portfolios. Everything in the swag bags from silk scarves to gold bangles to a jar of spices had been sourced in Zyria, showcasing their best merchants.

Within the speeches, she had the treasury minister praise her for being under budget with this party. He announced that she had asked for the savings to be donated to a traveling medical unit that would service some of the most difficult to access places in Zyria. It was met with an appropriate round of appreciative applause.

Her husband promptly upstaged her by announcing that a hospital wing to service women's health issues would be built in her name. Her reaction must have been priceless because everyone laughed and applauded even harder while she covered her hot cheeks with her hands.

It was a political gesture, she reminded herself. A means of ensuring she was accepted and welcomed and cemented into Zyria's history books.

She was still touched by the gesture, perhaps because he looked at her with sincere regard as he said, "I'm hoping you'll take an active role in this project. Your instincts and attention to detail are excellent."

"Did you mean that?" she asked as he seated himself next to her again.

"Of course." He seemed surprised by her question. "I've been kept apprised of every decision you've made here so far."

That was news. She had been quite convinced he hadn't thought of her more than twice since they'd met.

"You've done an excellent job," he said, sounding sincere. His gaze skimmed across the four hundred people dressed to the nines, jewelry sparkling and gold cutlery flashing as they dined on their first course beneath faux starlight. Landmarks were projected onto the walls beneath swathes of fabric to resemble looking out from a Bedouin tent on Zyria's landscape. The centerpieces were keepsake lanterns amid Zyrian flora and the scent of Zyrian incense hung on the air.

"I don't know that anyone will dare eat these chocolates, but they will certainly enjoy showing them off. Very ingenious." He tilted the treat that decorated each place setting. It was made of camel milk by a Zyrian chocolatier and shaped like Zyria and Khalia stuck together as one piece, the border only a subtle shift in color, not a dividing line. She had prevailed on her brother to send coffee and cinnamon from Khalia to flavor their side of it while the Zyrian was spiced with nutmeg and cardamom.

"It's a subtle yet brilliant touch."

Brilliant?

Don't be needy.

But she was. In her core, she was starved for validation. Which was exactly the problem with this marriage. She wanted—needed—to believe Karim valued her. That whatever he felt toward her was real and permanent.

He was in demand at all times, however. It was somewhat understandable that after his brief compliment, his attention went elsewhere. They didn't speak again until the plates had been cleared and they moved to the adjoining ballroom to begin the dancing.

Here she'd been a little freer with the Western influences, bringing in colored lights and a DJ who played current pop tunes from around the globe, but included many of the hits by Arab bands.

Their first dance was an older ballad, however, one Karim's mother had told her had been played at her wedding to Karim's father. It was meant as a reassurance to the older generation that things were changing but only a little.

Karim wore his ceremonial robes and she was in several layers of embroidered silk over a brocade gown with jewels in her hair, at her wrists, around her neck and even a bejeweled broach worn on a wide band around her middle.

Karim had to be very careful as he took her into his arms. He muttered something under his breath about hugging a cactus.

"I understood it to be an heirloom that all Zyrian

queens wear on special occasions," she said, affected by his closeness despite the fact he had to maintain enough distance not to catch his robes on the piece.

"My staff was too shy to explain it was designed as a chastity belt, worn when the king was not around to protect his interests."

"Talk about putting a ring on it," she said under her breath.

He snorted, the sound of amusement so surprising, she flashed a look upward in time to see the corner of his mouth twitch.

"Yes, well, the king is in the house so we'll dispense with it as soon as possible."

Her heart swerved in the crazy jitter of alarm and anticipation she'd been suffering as this day drew nearer. It was so silly! They were familiar with each other. She knew she would find pleasure with him.

But what happened after that? Would he go back to ignoring her? She wouldn't be able to stand it. How could she give herself to a man who would only rebuff her afterward?

Karim stole her away to her apartment as soon as he could, dismissing the staff that hovered to help undress her. He could handle that himself, thank you very much.

On his instruction, the rooms had been prepared with a fresh bath, rose petals, candles, cordial and exotic fruits. The music of gently plucked strings played quietly in the background. Silk pajamas had been left on the bed for both of them—and would be swept to the floor unused if he had his way.

Alone with his wife for the first time since she'd

blown his mind in his library the other day, he was fairly coming out of his skin with anticipation—not that he would admit to it. Oh, he knew damned well that part of him had been counting the minutes until he could release himself from his self-imposed restraint, but he barely acknowledged that. It was pure weakness to feel this way, damn it, but he couldn't put off consummation forever.

In fact, he had begun to rationalize that the reason he was growing obsessive about the moment of possession was merely because he hadn't yet done so. Once they made love, he wouldn't be so preoccupied by how delicious it might be.

That was the only reason urgency gripped him and put a gruff edge on his voice when he commanded her to turn around. "Let me relieve you of that thing."

She jolted a bit and didn't meet his eyes as she turned so he could remove the elaborate belt.

Her spine grew taller as he released the dozen tiny hook-and-eye fasteners. She drew a deep breath as he set it aside, then, when he touched her shoulders to remove her outer robe, she stiffened again and glanced warily over her shoulder.

He hesitated, but she shrugged to help him peel it away. It was surprisingly heavy with its detailed embroidery locking in pearls and other jewels. If anything, her tension grew as he eased it away, however.

She turned and folded her arms, now in a strapless gown bedecked with a band of silver and diamonds beneath the extravagant necklace that had been his wedding gift to her. She pressed her lips together, conveying wary uncertainty.

"What's wrong?"

"Nothing," she said a little too quickly, shoulders coming up in a shrug and staying in a defensive hunch.

He moved closer and had to tilt her chin up, then wait for her gaze to come to his. A tiny flinch plucked at her brows and her gaze swept away, anxious to avoid his.

"Galila," he murmured. "Are you being shy?" It seemed impossible, considering the intimacies they'd shared, but her mouth twitched.

She hitched a shoulder, nodding a little, lashes dropping to hide her gaze again.

"There's no rush," he assured her, even though it felt like a lie. Standing this close to her, feeling the softness of her cheek under the caress of his thumb, he didn't know how he had managed to wait this long. The starving beast inside him was waking and stretching, prowling in readiness to go on the hunt.

When he started to lower his mouth to hers, she stiffened with subtle resistance.

He drew back, experiencing something like alarm. Was she teasing him on purpose?

"I'm nervous, it's fine," she insisted, but she was still avoiding his gaze.

Her crown had been fitted with a silver and blue veil that draped over the rich, loose waves of her hair. She reached to remove it.

"I'll do it." He searched out the pins that secured it, distantly thinking he should have delegated this task to the one who'd put them in. It was an intricate process and she winced a couple of times, even though he was as gentle as he could be.

He persevered and finally was able to leave the crown and veil on a table. She ran her fingers through her hair—an erotic gesture at the best of times. Tonight, she was especially entrancing. The smooth swells of her breasts lifted against the blue velvet. Her heavily decorated ivory skirt shimmered, merely hinting at the lissome limbs it hid.

"You're so beautiful, it almost hurts the eyes." The words came from a place he barely acknowledged within himself, one where his desire for her was a craven thing that he could barely contain.

She dropped her hands in front of her. "I can't help the way I look."

"It's not a drawback," he said drily, moving to take up her hands and set them on his shoulders. His own then went to her rib cage, finding her supple as a dancer. Her heels put her at exactly the most comfortable height to dip his head and capture her mouth with his own.

A jolt of electricity seemed to jump between them, reassuring him even as his mouth stung and she made a sound of near pain. He quickly assuaged the sensation with a full, openmouthed kiss. The kind he'd been starving for. The kind that should have slaked something in him, but only stoked his hunger.

She began to melt into him and he felt mindlessness begin to overtake him, the same loss of control that had pinned him in place while she stole every last shred of his discipline that day in his library.

He tightened his hands on her and started to set her back a step, needing to keep a clear head.

She made a noise of hurt and the heels of her hands exerted pressure, urging him to release her altogether.

His reflexes very nearly yanked her back in close. Some primitive refusal to be denied was that close to overwhelming him.

The push-pull was startling enough to freeze him

with his hands still keeping her before him, so he could read her face.

"Do you not want—?" He had to look away, not ready to hear that she was rejecting him.

"I do, but—"

She did break from his hold then, brushing his hands off her and pacing away a few steps. The action raked something cold across him.

She turned back to hold out a beseeching hand. "I can't bear the games, Karim."

She looked stricken enough to cause a sharp sensation to pierce his heart.

"Make love to me if you want to. But don't… Don't tell me I'm beautiful, then act like you can't stand how I look. Don't kiss me like you can't get enough, then push me away as though I'm someone you dislike. Don't tell a roomful of people that you think I'm wonderful when you clearly think I'm not. I can't go through those ups and downs again. I can't."

He narrowed his eyes. "What are you talking about? I don't dislike you."

She closed her eyes. "It doesn't matter how you feel, just be honest about it. And consistent. Please. It's fine that you only want me a little, the way any man might respond to any available woman. Don't pander to me and act like…"

"What?" he prompted, bracing because he was afraid that he might have betrayed too much somewhere along the line. Definitely when she'd taken him in her mouth.

"I don't know," she said with a break in her voice. "I don't know how you feel. That's the issue. Sometimes you act as though you like me, but then…you don't."

"Of course, I like you, Galila." He swallowed, thinking he understood the issue here. In a gentler tone, he added, "But I told you in the beginning not to expect love from me."

"I'm not talking about love, Karim! I'm talking about basic regard. You've barely spoken to me since the day in your office. You act like it didn't even happen! Then you think saying a few nice things tonight—that I'm so beautiful you can't stand to look at me—and think that makes me want to…" She waved at the bed, then her arm dropped in defeat.

His heart skewed in his chest. "That's not the way I meant it, Galila."

"The worst part is, I still want to have sex with you. But be honest about how it will be afterward. If you're only going to ignore me until the next time an urge strikes, then don't arrange rose petals and candles and act like you want me to *feel* something tonight. Don't act like this is a special moment for either one of us. Not when you're only going to pretend I don't exist afterward."

He pinched the bridge of his nose. This was special. It was her first time. Did she think he didn't have some nerves about that? The responsibility to *make* it special?

"I wanted you to relax."

"Well, I can't." She shook off whatever melancholy was in her expression and reached to remove her earrings. "Let's just get it done so you can lock yourself back in your room."

"Get it done?" he repeated as a sick knot tightened in his gut. "I want our lovemaking to be a pleasure for you, Galila. Not a chore."

"I'm not like you! When we…do things, I feel it. Emotionally." She pressed her curled hand between her breasts. "And you're manipulating me with that. Maybe not on purpose. Maybe you don't even realize how badly you're knocking my feelings around, but you are. I can't do that for a night, Karim, let alone a lifetime. I accept that this is an arranged marriage, not one based on love. But don't act like you care and then prove that you don't. I can't bear that. Not again."

If she had plunged a knife into his lung, he wouldn't have winded him this badly. Her accusations were bad enough, but suddenly he was wondering if she had given her heart to another and been rejected. And if she had, why was he taking that far worse than he would have if she'd had other lovers physically?

"Who else did that to you?" He needed to know.

"It doesn't matter," she muttered, turning away to work bangles off her wrists.

"It's affecting our marriage. Our relationship." What the hell did he care about such things? She was handing him a free pass to make love to her and withhold any investment of deeper feelings. He ought to rejoice. Instead, he was aggrieved by the idea of her coming to their marriage bed withholding anything from him, especially the genuine excitement and delight she had seemed to take in their congress before.

Running a hand over his head, he demanded, "Who?"

She sighed and stayed silent a long time, while her jewelry went into a dish with soft clinks.

"In light of what we've learned about my mother recently," she began in a subdued voice, "I understand better why she was so ambivalent with my brothers. Why she pushed them away. She had given away a child she wanted to keep. That has to break something in you.

Maybe that's even why she eventually pushed me away, but it wasn't always like that. For years…"

Her shoulders slumped under an invisible weight.

"None of this really matters, Karim," she said faintly.

His ardor was well and truly doused. Short of an invasion that required him to protect his country, he could not imagine anything more important to him than what she was telling him right now.

"Continue," he commanded.

"It makes me sound very pathetic. As superficial as you think I am." She kept her back to him and spoke to her feet. "When I was a child, I felt very special. It was obvious to me that I was the one Mother loved. Father worshipped her and she gave him nothing. The boys learned to live without affection from her, but she adored me. She brushed my hair and dressed me so we looked alike. She took me everywhere with her and was always so proud and happy when people said I was pretty and looked like her."

"That makes you sound more like a pet than her child."

"I was. A living doll, maybe. If only I had stayed that way."

"What way? Young?"

"Preadolescent, yes. Once I started to become a woman, it stopped."

"What did?"

"Her love."

She clutched her elbows in clawlike fingers, manicured nails threatening to cut into the skin of her bare arms. He moved across to touch her, drawing her attention to it so she would stop hurting herself.

She gave a little shiver and flashed a distressed glance up to him, then stepped away, averting her face.

"How do you know she stopped loving you? What happened?"

"Instead of saying, *You're so beautiful*, she would say, 'Your perfume has soured.' Instead of saying, *I love how your smile is exactly like mine*, she would say, 'Your laugh is too high-pitched. That lipstick is not your color.'"

"Did you do something to anger her?"

"If I did, she never said outright what it was." Her tone grew bitter.

"Then why do you think—? Ah. You told me before that she didn't want to be called Grandmother," he recalled.

"She said those exact words one time when my father was telling me over a family dinner that I ought to marry."

"So she was jealous of your youth."

"Maybe even that my life was ahead of me. I've been thinking about her all day today, thinking she would have died rather than attend *my* wedding. She hated it when I was the center of attention and would always say, 'You're acting like Malak.' She really did hate him and wasn't afraid to show it."

Galila had never acknowledged that out loud, but it felt weirdly good to do so. Like lancing a wound so it could begin to heal.

"And now you have no opportunity to ask her about it. I do understand that frustration, you know."

She sent him a helpless look, one palm coming up.

"You see? You're doing it again. Making it seem like we have something in common, that you care what I might have been through. What happens in ten minutes, though? In an hour? In the morning? Will my feelings become inconsequential again?"

He looked away from her, uncomfortable as he viewed his behavior in a fresh light. He had been protecting himself—his whole country, he could argue—since Zyria had been impacted when his father threw his life away over a broken heart. But he hadn't seen that in protecting himself, he had been injuring her.

"Is it me, Karim?" she asked in a voice thick with dread. "I had nearly convinced myself that my mother's hurtful behavior was her own issue, but if you're doing the same thing, then there must be a flaw in *me*." Her voice cracked as she pointed at her breastbone. "Something that makes me impossible to love. What is it?"

Galila stood in a vice of agony while her husband stood unmoving, as a man made from marble. She didn't even think he breathed. Was he trying to spare her? Because he was alleviating none of her fears with that stoic expression.

Finally, he blinked and muttered, "There's nothing wrong with you. That's absurd."

"There you go. I'm absurd!" She felt exactly as she had in those first dark years when her mother had begun to pull away. "I know I'm a ridiculous person. My brothers told me all the time that I shouldn't be so needy and want to feel loved. I know that with some people, like you, there's no getting into their good graces, even when you once were loved by them. But I don't understand how I *lose* it. Is it things that I say? Am I supposed to stand in silence and allow myself to be admired? But why would anyone want to look at me? I'm not beautiful *enough*. My neck is too long and I have my mother's thighs. Is it because my nose is too pointy? Help me understand, Karim! I can't fix it if I don't know what the problem is."

"There is no problem," he said so firmly she could only take it as a knife in the heart because he clearly wasn't going to tell her.

She threw up her hands in defeat. "Fine. Let's just—" She waved at the bed, but tears came into her eyes. She didn't know if she could go through with it. All she could do was stand there, crushed by anguish, fighting not to break down.

"Galila. There is nothing wrong with you," he insisted, coming across to take her hands. "Look at me." He dipped his head and waited until she was looking into his eyes. "You're very engaging. Very easy to…"

His mouth tightened and she could see him pulling himself back behind some invisible wall.

She tried to pull away, but he tightened his grip on her hands.

"Listen. I find myself letting down my guard with you. That's not something I ever do. Not with anyone except perhaps my mother. Even then…it's not comfortable for me."

"Well, it's not comfortable for me to let down my guard only to be shut out afterward. That's why I'm still a virgin. That sort of intimacy isn't easy for me, either. Not unless I'm convinced my heart will be safe." She pulled her hands free and quarter-turned away. "Maybe that's what all relationships are, though? Maybe I am a fool, thinking there's some way to feel safe in one." She spun back. "But your mother and father were in love. It's possible, Karim."

He was the one to walk away this time, hand drawing down his face as he let out a harsh breath.

"I know what you're thinking," she said with despair frosting her insides. "That I'm ruining our honeymoon night. I don't mean to set ridiculous standards. I just…" *Find it all very disappointing. Heartbreakingly empty.* "I don't know how I'll live in this state of hurt for the rest of my life. How do you not care, then? Teach me *that*, Karim."

His shoulders flexed as though her words had struck like a whip across them. He shook his head, voice disembodied when he spoke.

"I have trained myself not to care, Galila. To keep my thoughts to myself and control my desires. A man in my position can't give in to urges and open up doorways to vulnerability. I can't, Galila. The kingdom depends on my strength." He turned to deliver that bad news in a voice that was calm and factual but kind, at least.

Her mouth trembled and she nodded. "I know. Look at my father, abdicating because he was so devastated by losing my mother, even after what she had done. I just don't know how to be like you, Karim, instead of like him."

"I don't want you to be like me," he said in a voice that was low and quiet, but carried an impact that seemed to go through her as a shock wave, shivering all her pieces into new alignments. "I like who you are, Galila."

"You don't even know me, Karim." Her eyes were hot, and she wanted so badly to believe him.

"Untrue. Look at this party tonight. It was a ridiculous expense, one where you could have made it all about yourself. Instead, you gave it meaning. You *are* beautiful, so beautiful you trick the mind into thinking that's all you are. Then you display intelligence and kindness and you navigate all aspects of my life—a life I fight to control every minute of every day—you walk through that obstacle course with a graceful lack of effort. It's astonishing to me how well you fit in."

"My mother should get the credit for preparing me for this life, not me," she pointed out, throat abraded by emotion.

"And humble on top of the rest."

"Karim, it's very nice of you to say these things, but—"

"I don't do platitudes, Galila," he cut in flatly. "I'm telling you what I have learned of you during our short union. You have qualities I didn't expect, but I never expected to have a partner at all. A wife, yes, but not someone who is a genuine support. It's the strangest thing to me. Do you understand that? I don't want to grow accustomed to your presence at my side. I never needed you before. Why should I need you now? But there it is. You make it easier to carry out my duties, even as I feel weak for allowing you to lift any of the load. It's a paradox I haven't worked out how to solve."

She was soaking up the mud with the rainwater, feeling the contradiction inside her while watching the dismay battle with resignation in his brutally handsome features.

"Do you understand that it's your reluctance to allow me to share in your life that is killing me? Every time you push me away and act like I'm more annoyance than necessity, I hurt. How do I relax and give myself to you tonight, then face your withdrawal tomorrow? When you've decided I've seen too much of you?"

His cheek ticked.

"I'm sorry," she whispered, shaking her head in defeat. "I don't think I can—"

"I won't," he cut in, tone thin and sharp as a dagger, one corner of his mouth pulling down into the deadly curve of a *jambiya* blade. He was tensile steel, pupils expanding and contracting with inner conflict—a warrior on the defensive, but ready and willing to attack.

"Won't…?"

"Shut you out. I won't," he vowed.

She searched his expression, anguished by the struggle she could see in him, disheartened by how clearly it went against the grain for him. "That's not a promise you want to make. I can see that much, Karim."

Why didn't he want to share himself with her?

His lips pulled back against his teeth.

"But I will." He came across to cup her cheek. His gaze dropped to her throat, where her pulse throbbed fast. His palm slid down to cover it, so her heartbeat was hitting the heel of his hand. "Because I would do almost anything to touch you." His voice was both graveled and velvety. "That is the crux of it. And I can't believe I am handing you that weapon."

He looked tortured, but if his statement was a weapon, it was one that disarmed her as thoroughly as him. Her eyes burned and the rest of her grew weak. With her own tentative trust building, she set her hand on his chest, where his heart hammered in fierce pounds that made her own echo in her ears.

"It's the same for me. You know it is," she whispered.

"Our souls may be destined for hell then, because I have tried to resist—"

He dipped his head and this time, when he dragged

his mouth across hers, she melted. The harsh truth was, she wanted him far more than she feared the detriment he might become to her well-being.

And how could she deny the hunger in his kiss? He was so unabashed it was as if he'd let himself off leash. His lips demanded while his tongue took and gave, making her whole body feel gripped in a force that was both energizing and weakening. The pulse that had raced in her throat grew to something she felt in the pit of her belly and at the juncture of her thighs. It was nervous anticipation. Knowledge that *this was it*.

Neither of them could be torn from the other now.

She clung to him, growing so hot, she whimpered in frustration because she didn't want to let him go to remove the rest of her clothing. Her one hand went to her back and tried to work the zipper.

He lifted his head, eyes glowing and avid, cheeks flushed, mouth wet and pulling in a nearly cruel grimace.

"We have time," he said roughly.

"I don't feel like we do," she said breathlessly, feeling overcome and anxious and—

With a feral noise, he scooped her up and strode to the bed. His angular features were warrior sharp, hawkish and fierce.

"This," he said as he set her on the mattress and leaned on the hands he braced beside her shoulders. "This is what scares the hell out of me. It's your first time and I feel like an animal. If I don't control it, who will, Galila?"

"Come here," she demanded. Begged. And set her hand behind his head, moaning in tortured joy when his weight came down on her along with the heat of his lips against hers.

They attacked each other with erotic passion, legs tangling in her gown as she tried to make space for him. Her fingers caught at the collar of his robe, pulling at it so she could taste his shoulder when he dragged his tongue down the side of her neck. Somehow her teeth set against his skin and she had to restrain herself from biting down, but she wanted so ferociously to mark him, it was a fight to keep herself to a scrape and a threat of pain.

"Go ahead," he said, lifting his head and revealing a dark smile that was so transfixing, she felt it like the sun hitting her bare skin. It lit her up inside and out, nearly blinding her. "Claw at me. Bite me. I want all of it. Whatever is inside you."

She dragged her nails down his back through his robe, then dug them into his buttocks, hard as steel but flexing at her touch to drive his firm flesh against her sensitive mound.

He cupped her head and held her still for another rapacious kiss. Again and again, he feasted on her, satisfying yet stoking. Driving them both wild until she was ready to cry, she was in a state of such heightened arousal.

"I need to feel you," she panted when his hot mouth went down her throat again. "Please, Karim."

His answer was to yank at her bodice, baring her breast to his greedy mouth. She arched, crying out at the sharp pull on her nipple.

"Too hard?" His breath bathed her skin in a tease.

"Never," she gasped, and dragged at his robe, trying to get beneath it.

He shifted, went after her other nipple with equal fervor while he began gathering her gown up her thighs. The second he found skin, his hand climbed unerringly to the lace that shielded her most intimate flesh.

He groaned as he traced over it. She whimpered at the caress that was desperately needed and not nearly enough.

"Karim," she begged.

"So ready for me." He rose to kiss her, but his hand stayed beneath her gown. "Do you think about that night my mouth was here? I do. All the time."

His finger slid beneath the silk, parting and caressing, making speech impossible.

"I think about you in my office, touching yourself as you pleasured me. I'm jealous." He probed gently, licking at her panting mouth as he carefully penetrated. "I think about being here like this with you, having you in every way possible because I want you to be *mine*."

"I am," she swore, opening her legs to invite his touch deeper.

"I take care of what's mine." He pushed the silk firmly aside, his thick finger making love to her while his thumb teased the knot of nerves that made her writhe in pleasure.

She was going to die, held by his caress on a molten ledge, teased and stroked, heat building until that was all she was. Heat. Blistering heat. She bit her lip, wanting the release but fighting it.

"Karim," she managed to breathe, stilling his hand. "I want to feel you. Do this together."

His cheekbones were sharp above cheeks drawn taut. All of him was tense and flexed. Even his lips were pulled back from his teeth in effort.

"Yes," he hissed and very, very carefully withdrew, then he began to tug at her gown.

It took forever. They kept stopping to kiss. To groan. To caress bared skin and whisper, "Oh, yes. You smell so good. You're so smooth here. So lovely. So strong."

Somehow, they managed to strip and she made a keening noise in her throat as they rolled together. The aching swells of her breasts flattened by his hard chest, the roughness of his thighs abrading the insides of hers was sheer magic. She hadn't known that being naked, skin to skin, sex to sex, would make her so weak. She hadn't known that his muscles and overwhelming size could be its own aphrodisiac, making her writhe in ecstasy simply because he was against her.

"Galila." His voice was an abrasive husk, savaged by the same limits of arousal that gripped her.

"I'm ready." She was going to weep. She was so achingly ready.

He slid against her, parting her folds, lined up for entry. And kissed her as he held himself there. He kissed her as though she was the most precious thing he had ever seen.

"No one else will ever give you this," he vowed against her mouth, brutally possessive, but truer words had never been spoken.

"No one could."

There was pressure, invasion. She stiffened a little in surprise, anticipating pain, bracing for it, but he kissed her so tenderly as he exerted that steady pressure.

For one second, as his implacable demand threatened pain, she thought, *I can't.* Then it was done and he seemed to become a part of her, mouth open over her trembling lips, thumb caressing her cheek. His hard shape inside her was strange, yet deeply wonderful.

"No one else will ever give me that," he said with awe and pride. He nibbled her jaw, brushed his lips at her temple, then kissed her once, very sweetly. Then again, this time with more purpose. When he came back a third time, she clung to his mouth with her own.

Their bodies shifted. There was tenderness where they were joined, but nothing more than she could handle, not when arousal was returning with inescapable tingles and clenches of desire.

He was right. This was a type of pleasure she couldn't give herself, couldn't have even imagined. She rubbed her face against his neck, wallowing in the weight of his hips, the way smoothing her inner thighs against his hips made him groan.

When he began to withdraw, she clung on with everything in her and he returned with a rush of sensation so acute she gasped.

"Oh," she breathed, beginning to understand.

"Yes," he said tightly, eyes deep pools, atavistic and regressive, yet he never lost control. He kept his pace slow, letting her get used to the feel of him forging his way, holding her well inside the concentric circles of pleasure that rang through her with each thrust.

She couldn't bear it, it was so good, and she turned her mouth against his iron-hard biceps, biting him. Only then did he make a primal noise and pick up the pace. The intensity redoubled. Her body undulated to receive him. The struggle to reach the pinnacle became a fight they fought together with ragged breaths and fisted hands and every ounce of strength they both possessed.

Then she was there, right there, the cataclysm a

breath away. She locked her heels at the small of his back, determined to keep him inside her forever. At least while the waves of pleasure rolled over her.

He pressed deep, holding himself flush against her as culmination arrived.

They clung then, holding on to each other as the acute tension released in a near painful rush of heat and such encompassing waves of pleasure she could hardly breathe. If her eyes were open, she was blind. If he said things, she only heard the rush of blood in her ears. What happened to him happened to her, stopping time and holding her transfixed. They were one in a way she hadn't known was possible.

It was utter perfection that couldn't be maintained forever, which was a tragedy, she decided, as the rush subsided and the pulses began to fade and she discovered tears on her cheeks.

That supreme ecstasy could be replicated, however. They pleasured each other into delirium twice more before she fell asleep, bound to him in a way that could never be undone.

Which made waking to an empty bed that much more excruciating.

He had promised not to rebuff her, but here she was, forsaken, abandoned and alone. Again.

CHAPTER SEVEN

KARIM HAD MADE a terrible mistake. He had known it
as he was offering a vow to Galila that put fissures in
his defenses against her. He had known it as he chose
to make that vow rather than put off consummation of
their marriage—which would have proven his mastery
over his corporeal desires.

He hadn't had the strength. Waiting until his wedding night, hanging on to control while he tried to understand her hesitation, had taken all his willpower.
When he had been pushed right up to the edge and
given the choice to protect himself or have her, he had
chosen to have her.

Which told him everything he needed to know about
how dangerous she was to him. Devastatingly dangerous.

Once hadn't been enough, either. Maybe if she had
expressed some reluctance or said she was tender, he
might have restrained himself, but she had been as eager
as him to bind their flesh irrevocably.

It wasn't until he woke in the dawn hours, aching
to take her a fourth time, that sanity had intruded on
the euphoria of honeymoon madness. She was slender,
delectable, infinitely erotic but new to lovemaking. He

had to find a shred of control, if only to continue calling himself human.

He left for his own apartment where he did everything he could to put himself back inside the armor he had worn until Galila had smashed him apart. He watched the sun come up, letting the brightness burn from his retina the image of her nubile curves. He listened to the morning numbers from overseas, drowning out the memory of her pleasured moans and cries. He showered the scent of her from his skin, then hated himself for all of it and wished himself back in her bed, feeling her warm, smooth skin stretching awake beside him.

He ordered their usual breakfast and had it served in the common dining room between their apartments, as it always was. He should have been sated and mellow. Instead, he was short on sleep and impatient with the staff as they hovered, each with their schedules and correspondence, their headlines and coffee urns.

Was the queen expected? Should they allow her to sleep? The questions were unending and struck him as unbearably intrusive. He gritted his teeth against ordering all of them out.

Despite his conflict, he lingered over his breakfast, full of self-loathing at the weakness he was displaying. His schedule had been emptied for the day after their reception as a courtesy. There was endless work in his office to be attended to and he shouldn't dally here like some besotted suitor, hoping to catch a glimpse of the object of his affection.

He was a man. One who ought to be in complete command of himself and the world around him. As he became aware of stirring behind the door to her room, he rose to leave.

* * *

Galila had barely been able to look at her own wan
face in the mirror, feeling quite a chump for falling for
Karim's promise. At least she had slept well past the
time when he normally left for the far side of the palace.
She would have the breakfast room to herself.

When she entered the small dining parlor, however,
he was standing by the table, reviewing something on
the tablet his aid was showing him. He flicked her a
glance, one that lasted barely a second, but she saw
the consternation in it. Read the lack of welcome in
his stiff posture.

Waking alone had been a slap. Walking in here to see
he had resumed his cloak of indifference was a kick in
the stomach. Having all that play out before the usual
assortment of hovering staff added insult to injury. Was
it really necessary that she parade her deflowered self
before a dozen people?

A case of acute vulnerability struck. Physically,
she was fine. She'd had a bath and was only feeling as
though she'd pushed herself with stretching poses, not
particularly tender from their lovemaking. But memory of their intimacy thinned her skin. She couldn't
bear to look at him, she was so dreading the coolness
in his eyes.

"Good morning." She gathered her shredded composure and found a distant smile. "I thought you would
be across the palace by now."

Silence.

She had the sense he was waiting for her to look at
him, but she pretended to take enormous care with se-
lecting cut fruit to add to her yogurt. She brushed away

the serving hand that would have poured date syrup over her flatbread.

When she reached for the coffee urn, one of the staff hurried to fill her cup, but Karim said sharply, "I'll do it. Leave us."

His tone was so hard, Galila started, then remained on her guard, gaze on her untasted breakfast.

The room cleared in a quick shuffle of feet and a closed door.

She sat with her hands in her lap, discovering she was afraid to move. Not because she feared him, but because she had silently wished they were alone and now discovered the downside of that. No one to hide behind. She didn't want to move and draw his attention.

"You're angry with me," he said.

She was angry with herself.

"Why would you think that?" she murmured, picking up her spoon.

"You're not looking at me."

She should have looked at him then, to prove she wasn't avoiding it, but her eyes were hot. She feared he would read the anguish in them. She had poured out her heart to him last night. She had shared her body in a way she had never done with any other man and now...

"Even if I were..." *It wouldn't matter*, she wanted to say, but couldn't face that harsh reality so head-on. It would hurt too much. "Just go, Karim."

"I would have made love to you all night, Galila," he said through his teeth. "Until we were both too weak to move. As it was, I was far too rough with you. How do you feel?"

He hadn't sat down again and she only had the nerve

to bring her gaze as far as the embroidery that edged his robe.

"Fine."

He sighed in a way that made her flinch, he sounded so impatient. Then he threw himself into the chair and his eyes were right there, leveled into hers like a strike of sunlight off water, penetrating so deep it hurt. Her eyes began to water and she blinked fast.

Through her wet lashes, she still saw the accusation behind his eyes. The way he searched her face as though trying to find a reason to hate her.

"I know a prevarication when I hear one," she said, her voice a scrape against the back of her throat. "You left because you'd had enough of me. Just go, Karim. It will be easier to stand being ignored if you're not doing it in person."

His hand closed into a fist. With a muttered curse, he unfurled it, then reached to take her wrist, the one that held her spoon. He tugged her to her feet and around the table where he pulled her into his lap.

She landed there stiffly, one elbow digging with resistance into his ribs, face forward as she gritted her teeth.

"What is this?" she demanded. "Some new form of torture where you assume that if I succumbed to you once, I'm yours whenever you want me?"

She very much feared she was. Her bones were already threatening to soften, her whole body wanting to relax into supple welcome, longing to melt into him, skin tingling for the sensation of his hands stroking over her.

"Definitely torture," he said, rubbing his beard into her neck so she shivered and squirmed in reaction.

His arms stayed locked around her, keeping her on his lap.

She put a little more pressure behind the sharpness of her elbow. "I'm actually hungry," she said pointedly.

"Eat, then," he invited, opening his arms and relaxing beneath her, but the way his hands settled on her hip and thigh told her he would restrain her if she tried to rise. "I will hold my wife and consider my inner failings."

"Sounds like I'll have time for dessert and a second cup of coffee." She didn't relax, still defensive even though his hands were settling, smoothing and massaging in a way that was kind of comforting, as though he wanted to offer and take pleasure in equal measures.

"Karim—"

"This is new territory for me, Galila. Don't expect my ease with this to happen overnight."

She let out a choke of humorless laughter. "Even though it was the deal you agreed to for that particular type of night? Are you just angling for more sex right now?"

His hands stalled. "Sex can wait until tonight."

Disappointment panged inside her even as he sighed toward the ceiling.

"I can stand depriving myself. Hurting you so badly you won't even look at me? That I cannot bear." His hands moved again, reassuring now then clenching possessively on her curves. "This level of passion isn't normal, you know. If you had had other lovers, you would know that and be as wary of it as I am." He dipped his head forward so his mouth was against her shoulder, whiskers tickling her skin.

She considered that as she spooned yogurt into her mouth. He wasn't offering her the open heart she wanted, but he was talking, at least. He had dismissed their audience. It was a small step, she supposed. One that allowed her to relax a little on his lap and enjoy the way he cradled her.

"You resent desiring me? That only makes me begrudge feeling attracted to you. That's not healthy, is it? Are we supposed to apologize for the pleasure we give each other?" She set petulant elbows on the table while she scraped at her yogurt bowl, deliberately jamming her buttocks deeper into his lap at the same time.

His hands gripped her hips and he drew a harsh breath.

She sent a knowing smirk into her bowl.

"Do you understand what you're inviting?" he asked mildly, opening his thighs a little so the shape of his aroused flesh dug firmly against her cheek.

"I believe you demonstrated that in great detail last night. Why do you think I'm so hungry? You'll have to let me finish my breakfast, though, before we satisfy other appetites. Otherwise, I'm liable to faint on you. Tell me something about yourself while you wait. What was your childhood like?"

"I didn't have one."

She started to rise, wanting to shift back to her own chair so she could look at him and gauge his expression as he spoke, but his hands hardened, keeping her on his lap. Keeping her with her back to him, she suspected.

"I didn't mean that to be an insensitive question," she said gently. "I thought, well, I supposed you might have played with cousins when you were young? Perhaps traveled when you were finishing your education?"

"My university was the throne of Zyria. When I wasn't with my tutors, I sat with my uncle, learning how to run my country. What did you do as a child?"

"Compared to that, it seems beyond childish. One of my favorite pastimes was learning pop songs. I have a decent voice and performed them for my mother's friends. I'm good with languages, too, which was another parlor trick she liked me to show off. I rode horses with my brothers and we camped in the desert with family sometimes. My childhood was fairly ideal. My teen years were more challenging."

"Why is that?"

She bit into the flatbread. It tasted like cardboard. For a moment, she thought about changing the subject, but maybe if he understood why she found his distance so hurtful...

"That's when she began to criticize me. I became obsessive about earning back her approval. I spent a ridiculous amount of time learning about fashion and makeup, trying to look more like her, thinking it would please her. I asked her to make every decision from my shade of lipstick to the shoes I wore. I kept thinking she couldn't disapprove of the way I looked if she made all my choices, but then she would say I was badgering her. Too needy. Everyone said it, my brothers especially. I felt like everyone hated me. It was awful."

Her scalp tickled as he idly played with her hair. "Did she send you away to Europe?"

"I begged my father to let me finish my schooling there. I couldn't take her moods. Even then, I was so careful to only be in the tabloids for good reasons.

Helping a children's hospital or whatever. Anytime I received good press, though, she would say I was up-staging her. Begging for attention. There was no pleasing her."

She tried to twist and look at him, but he didn't let her. He continued playing with her hair, lightly tugging, dipping his nose to inhale, breathing out against the side of her neck.

"How are we talking about me?" she asked. "Tell me what you like about ruling Zyria."

"I like providing stability. No ruler can make an entire populace happy all the time. The best I can do is avoid war and ensure my people are not suffering in poverty. If they can eat and send their children to school, get the care they need and a new refrigerator when the old one breaks, then I am winning the game."

"That's true. You can't *make* someone happy. Do you ever wish you had brothers or sisters?"

He didn't answer. When she tried to turn her head to look at him, his hand tightened in her hair, preventing her. She gave a little shrug of warning, but he wasn't hurting her. He didn't let go, though. After a long minute, he answered.

"There are times I have thought my life would have been easier if I'd had an older brother and the responsibility I carry had gone to him," he spoke with a hint of dry humor, but his tone was also very grave. "Perhaps a lot of things would have been different. I don't know. But I can't make a sibling happen, so there's no point wishing for it."

She waited, but he didn't say anything else.

She pushed aside her emptied plate and sipped her coffee. When she set it down, he shifted her sideways so her legs were across his and they were finally looking at each other.

His face was impassive, difficult to read, but she understood him a little better. He carried a country on his shoulders and had for a long time. If he was lonely, he had made it his friend. That was why he was having such trouble turning to her.

Smoothing her hand over the silky hairs on his jaw, she said very sincerely, "Thank you for telling me that." She pecked his lips with hers.

The light kiss turned his dark eyes molten. "Are you sufficiently rejuvenated?"

"I could be talked into returning to the bedroom."

"Here will do."

Karim had to be extremely careful with his inquiries, but he had learned more about Adir. In the three weeks since Zufar's wedding, Adir had married Amira, the bride who had been promised to Galila's brother. Rumor had it they were expecting.

An odd pang had hit him with the news. For years, Karim had been ambivalent about procreating. More than one of his cousins had the temperament to rule. Was it latent sibling rivalry that prompted a sudden desire to make an heir?

"What's wrong?" Galila's soft voice nudged him back to awareness of the view off her balcony as her scent arrived to cloud around him.

He glanced back into her apartment and discovered her maids had finally left them alone.

In another lifetime, which was mere days ago, he would have brushed off her inquiry with a brisk and conscienceless "Nothing." He wasn't required to explain his introspective moods to anyone.

But Galila's slender arms came around his waist as she inserted herself under his arm. Her pointy chin rested on his chest and she gazed up at him. The pretty bat of her lashes was an invitation to cast off his pensiveness and confide in her.

"There are things I would discuss with you if I could, but I can't," he said, surprised to discover it was true. He wanted to confide in her. It was yet another disturbing shift in his priorities. "It's confidential." He stroked the side of his thumb against her soft cheek to cushion his refusal.

"Hmm," she said glumly. "Bad?"

"Not violent, if that's what you mean."

"Trade embargoes or something," she guessed.

Did not acknowledging his potential successor to Zyria's throne count as an embargo? "Something like that."

"You can trust me, you know. I know I behaved indiscreetly the night we met, but I'm not usually so reckless. That was a special case. With a special man," she added, lips tilting into the smile that he fell for like a house of cards.

She hadn't had a drop of alcohol since the night they met, he had noted.

She shifted so they were front to front and rested her ear on his chest, sighing with contentment. His hands went to her back of their own accord, exploring her warm shape through the silk robe she wore over her nightgown.

This was becoming the norm for him—holding her. He wasn't a dependent man, but she was so tactile and affectionate, seeming to thrive on his touch, he couldn't resist petting and cuddling her.

"I don't regret telling you about him that night. Adir, I mean," she murmured.

He stalled in stroking across her narrow shoulders.

"I'm glad you're willing to listen. That *I* can trust *you*," she went on. "I'm still so shocked by Mother's affair and Adir. I keep wondering about Amira. How she even knew Adir well enough she would run away with him."

He almost told her the woman was married and expecting, but she would wonder how he came to know it.

"Did you know her well?" he asked instead, resuming his massage across her back.

"Her father is one of my father's oldest friends. She was promised to Zufar since she was born. I was looking forward to having her as a sister-in-law. And Zufar—you saw him on a really bad day. He can be gruff, but he would have done his best to be a good husband. I've asked him what he has learned of Adir, but he's so angry, he wants nothing to do with it. I don't know what to do. I want to be sure Amira is well and happy with her decision, but I can't very well make inquiries without spilling our family secrets, can I?" She leaned back to regard him. "See? I am capable of discretion."

"I'll see what I can learn," he promised, pleased when she grew visibly moved.

"You will? Thank you!"

He was growing so soft. He very much feared he was becoming infatuated with his wife, constantly wanting to put that light in her expression and feel her throw her arms around him like he was her savior.

He picked her up and took her to the bed, distantly wondering what she would say when he told her he had learned her friend was pregnant.

I don't desire your children.

He didn't know why that continued to sting when they made love so passionately every night. It was early days in their marriage and he ought to be pleased they were making love frequently without morning sickness or other health concerns curtailing their enjoyment of each other.

Still, as they stripped and began losing themselves in each other, he was aware of a deeper hunger that went beyond the drive for sexual satisfaction. Beyond his need to feel her surrender to him and take such joy at his touch. He wanted all of her. Every ringing cry, every dark thought, every tear and smile and whispered secret.

He suspected he wanted her heart.

Do I look pretty, Mama?

Galila was in the gown she intended to wear to stand next to her mother at the children's hospital gala. This used to be one of their favorite events, but for months now, her mother had been growing more and more critical. Galila didn't understand why.

She had tried very, very hard this time to be utterly flawless. Her gown was fitted perfectly to her growing bust and scrupulously trim waistline. Her hair fell in big barrel curls around her shoulders. Her makeup was light, since her mother still thought she was too young—at sixteen!—to wear it. Nail polish had been allowed for years, though. She had matched hers to the vibrant pink of her gown and wore heels, something the queen had also been arguing were too old for her.

She thought she looked as beautiful as she possibly could and smiled with hope, trying to prompt an answering one from her mother's stiff expression.

Her mother winced and gave her a pitying look. *I expect you to have better instincts, Galila. The green would be better and a nude shade on your lips.*

Rejection put a searing ache in the back of Galila's throat. She turned away to hide how crushed she was, waiting until her mother went back into her own closet before she reached for a tissue on the shelf and dabbed it beneath her eyes, trying to keep her makeup from running.

Why was her mother being so cruel lately? She stared blindly at the bookshelf, trying to make sense of her mother's change in attitude. She used to be all purrs and strokes, now she was claws and hisses. Just like...

The object before her blurred eyes came into focus. It was a bookend. Two slabs of ebony with a bright gold figure upon it. A lioness. She stood on her hind legs, one paw braced against the upright wall as she peered over the top, as if looking for her mate—

Galila sat up with a terrified gasp beside him, jolting Karim awake.

"What is it?" He reached out a hand in the dark, finding her naked back coated in sweat. The bumps of her spine stood up as she curled her back, hugging her knees protectively. Her heartbeat slammed into his palm from behind her ribs, drawing him fully out of slumber.

"Nightmare?" he guessed. "Come here. You're safe."

She only hugged herself into a tighter ball, tucking

her face into her knees, back rising and falling as she dragged long breaths into her lungs, as though she was being pursued.

He came up on an elbow, and rubbed her back, trying to ensure she was as awake as he was. "Are you in pain?"

"Just a bad dream." She didn't let him draw her under the covers, though. She pressed a clammy hand to his chest and pushed her feet toward the edge of the mattress. All of her shook violently, her reaction so visceral, his own body responded with a small release of adrenaline. He caught at her arm, ready to protect her against frightening shadows and monsters under the bed.

"What was it about?"

"I need a minute. Let me—" She left the bed and found her silk robe, pulling it on before she disappeared into the bathroom.

He was sleeping inordinately well these days, thanks to their regular and passionate lovemaking. The sated, sluggish beast in him wanted to lie back and drift into unconsciousness again, but he heard water running.

Concerned, he rose and followed her into the bathroom where the light blinded him. She had turned on the tap and buried her face in a towel to muffle her sobs. The cries were so violent, they racked her shoulders.

His scalp tightened. This reaction was off the scale. "Galila."

She hadn't heard him come in and gasped, lifting a face that was so white, his heart swerved in his chest.

"You look like a ghost," he said. Or she'd seen one. He tried to take her in his arms, but she wouldn't allow it.

"I'm sorry. I can't—" Her words ended in a choke. She set aside the towel and splashed the water on her face, then dried it only to hide behind the dark blue cloth again.

Her desire for distance surprised him. Stung, even. He was used to her turning to him for the least thing. He liked it.

"What was it about?" he insisted. "Tell me."

She couldn't. She was barely making sense of it herself. She wasn't even sure if it was a genuine memory. Dreams were pure imagination, weren't they?

Clenching her eyes shut, she tried to recall her mother's boudoir. Her bookshelves. Was it possible the lioness she had pictured so clearly had been conjured by the curiosity that was plaguing her? She wanted to know who her mother's lover had been, so she was inventing scenarios in her sleep.

Or was it real? The palace of her childhood was full of objets d'art. Masterpieces in oil, ivory, ceramic and yes, some were sculptures cast in gold. Could she mentally picture all of them? Of course not, especially the ones that had been in her parents' private rooms. She hadn't entered those much at all.

But she *had* gone to her mother that one afternoon, ahead of the children's hospital ball. That was a real memory. She distinctly remembered it because the ball had fallen right after her birthday. The pink gown had been a present to herself, one she had been certain her mother would approve of.

None of that was the reason she could hardly catch her breath, however.

What if it is true? What if her mother had owned the

other side of Karim's father's lion bookend? Did that prove Karim's father had been her lover? Or was it a bizarre coincidence?

"Galila."

Karim's tone demanded she obey him.

She opened her eyes and searched his gaze, but couldn't bring herself to ask if it was possible. How would he know? He'd been a child. And the suspicion was so awful, such a betrayal to his mother, she didn't want to speculate about it herself, let alone put it on him to wonder.

What would such an accusation do to this tentative connection they had formed? She couldn't bear to lose what was growing between them. He had married her to be a link between their two countries, not the catalyst for a rift that couldn't be mended.

With lashes wet with helplessness, she said very truthfully, "I don't want to think of it." She held out her hand. "Make love to me," she whispered. "Make me forget."

He was too sharp not to recognize she was putting him off, but he let her plaster herself across his front and draw his head down to kiss him.

Within seconds, he took command of their lovemaking, taking her back to bed where they were both urgent in a way that was new and agonizing, as if he felt the pull of conflict within her. Impending doom. He dragged his mouth down her body, pleasured her to screaming pitch and kept her on the edge of ecstasy, then rolled her onto her knees. She gripped the headboard in desperate hands as he thrust into her from behind, but even after she shuddered in release, he wasn't done. He aroused her all over again, his own body taut and hotter than a branding iron when he finally settled over her and drew her thighs to his waist.

Now he was everything, her entire world, filling her, possessing her, driving her to new heights that they reached together, so intense she sobbed in glory.

Spent, she fell asleep in his arms, clinging to his damp body as if he could save her from her own sub-conscious.

But the lioness stalked her into the morning light.

When she woke, she knew what she had to do.

"Are you sure you're all right?" Karim asked twice over breakfast. It was usually a private meal now. He let their aids in when they were nursing their second cup of cof-fee, rarely before. "You'll feel better if you talk it out."

"It's silly," she prevaricated, but couldn't find the dismissive smile she needed. "Just a silly dream."

He knew she was lying to him. She could tell by the grim frown overshadowing his stern gaze. It chilled her heart to disappoint him and even worse, deserve his consternation.

"I don't want to relive it," she said, miserable at not being able to share.

His mouth twitched with dismay, but he let the sub-ject drop. A few minutes later, he rose to start his day.

When she was certain he was on the far side of the palace, she texted Niesha, Zufar's wife and the new Queen of Khalia. With so much going on, she had barely absorbed her brother's email yesterday concerning his new wife and the startling possibility she could be the lost Princess of Rumadah.

It wouldn't have surprised her in the least if Niesha hadn't returned her message, preferring to take time to absorb her own life changes, but she video-called Galila a short time later. Galila dismissed the maid in her room and answered, forcing herself to strike a casual pose on the end of a sofa, as if she wasn't wound so tightly with nerves she was ready to snap. It took everything in her to get through a few gentle inquiries after Niesha's situation and well-being.

"Thank you so much for calling me back," Galila said when she felt she could steer the conversation to her own interests. "I don't know what made me think of a particular keepsake of my mother's, but I wondered if it was on the shelf in your room? Would you be able to show me? It's an ebony bookend with a lioness cast in gold."

"I'm so sorry," Niesha said. "All her rooms have been completely redecorated, but your mother's things were boxed up and put into storage. Nothing was discarded. It's all safe."

"No apology is necessary. Of course, you made it your own." Galila spared a brief thought for how odd it must be for Niesha to be living as a queen, rather than a maid. They were equals now and Galila had to remember that, but she was fixated on learning the truth. "Do you recall seeing a bookend with a lioness, though?"

"I don't recall it, no. Let me check with Zufar. I'm sure he'll agree you should be the one to have her things. I'll have them shipped to you."

It wasn't exactly the answer she wanted. Galila had hoped to solve the mystery in seconds. Instead, she had to act like it was a trifling thing, not an obsessive worry.

"Whenever you have time," she said with a flick of her hand. "I don't want to disturb you when you have so much going on."

The more Galila thought about it, however, the more she was convinced that Karim's father, King Jamil, had been her mother's lover. The timing fit with Adir's age and her own father's diplomatic tour. A brief glance at Zyria's history online confirmed that Karim's father had died very shortly after her father had returned to Zyria.

Had his death been a catalyst for her mother telling her father about her pregnancy? Had Jamil's accident even been an accident?

She couldn't help dwelling on every possibility as she waited for the boxes to arrive.

What if Karim's father had been her mother's lover? That would mean Adir was Karim's half brother, too. How would he react to *that* news?

Not that she could burden him with any of this. Definitely not until she had more evidence than a spooky dream.

But if it did turn out to be true, was it wise to tell him? He would have to keep it from his mother, who still held Jamil so close to her heart. What of the political ramifications? Zufar was already dealing with an embittered man who blamed him for the loss of his birthright. She couldn't subject Karim to the same.

A sensible woman would leave the mystery unsolved, but she couldn't let it go. At the same time, keeping all of this inside her was like trying to ignore an abscess. It throbbed and ached in the back of her throat, flaring up and subsiding as she pretended to Karim that she was fine, all the while waiting on tenterhooks for news that the shipment of boxes had arrived.

A week later, rather than bother Niesha again, she

had her assistant speak to the palace in Khalia. The boxes had finally left and should arrive in a day or two.

Somehow, knowing they were on their way was far worse than if they hadn't left.

"Should I cancel our dinner engagement tonight?" Karim asked over breakfast.

"Pardon?" Galila's gaze came back from staring at nothing and focused on him. She seemed to become aware that her coffee was halfway to her mouth and set it down without tasting it. "Why would you do that?" she asked.

Because she had been positively vacant the last few days. He wanted to know why. This was usually her favorite time of day, when she had him all to herself. She usually flirted and chattered, reminded him to call his mother and asked if he had any preferences for upcoming menu choices. She might sidle up to his chair and kiss him if she was feeling particularly sensual.

She'd become downright remote of late, though.

He hated it.

"You're not yourself. Is there something we should discuss?"

"What? No! I'm completely fine." A blatant lie. "Just…distracted. Should I let the staff in?" She rose to do it.

"Does it have to do with Adir? Because I have news."

"You do?" She swung back, interest sharp.

"He married Amira. She's expecting. Sooner than one would anticipate, given she was supposed to marry your brother a month ago," he added drily. "My reports are that they're quite happy."

"Oh. I thought she must have had some sort of relationship with him, to be willing to go with him like that. It's good to know she's well." She stood with her hands linked before her, still taking it in, chewing her lip and pleating her brow. "That's all you learned?"

For some reason, the way her gaze searched his caused the hair on the back of his neck to stand up.

"Yes." The word *why?* stayed locked in his throat.

With a thoughtful nod, she let in their staff, curtailing further discussion.

Galila wanted the lion on hand to compare to the lioness when—*if*—it arrived. Would Karim miss it if she removed it from his study? At the very least, she needed a fresh look at it. She wanted to search for a signature or an identifying engraving or seal—anything that might prove it was one of a pair.

She would take a few photos on her phone, she decided, as she crossed to the far side of the palace.

Karim had left their breakfast room about an hour ago for his day of royal duties. Would he cancel their dinner? She wasn't sure how she felt about that. Her mind was a whirlwind these days, one where she could barely take in what Karim had said about Adir and Amira when she was so focused on discovering who Adir's father was. Obviously her distraction was beginning to show, but she couldn't tell Karim what was bothering her until she could provide a definitive answer.

Much like the first time when she had arrived without warning, she was invited to wait in his study. She again insisted he should not be interrupted. She wanted to be alone for this.

The bookend was exactly where she had seen it the

first time. It was surprisingly heavy. She turned it this
way and that on the shelf, taking photos, then tilted it
to look at the bottom.

There was a date that fell a few weeks into Galila's
father's trip away. The artist was someone she didn't
know, but she would look up the name later. Where
was he located? Zyria? Khalia? Somewhere in between
where lovers might meet?

Most tellingly, the piece was called *Where Is She?*

Her heart began to thump as she instinctively guessed
the other would be called *Where Is He?*

"They just told me you were waiting."

Karim's voice startled her so badly she dropped the
bookend, narrowly missing her foot and crying out with
alarm as she leaped back from it.

"Did it hit you?" Karim grasped at her arm to steady
her, then crouched, trying to examine her foot.

Galila stumbled back, certain her guilty conscience
gleamed bright as full moon on a clear night. "I'm fine,"
she stammered. "Did I break it? I'm so sorry. I didn't
hear you come in."

"Worry about your foot." He picked up the bookend
and rose, turning it over and weighing it in his hand.
"I don't think a nuclear bomb could hurt this thing, but
you would be in a cast if it had landed on your toes.
What was so engrossing about it?"

"I don't know," she babbled, finding it increasingly
impossible to lie to him, especially when she had been
working so hard to coax him to open up to her. "It's just
a very well-crafted piece, don't you think?"

He narrowed his eyes and studied it more closely,
reading the bottom before slowly setting it on the shelf
and nudging it up against the books.

"It belonged to your father, I imagine? I would feel horrible if I had dented it."

"It's fine." He folded his arms and frowned at her. "What did you need?"

"I—" She couldn't say *Nothing.* Not when she had said she needed to speak to him and would wait here for a private audience. Last night, when she had decided to come here to examine the bookend, she had conjured a question about Adir and Amira, but he had answered that this morning. They had private conversations every day over breakfast. She had no good excuse for being here.

Fighting to keep her gaze from drifting back to the lion, she racked her brain.

"Is it whatever you've been hiding from me?"

Her heart took a hard bounce, causing her voice to stutter. "W-what?"

She knew damned well her gaze was rife with culpability as it rose to his. She watched his own narrow like a predatory bird swooping into a nose dive.

"You think I can't tell? We're so attuned, I sense the slightest shift in the cadence of your breath and the change of scent on your skin. You're worried about something. You avoid my eyes—" He muttered an imprecation. "You're doing it now. *Look at me.*"

She couldn't. Guilt weighed her lashes along with her shoulders and even her head on her neck. She couldn't tell him, though. Not until she knew for sure.

This morning, when he had mentioned Adir, she had wondered if he had learned Adir was his half brother. Now, through her panic, she recalled something else that had penetrated the edges of her mind during that conversation. A suspicion that had been overshadowed by her turmoil over a pair of bookends.

It was something she wasn't quite ready to acknowledge because she could be just as wrong about that as she might be about his father. But she would rather speculate on that than the other.

"I think I'm pregnant."

CHAPTER EIGHT

KARIM HEARD THE words but they didn't make sense. They weren't bad, just astonishing. "How?"

She rolled her eyes. "Do not tell me to have 'the talk' with you. Not the way we've been carrying on."

He couldn't help smirking at that, but then frowned in confusion. "I said you could use birth control. You said you wanted to."

"Yes, well." She wrinkled her nose and gave her hair a self-conscious flip. "I was annoyed with you the day I came in here to discuss that. The doctor was very patronizing, making it sound like I *had* to take something. As if it was your decision that I shouldn't conceive. You'll recall that we weren't even having sex at the time…" She looked at her manicure, embarrassed by her pique that day, but also blushing at how uninhibited she'd been with him.

"I remember." His voice held a warm, delicious undertone, one that made her toes curl. "So you didn't go on anything?"

"I had a small tantrum about it at the doctor's, then came here. I kept thinking I should go back and get it sorted, but I don't care for him, so I never did."

"He's been my doctor all my life. He's very thorough."

"And I'm sure you would enjoy discussing your personal life with my female doctor back in Khalia, who is also very thorough," she said pertly.

"Point taken. See if she wants to relocate."

"I've had preliminary discussions about the women's health center and met some excellent female doctors here in Nabata. I only have to ask my assistant to book me an appointment, but—you're going to think me the biggest idiot alive, Karim. You're going to say I'm the one who needed 'the talk.'"

"Why?" He frowned.

"I honestly didn't think it would happen so fast," she admitted with a groan. "I've been ignoring the signs because I feel quite stupid for thinking I could have sex and get around to starting birth control when I felt like making a visit to a new doctor a priority. I'm a grown woman. *I know better.*"

He laughed. It was a brief chuckle that was more of a pair of staccato exhales, but it made her insides blossom in sweetly smug triumph for squeezing that carefree noise out of him.

His amusement lingered in his expression as he shook his head in wry disbelief at her. In fact, he was so handsome in that moment, she tipped a little further into love with him.

A little further? Oh, dear. Yes. She was quite in love with him, she realized with a stutter of her heart. She looked to the floor, letting her hair fall forward to curtain her face and hide that she was coming to terms with a *lot* lately. How had she been so foolish as to do that though? The very thing she feared most—yearning for someone she loved to love her back—was now the definition of her marriage.

With that burning ache for a return of her affections pressing outward in the base of her throat, she asked, "Are you angry?"

"Of course not! I'm astounded, but thrilled. You told me you didn't desire my children."

"I was angry." She wrinkled her nose in apology. "It turns out, I do want your baby, Karim. Very much." So much, the magnitude of it pushed bright tears into her eyes.

His expression of utter bemusement turned tender as he cupped her face. His gaze was quite solemn.

"I've been thinking lately that we ought to be trying to conceive, waiting for the right time to bring it up. I'm very happy with this news, Galila. I only wish you had felt you could trust me with it sooner. Is this why you've been so distracted? You thought I wouldn't approve?"

She shrugged, feeling evasive as she buried her face in his shoulder, but enormous feelings were overtaking her. Love, a kind she had never before experienced, had a breadth and depth that terrified even as it exhilarated her. Anticipation of their growing family swelled excitedly in her while profound despair countered her buoyancy. He had said he would never love her. Overshadowing all of that was the secret of his father's possible affair with her mother, the weight of it heavy enough to crush her flat.

He closed his arms around her, though, and kissed her with such incredible sweetness, her world righted itself for a few precious seconds.

"I'm glad you're pleased," she said against his mouth.

"That's two good memories you've given me in this room to replace my bad one."

She was so startled by that statement she drew back and studied him.

He clearly regretted his remark at once. She watched his expression close up. His jaw hardened and his lips sealed themselves into a tight line.

Ah, this man of hers. He was capable of opening up, but only in very brief and narrow peeks. She traced the hollow of his rigid spine through his shirt, saying quietly, "I wondered."

He grimaced and his gaze struck the curtains that hid the balcony beyond.

"Do you have many memories of him? Six is so young."

"Too young for a memory like that," he said flatly, almost as if he'd seen his father's body, but surely not. Who would allow such a thing?

She started to ask, but he kissed each of her eyes closed. "Shall we make another pleasant memory in here?" His mouth sought hers.

She let him erase the troubling thoughts lingering in her psyche, but it was temporary. She hadn't been completely honest with him and couldn't be.

Not until she had found the lion's mate.

Galila belatedly realized how tasteless it was to have her mother's things shipped to her in Zyria. She wound up requesting they be left in a storage room in the lower palace, rather than in the royal chambers.

Then she had to wait until she had a free afternoon, which didn't happen until she had had her doctor's appointment and her pregnancy confirmed.

That had prompted a flurry of additional appointments with key staff who would keep the news confidential but begin preparations for the upcoming heir. She and Karim even squeezed in a day trip to inform his mother, who was beside herself at the news.

Finally, five days later, Galila was able to go with her assistant down to the roomful of boxes and begin sifting through them. They were labeled but very generally— Books, Art and Heirlooms—all words that could indicate the box held the bookend she sought.

Her assistant was beginning to nag her about being on her feet too long when she squeezed something hard and vaguely animal-shaped through a careful wrapping of linen. She asked her helpers to leave her alone for a few moments.

Stomach tight and curdling, she lifted out the heavy piece. Her hands shook as she unwound the linen.

It was the lioness, exactly as she had dreamed it.

Not risking her foot this time, she kept it on the table and tilted it enough to see the same artist's signature, the same date and the inscription *Where Is He?*

She drew a shaken breath. What should she do now?

Galila was still not herself. Was it the baby? Karim wondered.

She had had the pregnancy confirmed and the obvious signs were there, now that he made a point to notice them. She hadn't had a cycle and her breasts were tender. A brief glance online told him moodiness and forgetfulness weren't uncommon.

If he didn't know better, however, he would think she was drunk, she was so absentminded, leaving the making of conversation with their guests to him. He could tell the older couple was surprised by her wan smiles and quiet introspection. They had met her before and knew she was typically animated and engaging.

Finally, the wife of the minister said something about Galila suffering the pressure of producing an heir. Galila snapped out of her daze to blush and Karim was certain they immediately put her distraction down to pregnancy. They left with smug smiles, convinced they held a state secret.

"Our news will be rumored on every station tomorrow," he said as he followed her into her rooms.

She gave him a startled look. "What news?"

He stared at her. "What is going on with you?"

Her entire being seemed to deflate. "I have to talk to you about something and I don't know how."

The anguish in her expression made his heart lurch. "Is it the baby?"

How could he be instantly devastated when he'd barely begun to absorb this new reality?

"No. I'm perfectly fine. Not even iron deficient or suffering much morning sickness. The baby and I are completely healthy. No, this is something else entirely." She touched her forehead. "Come. I have to show you something."

They dismissed the staff and she took him into her bedroom where she knelt to open a lower drawer. She lifted out a wrapped object that was obviously heavy.

He bent to take it from her and saw the anxiety that leaped into her expression as he picked it up, as if she wanted to snatch it back.

"What is it?" Its density and bulk felt vaguely familiar.

She waved at the bed and he set it there to let her unwrap it. She did, slowly. With dread, even. He heard her swallow as she revealed glimpses of ebony and gold.

It was a bookend, one he recognized as similar to the one that had so engrossed her in his office. The two polished black slabs set at an angle were identical to his, but the lioness cast in gold on this one was in a different position, peering over the top of the wall, rather than around the side.

She had distracted him with pregnancy news, but that had been subterfuge. *This* had been her reason for coming to his office last week. He didn't care to be lied to, but that wasn't what made his scalp prickle so hard it felt as though it was coming off.

"An early birthday present?" He wasn't a flippant man. The remark came out abraded by the gravel in his throat. The pit of his gut was turning sour. "Where did it come from?"

He already knew, even before she looked up at him with misery and regret pulling at her features. Her knuckles were white and sharp as teeth where she clutched the linen in her fist.

"It belonged to my mother."

He closed his eyes. Now came the fury.

"Who else have you told?"

Galila frowned in confusion. "What do you mean, who have I told? Karim, do you understand what I'm telling *you*?"

"Yes," he clipped out.

She had expected more disbelief and shock, not an immediate leap to damage control. She had agonized all day, since pulling this from the box, about whether to tell him. She had then braced herself for having to convince him, once he realized what she suspected. This was, after all, circumstantial evidence. Strong but not definitive. Of course, he would have doubts. She still wasn't ready to believe it.

How could he get there so fast without working through all the reasons that this proved nothing?

"Maybe you should sit down," she said. "Because I don't think you realize what this might mean."

"It matches the one that belonged to my father. *I know what it means*, Galila. I didn't think there was proof of their affair. That there was a way for it to be pieced together. What did you tell them in Khalia about this?" His voice was scythe-sharp, cutting off her reach for other explanations and leaving her weak excuses on the ground. He was so tall and intimidating in that moment, she stumbled back a step.

She kept going, backing away until her knees found the chair where she threw her robe when she climbed into bed. She plopped into it.

"Am I to understand you *knew*?" She was like a fish gasping for air, jaw working, eyes goggling.

"Of course I knew! Why do you think I married you?"

She was glad she was sitting down. His words bowled her over. She felt each of the buttons in the upholstery digging into her back.

"That's why you came on to me at Zufar's wedding? Why you coerced him into agreeing to our marriage? To hide this secret?" She thought being a political pawn had been bad. She wasn't even *that* expedient! Their marriage was a gag order, nothing more.

"Do you understand the ramifications if this gets out?" he went on. "It could start a war!"

She had never seen him this aggressive, shoulders bunched, face so hard there was nothing of the tender lover she had slept beside. He was not a man at all. He was a warrior defending his kingdom.

"My parents' marriage was a peace treaty with tribesmen who backed her father," he added in a clipped tone. "They support me, but grudgingly. If they found out my father cheated on her? That he had a child with another woman? Who knows what sort of retaliation they would take against me. Or Adir."

He paced away and his hand cut through the air.

"Who even knows what kind of man Adir is? He's already shown himself willing to take revenge against your brother for your mother's actions. What would he do to me and Zyria? Then there is your brother Zufar."

He spun to confront her.

"Zyria and Khalia have been in a cold war for years. Your mother's doing, I am sure, since my uncle's overtures after my father's death were always shut down. *I* knew why the relationship between our countries went stale." He tapped the center of his chest. "I never tried to reach out when I took the throne, knowing there was no point. But after your mother passed, I was suddenly invited to your brother's wedding. We are finally in a position to mend fences between our countries and you want to tell him *this*?"

"No!" she cried. "I haven't told Zufar or anyone. I've been agonizing about telling *you*." She had been trying to protect him, didn't he see that?

"How you even—" He ran his hand down his face and glared at the bookend.

"How did *you* know?" she asked.

"My father told me," he spat with great bitterness. "The night he died. Your mother cut off their affair and he got himself blind drunk. If only he had blacked out, but no. He sat there and told me in great detail how deeply he was suffering a broken heart. Said he loved my mother, but not the way he loved Namani. His feelings for her were beyond what he thought possible."

His tortured memory of that night threw harsh shadows into his face.

"He'd thought she felt the same, but she broke it off. He couldn't go on without her. Refused to."

Galila tried to speak and realized her hand was over her mouth. She lowered it. "You were six years old. What was he thinking, putting all of that on you?"

"He wasn't thinking. He was out of his mind with agony."

Karim's own agony was written in deep lines of anguished grief, painful memory and a lifetime of confusion and regret.

"It was years before I understood it properly, but he wanted me to know why he was leaving it all in my hands. He couldn't leave a note. My mother would have seen it."

"Are you saying—Karim," she breathed, gripping the arms of her chair and leaning forward. "His death was deliberate." *Please, no.*

He flashed one tortured flare of his gaze her direction, then showed her his grim profile. "My mother can never know. I've always let her believe he stumbled."

"You *saw* that?" The words tore a strip from the back of her heart to the back of her throat, leaving a streak of burning anguish on his behalf. "That's horrible! He never should have—"

Her entire composure was crumpling in empathy for him. She rose anyway, but he stiffened as she approached, telling her he didn't want her comfort. It was an excruciating rejection.

"Karim…" She held out a hand. "I had to tell you, but I would never, ever tell anyone any of this. Certainly not your mother."

He jerked his chin in a nod of acknowledgment, but when she came closer, he again stiffened and held up a hand this time, warding her off.

His harshly voiced declaration came back to her. *Why do you think I married you?* Surely, they had built something beyond that, though? She was carrying his child.

"I'm going to put that in my personal safe," he said. "I don't want anyone else to see it and come to the same conclusions you have."

"Of course." She moved to take up the linen, but he took it from her and wrapped it himself, disappearing to his own side.

She stood there waiting for his return. And waited and waited.

He didn't come back.

Galila entered the breakfast room to find a handful of aides doing exactly what her husband wanted them to do—they were creating a buffer between him and his wife.

She had spent a restless night missing his heat beside her in the bed, trying to take in the fact Karim had known all along that his father had had an affair with her mother. That he had lied to her about his reasons for marrying her and hadn't trusted her enough to tell her the truth. Not until she figured it out for herself.

Now she had, he was turning his back on her again. Why? Shouldn't this shared secret draw them closer?

As she sank into her chair, he rose, almost as if they were on different ends of a child's seesaw.

"I have a busy morning," he said, looking to the door rather than at her. "If you have questions about our schedule with the duke and duchess, we should cover that now, before we greet them at the airport."

Why do you think I married you?

They had grown close despite his initial motives, though. Hadn't they? He had seemed happy about her pregnancy. Until last night, they had made love unreservedly. That meant she was a source of pleasure for him, didn't it? Surely, he felt *something* toward her? He wasn't going to reject her out of hand, now that she had uncovered the truth about his father's infidelity. Was he?

He didn't give her time to ask any of her questions, rushing out to start his day. They were both tied up for the next few days as they hosted several dignitaries around an international competition for child athletes recovering from land mines and other war-related injuries.

Galila did what she had done for years. She ensured her appearance was scrupulously balanced between flawless elegance and warm benevolence. The cameras adored her. All of Zyria praised Karim for his choice in bride. They dubbed her the Queen of Compassion.

She was miserable, taking no pleasure in the adulation. Thankfully, the car windows were tinted and the madly waving crowd couldn't see that she wore such a long face.

Karim finished his call beside her, one he hadn't needed to make. It was yet another brick in the wall he was building against her.

Before he could cement another into place, she asked,

"Are you so angry with me for figuring it out that you can't even speak to me about it?"

He paused in placing another call. "There's nothing left to say."

"Is there nothing left of our marriage, either? Because you're avoiding me. You're—" He was avoiding their bed.

He sighed. It was the sigh that cut through her like a blade. *Don't be needy*, it said.

"Why aren't you sleeping with me?" She swung her face toward him, refusing to guess at his reasons. "Is it because I'm pregnant? Because you don't trust me? Because you're angry? What did I do to make you turn your back on me, Karim?"

"Nothing," he said from behind clenched teeth. "I was simply reminded by our…discussion the other night that…" He polished the screen of his phone on his thigh. "This passion between us is dangerous," he stated more firmly.

She studied his craggy profile. He was staring straight ahead at the closed privacy window. There might as well be one between them, holding her apart from his thoughts and feelings. From his heart.

"Is that all it is?" She felt as though she inched onto thin ice. "Because I had begun to hope it was more than merely passion."

His jaw pulsed. "I told you not to expect that."

Don't be needy.

Swallowing, she looked to the palm trees that lined the boulevard as they approached the palace. The archway and fountain, the flower garden and flags, the columns and carpeted steps that formed the impressive entrance of the Zyrian palace.

He offered her a home as beautiful as the one she'd grown up in, and as equally empty of love.

"Why?" Her voice broke. "I don't understand why I should never expect to feel loved, Karim. What is wrong with me that I must lower my expectations and stop believing I deserve that?"

"It's not you." The car stopped and he said, "I don't want to talk about this right now."

"You don't want to talk about it ever. Be honest about that much, please." She slid out of the car as the door was opened for her.

Karim threw himself from the far side and flashed her a look across the roof of the car, one that accused her of pushing him to the very limits of his control.

"You want me to be honest? Come, then." He snapped his fingers at her as he started down the walkway alongside the palace.

She knew eyes followed them, but they were left to walk alone through the garden and around the corner of the public wing to the side of the palace that faced the sea. Here the grounds were a narrow band of beach, a triangle of garden and a courtyard—

Oh. She realized where they were when he stopped in the middle of a ruthlessly straight path and looked upward.

"Karim," she breathed. The sun beat down on them so hot it dried the air in her lungs. Her shoulders stung through the silk of her dress and her scalp tingled as though burning along the part in her hair.

"He was so *in love*—" his inflection made the emotion sound like a case of leprosy "—he could not live without her. He preferred to plunge to his death, *in front of his son*, than face another day without her. Is that what you want me to feel for you, Galila? Unable to live without you?"

The reflection off the building was so hot it burned her face, even though the sun was behind her.

"They weren't able to be together." And she knew her mother. There was every chance she didn't love Jamil in the same way, not that she would dare say so. "Our situation is different. I—I'm falling in love with you."

His body jolted as though struck. "Do not," he said grittily. "We have the foundation for something that can work. If we hold ourselves at arm's length."

"No, we don't!" She grabbed his sleeve and shook his arm, as if she could shake some sense into him. "We almost did and now you're pushing me away again. Karim, are you really saying you will never love me? That you would rather break *my* heart by refusing to? By your logic, that means I should go drown myself right now." She thumbed toward the nearby waves washing the shore.

His gaze flashed from her to the water. He flinched, then his expression hardened. "I'm putting a stop to your feelings before they get any worse."

Worse? He really didn't understand love at all. Which was, perhaps, the real problem.

"You aren't just refusing to love me, you *can't*. Can you?" He didn't know how.

"Cannot and will not. I'm protecting both of us. All of Zyria."

He had told her this before, but some tiny thing inside her—smaller even than the child she carried—had hoped. Now she knew how foolish that hope had been. Now she believed him when he said he would never love her.

Her next breath was deep. It was the kind one took to absorb the sting of a deep cut or the reverberation from a cracked head. The kind that felt like a knife going into her throat and staying there.

"Very well, then."

CHAPTER NINE

KARIM ROSE AND prowled through the dark to the door to Galila's bedroom, paused, turned back and sat in the chair, elbows braced on his splayed thighs.

He was hard, so hungry for her he was sweating and panting with need, but he made himself resist the lure of her. The weakness that going to her would represent.

She might not welcome him anyway. He had ground her heart beneath his heel a few days ago and she'd been walking around like a ghost ever since. He loathed himself for doing it, but clung to the truth he had spoken. They had a child on the way. He had to keep a level head on his shoulders for the next two decades, at least.

Two decades of meting out their lovemaking in small measures to prove to himself he didn't need her like air and water. Twenty years of averting his gaze from her laughing expression so he wouldn't be tempted. Of listening to the falsely cheerful tone she used when she was hurting and trying not to let it show.

Of knowing he was breaking her heart.

She had said she was falling in love with him.

He closed his eyes, savoring those words before

pushing them to the furthest reaches of his consciousness. Whatever she felt was so new, she would be able to recover from his rejection. He was sure of it.

He had to believe it.

Unable to sleep and quite sure he would go to her if he stayed, he dressed and went to his office across the palace. It wasn't even sunrise. He ate an early breakfast in his library, a room where she permeated the walls, layering over old memories like a clean coat of paint, then started his work day.

He was little better than a ghost himself, unable to say later what he had accomplished. The entire day was an exercise in deprivation. He counted the minutes until he would see her. It was exactly the sort of weakness he dreaded in himself, but he finally began to breathe again when he entered his apartment to dress for their dinner with a general and his wife.

That was when he was informed Galila wouldn't be joining them.

"The queen was feeling under the weather and canceled all her engagements for the rest of the week," her assistant informed him.

Shock and concern washed through him in a sickly wave.

"Why wasn't I informed?" He started to brush past her into Galila's rooms.

"She's not here, Your Highness," the woman quickly said. "I thought—it must be my mistake. I understood she intended to speak to you before she left."

Something inside him snapped. Broke. Exploded. "Where the hell did she go?"

The girl fell back a step, eyes wide. "I believe she went to stay with your mother."

* * *

Galila was beating herself up for being the neediest wimp alive, scurrying off for TLC in the desert palace.

She discovered, however, that being needy could be a good thing. Sometimes a person needed someone to coddle and fuss over. Galila's low spirits pulled a maternal instinct from Karim's mother that put a smile of warmth on the older woman's face. A brightness of purpose.

"I'm so glad you came to me. Of course, you should come anytime you feel a need to get away," Tahirah said in response to Galila's apology for imposing. "You'll be a new mother soon. Learn to let people take care of you."

Her spoiling and attention was so sincere, Galila wanted to cry with gratitude. Here was the mother she desperately needed. They talked pregnancy and babies and the challenge of running a palace and the endless social obligations of royal duties.

She was still scorched by Karim's refusal to love her, but at least she had someone who seemed genuinely happy to bond with her. Her heart would still be in two pieces, but at least those pieces could be offered to his mother and the child he gave her. Her life would not be completely devoid of love.

Those broken pieces of her heart jangled when Karim rang through on a video call as she was dressing for dinner. She dismissed her maid and answered.

He looked surprisingly incensed. "What are you doing there?" he snapped.

"I was going to discuss this with you over breakfast this morning, but you weren't there." Completely true, but rather than seek him out or text him or try to inform him via the many other avenues of communication available at the palace, she had slipped away like a criminal. "I'm not here to tell her anything, if that's what you're worried about. I just needed some time."

"For what?"

"To think about how I'm going to accept the kind of marriage you've offered."

"We went over this in the early days, Galila. It will be fine."

"For you. But I fell in love with you. I didn't expect that to happen, but it did. And you don't feel the same. Can't. So I need to think about all of that."

"And do what?" His tone sharpened. "If you think you're going back to Khalia, or taking my child to Europe—"

"If I wanted to do that, I would already be there, wouldn't I? I came to your mother's, Karim. That's as far as I plan on taking your child without your permission. We're having a lovely visit so let me be."

His mouth tightened. "When are you coming back?"

"I haven't decided."

"I'll send the helicopter tomorrow."

"I just got here! Why would you even want me to come back? We're not sleeping together. You barely speak to me. I'm surprised you noticed I was gone."

His nostrils flared as he drew a deep, patience-seeking breath.

"What?" she goaded. "You don't even like when I help with your royal duties. You said so. I make you feel weak. You never needed me before we married and still don't want to, judging by the way you've been treating me. Go back to your old life, then. Pretend I don't exist."

"Galila, if you're trying to provoke some kind of reaction—"

"I know that's impossible! You feel nothing, Karim! We both know you're not going to kill yourself if I stay a few days with your mother so that's exactly what I'm doing."

She jammed the button to end the call.

Then she threw the phone across the room. It hit a marble column, shattering the screen.

"Her Highness has broken her phone," Galila's assistant informed Karim the next morning. "A new one is on its way. She'll be back online this afternoon, I'm sure. In the meanwhile, you'll have to message her through your mother. May I also ask…? There are a number of agenda items I needed to discuss with her, but in her absence, will you approve these?"

Karim went through them quickly, resenting every second of it. Why? Not because he didn't want to review the preliminary budget for the women's health center. He would have to do that eventually anyway, but because he was staring at an empty chair, speaking instead of listening.

We both know you won't kill yourself…

He forced himself to proceed through his day, thinking of her constantly. He kept making mental notes to share things with her only to realize he wouldn't see her later. He wouldn't watch her painted mouth as she entertained their guests, wouldn't stand with pride beside her, wouldn't set his hand in the middle of her back just so the silken fall of her hair would caress his skin.

By the time he was alone in his library, he was thinking for the first time in his life how good a shot of whiskey might taste.

Furious, he yanked open the curtain and glared at the balcony. Instead of seeing his father there, he saw Galila, tall and strong, chin up, eyes on the horizon.

By your logic, I should drown myself.

Was she hurting? Was that why she had run away? Breaking her heart had never been his intention. Collateral damage was inevitable in life, but he tried not to purposefully hurt anyone. Galila, with her spirit and compassion and sharp intelligence, deserved every speck of the adoration she earned.

She had definitely earned his respect, not only solving the mystery of her mother's lover, but protecting that secret as diligently as he always had. She had been reluctant to tell *him*, and he knew how heavy the load was on that.

It was considerably lighter these days, he realized. Because he had shared it with her? Or because he was carrying a different load on his conscience? Her bruised heart crushed like a piano atop his own.

He turned to stare at the lion on the bookshelf, the one engraved with the words *Where Is She?*

The same question clawed inside him. His mate was in a palace in the desert. She might as well be locked in a vault the way the lioness was. Locked in the dark for safekeeping. Endlessly searching for her mate while this one eternally waited here.

Apart.

Why? Why did it have to be this way?

With a snarl, he grabbed the bookend, tempted to throw it through the glass doors and over the balcony, into the sea.

Instead, he carried it with him to his empty bedroom.

* * *

Galila was treading water in the infinity pool that overlooked the oasis when she heard her maid make a startled noise. She dragged her gaze from the sand dunes and palms, swirling in the water to face the paved courtyard that surrounded the pool.

Her husband picked up her robe off the chair while her maid scampered away.

Her chin was in the water and Galila very nearly sucked a mouthful into her lungs, managing at the last second to merely swallow a taste of chlorine.

"Come," Karim said, shaking out her robe. "I want to talk."

She hesitated, then kicked herself into a glide toward the steps, self-conscious as she climbed them. Her body hadn't changed. She was barely pregnant, but she didn't know which would be worse—his avid gaze or a disinterested one.

He gave her a rapacious one. His features hardened as his attention followed the flow of water off her shoulders, between her breasts and across her quivering belly, over the triangle of green-blue bikini bottoms and down her thighs and calves.

Shaken, she couldn't find a voice to ask what he was doing there. She turned to thread her arms into the sleeves of the robe, then caught the edges and folded them across her front. The silk clung to her wet skin, warm despite being in the shade.

He didn't let her step away. His arms closed around her and held her before him, damp hair under his chin. He trapped her arms in a crisscross before she could get the belt tied.

"Karim—"

"Shh," he commanded softly. "Let me feel you. I need to know that you are here."

"You knew exactly where I was." She didn't know why, but her heart began to pepper even harder in her chest. Her body twitched with uncertainty. Relax? Remain on guard? "Why are *you* here, Karim?"

"To tell you that we don't have to repeat history. We shouldn't."

"In what way? Because you've already made it clear you won't allow yourself to feel anything toward me," she said with a jagged edge on her voice. Most especially not the depth of love his father had felt for her mother.

His arms tightened and his beard brushed her wet cheek as he spoke against her skin. "I don't know that I had a choice in how I feel about you. From the moment I saw you, I was transfixed."

Her insides juddered in reaction while she recalled that luminescent moment of turning to see him watching her.

"So was I," she whispered in stark honesty.

"The difference is, you were willing to accept how I made you feel. I was never going to allow myself to be this vulnerable, Galila. I knew I couldn't afford it. I had to fight it."

"Because you don't trust me." She pushed out of his arms and turned to confront him.

"Be careful," he said through gritted teeth, glancing toward an upper balcony to indicate they could be overheard by his mother at any moment.

"I know," she hissed. "But that secret is the reason you married me, yet you withheld it from me. Even when things changed. At least, I thought things were changing." She touched where her heart was a cracked and brittle thing in her chest. "You made me think we were growing close, that we could trust one another, but no. You were keeping secrets, refusing to care..." Her voice trailed into a whisper. The despair that had been stalking her crept close enough to swallow her whole.

"Galila." He tried to reach for her.

She held him off with an upraised hand, too raw to accept his touch without crying under the agony of a caress that wasn't genuine tenderness or affection.

He flinched at her rejection.

"I trust you," he said gravely. "If I didn't, I wouldn't have let you stay here like this. I know you'll guard what you know as carefully as I do. I wouldn't be having a child with you if I didn't trust you."

"But you don't trust me with your heart! What do you think I'm going to do with it? Treat it as badly as you treat mine?"

He snapped his head back, breath hissing in with shock, as though she had struck far deeper than he had imagined anyone could.

There was no satisfaction in it. It made her feel small. She looked to the arid sands of the desert, a perfect reflection of their future.

"I'm not trying to hurt you," she murmured. "I'm just not ready to be with you and act like I'm happy when I'm not."

"You won't be until you come back to me, Galila. We have to be together."

She started to shake her head, but he spoke with more insistence.

"The denial is what does the damage. Pushing you

away is killing me." His tone was an odd mix of vehemence and tenderness.

She glanced at him, not wanting the unfurling of
hope again, only to open herself for a stomping.

"You were right," he continued. "I won't kill myself
over your absence."

And there it was. Her heart went into free fall toward
a shattering impact.

"I will come after you and fight to keep you. I *am*
fighting for you." His possessive words, the light of anguished need in his expression, was a hand that thrust
out and caught her heart before it hit the ground, dragging it into his possession so it would be his forever.
"Come home."

Her mouth trembled. "I want to, but—"

"I love you, Galila."

Her knees weakened.

He caught her with real hands this time, grasping
her upper arms and holding her in front of him so all
she saw was him. His features were hard, but cast in
angles of concern and repentance. His eyes gleamed
dark and solemn, but they were open windows to his
soul, holding back none of the brilliant light within
him. A light that shone with ardent, aching love as he
scanned her features.

It was such a startling, intimate look into his own
heart, hot tears of emotion brimmed in her eyes and a
lump formed in her throat.

The rest of her crumbled. Not in a bad way. In the
best possible way, even though she was quite sure it
was her least elegant look ever. Her chin crinkled and
she had to bite her lips while tears of joy and love over-
flowed her eyes. Her face was clean of makeup, her hair

skimmed flat, her robe damp and ruffled as she hugged herself into him. Hard.

"I love you, too," she choked. "So much."

She lifted her mouth and he brought his head down. Their lips met in a kiss that made her cry out at the power of it. The sweet perfection. He kissed her the way he had that first night in the garden outside the palace of Khalia. Like he was released from years of restraint.

She returned his passion with her own overwhelming need for him, ignoring the aching tenderness in her breasts in favor of pressing closer and closer—

"Karim!" his mother called sharply from an upper terrace. "*The servants*. Take that to your room."

He pulled away from their kiss as they both broke into laughter.

CHAPTER TEN

KARIM WOKE DISORIENTED in the darkness of a tent. He was quickly distracted by his wife's exploring touch over his body. She was staking a claim here in the dark, taking her time, teasing him with the swish of her hair across his skin, kissing and arousing him.

His hands sought her breasts and he remembered at the last moment to be extra gentle, letting her press into his touch as much as she could bear.

"I thought you were too tired for this," he whispered in the dark, longing to suck on her nipples, but he could only tongue them or she cried, they were so sensitive.

"I was." She sighed. "Then I woke up and I didn't want to sleep. *I want you.*"

She straddled him so he felt her nest against his shaft. It had been a long day of travel finding this particular tribe. They'd been welcomed warmly and given the royal treatment, but Galila was in a delicate condition and had turned in early.

She was proving very resilient now, though. He held himself in position as he felt her seeking to take him inside her heat.

They both sighed as she seated herself on him, her heat snug around his pulsing shaft. She began an undulation that made him bite back a groan of supreme pleasure. They didn't have wind and the pepper of whipped sand to disguise their carnal noises this time.

Catching back her own moans of pleasure, she gave herself to him without reserve. He did the same, lifting his hips to meet the return of hers. Her fingernails dug into his chest where she braced herself and hit her peak quickly, the power of it so acute, she pulled him over with her.

He was sorry for it to be over so quickly, but they were practically in public. It was close to dawn and the arrival of other royal guests could happen any time. Today, tomorrow. It might be in a few days, they had been told, but eventually Adir would show up with his wife.

As their personal storm receded, Galila lay sleepily upon him, still joined with him. Her lips grazed his damp skin as she spoke.

"What do you think he will say?"

"I don't know," he said truthfully. That was what he was here to find out.

Galila was watching a new mother demonstrate the proper way to swaddle an infant when excited voices drew her attention to the arriving party.

"Amira!" She leaped to her feet with excitement. Her friend was considerably further along than she was, showing well into her second trimester.

Amira hugged her warmly, but it was the beaming smile on her face that put Galila most at ease. She hadn't seen Adir since the shocking morning of Zufar's wedding. He still had the dangerous air about him and watched her closely as she reunited with Amira, but when he gazed on his wife, he revealed a glimpse of tenderness that warmed Galila's heart.

That softness disappeared between one blink and the next as he flicked his gaze from her to Karim. His stance shifted imperceptibly, almost as if he felt Karim was an enemy he had to watch for sudden moves.

Karim wore the same air of armed caution, unabashed in the way he took Adir's measure.

"Meet my husband," Galila invited Amira, stepping back to Karim's side as she made the introductions.

The resemblance between Karim and Adir wasn't obvious, but she was looking for it and saw the way Karim noted their similar height and scanned a brow and a jaw that matched his own. Seeing their profiles reflected like that, the similarity was undeniable to her. Strange and endearing, especially because she saw a hint of her brothers in Adir as well.

"What business do you have with me?" Adir asked Karim.

"My wife wanted to see her friend, to assure herself she was well." He nodded at Amira.

"Very," Adir said flatly. "As you can see."

Amira patted her baby bump. "All three of us are very happy."

"I'm glad," Galila said. "But we also wanted to speak with you, Adir. About…" She looked to Karim. This was such a delicate matter. "It's a private matter. We have something for you. But I think…" She looked between Adir and Amira, able to see the obvious connection between husband and wife. "Amira, you should come, too."

They entered the tent that Galila and Karim occupied. Amira accompanied them, a confused look on her face. Galila gave her hand a small squeeze and offered a smile of reassurance as she lowered to the cushions with her.

Adir waited while Karim brought the parcel they'd carried into the desert with them, then sat as Karim did.

The bookends were both wrapped carefully in linen. Galila helped Karim unravel them until the lion and lioness were both revealed.

Karim set the lion on the mat before Adir. Then he took the heavy lioness from Galila and braced the two upright walls back to back.

Now it looked as though the male lion gazed on his mate with a casual check-in. *Stay close, sweetheart.* She peered over at him. *I'm right here, darling.*

"A wedding gift?" Adir said, voice somewhere between dry sarcasm and suspicion. But it was clear he saw the value in the pieces and found it odd they were offering such a treasure to him.

Galila licked her lips. "This one belonged to my mother."

Karim's cheeks went hollow before he nodded at the lion. "The other was my father's. We think you should have them."

Adir's brows slammed together.

Amira gasped. "Are you saying…?"

Karim nodded once, curt. He was wary, she could tell, because she knew her husband well these days. She wanted to take his hand, but there were still times where he needed his walls. This was one of them.

Adir looked between them, astonished. He picked up both pieces and turned them over.

"There's nothing to prove it," Karim said. "Except that I know it to be true."

"That your father is—"

"Was. He passed away when I was six. A few months before you were born."

Adir drew a harsh breath. "You're saying we're brothers?" He was clearly astounded, but studied Karim with more interest.

Karim was doing the same to him. "I didn't know there was a child. Not until the night of Zufar's wedding, when Galila told me."

"These are so beautiful," Amira murmured, taking up the lioness.

"Are you sure you want to give them up?" Adir looked between them.

"It's best if questions aren't asked in my palace about how we found the mate," Karim said. "And it seems right that you should have something of them."

Adir nodded and set aside the lion, thoughtful. "Volatile information, indeed. Thank you for entrusting me with it." He shot a look at Galila and the corner of his mouth quirked. "Good thing I never intend to talk about this, since I would have to tell people that my brother and sister are married."

She gave his knee a nudge. "Exactly the sort of misplaced remark I expect from a brother."

His mouth quirked and he looked to Karim again. "I've always wondered who my father might be. What was he like?"

"That was a wonderful trip, but it's good to be home," Galila said as they entered their apartment. The doors between their rooms were rarely closed these days.

"What are you most excited for? A proper bath? Or Wi-Fi?"

"Privacy with my husband," she said, pinching at his stomach as she walked past him toward the bathroom. "Join me in the bath?"

"Love to. I'll be in as soon as I check—" He cut himself off with a sharp curse.

Galila swung back, instantly concerned. "What's wrong?"

"I don't know if it's *wrong*, but your brother has abdicated."

"Zufar? *Why?*"

"To rule Rumadah, Niesha's home country."

"What?" Her ears rang under the news. "Then who is king of Khalia?"

His head came up. "Your brother Malak."

She blinked in shock. "God help us all."

* * * * *

LET'S TALK
Romance

For exclusive extracts, competitions
and special offers, find us online:

Get in touch on 01413 063232